Beatrice Boville
And
Other Stories

by

Ouida

Beatrice Boville And Other Stories
by Ouida

ISBN: 978-93-60465-21-6

Published by

DOUBLE 9 BOOKS

2/13-B, Ansari Road
Daryaganj, New Delhi – 110002
info@double9books.com
www.double9books.com
Tel. 011-40042856

ABOUT THE AUTHOR

English novelist Ouida wrote novels. Ouida authored almost forty novels over her career in addition to articles, children's books, and short tales. She was a moderately successful woman who led a luxurious lifestyle and entertained many famous writers of the day. In her most well-known book, Under Two Flags (1867), she wrote about the British in Algeria. Ouida strongly connected with the French colonists, and it showed support for them as well as, to some measure, for the Arabs. The book was six times filmed and turned into a stage adaptation. In most of Asia, her 1872 book A Dog of Flanders is regarded as a children's classic. Her novel Signa was cited by American writer Jack London as a contributing factor to his success in writing. She later fell into poverty as a result of her opulent lifestyle, and her artwork was auctioned off to cover her bills. Her illness claimed her life in Italy. Her birthplace, Bury St Edmunds, saw a public subscription soon after her passing, and a fountain for horses and dogs was named in her honor.

CONTENTS

I
OF EARLSCOURT'S FIANCEE

"To compass her with sweet observances,
To dress her beautifully and keep her true."

That, according to Mr. Tennyson's lately-published opinion, is the devoir of that deeply-to-be-pitied individual, l'homme marié. Possibly in the times of which the Idyls treat, Launcelot and Gunevere *might* have been the sole, exceptional mauvais sujets in the land, and woad, being the chief ingredient in the toilet-dress, mightn't come quite so expensive. But nowadays "sweet observances," rendered, I presume, by gifts from Hunt and Roskell's and boxes in the grand tier, tell on a cheque-book so severely; "keeping her true" is such an exceedingly problematical performance, to judge by Sir C. C.'s breathless work, and "dressing her beautifully" comes so awfully expensive, with crinoline and cashmeres, pink pearls, and Mechlin, and the beau sexe's scornful repudiation, not alone of a faded silk, like poor Enid's, but of the handsomest dress going, if it's damned by being "seen twice," that I have ever vowed that, plaise à Dieu, I will never marry, and with heaven's help will keep the vow better than I might most probably keep the matrimonial ones if I took them. Yet if ever I saw a woman for whom I could have fancied a man's committing that semisuicidal act, that woman was Beatrice Boville. Not for her beauty, for, except one of the loveliest figures and a pair of the most glorious eyes, she did not claim much; not for her money, for she had none; not for her birth, for on one side that was somewhat obscure; but for *herself*; and had I ever tried the herculean task of dressing anybody beautifully and keeping anybody true, it should have been she, but for the fact that when I knew her first she was engaged to my cousin Earlscourt. We had none of us ever dreamt he would marry, for he had been sworn to political life so long, given over so utterly to the battle-ground of St. Stephen's and the intrigues of Downing Street, that the ladies of our house were sorely wrathful when they heard that he had at last fallen in love and proposed to Beatrice Boville, who, though she was Lady Mechlin's niece, was the daughter of a West Indian who had married her mother, broken her heart, spent her money, deserted her, and never been heard of since; the more wrathful as they had no help for themselves, and were obliged to be contented with distinguishing her with refreshing appellations of a "very clever schemer," evidently a "perfect intrigante," and similar epithets with which their sex is driven for consolation under such trying circumstances. It's a certain amount of relief to us to call a man who has cut us down in a race "a stupid owl; very little in him!" but it is mild gratification to that enjoyed by ladies when they retaliate for injury done them by that delightful bonbon of a sentence, "No doubt a most artful person!" You see it conveys so much and proves three things in one—their own artlessness, their enemy's worthlessness, and their victim's folly. Being with Earlscourt at the time of his "singularly unwise, step," as they phrased it, I knew that he wasn't trapped in any way, and that he was loved irrespectively of his social rank; but where was the good of telling that to deeply-injured and perforce silenced ladies? "They knew better;" and when a woman says that, always bow to her superior judgment, my good fellow, even when she knows better than you what you did with yourself last evening, and informs you positively you were at that odious Mrs. Vanille's opera supper, though, to the best of your belief, you never stirred from the U. S. card-room; or you will be voted a Goth, and make an enemy for the rest of your natural life.

In opposition to the rest of the family, I thought (and you must know by this time, amis lecteurs, that I hardly think marriage so enjoyable an institution as some writers do, but perhaps a little like a pipe of opium, of which the dreams are better than the awakening)—I thought that he could hardly have done better, as far as his own happiness went, as I saw her standing by him one evening in the window of Lady Mechlin's rooms at Lemongenseidlitz, where we all were that August, a brilliant, fascinating woman already, though then but nineteen, noble-hearted, frank, impetuous, with something in the turn of her head and the proud glance of her eyes, that told you, you might trust her; that she was of the stuff to keep her word even to her own hinderance; that neither would she tell a lie, nor brook one imputed to her; that she might err on the side of pride, on the side of meanness never; that she might have plenty of failings, but not anything petty, low, or ungenerous among them. The evening sun fell on them as they stood, on her high, white forehead, with its chestnut hair turned off it as you see it in old pictures, which Earlscourt was touching caressingly with his hand as he talked to her. They seemed well suited, and yet—his fault was pride, an unassailable, unyielding pride; hers was pride, too, pride in her own truth and honor, which would send you to the deuce if you ever presumed to doubt either; and I wondered idly as I looked at them, whether those two prides would ever come in conflict, and if so, whether either of them would give in in such a case—whether there would be submission on one side or on both, or on neither? Such metaphysical and romantic calculations are not often my line; but as they stood together, the sun faded off, and a cold, stormy wind blew up in its stead, which, perhaps, metaphorically suggested the problem to me. As one goes through life one gets up to so many sunny, balmy, cloudless days, and so often before the night is down gets wetted to the skin by a drenching shower, that one contracts an uncomfortable habit when the sun *does* shine, of looking out for squalls, a fear that, sans doute, considerably damps the pleasures of the noon. But the fear is natural, isn't it, more's the pity, when one has been often caught?

I chanced to ask her that night what made her so fond of Earlscourt. She turned her fearless, flashing eyes half laughingly, half haughtily on me, the color brighter in her face:

"I should have thought you would rather have asked how could I, or any other woman whom he stooped to notice, fail to love him? There are few hearts and intellects so noble: he is as superior to you ball-room loungers, you butterfly flutterers, as the stars to that chandelier."

"Bien obligé!" laughed I. "But that is just what I meant. Most young ladies are afraid of him; you never were?"

She laughed contemptuously.

"Afraid! You do not know much of me. It is precisely his giant intellect that first drew me to him, when I heard his speech on the Austrian question. Do you remember how the Lords listened to him so quietly that you could have heard a feather fall? I like that silence of theirs when they hear what they admire, better than I do the cheers of the other house. Afraid of him! What a ludicrous idea! Do you suppose I should be afraid of any one? It is only those who are conceited or cowardly, who are timid. If you have nothing to assume, or to conceal, what cause have you to fear? I love, honor, reverence Lord Earlscourt, God knows; but fear him—never!"

"Not even his anger, if you ever incurred it?" I asked her, amused with her haughty indignation.

"Certainly not. Did I merit it, I would come to him frankly, and ask his pardon, and he would give it; if I did not deserve it, *he* would be the one to repent."

She looked far more attractive than many a handsomer woman, and infinitely more noble than a more tractable one. She was admirably fitted for Earlscourt, if he trusted her; but it was just possible he might some day *mis*trust and *mis*understand her, and then there might be the devil to pay!

II
THE FIRST SHADOW

Lemongenseidlitz was a charming little Bad. Beatrice Boville and her aunt Lady Mechlin, Earlscourt and I, had been there six weeks. His brother peers—of whom there were scores at Lemongenseidlitz—complimented Earlscourt on his fiancée.

"So you're caught at last?" said an octogenarian minister, who was as sprightly as a schoolboy. "Well, my dear fellow, you might have gone higher, sans doute, but on my honor I don't think you could have done better."

It was the universal opinion. Beatrice was not the belle of the Bad, because there were dozens of beautiful women, and beautiful she was not; but she was more admired than any of them, and had Earlscourt wanted voices to justify his choice he would have had them, but he didn't; he was entirely independent of the opinions of others, and had he chosen to set his coronet on the brows of a peasant girl, would have cared little what any one thought or said. We all of us enjoyed that six weeks. Lady Mechlin lost to her heart's content at roulette, and was as complacent over her losses as any old dowager could be. Beatrice Boville shone best, as nice natures ever do, in a sunny atmosphere; and if she had any faults of impatient temper or pride, there was nothing to call them forth. Earlscourt, cold politician though he'd been, gave himself up entirely to the warmer, brighter existence, which he found in his new passion; and I, not being in love with anybody, made the pleasantest love possible wherever I liked. We all of us found a couleur de rose tint in the air of little Lemongenseidlitz, and I'd quite forgotten my presentiment, when, one night at the Kursaal, a cloud no bigger than a man's hand came up on the sunny horizon, and put me in mind of it.

Earlscourt came into the ball room rather late; he had been talking with some French ministers on some international project which he was anxious to effect, and asked Lady Mechlin where Beatrice was.

"She was with me a moment ago; she is waltzing, I dare say," said the old lady, whose soul was hankering after the ivory ball.

"Very likely," he answered, as he looked among the dancers for her; he was restless without her, though he would have liked none to see the weakness, for he was a man who felt more than he told. He could not see her, and went through the rooms till he found her, which was in a small anteroom alone. She started as he spoke to her, and a start being a timorous and nervous thing of which Beatrice Boville was never guilty, he drew her to him anxiously.

"My darling, has anything annoyed you?"

She answered him with her habitual candor:

"Yes; but I cannot tell you what, just now."

"Cannot tell me! and why?"

"Because I cannot. I can give no other reason. It is nothing of import to you, or you are sure I should not keep it from you."

"Yes; but I am equally sure that anything that concerns you *is* of import to me. To whom should you tell anything, if not to me? I do not like concealment, Beatrice."

His tone was grave; indeed, too much like reproof to a fractious child to suit Beatrice's pride. She drew away from him.

"Nor I. You must think but meanly of me if you can impute anything like concealment to me."

"How can I do otherwise? You tell me you have been annoyed, and refuse to say how, and by whom. Is that anything but concealment? If any one has offended or insulted you, I ought to be the first you came to. A woman, Beatrice, should have nothing hidden from the man who is, or will be, her husband."

She threw her arms around him. Her moods were variable as a child's. Perhaps this very variability Earlscourt hardly understood, for it was utterly opposed to his own character: you always found him the same; *she* would be all storm one moment, all sunshine the next.

"Do you suppose I would hide anything from you? Do you think for a moment I would hold back anything you had a right to know? You might look into my heart; there would be no thought or feeling there I should wish to keep from you. But if you exact confidence, so do I. Would you think of taking as your wife one you could not trust?"

He answered her a little sternly:

"No; if I once ceased to believe in your truth or honor, as I believe in my own, I should part from you forever, though God knows what it would cost me!"

"God knows what it would cost *me!* But I give you free leave. The instant you find a flaw in either, I am no longer worthy of your love; withdraw it, and I will never complain. But trust me you must and will; I merit your confidence, and I exact it. Look at me, Ernest. Do you believe I could ever deceive you?"

He looked into her eyes long and earnestly.

"No. When you do, your eyes will droop before mine. I trust you, Beatrice, fully, and I know you will never wrong it."

She clung to him with caressant softness, softer in her than in a meeker-spirited woman, as she whispered, 'Never!' and a man would need have been obtuse and skeptical, indeed, who could then have doubted her. And so that cloud blew over, for a time, at the least—trusted, Beatrice Boville was soft and gentle as a lamb; mistrusted or misjudged, she was fiery as a young lioness, and Earlscourt, I thought, though originally won by her intellect, held her too much as a child to fully understand her character, and to see that, though she was his darling and plaything, she was also a passionate, ardent, proud-spirited woman, stung by injustice and impatient of doubt. No two people could be more fitted to make each other's happiness, yet it struck me that it was just possible they might make each other's misery very completely, through want of comprehension on the one side, through want of explanation on the other.

"Your marriage is fixed, isn't it, Earlscourt?" asked his sister, Lady Clive Edghill, who had come to Lemongenseidlitz, and, though compelled by him, as he compelled all the rest of the family, to show Beatrice strict courtesy, disliked her, because she was not an advantageous match, was much too young in their opinion, and had no money—the gravest crimes a woman can have in the eyes of any man's relatives. "The 14th! Indeed! yours is a very short engagement!"

"Is there any reason why it should be longer?"

"O, dear, no! none that I am aware of. I wish, earnestly, my dear Earlscourt, I could congratulate you more warmly; but I can never say what I do not feel, and I had so much hoped—"

"My dear Helena, as long as I have so much reason to congratulate myself, it matters very little whether you do or do not," smiled Earlscourt. He was too much of a lion to be stung by gnats.

"I dare say. I sincerely trust you may ever have reason. But I heard some very disagreeable things about that Mr. Boville, Beatrice's father. Do you know that he was in a West India regiment, but was deprived of his commission even there?—a perfect blackleg and sharper, I understand. I suppose she has never mentioned him to you?"

"You are very much mistaken; all that Beatrice knows of him, I know; that is but little, for Lady Mechlin took her long ago, when her mother died, from such unfit guardianship. Beatrice is as open as the day—"

"Indeed! A little too frank, perhaps?"

"Too frank? That is a paradox. No one can have too much candor. It is not a virtue of your sex, but it is one, thank God! which she possesses in a rare degree, though possibly it gains her enemies where it should gain her friends."

"Still frankness *may* merge into indiscretion," said Helena, musingly.

"I doubt it. An indiscreet woman is never frank, for she has always the memory of silly things said and done which require concealment."

"I was merely thinking," Helena went on, regardless of a speech which she did not perhaps relish, pour cause, "merely from my deep interest in you, and my knowledge of all you will wish your wife to be, that perhaps Beatrice might be, in pure insouciance, a little too careless, a little too candid for so prominent a position as she will occupy. Last night, in passing a little anteroom in the Redoute, I saw her in such extremely earnest conversation with a man, a handsome man, about your height and age, and—"

The anteroom! Earlscourt thought, with a pang, of the start she had given when he entered it the previous night. But he was not of a jealous temperament, nor a curious one; his mind was too constantly occupied with great projects and ambitions to be capable of joining petty things together into an elaborate mosaic; he had no petitesses himself, and trifles passed unheeded. He interrupted her decidedly:

"What is there in that to build a pyramid of censure from? Doubtless it was one of her acquaintances—probably one of mine also. I should have thought you knew me better, Helena, than to attempt this gossiping nonsense with me."

"O, I say no more. I only thought you, of all men, would wish Cæsar's wife to be above—"

The gnat-strings had been too insignificant to rouse him before, but at this one his eyebrows contracted, and he rose.

"Silence! Never venture to make such a speech as that to me again. In insulting Beatrice you insult me. Unless you can mention her in terms of proper respect and reverence, never presume to speak her name to me again. Her enemies are my enemies, and, whoever they may be, I will treat them as such."

Helena was sorely frightened; if she held anybody in veneration it was Earlscourt, and she would never have ventured so far with him but for the causeless hate she had taken to Beatrice, simply because Lady Clive had decided long ago that her brother was too voué to public life ever to marry, and that her son would succeed to his title. She was sorely frightened, but she comforted herself—the little thorn she had thrust in might rankle after a while; as pleasant a consolation under failure as any lady could desire.

Beatrice was coming along the corridor as Earlscourt left Helena's rooms, which were in the same hotel as Lady Mechlin's. She was stopping to look out of one of the windows at the sunset; she did not see him at first, and he watched her unobserved, and smiled at the idea of associating anything deceitful with her—smiled still more at the idea when she came up to him, with her frank, bright, regard, lifting her face for a caress, and patting both her hands through his arm. Accustomed to chill and reserved women in his own family, her abandon had a great charm for him; but perhaps it led him into his error in holding her still as half a child.

"You have been seeing my enemy?" she said, laughingly. "Your sister does not like me, does she?"

"Not like you! Why should you think so? She may not like my marrying, perhaps, because she had decided for me that I should never do so; and no woman can bear any prophecies she makes to prove wrong."

"Very possibly that may be one reason; but she does not think me good enough for you."

Her tips curved disdainfully, and Earlscourt caught a glimpse of her in her fiery mood. He laughed at her where, with her, he had better have admitted the truth. Beatrice had too much pride to be wounded by it, and far too much good sense to measure herself by money and station.

"Nonsense, Beatrice; I should have thought you too proud to suppose such a thing," he said, carelessly.

"It is the truth, nevertheless."

"More foolish she, then; but if you and I do not, what can it signify?"

"Nothing. As long as I am worthy of you in your eyes, what others think or say is nothing to me. I honor you too much to make the gauge between us a third person's opinion; or measure you or myself by a few stops higher or lower in the social ladder. Your sister thinks me below you in rank, soit! She is right; I am quite ready to admit it; but that I am your equal in all that makes men and women equal in the sight of Heaven, I know. When she finds me unworthy of you in thought or deed, then she may call me beneath you—not till then."

Her cheeks were flushed; he could hear her quick breathings, and in her vehemence and haughty indignation she picked the petals of her bouquet de corsage to pieces and flung them away. Another time he would have thought how well her pride became her, and given her some fond reply. Just now the thorn rankled as Lady Clive had hoped, and he answered her gravely, in the tone which it was as unwise to use to her as to prick a thorough-bred colt with both spurs.

"You are quite right. Were I a king, you would be my equal as long as your heart was mine, your mind as noble, and your character as unsullied as I hope them to be now."

She turned on him rapidly with the first indignant look she had ever given to him.

"*Hope!* You might say *know*, I think!"

"I would have said 'know,' and meant it too, yesterday."

"Yesterday? What do you mean? Why am I less worthy your confidence to-day than yesterday?"

She looked wonderingly at him, her eyes full of inquiry and bewilderment. It was marvellous acting, if it was acting; yet he thought she could scarcely have so soon forgotten their scene in the anteroom the previous night. They had now come into the salon; he left her side and walked to the mantel-piece, leaning his arm on it, and speaking coldly, as he had never done to her since they first met.

"Beatrice, do not attempt to act with me. You cannot have forgotten what we said in the anteroom last night. Nothing assumed ever deceives me, and you only lower yourself in my estimation."

She clinched her hands till the rings he had given her crushed together.

"Act! assume! Great Heaven, how dare you speak such words to me?"

"Dare? You speak like an angry child, Beatrice. When you are reasonable I will answer you."

The tears welled into her eyes, but she would not let them fall.

"Reasonable? Is there anything unreasonable in resenting words utterly undeserved? Would you be calm under them yourself, Lord Earlscourt? I remember now what you mean by yesterday; I did not remember when I asked you. Had I done so I should never have simulated ignorance and surprise. Only last night you promised to trust me. Is this your trust, to accuse me of artifice, of acting, of falsehood? I would bear no such imputation from any one, still less from you, who ought to know me so well. What happiness can we have if you—"

She stopped, the tears choking her voice, but he did not see them; he only saw her indignant attitude, her flushed cheeks, her flashing eyes, and put them down to her girlish passion.

"Calm yourself, Beatrice, I beg. This sort of scene is very distasteful to me; to figure in a lover's quarrel hardly suits me. I am not young enough to find amusement in disputation and reconciliation, sparring one moment and caresses the next. My life is one of grave pursuits and feverish ambitions; I am often harassed, annoyed, worn out in body and mind. What I hoped for from you was, to borrow the gayety and brightness of your own youth, to find rest, and happiness, and distraction. A life of disputes, reproaches, and misconstruction, would be what I never would endure."

Beatrice was silent; she leaned her forehead on her arms and did not answer him. His tone stung her pride, but his words touched her heart. Her passion was always short-lived, and no evil spirit possessed her long. She rebelled against the first part of his speech with all her might, but she softened to the last. She came up to him with her hands out.

"I had no right to speak so impatiently to you. God knows, to make your life happy will be my only thought, and care, and wish. If I spoke angrily, forgive me!"

Earlscourt knew that the nature so quick to acknowledge error was worth fifty unerring and unruffled ones; still he sighed as he answered her,—

"My dear child, I forgive you. But, Beatrice, there is no foe to love so sure and deadly as dissension!" And as he drew her to him and felt her soft warm lips on his, he thought, half uneasily yet, "She has never told me who annoyed her—never mentioned her companion in the anteroom last night."

Lady Clive had her wish; the thorn festered as promisingly as she could have desired. Ce n'est que le premier pas qui coûte in quarrels as in all else. Dispute once, you are very sure to dispute again, whether with the man you hate or the woman you love.

III
HOW PRIDE SOWED AND REAPED

It only wanted three weeks to Beatrice Boville's marriage. We were all to leave Lemongenseidlitz together in a fortnight's time for old Lady Mechlin's house in Berks, where the ceremony was to take place.

"Earlscourt is quite infatuated," said Lady Clive to me one evening. "Beatrice is very charming, of course, but she is not at all suited to him, she is so fiery, so impetuous, so self-reliant."

"I think you are mistaken," said I. I admired Beatrice Boville—comme je vous ai dit—and I didn't like our family's snaps and snarls at her. "She may be impetuous, but, as her impulses are always generous, that doesn't matter much. She is only fiery at injustice, and, for myself, I prefer a woman who can stand up for her own rights and her friends' to one who'll sit by in—you'll call it meekness, I suppose? I call it cowardice and hypocrisy—to hear herself or them abused."

"Thank you, mon ami," said Beatrice's voice at my elbow, as Lady Clive rose and crossed the room. "I am much obliged for your defence; I couldn't help hearing it as I stood in the balcony, and I wish very much I deserved it. I am afraid, though, I cannot dispute Helena's verdict of 'fiery,' 'impetuous,'—"

"And self-reliant?" I asked her. She laughed softly, and her eyes unconsciously sought Earlscourt, who was talking to Lady Mechlin.

"Well? Not quite, now! But, by the way, why should people charge self-reliance on to one as something reprehensible and undesirable? A proper self-reliance is an indispensable ground-work to any success. If you cannot rely upon yourself, upon your power to judge and to act, you must rely upon some other person, possibly upon many people, and you become, perforce, vacillating and unstable.

'To thine own self be true,
And it shall follow, as the day the night,
Thou canst not then be false to any man.'"

As she spoke a servant brought a note to her, and I noticed her cheeks grow pale as she saw the handwriting upon it. She broke it open, and read it hastily, an oddly troubled, worried look coming over her face, a look that Earlscourt could not help but notice as he stood beside her.

"Is there anything in that letter to annoy you, Beatrice?" he asked, very naturally.

She started—rather guiltily, I thought—and crushed the note in her hand.

"Whom is it from? It troubles you, I think. Tell me, my darling, is it anything that vexes or offends you?" he whispered, bending down to her.

She laughed, a little nervously for her, and tore the note into tiny pieces.

"Why do you not tell me, Beatrice?" he said again, with a shade of annoyance on his face.

"Because I would rather not," she said, frankly enough, letting the pieces float out of the window into the street below. The shadow grew darker in his face; he bent his head in acquiescence, and said no more, but I don't think he forgot either the note or her destroyal of it.

"I thought there was implicit confidence *before* marriage whatever there is after," sneered his sister, as she passed him. He answered her calmly:—

"I should say, Helena, that neither before nor after marriage would any man who respected his wife suffer curiosity or suspicion to enter into him. If he do, he has no right to expect happiness, and he will certainly not go the way to get it."

That was the only reply he gave Lady Clive, but her thorn No. 2 festered in him, and when he bade Beatrice good night, standing alone with her in the little drawing room, he took both her hands in his, and looked straight into her eyes.

"Beatrice, why would you not let me see that note this evening?"

She looked up at him as fearlessly and clearly.

"If I tell you why, I must tell you whom the note was from, and what it was about, and I would much rather do neither as yet."

"That is very strange. I dislike concealment of all kinds, especially from you, who so soon will be my wife. It is inconceivable to me why you should need or desire any. I thought your life was a fair open book, every line of which I might read if I desired."

Beatrice looked at him in amazement.

"So you may. Do you suppose, if I had any secret from you that I feared you should know, I could have a moment's peace in your society, or look at you for an instant as I do now? I give you my word of honor that there was nothing either in the note that concerns you, or that you would wish me to tell you. In a few days you shall know all that was in it, but I ask you as a kindness not to press me now. Surely you do not think me such a child but that you can trust me in so small a trifle. If you say I am not worthy of your confidence, you imply that I am not worthy of your love. You spoke nobly to your sister just now, Ernest; do not act less nobly to me."

He could not but admire her as she looked at him, with her fearless, unshadowed regard, her head thrown a little back, and her attitude half-commanding, half-entreating. He smiled in spite of himself.

"You are a wayward, spoiled child, Beatrice. You must have your own way?"

She gave a little stamp of her foot. She hated being called a spoiled child, specially by him, and in a serious moment.

"If I have my own way, have I your full confidence too?"

"Yes; but, my dear Beatrice, the only way to gain confidence is never to excite suspicion." And Lady Clive's thorn rankled à ravir; for even as he pressed his goodnight kisses on her lips, he thought, restlessly, "Shall we make each other happy?—am I too grave for her?—and is she too wilful for me? I want rest, not contention."

The night after that there was a bal-masqué at the Redoute. I was just coming out of my room as Beatrice came down the corridor; She had her mask in her hand, her dress was something white starred with gold, and round her hair she had a little band of pearls of Earlscourt's gift. I never saw her look better, specially when her cheeks flushed and her eyes brightened as Earlscourt opened his door next mine, and met her. He did not see me, the corridor was empty, and he bent down to her with fond words and caresses.

"Do I look well?" she said, with child-like delight.

"I am so glad, Ernest, I want to do you honor."

In that mood he understood her well enough, and he pressed her against his heart with the passion that was in him, whose strength he so rarely let her see. Then he drew her hand through his arm, and led her down the stairs; and, as I laughed to find to what lengths our cold statesman could come at last, I thought Lady Clive's thorns would be innocuous, however well planted.

Earlscourt never danced; nothing but what was calm and stately could possibly have suited him; but Beatrice did, and waltzed like a Willis, (though she liked even better than that standing on his arm and talking with his friends—diplomatic, military, and ministerial—on all sorts of questions, most of which she could handle nearly as well as they;) and about the middle of the evening, while she was waltzing with some man or other who had begged to be introduced to her, Earlscourt left the ball-room for ten minutes in earnest conversation with one of the French ministers, who was leaving the next morning. As he came back again, I asked him where Beatrice was, because Powell, of the Bays, was bothering my life out to introduce him to her.

"In the ball room, isn't she? She is with Lady Mechlin, of course, if, the waltz is over."

A familiar voice stopped him.

"She is not in the ball room. Go where you found her the other night, and see if Cæsar's promised wife be above suspicion!"

I could have sworn the voice was Lady Clive's; a pink domino passed us too fast for detention, but Earlscourt's lips turned white at the subtle whisper, and he muttered a fierce oath—fiercer from him, because he's never stirred into fiery expletives. "There is some vile plot against her. I must sift it to the bottom;" and, pushing past me, he entered the ball room. Beatrice was not there; and wending his way through the crowd, he went in through several other apartments leading off to the right, and involuntarily I followed him, to see what the malicious whisper of the pink domino had meant. Earlscourt lifted the curtain that parted the anteroom from the other chamber—lifted it to see Beatrice Boville, as the pink domino had prophesied, and not alone! With her was a man, masked, but about Earlscourt's height, and seemingly about his age, who, as he saw us, let go her hand with a laugh, turned on to a balcony, which was but a yard or so from the street, and dropped on to the pave below. Beatrice started and colored, but I thought she must be the most desperate actress going, for she came up to Earlscourt with a smile, and was about to put her hand through his arm, but he signed her away from him.

"Your acting is quite useless with me. I am not to be blinded by it again. I have believed in your truth as in my own—"

"So you may still. Listen to me, Ernest!"

"Hush! Do not add falsehood to falsehood."

He spoke sternly and coldly; his pride, which was as strong as his love for her, would not gratify her by a sign of the torture within him, and even in his bitterest anger Earlscourt would never have been ungentle to a woman. That word acted like an incantation on her, the blood crimsoned her temples, her eyes literally flashed fire, and she threw back her head with the haughty, impatient gesture habitual to her.

"Falsehood? Three times of late you have used that word to me."

"And why? Because you merited it."

She stood before him, the indignant flush hotter still upon her cheeks, her lips curved into scornful anger. If she was an actress, she knew her rôle to perfection.

"Do you speak that seriously, Lord Earlscourt? Do you believe that I have lied to you?"

"God help me! What else can I believe?" he muttered, too low for her to hear it.

She asked him the question again, fiercely, and he answered her briefly and sternly, —

"I believe that all your life with me has been a lie. I trusted you implicitly, and how do you return it? By carrying on clandestine intercourse with another man, giving him interviews that you conceal from me, having letters that you destroy, doubtless receiving caresses that you take care are unwitnessed; while you dare to smile in my face, and to dupe me with child-like tenderness, and to bid me 'trust' you and believe in you! Love shared to me is worthless, and on my wife, Beatrice, no stain must rest!"

As he spoke, a dark shadow spread over her countenance, her evil spirit rose up in her, and her bright, frank, fearless face grew almost as hard and cold as his, while her teeth were set together, till her lips, usually soft and laughing, were pressed into one straight haughty line.

"Since you give me up so easily, far be it from me to dispute your will. We part from this hour, if you desire it. My honor is as dear to me as yours to you, and to those who dare to suspect it I never stoop to defend it!"

"But, my God! Beatrice, what *am* I to believe?"

"Whatever you please!"

"What I please! Child, you must be mad. What *can* I believe, but that you are the most perfect of all actresses, that your art is the greatest of all sins, the art that clothes itself in innocence, and carries would-be truth upon its lips. Prove to me that I wrong you!"

She shook her head; the devil in her had still the victory; her eyes glittered, and her little teeth were clinched together.

"What I exact is trust without proof. I am not your prisoner, Lord Earlscourt, to be tried coldly, and acquitted if you find legal evidence of innocence; convicted, if there be a link wanting. If you choose to trust me, I have told you often your trust will never be wronged; if you choose to condemn me, do. I shall not stoop to show you your injustice."

Earlscourt's face grew dark and hard as hers, but it was wonderful how well his pride chained down all evidence of suffering; the only sign was in the hoarseness of, and quiver in, his voice.

"Say nothing more—prevarication is guilt! God forgive you, Beatrice Boville! If you loved me, and knelt at my feet, I would not make you my wife after the art and the lies with which you have repaid my trust. Thank God, you do not already bear my name and my honor in your hands!"

With those words he left her. Beatrice stood still in the same place, her lips set in one scornful line, her eyes glittering, her brow crimson, her whole attitude defiant, wronged, and unyielding. Earlscourt passed me, his face white as death, and was out of sight in a second. I waited a moment, then I followed my impulse, and went up to her.

"Beatrice, for Heaven's sake, what is all this?"

She turned her large eyes on me haughtily.

"Do *you* believe what your cousin does?"

I answered her as briefly:—

"No, I do not. There is some mistake here."

She seized my arm, impetuously:—

"Promise me, on your honor, never to tell what I tell to you while I live. Promise me, on your faith as a gentleman."

"On my honor, I promise. Well?"

"The man whom you saw with me to-night is my father. Lord Earlscourt chose to condemn me without inquiry; so let him! But I tell you, that you may tell him if I die before him, that he wronged me. You know Mr. Boville's—my father's—character. I had not seen him since I was a child, but when he heard of my engagement to Lord Earlscourt he found me out, and wanted to force himself on him, and borrow money of him, and—" She stopped, her face was crimson, but she went on, passionately. "All my efforts, of course, were to keep them apart, to spare my father such degradation, and your cousin such an application. I could not tell Lord Earlscourt, for he is generous as the winds, and I knew what he would have done. My note was from my father; he wanted to frighten me into introducing him to Lord Earlscourt, but he did not succeed. I would not have your cousin disgraced or pained by—Arthur, that is all my crime! No very great one, is it?" And she laughed a loud, bitter laugh, as unlike her own as the stormy shadow on her face was like the usual sunshine.

"But, great Heaven! why not have told this to Earlscourt?"

She signed me to silence with a passionate gesture.

"No! He dishonored me with suspicion; let him go. I forbid you ever to breathe a word of what I have told you to him. If he has pride, so have I. He would hold no dishonor greater than for another man to charge him with a lie. My truth is as untainted as his, and my honor as dear to me. He accused me wrongly; let him repent. I would have loved and reverenced him as never any woman yet could do; but once suspected, I could find no happiness with him. His bitter words are stamped into my heart. I shall never forget—I doubt if I shall ever forgive—them. I can bear anything but injustice or misconception. If any doubt me, they are free to do so; theirs is the sin, not mine. As he has sown so must he reap, and so must I!" A low, gasping sob choked her voice, but she stood like a little Pythoness, the pearl gleaming above her brow, her eyes unnaturally bright, the color burning in her face, her attitude what it was when he left her, defiant, wronged, unyielding. She swept away from me to a man who was coming through the other room, and he stared at her set lips and her gleaming eyes as she asked him, carelessly, "Count Avonyl, will you have the kindness to take me to Lady Mechlin?"

That was the last I saw of her. She left the Bad with her aunt as soon as the day dawned, and when I went to our hotel, I found that Earlscourt had ordered post-horses immediately he quitted the ball room, and gone—where he did not leave word. So my presentiment was verified; the pride of both had come in conflict, and the pride of neither had succumbed. How long it would sustain and satisfy them, I could not guess; but Lady Clive smiled again, as sweetly as ladies ever do when their thorns have thriven and brought forth abundant fruit. Some other time I will tell you how I saw Beatrice Boville again; but I often thought of

"Pauline, by pride

Angels have fallen ere thy time!"

when I recalled her with the pearls above her brow, and her passionate, gleaming eyes, and her fearless, scornful, haughty anguish, as she had stood before me that night when Pride *v.* Pride caused the wreck of both their lives.

IV
WHERE I SAW BEATRICE BOVILLE AGAIN

I don't belong to St. Stephen's myself, thank Heaven. Very likely they would have returned me for the county when the governor departed this life had I tried them; but as I generally cut the county, from not being one of the grass countries, and as I couldn't put forward any patriotic claims like Mr. Harper Twelvetrees, (who, as he's such a slayer of vermin, thought, I suppose, that he'd try his hand at the dry-rot and the red tapeworms, which, according to cotton grumblers, are sapping the nation,) I haven't solicited its suffrages. The odds at Tattersall's interest me more than the figures of the ways and means; and Diophantus's and Kettledrum's legerdemain at Newmarket and Epsom is more to my taste than our brilliant rhetorician's with the surplus. I don't care a button about Lord Raynham and Sir C. Burrell's maids-of-all-work; they are not an attractive class, I should say, and, if they like to amuse their time tumbling out of windows, I can't see for the life of me why peers and gentlemen should rush to the rescue like Don Quixote to Dulcinea's. And as for that great question, Tea v. Paper, bohea delights the souls of old ladies and washerwomen—who destroy crumpets and character over its inebriating cups, and who will rush to crown Lord Derby's and Mr. Disraeli's brows with laurels if they ever go to the country with a teapot blazoned on their patriotic banners—more than it does mine, which prefers Bass and Burgundy, seltzer and Sillery; and, though I dare say Brown, Jones, and Robinson find the Divorce News exciting, and paper collars very showy and economical, as I myself am content with the *Times* and its compeers, and think, with poor Brummel, that life without daily clean linen were worthless, *that* subject doesn't absorb me as it does those gentlemen who find "the last tax of knowledge" so grandiloquent and useful a finishing period. So I have never stood for the county, nor essayed to stand for it, seeing that to one Bernal Osborne there are fifty prosers in St. Stephen's, and to be bored is, to a butterfly flutterer, as the young lady whose name heads this paper once obligingly called me, torture unparalleled by anything short of acid wine or the Chinese atrocities, though truly he who heads our Lower House with his vernal heart and his matchless brain were enough to make any man, coxcomb or hero, oppositionist or ministerialist, proud to sit in the same chamber with him. But there are nights now and then, of course, when I like to go to both Houses, to hear Lord Derby's rich, intricate oratory, or Gladstone's rhetoric, (which has so potent a spell even for his foes, and is yet charged so strangely against him as half a crime; possibly by the same spirit with which plain women reproach a pretty one for her beauty: what business has he to be more attractive than his compeers? of course it's a péché mortel in their eyes!) and when Mrs. Breloques, who is a charming little woman, to whom no man short of a Goth could possibly say "No" to any petition, gave me a little blow with her fan, and told me, as I valued her friendship, to get an order and take her and Gwen to hear the Lords' debate on Tuesday, when my cousin Viscount Earlscourt, one of the best orators in the Upper House, was certain to speak, of course I obliged her. Her sister Gwen, who was a girl of seventeen, barely out, and whom I wished at Jerico, (three is so odious a number, one of the triad must ever be de trop,) was wrathful with the Upper House; it in no wise realized her expectations; the peers should have worn their robes, she thought, (as if the horrors of a chamber filled with Thames odors in June wasn't enough without being bored with velvet and ermine) she would have been further impressed by coronets also; they had no business to lounge on their benches as if they were in a smoking-room; they should have declaimed like Kean, not spoken colloquially; and—in fact, they shouldn't have been ordinary men at all. I think a fine collection from Madame Tussaud's, with a touch of the Roman antique, would have been much more to Gwen's ideal, and she wasn't at all content till Earlscourt rose; he reconciled her a little, for he had a grand-seigneur air, she said, that made up for the incongruities of his dress. It was a measure that he had much at heart; he had exerted for it all his influence in the cabinet, and he was determined that the bill should pass the Lords, though the majority inclined to throw it out. As he stood now against the table, with his calm dignity of gesture, his unstrained flow of words, and his rich and ringing voice, which could give majesty to commonplace subjects, and sway even an apathetic audience as completely as Sheridan's Begum speech, every one in the House listened attentively, and each of his words fell with its due weight. I heard him with pride, often as I had done so before, though I noticed with pain that the lines in his forehead and his mouth were visibly deepened; that he seemed to speak with effort, for him, and looked altogether, as somebody had said to me at White's in the morning, as if he were wearing out, and would go down in his prime, like Canning and Pitt.

"Lord Earlscourt looks very ill—don't you think so?" said Lelia Breloques.

As I answered her, I heard a sharp-wrung sigh, and I looked for the first time at the lady next me. I saw a delicate profile, lips compressed and colorless, chestnut hair that I had last seen with his pearls gleaming above it: I saw, en deux mots, Beatrice Boville for the first time since that night eight months before, when she had stood before me in her passion and her pride. She never took her eyes off Earlscourt while he spoke, and I wondered if she regretted having lost him for a point of honor. Had she grown indifferent to him, that she had come to his own legislative chamber, or was her love so much stronger than her pride that she had sought to see him thus rather than not see him at all? When his speech was closed, and he had resumed his place on the benches, she leaned back, covering her eyes with her hand for a moment: and, as I said aloud (more for her benefit than Mrs. Breloques's) my regret that Earlscourt would wear himself out, I was afraid, in his devotion to public life, Beatrice started at the sound of my voice, turned her head hastily, and her face was colorless enough to tell me she had not gratified her pride without some cost. Of course I spoke to her; she had been a favorite of mine always, and I had often wished to come across her again; but beyond learning that she was with Lady Mechlin in Lowndes Square, and had been spending the winter at Pau for her aunt's health, I had no time to hear more, for Lelia, having only come for Earlscourt's speech, bade me take her to her carriage, while Beatrice and her party remained for the rest of the debate; but the rencontre struck me as so odd, that I believe it occupied my thoughts more than Mrs. Breloques liked, who got into her carriage in not the best of humors, and asked me if *I* was going in for public life that I'd grown so particularly unamusing. We're always unamusing to one woman if we're thinking at all about another.

"Do you know who was at the House to-night, Earlscourt, to hear your speech?" I asked him, as I met him, a couple of hours afterwards, in one of the passages, as he was leaving the House. He had altered much in eight months; he stooped a little from his waist; he looked worn, and his lips were pale. Men said his stamina was not equal to his brain; physicians, that he gave himself too much work and too little sleep. I knew he was more wrapped in public life than ever; that in his place in the government he worked unwearyingly, and that he found time in spare moments for intellectual recreation that would have sufficed for their life's study for most men. Still, I thought possibly there might be a weakness still clinging round his heart, though he never alluded to it; a passion which, though he appeared to have crushed it out, might be sapping his health more than all his work for the nation.

"Do you mean any one in particular? Persigny said he should attend, but I did not see him."

"No, I meant among the ladies. Beatrice Boville was in the seat next me." I had no earthly business to speak of her so abruptly, for when I had seen him for the first time after he left the Bad when Parliament met that February, he had forbidden me ever to mention her name to him, and no allusion to her had ever passed his lips. The worn, stern gravity, that had become his habitual expression, changed for a moment; bullet-proof he might be, but my arrow had shot in through the chain links of his armor; a look of unutterable pain, eagerness, anxiety, passion, passed over his face; but, whatever he felt, he subdued it, though his voice was broken as he answered me:—

"Once for all, I bade you never speak that name to me. Without being forbidden, I should have thought your own feeling, your own delicacy, might—"

"Have checked me? O, hang it, Earlscourt, listen one second without shutting a fellow up. I never broached the subject before, by your desire; but, now I have once broken the ice, I must ask you one question: Are you sure you judged the girl justly? are you sure you were not too quick to slan—"

He pressed his hand on his chest and breathed heavily as I spoke, but he wouldn't let me finish.

"That is enough. Would any man sacrifice what he held dearest wantonly and without proof? She is dear to me *now*. You are the only living being so thoughtless or so merciless as to force her name upon me, and rake up the one folly, the one madness, the one crowning sorrow of my life. See that you never dare bring forward her name again."

He went out before me into the soft night air. His carriage was waiting; he entered it, threw himself back on its cushions, and was driven off before I had time to break my word of honor to Beatrice Boville, which I felt sorely tempted to do just then. Who among the thousands that heard his briliant speech that night, or read it the next morning, who saw him pass in his carriage, and had him pointed out to them as the finest orator of his day, or dined with him at his ministerial dinners at his house in Park Lane, would have believed that, with all his ambition, fame, honors, and attainments, the one cross, the one shadow, the one dark thread, in the successful stateman's life, was due to a woman's hand, and that underneath all his strength lay that single weakness, sapping and undermining it?

"*Did you* see that girl Boville at the House last night?" Lady Clive (who had smiled most sweetly ever since her thorns had brought forth their fruit— her son *would* be his heir—Earlscourt would never marry now!) said to me, the next day, at one of the Musical Society concerts. "Incredible effrontery, wasn't it, in her, to come and hear Earlscourt's speech? One would have imagined that conscience and delicacy might have made her reluctant to see him, instead of letting her voluntarily seek his own legislative chamber, and listen coolly for an hour and a half to the man whom she misled and deceived so disgracefully."

I laughed to think how long a time a woman's malice *will* flourish, n'importe how victorious it may have been in crushing its object, or how harmless that object may have become.

"You are very bitter about her still, Lady Clive. Is that quite fair? You know you were so much obliged to her for throwing Earlscourt away. You want Horace to come in for the title, don't you?" Which truism being unpalatable, Lady Clive averred that she had no wish on earth but for Earlscourt's happiness; that of course she naturally grieved for his betrayal by that little intrigante, but that had his marriage been a well-advised one, nobody would have rejoiced more, etc., etc., and bade me be silent and listen to Vieuxtemps, both of which commands I obeyed, pondering in my own mind whether I should go and call in Lowndes Square or not: if anybody heard of it, they would think it odd for me alone, of all the family, to continue acquainted with a girl whom report (circulated through Lady Clive) said had used Earlscourt so ill, and wrong constructions might get put upon it; but, thank God! I never have considered the qu'en dira-t-on. If constructions are wrong, to the deuce with them! they matter nothing to sensible people; and the man who lives in dread of "reports" will have to shift his conduct as the old man of immortal fable shifted his donkey, and won't ever journey in any peace at all. If anybody remarked my visiting Lowndes Square, I couldn't help it: I wanted to see Beatrice Boville again, and to Lowndes Square, after the concert, I drove my tilbury accordingly, which, as that turn-out is known pretty tolerably in those parts, I should be wisest to leave behind me when I don't want my calls noticed. By good fortune, I saw Beatrice alone. They were going to drive in the Park, and she was in the drawing room, dressed and waiting for her aunt. She was not altered: at her age sorrow doesn't tell physically as it does at Earlscourt's. In youth we have Hope; later on we know that of all the gifts of Pandora's box none are so treacherous and delusive as the one that Pandora left at the bottom. True, Beatrice had none of that insouciant, shadowless brightness that had been her chief charm at Lemongenseidlitz, but she was one of those women whose attractions, dependent on fascination, not on beauty, grow more instead of less as time goes on. She met me with a trace of embarrassment; but she was always self-possessed under any amount of difficulties, and stood chatting, a trifle hurriedly, of all the subjects of the year, of anything, I dare say, rather than of that speech the night before, or of the secret of which I was her sole confidant. But I was not going to let her off so easily. I had come there for a definite purpose, and was not going away without accomplishing it. I was afraid every second that Lady Mechlin might come down, or some visitor enter, and as she sat in a low chair among the flowers in the window, leant towards her, and plunged into it *in medias res.*

"Miss Boville, I want you to release me from my promise."

She looked up, her face flushing slightly, but her lips and eyes shadowed already with that determined pride and hauteur that they had worn the last time I had seen her. She did not speak, but played with the boughs of a coronella near her.

"You remember" (I went on speaking as briefly as possible, lest the old lady's toilet should be finished, and our tête-à-tête cut short) "I gave you my word of honor never to speak again of what you told me in the Kursaal last autumn until you gave me leave; that leave I ask you for now. Silence lies in the way of your own happiness, I feel sure, and not alone of yours. If you give me carte blanche, you may be certain I shall use it discreetly and cautiously. You made the prohibition in a moment of heat and passion; withdraw it now—believe me, you will never repent."

The flush died out of her cheeks as I spoke; but her little, white teeth were set together as they had been that night, and she answered me bitterly,—

"You ask what is impossible; I cannot, in justice to myself, withdraw it. I would never have told you, but that I deemed you a man of honor, whom I could trust."

"I do not think I have proved myself otherwise, Beatrice. I have kept my word to you, when I have been greatly tempted to break it, when I have doubted whether it were either right or wise to stand on such punctilio, when greater stakes were involved by my silence. Surely, if you once had elevated mind enough to comprehend and admire such a man as Earlscourt, and be won by the greatness of his intellect to prefer him to younger rivals, it is impossible you can have lowered your taste and found any one to replace him. No woman who once loved Earlscourt could stoop to an inferior man, and almost all men *are* his inferiors; it is impossible you can have grown cold towards him."

She turned her eyes upon me luminous with her old passion—the color hot in her cheeks, and her attitude full of that fiery pride which became her so infinitely well.

"*I* changed!—*I* grown cold to him! I love him more than all the world, and shall do to my grave. Do you think that any who heard him last night could glory in him as I did? Did you think any physical torture would not have been easier to bear than what I felt when I saw his face once more, and thought of what we *should have been* to one another, and of what we *are*? We women have to act, and smile, and wear a calm semblance, while our hearts are bursting; and so you fancy that we never feel."

"But, great Heavens! Beatrice, if you love Earlscourt like this, why not give me leave to tell him? Why not write to him yourself? A word would clear you, a word restore you to him. Your anger, your pride, he would forgive in a moment."

I'm a military man, not a diplomatist, or I shouldn't have added that last sentence.

She rose, and looked at me haughtily and amazedly.

"It is I who have to forgive, not he. I wronged him in no way; he wronged me bitterly. He dared to misjudge, to suspect, to insult me. I shall never stoop to undeceive him. He gave me up without a trial. I never will force myself upon him. He thanked God I was not his wife—could I seek to be his wife after that? Love him passionately I do, but forgive him I do *not*! I forbid you, on your faith as a gentleman, ever to tell him what I told you that night. I trusted to your honor; I shall hold you *dis*honored if you betray me."

Just as she paused an open carriage rolled past. I looked down mechanically; in it was Earlscourt lying back on his cushions, returning, I believe, from a Cabinet Council. There, in the street, stood my tilbury, with the piebald Cognac that everybody in Belgravia knew. There, in the open window, stood Beatrice and I; and Earlscourt, as he happened to glance upwards, saw us both! His carriage rolled on; Beatrice grew as white as death, and her lips quivered as she looked after him; but Lady Mechlin entered, and I took them down to their barouche.

"You are determined not to release me from my promise?" I asked Beatrice, as I pulled up the tiger-skin over her flounces.

She shook her head.

"Certainly not; and I should think you are too much of a gentleman not to hold a promise sacred."

Pride and determination were written in every line of her face, in the very arch of her eyebrows, the very form of her brow, the very curve of her lips—a soft, delicate face enough otherwise, but as expressive of indomitable pride as any face could be. And yet, though I swore at her as I drove Cognac out of the square, I couldn't help liking her all the better for it, the little Pythoness! for, after all, it was natural and very intelligible to me—she had been misjudged and wrongly suspected, and the noblest spirits are always the quickest to rebel against injustice and resent false accusation.

V

HOW IN PERFECT INNOCENCE I PLAYED THE PART OF A RIVAL

The season whirled and spun along as usual. They were having stormy debates in the Lower House, and throwing out bills in the Upper; stifled by Thames odors one evening, and running down to Epsom the next morning; blackguarding each other in parliamentary language—which, on my honor, will soon want duels revived to keep it within decent breeding, if Lord Robert Cecil and others don't learn better manners, and remember the golden rule that "He alone resorts to vituperation whose argument is illogical and weak." We, luckier dogs, who weren't slaves to St. Stephen's, nor to anything at all except as parsons and moralists, with whom the grapes sont verts et bons pour des goujats, said to our own worldly vitiated tastes and evil leanings, spent our hours in the Ring and the coulisses, White's and the United, crush balls and opera suppers, and swore we were immeasurably bored, though we wouldn't have led any other life for half a million. The season whirled along. Earlscourt devoted himself more entirely than ever to public life; he filled one of the most onerous and important posts in the ministry, and appeared to occupy himself solely with home politics and foreign politics. Lady Mechlin, only a baronet's widow, though she had very tolerable society of her own, was not in *his* monde; and Beatrice Boville and he, with only Hyde Park Corner between them, might as well, for any chance of rapprochement, have been severally at Spitzbergen and Cape Horn. Two or three times they passed each other in Pall-Mall and the Ride; but Earlscourt only lifted his hat to Lady Mechlin, and Beatrice set her little teeth together, and wouldn't have solicited a glance from him to save her life. Earlscourt was excessively distant to me after seeing my tilbury at her door; no doubt he thought it strange for me to have continued my intimacy with a woman who had wronged him so bitterly. He said nothing, but I could see he was exceedingly displeased; and the more I tried to smooth it with him, the more completely I seemed to set my foot in it. It was exceedingly difficult to touch on any obnoxious subject with him; he was never harsh or discourteous, but he could freeze the atmosphere about him gently, but so completely, that no mortal could pierce through it; and, fettered by my promise to her and his prohibition to me, I hardly knew how to bring up her name. As the Fates would have it, I often met Beatrice myself, at the Regent Park fêtes, at concerts, at a Handel Festival at Sydenham, at one or two dinner parties; and, as she generally made way for me beside her, and was one of those women who are invariably, though without effort, admired and surrounded in any society, possibly people remarked it—possibly our continued intimacy might have come round to Earlscourt, specially as Lady Clive and Mrs Breloques abused me roundly, each à sa mode, for countenancing that "abominable intrigante." I couldn't help it, even if Earlscourt took exception at me for it. I knew the girl was not to blame, and I took her part, and tried my best to tame the little Pythoness into releasing me from my promise. But Beatrice was firm; had she erred, no one would have acknowledged and atoned for it quicker, but innocent and wrongly accused, she kept silent, coûte que coûte, and in my heart I sympathized with her. Nothing stings so sharply, nothing is harder to forgive, than injustice; and, knowing herself to be frank, honorable, and open as the day, his charge of falsehood and deception rankled in her only more keenly as time went on. Men ran after her like mad; she had more of them about her than many beauties or belles. There was a style, a charm, a something in her that sent beauties into the shade, and by which, had she chosen, she could soon have replaced Earlscourt. Still, it needed to be no Lavater to see, by the passionate gleam of her eyes and the haughty pride on her brow, that Beatrice Boville was not happy.

"Why *will* you let pride and punctilio wreck your own life, Beatrice?" I asked her, in a low tone, as we stood before one of Ed. Warren's delicious bits of woodland in the Water-Color Exhibition, where we had chanced to meet one day. "That he should have judged you as he did was not unnatural. Think! how was it possible for him to guess your father was your companion? Remember how very much circumstances were against you."

"Had they been ten times more against me, a man who cared for me would have believed in me, and stood by me, not condemned me on the first suspicion. It was unchivalrous, ungenerous, unjust. I tell you, his words are stamped into my memory forever. I shall never forgive them."

"Not even if you knew that he suffered as much and more than you do?"

She clinched her hands on the rolled-up catalogue with a passionate gesture.

"No; because he *misjudged* me. Anything else I would have pardoned, though I am no patient Griselda, to put up tamely with any wrong; but *that* I never could—I never would!"

"I regret it, then. I thought you too warm and noble-hearted a woman to retain resentment so long. I never blamed you in the first instance, but I must say I blame you now."

She laughed, a little contemptuously, and glanced at me with her haughtiest air; and on my life, much as it provoked one, nothing became her better.

"Blame me or not, as you please—your verdict will be quite bearable, either way. I am the one sinned against. I can have nothing explained to Lord Earlscourt. Had he cared for me, as he once vowed, he would have been less quick then to suspect me, and quicker now to give me a chance of clearing myself. But you remember he thanked God I had not his name and his honor in my hands. I dare say he rejoices at his escape."

She laughed again, turning over the catalogue feverishly and unconsciously. *Those* were the words that rankled in her; and it was not much wonder if, to a proud spirit like Beatrice Boville's, they seemed unpardonable. As I handed her and Lady Mechlin into their carriage when they left the exhibition, Earlscourt, as ill luck would have it, passed us, walking on to White's, the fringe of Beatrice's parasol brushed his arm, and a hot color flushed into her cheeks at the sudden rencontre. By the instinct of courtesy he bowed to her and Lady Mechlin, but passed up Pall-Mall without looking at Beatrice. How well society drills us, that we meet with such calm impassiveness in its routine those with whom we have sorrowed and joyed, loved and hated, in such far different scenes!

Their carriage drove on, and I overtook him as he went up Pall-Mall. He was walking slowly, with his hand pressed on his chest, and his lips set together, as if in bodily pain. He looked at me, as I joined him, with an annoyed glance of unusual irritation for him, for he was always calm and untroubled, punctiliously just, and though of a proud temper, never quick to anger.

"You passed that girl wonderfully coldly, Earlscourt," I began, plunging recklessly into the thick of the subject.

"Coldly!" he repeated, bitterly. "It is very strange that you will pursue me with her name. I forbade you to intrude it upon me; was not that sufficient?"

"No; because I think you judged her too harshly."

"Think so, if you please, but never renew the topic to me. If she gives you her confidence, enjoy it. If you choose, knowing what you do, to be misled by her, be so; but I beg of you to spare me your opinions and intentions."

"But why? I say you *do* misjudge her. She might err in impatience and pride; but I would bet you any money you like that you would prove her guilty of no indelicacy, no treachery, no underhand conduct, though appearances might be against her."

"*Might* be! You select your words strangely; you must have some deeper motive for your unusual blindness. I desire, for the last time, that you cease either the subject to me, or your acquaintance with me, whichever you prefer."

With which, he went up the steps of White's, and I strolled on, amazed at the fierce acrimony of his tone, utterly unlike anything I had ever heard from him, wished their pride to the devil, called myself a fool for meddling in the matter at all, and went to have a quiet weed in the smoking-room of the U. S. to cool myself. I was heartily sick of the whole affair. If they wanted it cleared, they must clear it themselves—I should trouble myself no more about it. Yet I couldn't altogether dismiss Beatrice's cause from my mind. I thought her, to say the truth, rather harshly used. I liked her for her fearless, truthful, impassioned character. I liked her for the very courage and pride with which she preferred to relinquish any chance of regaining her forfeited happiness, rather than stoop to solicit exculpation from charges of which she knew she was innocent. Perhaps, at first, she did not consider sufficiently Earlscourt's provocation, and perhaps, now, she was too persisting in her resentment of it; still I liked her, and I was sorry to see her, at an age when life should have been couleur de rose, to one of her gay and insouciant nature, with a weary, passionate look on her face that she should not have had for ten years to come—a look that was rapidly hardening into stern and contemptuous sadness.

"You tell me I am too bitter," she said to me one day, "how should I be otherwise? I, who have wronged no one, and have never in my life done anything of which I am ashamed, am called an intrigante by Lady Clive Edghill, and get ill-will from strangers, and misconstructions from my friends, merely because, thinking no harm myself, it never occurs to me that circumstances may look against me; and, hating falsehood, I cannot lie, and smile, and give soft words where I feel contempt and indignation. Mrs. Breloques yonder, with whom les présens ont toujours raison, and les absens ont toujours tort, who has honeyed speeches for her bitterest foes, and poisoned arrows (behind their back) for her most trusting friends, who goes to early matins every morning, and pries out for a second all over the top of her prayer-book, who kisses 'darling Helena,' and says she 'never looked so sweetly,' whispering en petit comité what a pity it is, when Helena is so passée, she *will* dress like a girl just out—she is called the sweetest woman possible—so amiable! and is praised for her high knowledge of religion.

You tell me I am too bitter. I think not. Honesty does *not* prosper, and truth is at a miserable discount; straightforward frankness makes a myriad of foes, and adroit diplomacy as many friends. If you make a prettily-turned compliment, who cares if it is sincere? if you hold your tongue where you cannot praise, because you will not tell a conventional falsehood, the world thinks you very ill-natured, or odiously satirical. Society is entirely built upon insincerity and conventionality, from the wording of an acceptance of a dinner invitation, where we write 'with much pleasure,' thinking to ourselves 'what a bore!' to the giant hypocrisies daily spoken without a blush from pulpit and lectern, and legitimatized both as permissible and praiseworthy. To truth and unconventionality society of course is adverse; and whoever dares to uphold them must expect to be hissed, as Paul by the Ephesians, because he shivered their silver shrines and destroyed the craft by which they got their wealth."

Beatrice was right; her truth and fearlessness were her enemies with most people, even with the man who had loved her best. Had she been ready with an adroit falsehood and a quick excuse, Earlscourt's suspicions would never have been raised as they were by her frank admission that there was something she would rather not tell him, and her innocent request to be trusted. That must have been some very innocent and unworldly village schoolmaster, I should say, who first set going that venerable proverb, "Honesty is the best policy." He must have known comically little of life. A diplomatist who took it as his motto would soon come to grief, and ladies would soon stone out of their circles any woman bête enough to try its truth among them. There is no policy at greater discount in the world, and straightforward and candid people stand at very unequal odds with the rest of humanity; they are the one morsel of bread to a hogshead of sack, the handful of Spartans against a swarm of Persians, and they get the brunt of the battle and the worst of the fight.

VI
HOW PRIDE BOWED AND FELL

Beyond meeting Earlscourt at White's, or, for an hour, at the réunion of some fair leader of ton, I scarcely saw him that season, for he was more and more devoted to public life. He looked wretchedly ill, and his physicians said if he wished to live he must go to the south of France in July, and winter at Corfu; but he paid them no heed; he occupied himself constantly with political and literary work, and grudged the three or four hours he gave to sleep that did him little good.

"Will you get me admittance to the Lords to-morrow night?" Beatrice asked me, one morning, when I met her in the Ride. I looked at her surprised.

"To the Lords? Of course, if you wish."

"I do wish it." Her hands clinched on her bridle, and the color flushed into her face, for Earlscourt just then passed us, riding with one of his brother ministers. He looked at us both, and his face changed strangely, though he rode on, continuing his conversation with the other man, while I went round the turn with Beatrice and the other fellows who were about her; le fruit défendu is always most attractive, and Beatrice's profound negligence of them all made them more mad about her than all the traps and witcheries, beguilements and attractions, that coquettes and beauties set out for them. She rode beautifully; and a woman who *does* sit well down on her saddle, and knows how to handle her horse, never looks better than en Amazone. Earlscourt met her three times at the turn of the Ride; and though you would not have told that he was passing any other than an utter stranger, I think it must have struck him that he had lost much in losing Beatrice Boville. I was riding on her off-side each time when we passed him. As I say, I never, thank God! have cared a straw for the qu'en dira-t-on? and if people remarked on my intimacy with my cousin's cast off fiancée, so they might, but to Earlscourt I wished to explain it more for Beatrice's sake than my own; and as I rode out by Apsley House afterwards, I overtook him, and went up to Piccadilly with him, though his manner was decidedly distant and chill, so pointedly so that it would have been rude, had he not been too entirely a disciple of Chesterfield to be ever otherwise than courteous to his deadliest foe; but, disregarding his coldness, I said what I intended to say, and began an explanation that I considered only due to him.

"I beg your pardon, Earlscourt, for intruding on you a topic you have forbidden, but I shall be obliged to you to listen to me a moment. I wish to tell you my reasons for what, I dare say, seems strange to you, my continued intimacy with—"

But I was not permitted to end my sentence; he divined what I was about to say, and stopped me, with a cold, wearied air.

"I understand; but I prefer not to hear them. I have no desire to interfere with your actions, and less to be troubled with your motives. Of course, you choose your friendships as you please. All I beg is, that you obey the wish I expressed the other day, and intrude the subject no more upon me."

And he bade me good morning, urged his mare into a sharp canter, and turned down St. James's Street. How little those in the crowd, who looked at him as he rode by, pointing him out to the women with them as Viscount Earlscourt, the most eloquent debater in the Lords, the celebrated foreign minister, author, and diplomatist, guessed that a woman's name could touch and sting him as nothing else could do, and that under the calm and glittering upper-current of his life ran a dark, slender, unnoticed thread that had power to poison all the rest! Those women, mon ami!—if we *do* satirize them a little bit now and then, are we doing any more than taking a very mild revenge? Don't they make fools of the very best and wisest of us, play the deuce with Cæsar as with Catullus, and make Achilles soft as Amphimachus?

The next morning I met Beatrice at a concert at the Marchioness of Pursang's. Lady Pursang would not have been, vous concevez, on the visiting list of Lady Mechlin, as she was one of the crème de la crème, but she had met Beatrice the winter before at Pau, had been very delighted with her, and now continued the acquaintance in town. I happened to sit next our little Pythoness, who looked better, I think, that morning, than ever I saw her, though her face was set into that disdainful sadness which had become its habitual expression. She liked my society, and sought it, no doubt, because I was the only link between her and her lost past; and she was talking with me more animatedly than usual, thanking me for having got her admittance to the Lords that night, during a pause in the concert, when Earlscourt entered the room, and took the seat reserved for him, which was not far from ours. Music was one of his passions, the only délassement, indeed, he ever gave himself now; but to-day, though ostensibly he listened to Alboni and Arabella Goddard, Hallé and Vieuxtemps, and talked to the marchioness and other women of her set, in reality he was watching Beatrice, who, her pride roused by his presence, laughed and chatted with me and other men with her old gay abandon, and, impervious to déréglement though he was, I fancy even *he* felt it a severe trial of his composure when Lady Pursang, who had been the last five years in India with her husband, and who was ignorant of or had forgotten the name of the girl Earlscourt was to have married the year before, asked him, when the concert was over, to let her introduce him to her, yet Beatrice Boville, bringing him in innocent cruelty up to that little Pythoness, with whom he had parted so passionately and bitterly ten months before! Happy for them that they had that armor which the Spartans called heroism, the stoics philosophy, and we—simply style good breeding, or they would hardly have gone through that ordeal as well as they did when she introduced them to each other as strangers!—those two who had whispered such passionate love words, given and received such fond caresses, vowed barely twelve months before to pass their lifetime together! Happy for them they were used to society, or they would hardly have bowed to each other as calmly and admirably as they did, with the recollection of that night in which they had parted so bitterly, so full as it was in the minds of both. Beatrice was standing in one of the open windows of the little cabinet de peinture almost empty, and when the marchioness moved away, satisfied that she had introduced two people admirably fitted to entertain one another, Earlscourt, with people flirting and talking within a few yards of him, was virtually alone with Beatrice— for there is, after all, no solitude like the solitude of a crowd—and *then*, for the first time in his life, his self-possession forsook him. Beatrice was silent and very pale, looking out of the window on to the Green Park, which the house overlooked, and Earlscourt's pride had a hard struggle, but his passion got the better of him, malgré lui, and he leaned towards her.

"Do you remember the last night we were together?"

She answered him bitterly. She had not forgiven him. She had sometimes, I am half afraid, sworn to revenge herself.

"I am hardly likely to forget it, Lord Earlscourt."

He looked at her longingly and wistfully; his pride was softened, that granite pride, hitherto so unassailable! and he bent nearer to her.

"Beatrice! I would give much to be able to wash out the memories of that night—to be proved mistaken—to be convicted of haste, of sternness—"

The tears rushed into her eyes.

"You need only have given one little thing—all I asked of you—trust!"

"Would to God I dare believe you now! Tell me, answer me, did I judge you too harshly? Love at my age never changes, however wronged; it is the latest, and it only expires with life itself. I confess to you, you are dearer to me still than anything ever was, than anything ever will be. Prove to me, for God's sake, that I misjudged you! Only prove it to me; explain away what appeared against you, and we may yet—"

He stopped; his voice trembled, his hand touched hers, he breathed short and fast. The Pythoness was very nearly tamed; her eyes grew soft and melting, her lips trembled; but pride was still strong in her. At the touch of his hand it very nearly gave way, but not wholly; it was there still, tenacious of its reign. She set her little teeth obstinately together, and looked up at him with her old hauteur.

"No, as I told you then, you must believe in me *without* proof. I have not forgotten your bitter words, nor yet forgiven them. I doubt if I ever shall. You roused an evil spirit in me that night, Lord Earlscourt, which you cannot exorcise at a moment's notice. Remember what was your own motto, 'An indiscreet woman is never frank,'—yet from my very frankness you accused me of indiscretion, and of far worse than indiscretion—"

"My God! if I accused you falsely, Beatrice, forgive me!"

He must have loved her very much to bow his pride so far as that. He was at *her* feet—at *her* mercy now; he, whom she had vainly sued, sued her; but a perverse, fiery devil in her urged her to take her own revenge, compelled her to throw away her own peace.

"You should have asked me that ten months ago; it is too late now."

His face dyed white, his eyes filled with passionate anguish. He crushed her hand in his.

"Too late! Great Heavens! Answer me, child, I entreat you—I beseech you—is it 'too late' because report is true that you have replaced me with your cousin—that you are engaged to Hervey? Tell me truth now, for pity's sake. I will be trifled with no longer."

Beatrice threw back her haughty little head contemptuously, though ladies *don't* sneer at the idea of being liées with me generally, I can assure you. Her heart throbbed triumphantly and joyously. She had conquered him at last. The man of giant intellect and haughty will had bowed to her. She held him by a thread, he who ruled the fate of nations!—and she loved him so dearly! But the Pythoness was not wholly tamed, and she could not even yet forget her wrongs.

"You told me before I spoke falsehoods to you, Lord Earlscourt; my word would find no more credence now."

He looked at her, dropped her hand, and turned away, before Beatrice could detain him. Five minutes after he left the house. Little as I guessed it, he was jealous of me—I! who never in my own life rivalled any man who wished to *marry*! Beatrice had fully revenged herself. I wonder if she enjoyed it quite as much as she had anticipated, as she stood where he had left her looking out on the Green Park?

I went with Beatrice and her party to the Lords that night; it was the tug of war for the bill which Earlscourt was so determined should pass, and a great speech was expected from him. We were not disappointed. When he rose he spoke with effort, and his oratory suffered from the slight hoarseness of his voice, for half the beauty of his rhetoric lay in the flexibility and music of his tones; still, it was emphatically a great speech, and Beatrice Boville listened to it breathlessly, with her eyes fixed on the face—weary, worn, but grandly intellectual—of the man whom Europe reverenced, and she—a girl of twenty!—ruled. Perhaps her heart smote her for the lines she had added there; perhaps she felt her pride misplaced to him, great as he was, with his stainless honor and unequalled genius; perhaps she thought of how, with all his strength, his hand had trembled as it touched hers; and how, with all her love, she had been wilful and naughty to him a second time. His voice grew weaker as he ended, and he spoke with visible effort; still it was one of his greatest political triumphs: his bill passed by a large majority, and the papers, the morning after, filled their leading articles with admiration of Viscount Earlscourt's speech. But before those journals were out, Earlscourt was too ill almost to notice the success of his measures: as he left the House, the presiding devil of beloved Albion, that plays the deuce with English statesmen as with Italian cantatrices,—the confounded east wind,—had caught him, finished what over-exertion had begun, and knocked him over, prostrated with severe bronchitis. What pity it is that the body *will* levy such cruel black mail upon the mind; that a gust of wind, a horse's plunge, the effluvia of a sewer, the carelessness of a pointsman, can destroy the grandest intellect, sweep off the men whose genius lights the world, as ruthlessly as a storm of rain a cloud of gnats, and strike Peel and Canning, Macaulay and Donaldson, in the prime of their power, as heedlessly as peasants little higher than the brutes, dull as the clods of their own valley, who stake their ambitions on a surfeit of fat bacon, and can barely scrawl their names upon a slate!

Unconscious that Earlscourt's jealousy had fastened so wrongly upon me, I was calling upon Beatrice late the next morning, ignorant myself of his illness, when his physician, who was Lady Mechlin's too, while paying her a complimentary visit, regretted to me my cousin's sudden attack.

"Lord Earlscourt would speak last night," he began. "I entreated him not; but those public men are so obstinate; to-day he is very ill—very ill indeed, though prompt measures stopped the worst. He has risen to dictate something of importance to his secretary; he would work his brain if he were dying; but it has taken a severe hold on him, I fear. I shall send him somewhere south as soon as he can leave the house, which will not be for some weeks. He would be a great loss to the country. We have not such another foreign minister. But I admit to you, Major Hervey—though of course I do not wish it to go further—that I *do* think very seriously of Lord Earlscourt's state of health."

Beatrice heard him as she sat at her Davenport; her face grew white, and her eyes filled with great anguish. She thought of his words to her only the day before, and of how her pride had repelled him a second time. I saw her hand clinch on the pen she was playing with, and her teeth set tight together, her habitual action under any strong emotion, thinking to herself, no doubt, "And my last words to him were bitter ones!"

When the physician had left, I went up to her.—

"Beatrice, you must let me tell him *now*!"

She did not answer, but her hand clinched tighter on the pen-handle.

"His life is in your hands; for God's sake relinquish your pride."

But her pride was strong in her, and dear to her still, strong and dear as her love; and the two struggled together. Earlscourt had bowed *his* pride to her; but she had not yielded up her own, and it cost her much to yield it even now. All the Pythoness in her was not tamed yet. She was silent—she wavered—then her great love for him vanquished all else. She rose, white as death, her passionate eyes full of unshed tears, the bitterest, yet the softest, Beatrice Boville had ever known.

"Take me to him. No one shall tell him but myself."

Earlscourt was lying on a couch in his library; he had been unable to dictate or to write himself, for severe remedies had prostrated him utterly, and he could not speak above his breath, though he was loath to give up, and acknowledge himself as ill as he was. His eyes were closed, his forehead knitted together in pain, and his labored breathing told plainly enough how fiercely his foe had attacked him, and that it was by no means conquered yet. He had not slept all night, and had fallen into a short slumber now, desiring his attendants to leave him. I bade the groom of the chambers let us enter unannounced, and, opening the door myself, signed to Beatrice to go in, while her aunt and I waited in the anteroom. She stopped a moment at the entrance; her pride had its last struggle; but he turned restlessly, with a weary sigh, and by that sigh the Pythoness was conquered. Beatrice went forward and fell on her knees beside his sofa, bending down till her lips touched his brow, and her hot tears fell on his hands.

"I was too proud last night to tell you you misjudged me. I have no pride now. I am your own—wholly your own. I never loved, I never should love, any but you. I forgive you now. O, how could you ever doubt me? Lord Earlscourt—Ernest—may we not yet be all we once were to one another?"

Awakened by her kisses on his brow, bewildered by her sudden appearance, he tried to rise, but sank back exhausted. He did not disbelieve her now. He had no voice to speak to her, no strength to answer her; but he drew her down closer and closer to him, as she knelt by him, and, as her heart beat once more against his, the little Pythoness, tamed at last, threw her arms round him and sobbed like a child on his breast. And so—Beatrice Boville took her best Revenge!—while I shut the library door, invited Lady Mechlin to inspect Earlscourt's collection of French pictures, and asked what she thought of *Punch* this week.

I don't know what his physicians would have said of the treatment, as they'd recommended him "perfect quiet;" all I do know is, that though Earlscourt went to the south of Europe as soon as he could leave the house, Beatrice Boville went with him; and he took his place on the benches and in the cabinet this season, without any trace of bronchia, or any sign of wearing out.

Lady Clive, I regret to say, "does not know" Lady Earlscourt: anything for her beloved brother she *would* do, were it possible; but she hopes we understand that, for her daughters' sakes, she feels it quite impossible to countenance that "shocking little intrigante."

A LINE IN THE "DAILY"

WHO DID IT, AND WHO WAS DONE BY IT

"Lieutenant-Colonel Fairlie's troop of Horse Artillery is ordered to Norwich to replace the 12th Lancers, en route to Bombay."—Those three lines in the papers spread dismay into the souls of Norfolk young ladies, and no less horror into ours, for we were very jolly at Woolwich, could run up to the Clubs and down to Epsom, and were far too material not to prefer ball-room belles to bluebells, strawberry-ice to fresh hautboys, the sparkle of champagne-cups to all the murmurs of the brooks, and the flutter of ballet-girls' wings to all the rustle of forest-leaves. But, unhappily, the Ordnance Office is no more given to considering the feelings of their Royal Gunners than the Horse Guards the individual desires of the two other Arms; and off we went to Norwich, repining bitterly, or, in modern English, swearing hard at our destinies, creating an immense sensation with our 6-pounders, as we flatter ourselves the Royals always contrive to do, whether on fair friends or fierce foes, and were looked upon spitefully by the one or two young ladies whose hearts were gone eastwards with the Twelfth, smilingly by the one or two hundred who, having fruitlessly laid out a great deal of tackle on the Twelfth, proceeded to manufacture fresh flies to catch us.

We soon made up, I think, to the Norwich girls for the loss of the Twelfth. They set dead upon Fairlie, our captain, a Brevet Lieutenant-Colonel, and a C. B. for "services in India," where he had rivalled Norman Ramsay at Fuentes d'Onor, had had a ball put in his hip, and had come home again to be worshipped by the women for his romantic reputation. They made an immense deal, too, of Levison Courtenay, the beauty of the troop, and called Belle in consequence; who did not want any flummery or flirtation to increase his opinion of himself, being as vain of his almond eyes as any girl just entered as the favorite for the season. There were Tom Gower, too, a capital fellow, with no nonsense about him, who made no end of chaff of Belle Courtenay; and Little Nell, otherwise Harcourt Poulteney Nelson, who had by some miracle escaped expulsion both from Carshalton and the College; and *votre humble serviteur* Phil Hardinge, first lieutenant; and one or two other fellows, who having cut dashing figures at our Woolwich reviews, cantering across Blackheath Common, or waltzing with dainty beauties down our mess-room, made the Artillery welcome in that city of shawls and oratorios, where according to the Gazetteer, no virtuous person ought to dwell, that volume, with characteristic lucidity, pronouncing its streets "ill-disposed."

The Clergy asked us to their rectories — a temptation we were often proof against, there being three noticeable facts in rectories, that the talk is always slow, "the Church" being present, and having much the same chilling effect as the presence of a chaperone at a tête-à-tête; the daughters generally ugly, and, from leading the choir at morning services, perfectly convinced that they sing like Clara Novello, and that the harmonium is a most delightful instrument; and, last and worst, the wines are almost always poor, except the port which the reverend host drinks himself, but which, Dieu merci! we rarely or never touch.

The County asked us, too; and there we went for good hock, tolerable-looking women, and first-rate billiard-tables. For the first month we were in Norfolk we voted it unanimously the most infernally slow and hideous county going; and I dare say we made ourselves uncommonly disagreeable, as people, if they are not pleased, be they ever so well bred, have a knack of doing.

Things were thus quiescent and stagnant, when Fairlie one night at mess told us a bit of news.

"Old fellows, whom do you think I met to-day?"

"How should we know? Cut along."

"The Swan and her Cygnets."

"The Vanes? Oh, bravo!" was shouted at a chorus, for the dame and demoiselles in question we had known in town that winter, and a nicer, pleasanter, faster set of women I never came across. "What's bringing them down here, and how's Geraldine?"

"Vane's come into his baronetcy, and his place is close by Norwich," said Fairlie; "his wife's health has been bad, and so they left town early; and Geraldine is quite well, and counting on haymaking, she informed me."

"Come, that is good news," said Belle, yawning. "There'll be one pretty woman in the county, thank Heaven! Poor little Geraldine! I must go and call on her to-morrow."

"She has existed without your calls, Belle," said Fairlie, dryly, "and don't look as if she'd pined after you."

"My dear fellow, how should you know?" said Belle, in no wise disconcerted. "A little rogue soon makes 'em look well, and as for smiles, they'll smile while they're dying for you. Little Vane and I were always good friends, and shall be again—if I care."

."Conceited owl!" said Fairlie, under his moustaches. "I'm sorry to hurt your feelings, then, but your pretty 'friend' never asked after you."

"I dare say not," said Belle, complacently. "Where a woman's most interested she's always quietest, and Geraldine——"

"Lady Vane begged me to tell you you will always be welcome over there, old fellows," said Fairlie, remorselessly cutting him short. "Perhaps we shall find something to amuse us better than these stiltified Chapter dinners."

The Vanes of whom we talked were an uncommonly pleasant set of people whom we had known at Lee, where Vane, a Q. C., then resided, his prospective baronetcy being at that time held by a third or fourth cousin. Fairlie had known the family since his boyhood; there were four daughters, tall graceful women, who had gained themselves the nickname of The Swan and her Cygnets; and then there were twins, a boy of eighteen, who'd just left Eton; and the girl Geraldine, a charming young lady, whom Belle admired more warmly than that dandy often admired anybody besides himself, and whom Fairlie liked cordially, having had many a familiar bit of fun with her, as he had known her ever since he was a dashing cadet, and she made her *début* in life in the first column of the *Times*. Her sisters were handsome women; but Geraldine was bewitching. A very pleasant family they were, and a vast acquisition to us. Miss Geraldine flirted to a certain extent with us all, but chiefly with the Colonel, whenever he was to be had, those two having a very free-and-easy, familiar, pleasant style of intercourse, owing to old acquaintance; and Belle spent two hours every evening on his toilette when we were going to dine there, and vowed she was a "deuced pretty little puss. Perhaps she might—he wasn't sure, but perhaps (it would be a horrid sacrifice), if he were with her much longer, he wasn't sure she mightn't persuade him to take compassion upon her, he *was* so weak where women were concerned!"

"What a conceit!" said Fairlie thereat, with a contemptuous twist of his moustaches and a shrug of his shoulders to me. "I must say, if I were a woman, I shouldn't feel over-flattered by a lover who admired his own beauty first, and mine afterwards. Not that I pretend to understand women."

By which speech I argued that his old playmate Geraldine hadn't thrown hay over the Colonel, and been taught billiards by him, and ridden his bay mare over the park in her evening dress, without interesting him slightly; and that—though I don't think he knew it—he was deigning to be a trifle jealous of his Second Captain, the all-mighty conqueror Belle.

"What fools they must be that put in these things!" yawned Belle one morning, reading over his breakfast coffee in the *Daily Pryer* one of those "advertisements for a wife" that one comes across sometimes in the papers, and that make us, like a good many other things, agree with Goldsmith:

Reason, they say, belongs to man,

But let them prove it if they can;

Wise Aristotle and Smiglicious,

By ratiocinations specious,

Have strove to prove with great precision,

With definition and division,

Homo est ratione præditum,

But for my soul I cannot credit 'em.

"What fools they must be!" yawned Belle, wrapping his dressing-gown round him, and coaxing his perfumy whiskers under his velvet smoking-cap. Belle was always inundated by smoking-caps in cloth and velvet, silk and beads, with blue tassels, and red tassels, and gold tassels, embroidered and filigreed, rounded and pointed; he had them sent to him by the dozen, and pretty good chaff he made of the donors. "Awful fools! The idea of advertising for a wife, when the only difficulty a man has is to keep from being tricked into taking one. I bet you, if I did like this owl here, I should have a hundred answers; and if it was known it was I——"

"Little Geraldine's self for a candidate, eh?" asked Tom Gower.

"Very possibly," said Belle, with a self-complacent smile. "She's a fast little thing, don't check at much, and she's deucedly in love with me, poor little dear—almost as much trouble to me as Julia Sedley was last season. That girl all but proposed to me; she did, indeed. Never was nearer coming to grief in my life. What will you bet me that, if I advertise for a wife, I don't hoax lots of women?"

"I'll bet you ten pounds," said I, "that you don't hoax one!"

"Done!" said Belle, stretching out his hand for a dainty memorandum-book, gift of the identical Julia Sedley aforesaid, and entering the bet in it—"done! If I'm not asked to walk in the Close at noon and look out for a pink bonnet and a black lace cloak, and to loiter up the market-place till I come across a black hat and blue muslin dress; if I'm not requested to call at No. 20, and to grant an interview at No. 84; if I'm not written to by Agatha A. with hazel, and Belinda B. with black, eyes—all coming after me like flies after a sugar-cask, why you shall have your ten guineas, my boy, and my colt into the bargain. Come, write out the advertisement, Tom—I can't, it's too much trouble; draw it mild, that's all, or the letters we shall get will necessitate an additional Norwich postman. By George, what fun it will be to do the girls! Cut along, Tom, can't you?"

"All right," said Gower, pushing away his coffee-cup, and drawing the ink to him. "Head it 'Marriage,' of course?"

"Of course. That word's as attractive to a woman as the belt to a prize-fighter, or a pipe of port to a college fellow."

"'Marriage.—A Bachelor——'"

"Tell 'em a military man; all girls have the scarlet fever."

"Very well—'an Officer in the Queen's, of considerable personal attractions——'"

"My dear fellow, pray don't!" expostulated Belle, in extreme alarm; "we shall have such swarms of 'em!"

"No, no! we must say that," persisted Gower—"'personal attractions, aged eight-and-twenty——'"

"Can't you put it, 'in the flower of his age,' or his 'sixth lustre'? It's so much more poetic."

"'—the flower of his age,' then (that'll leave 'em a wide range from twenty to fifty, according to their taste), 'is desirous of meeting a young lady of beauty, talent, and good family,'—eh?"

"Yes. All women think themselves beauties, if they're as ugly as sin. Milliners and confectioner girls talk Anglo-French, and rattle a tin-kettle piano after a fashion, and anybody buys a 'family' for half-a-crown at the Heralds' Office—so fire away."

"'—who, feeling as he does the want of a kindred heart and sympathetic soul, will accord him the favor of a letter or an interview, as a preliminary to the greatest step in life.'"

"A step—like one on thin ice—very sure to bring a man to grief," interpolated Belle. "Say something about property; those soul-and-spirit young ladies generally keep a look-out for tin, and only feel an elective affinity for a lot of debentures and consols."

"'The advertiser being a man of some present and still more prospective wealth, requires no fortune, the sole objects of his search being love and domestic felicity.' Domestic felicity—how horrible! Don't it sound exactly like the end of a lady's novel, where the unlucky hero is always brought to an untimely end in a 'sweet cottage on the banks of the lovely Severn.'"

"'Domestic felicity'—bah! What are you writing about?" yawned Belle. "I'd as soon take to teetotalism: however, it'll tell in the advertisement. Bravo, Tom, that will do. Address it to 'L. C., care of Mrs. Greene, confectioner, St. Giles Street, Norwich.' Miss Patty'll take the letters in for me, though not if she knew their errand. Tip seven-and-sixpence with it, and send it to the *Daily Pryer*."

We did send it to the *Daily*, and in that broadsheet we all of us read it two mornings after.

> MARRIAGE.—A Bachelor, an Officer of the Queen's, of considerable personal attractions, and in the flower of his age, is desirous of meeting a young lady of beauty, accomplishments, and good family, who, feeling as he does the want of a kindred heart and sympathetic soul, will accord him the favor either of a letter or an interview, as a preliminary to the greatest step in life. The advertiser being a man of some present and still more prospective wealth, requires no fortune, the sole objects of his search being love and domestic felicity. Address, L. C., care of Mrs. Greene, confectioner, St. Giles Street, Norwich.

"Whose advertisement do you imagine that is?" said Fairlie, showing the *Daily* to Geraldine, as he sat with her and her sisters under some lilac and larch trees in one of the meadows of Fern Chase, which had had the civility, Geraldine said, to yield a second crop of hay expressly for her to have the pleasure of making it. She leaned down towards him as he lay on the grass, and read the advertisement, looking uncommonly pretty in her dainty muslin dress, with its fluttering mauve ribbons, and a wreath she had just twisted up, of bluebells and pinks and white heaths which Fairlie had gathered as he lay, put on her bright hair. We called her a little flirt, but I think she was an unintentional one; at least, her agaceries were, all as unconscious as they were—her worst enemies (*i. e.* plain young ladies) had to allow—unaffected.

"How exquisitely sentimental! Is it yours?" she asked, with demure mischief.

"Mine!" echoed Fairlie, with supreme scorn.

"It's some one's here, because the address is at Mrs. Greene's. Come, tell me at once, monsieur."

"The only fool in the Artillery," said Fairlie, curtly: "Belle Courtenay."

"Captain Courtenay!" echoed Geraldine, with a little flush on her cheeks, caused, perhaps, by the quick glance the Colonel shot at her as he spoke.

"Captain Courtenay!" said Katherine Vane. "Why, what can he want with a wife? I thought he had *l'embarras de choix* offered him in that line; at least, so he makes out himself."

"I dare say," said Fairlie, dryly, "it's for a bet he's made, to see how many women he can hoax, I believe."

"How can you tell it is a hoax?" said Geraldine, throwing cowslips at her greyhound. "It may be some medium of intercourse with some one he really cares for, and who may understand his meaning."

"Perhaps you are in his confidence, Geraldine, or perhaps you are thinking of answering it yourself?"

"Perhaps," said the young lady, waywardly, making the cowslips into a ball, "there might be worse investments. Your *bête noire* is strikingly handsome; he is the perfection of style; he is going to be Equerry to the Prince; his mother is just married again to Lord Chevenix; he did not name half his attractions in that line in the *Daily*."

With which Geraldine rushed across the meadow after the greyhound and the cowslip ball, and Fairlie lay quiet plucking up the heaths by the roots. He lay there still, when the cowslip ball struck him a soft fragrant blow against his lips, and knocked the Cuba from between his teeth.

"Why don't you speak?" asked Geraldine, plaintively. "You are not half so pleasant to play with as you were before you went to India and I was seven or eight, and you had La Grace, and battledoor and shuttlecock, and cricket, and all sorts of games with me in the old garden at Charlton."

He might have told her she was much less dangerous then than now; he was not disposed to flatter her, however. So he answered her quietly,

"I preferred you as you were then."

"Indeed!" said Geraldine, with a hot color in her cheeks "I do not think there are many who would indorse your complimentary opinion."

"Possibly," said Fairlie, coldly.

She took up her cowslips, and hit him hard with them several times.

"Don't speak in that tone. If you dislike me, you can say so in warmer words, surely."

Fairlie smiled *malgré lui*.

"What a child you are, Geraldine! but a child that is a very mischievous coquette, and has learned a hundred tricks and *agaceries* of which my little friend of seven or eight knew nothing. I grant you were not a quarter so charming, but you were, I am afraid—more true."

Geraldine was ready to cry, but she was in a passion, nevertheless; such a hot and short-lived passion as all women of any spirit can go into on occasion, when they are unjustly suspected.

"If you choose to think so of me you may," she said, with immeasurable hauteur, sweeping away from him, her mauve ribbons fluttering disdainfully. "I, for one, shall not try to undeceive you."

The next night we all went up to a ball at the Vanes', to drink Rhenish, eat ices, quiz the women, flirt with the pretty ones in corners, lounge against doorways, criticise the feet in the waltzing as they passed us, and do, in fact, anything but what we went to do—dance,—according to our custom in such scenes.

The Swan and her Cygnets looked very stunning; they "made up well," as ladies say when they cannot deny that another is good-looking, but qualify your admiration by an assurance that she is shockingly plain in the morning, and owes all to her milliner and maids. Geraldine, who, by the greatest stretch of scepticism, could not be supposed "made up," was bewitching, with her sunshiny enjoyment of everything, and her untiring waltzing, going for all the world like a spinning-top, only a top tires, and she did not. Belle, who made a principle of never dancing except under extreme coercion by a very pretty hostess, could not resist her, and Tom Gower, and Little Nell, and all the rest, not to mention half Norfolk, crowded round her; all except Fairlie, who leaned against the doorway, seeming to talk to her father or the members, or anybody near, but watching the young lady for all that, who flirted not a little, having in her mind the scene in the paddock of yesterday, and wishing, perhaps, to show him that if he did not admire her more than when she was eight, other men had better taste.

She managed to come near him towards the end of the evening, sending Belle to get her an ice.

"Well," she said, with a comical *pitié d'elle-même*, "do you dislike me so much that you don't mean to dance with me at all? Not a single waltz all night?"

"What time have you had to give me?" said Fairlie, coldly. "You have been surrounded all the evening."

"Of course I have. I am not so disagreeable to other gentlemen as I am to you. But I could have made time for you if you had only asked for it. At your own ball last week you engaged me beforehand for six waltzes."

Fairlie relented towards her. Despite her flirting, he thought she did not care for Belle after all.

"Well," he said, smiling, "will you give me one after supper?"

"You told me you shouldn't dance, Colonel Fairlie," said Katherine Vane, smiling.

"One can't tell what one mayn't do under temptation," said Fairlie, smiling too. "A man may change his mind, you know."

"Oh yes," cried Geraldine; "a man may change his mind, and we are expected to be eminently grateful to him for his condescension; but if *we* change our minds, how severely we are condemned for vacillation: 'So weak!' 'Just like women!' 'Never like the same thing two minutes, poor things!'"

"You don't like the same thing two minutes, Geraldine," laughed Fairlie; "so I dare say you speak feelingly."

"I changeable! I am constancy itself!"

"Are you? You know what the Italians say of 'ocche azzure'?"

"But I don't believe it, monsieur!" cried Geraldine:

"Blue eyes beat black fifty to seven,

For black's of hell, but blue's of heaven!"

"I beg your pardon, mademoiselle," laughed Fairlie:

"Done, by the odds, it is not true!

One devil's black, but scores are blue!"

He whirled her off into the circle in the midst of our laughter at their ready wit. Soon after he bid her good night, but he found time to whisper as he did so.

"You are more like *my* little Geraldine to-night!"

The look he got made him determine to make her his little Geraldine before much more time had passed. At least he drove us back to Norwich in what seemed very contented silence, for he smoked tranquilly, and let the horses go their own pace—two certain indications that a man has pleasant thoughts to accompany him.

I do not think he listened to Belle's, and Gower's, and my conversation, not even when Belle took his weed out of his mouth and announced the important fact: "Hardinge! my ten guineas, if you please. I've had a letter!"

"What! an answer? By Jove!"

"Of course, an answer. I tell you all the pretty women in the city will know my initials, and send after me. I only hope they *will* be pretty, and then one may have a good deal of fun. I was in at Greene's this morning having mock-turtle, and talking to Patty (she's not bad-looking, that little girl, only she drops her 'h's' so. I'm like that fellow—what's his name?—in the 'Peau de Chagrin:' I don't admire my loves in cotton prints), when she gave me the letter. I left it on my dressing-table, but you can see it to-morrow. It's a horrid red daubed-looking seal, and no crest; but that she mightn't use for fear of being found out, and the writing is disguised, but that it would be. She *says* she has the three requisites; but where's the woman that don't think herself Sappho and Galatea combined? And she was nineteen last March. Poor little devil! she little thinks how she'll be done. I'm to meet her on the Yarmouth road at two, and to look out for a lady standing by the first milestone. Shall we go, Tom? It may lead to something amusing, you know, though certainly it won't lead to marriage."

"Oh! we'll go, old fellow," said I. "Deuce take you, Belle! what a lucky fellow you are with the women."

"Luckier than I want to be," yawned Belle. "It's a horrid bore to be so set upon. One may have too much of a good thing, you know."

At two the day after, having refreshed ourselves with a light luncheon at Mrs. Greene's of lobster-salad and pale ale, Belle, Gower, and I buttoned our gloves and rode leisurely up the road.

"How my heart palpitates!" said Belle, stroking his moustaches with a bored air. "How can I tell, you know, but what I may be going to see the arbiter of my destiny? Men have been tricked into all sorts of tomfoolery by their compassionate feelings. And then—if she should squint or have a turn-up nose! Good Heavens, what a fearful idea! I've often wondered when I've seen men with ugly wives how they could have been cheated into taking 'em; they couldn't have done it in their senses, you know, nor yet with their eyes open. You may depend they took 'em to church in a state of coma from chloroform. 'Pon my word, I feel quite nervous. You don't think the girl will have a parson and a register hid behind the milestone, do you?"

"If she should, it won't be legal without a license, thanks to the fools who turn Hymen into a tax-gatherer, and won't let a fellow make love without he asks leave of the Archbishop of Canterbury," said Gower. "Hallo, Belle, here's the milestone, but where's the lady?"

"Virgin modesty makes her unpunctual," said Belle, putting up his eye-glass.

"Hang modesty!" swore Tom. "It's past two, and we left a good quarter of that salad uneaten. Confound her!"

"There are no signs of her," said I. "Did she tell you her dress, Belle?"

"Not a syllable about it; only mentioned a milestone, and one might have found a market-woman sitting on that."

"Hallo! here's something feminine. Oh, good gracious! this can't be it, it's got a brown stuff dress on, and a poke straw bonnet and a green veil. No, no, Belle. If you married her, that *would* be a case of chloroform."

But the horrible brown stuff came sidling along the road with that peculiar step belonging to ladies of a certain age, characterized by Patty Greene as "tipputting," sweeping up the dust with its horrible folds, making straight *en route* for Belle, who was standing a little in advance of us. Nineteen! Good Heavens! she must have been fifty if she was a day, and under her green veil was a chestnut front—yes, decidedly a front— and a face yellow as a Canadian's, and wrinkled as Madame Pipelet's, made infinitely worse by that sweet maiden simper and assumed juvenility common to *vieilles filles*. Up she came towards poor Belle, who involuntarily retreated step by step till he had backed against the milestone, and could get no farther, while she smiled up in his handsome face, and he stared down in her withered one, with the most comical expression of surprise, dismay, and horror that had ever appeared on our "beauty's" impassive features.

"Are you—the—the—L. C.?" demanded the maiden of ten lustres, casting her eyes to the ground with virgin modesty.

"L. C. ar——My dear madam, I don't quite understand you," faltered Belle, taken aback for once in his life.

"Was it not you," faltered the fair one, shaking out a pocket-handkerchief that sent a horrible odor of musk to the olfactory nerves of poor Belle, most fastidious connoisseur in perfume, "who advertised for a kindred heart and sympathetic soul?"

"Really, my good lady," began Belle, still too aghast by the chestnut front to recover his self-possession.

"Because," simpered his inamorata, too agitated by her own feelings to hear his horrible appellative, keeping him at bay there with the fatal milestone behind him and the awful brown stuff in front of him—"because I, too, have desired to meet with some elective affinity, some spirit-tie that might give me all those more subtle sympathies which can never be found in the din and bustle of the heartless world; I, too, have pined for the objects of your search—love and domestic happiness. Oh, blessed words, surely we might—might we not?——"

She paused, overcome with maidenly confusion, and buried her face in the musk-scented handkerchief. Tom and I, where we stood *perdus*, burst into uncontrollable shouts of laughter. Poor Belle gave one blank look of utter terror at the *tout ensemble* of brown stuff, straw poke, and chestnut front. He forgot courtesy, manners, and everything else; his lips were parted, with his small white teeth glancing under his silky moustaches, his sleepy eyes were open wide, and as the maiden lady dropped her handkerchief, and gave him what she meant to be the softest and most tender glance, he turned straight round, sprang on his bay, and rushed down the Yarmouth road as if the whole of the dignitaries of the church and law were tearing after him to force him *nolens volens* into carrying out the horrible promise in his cursed line in the *Daily*. What was Tom's and my amazement to see the maiden lady seat herself astride on the milestone, and join her cachinnatory shouts to ours, fling her green veil into a hawthorn tree, jerk her bonnet into our faces, kick off her brown stuff into the middle of the road, tear off her chestnut front and yellow mask, and perform a frantic war-dance on the roadside turf. No less a person than that mischievous monkey and inimitable mimic Little Nell!

"You young demon!" shouted Gower, shrieking with laughter till he cried. "A pretty fellow you are to go tricking your senior officer like this. You little imp, how can you tell but what I shall court-martial you to-morrow?"

"No, no, you won't!" cried Little Nell, pursuing his frantic dance. "Wasn't it prime? wasn't it glorious? wasn't it worth the Kohinoor to see? You won't go and peach, when I've just given you a better farce than all old Buckstone's? By Jove! Belle's face at my chestnut front! This'll be one of his prime conquests, eh? I say, old fellows, when Charles Mathews goes to glory, don't you think I might take his place, and beat him hollow, too?"

When we got back to barracks, we found Belle prostrate on his sofa, heated, injured, crestfallen, solacing himself with Seltzer-and-water, and swearing away anything but mildly at that "wretched old woman." He bound us over to secrecy, which, with Little Nell's confidence in our minds, we naturally promised. Poor Belle! to have been made a fool of before two was humiliation more than sufficient for our all-conquering *blondin*. For one who had so often refused to stir across a ball-room to look at a Court beauty, to have ridden out three miles to see an old maid of fifty with a chestnut front! The insult sank deep into his soul, and threw him into an abject melancholy, which hung over him all through mess, and was not dissipated till a letter came to him from Mrs. Greene's, when we were playing loo in Fairlie's room. That night Fairlie was in gay spirits. He had called at Fern Chase that morning, and though he had not been able to see Geraldine alone, he had passed a pleasant couple of hours there, playing pool with her and her sisters, and had been as good friends as ever with his old playmate.

"Well, Belle," said he, feeling good-natured even with him that night, "did you get any good out of your advertisement? Did your lady turn out a very pretty one?"

"No: deuced ugly, like the generality," yawned poor Belle, giving me a kick to remind me of my promise. Little Nell was happily about the city somewhere with Pretty Face, or the boy would scarcely have kept his countenance.

"What amusement you can find in hoaxing silly women," said Fairlie, "is incomprehensible to me. However, men's tastes differ, happily. Here comes another epistle for you, Belle; perhaps there's better luck for you there."

"Oh! I shall have no end of letters. I sha'n't answer any more. I think it's such a deuced trouble. Diamonds trumps, eh?" said Belle, laying the note down till he should have leisure to attend to it. Poor old fellow! I dare say he was afraid of another onslaught from maiden ladies.

"Come, Belle," said Glenville; "come, Belle, open your letter; we're all impatience. If you won't go, I will in your place."

"Do, my dear fellow. Take care you're not pounced down upon by a respectable papa for intentions, or called to account by a fierce brother with a stubby beard," said Belle, lazily taking up the letter. As he did so, the melancholy indolence on his face changed to eagerness.

"The deuce! the Vane crest!"

"A note of invitation, probably?" suggested Gower.

"Would they send an invitation to Patty Greene's? I tell you it's addressed to L. C.," said Belle, disdainfully, opening the letter, leaving its giant deer couchant intact. "I thought it very likely; I expected it, indeed — poor little dear! I oughtn't to have let it out. Ain't you jealous, old fellows? Little darling! Perhaps I may be tricked into matrimony after all. I'd rather a presentiment that advertisement would come to something. There, you may all look at it, if you like."

It was a dainty sheet of scented cream-laid, stamped with the deer couchant, such as had brought us many an invitation down from Fern Chase, and on it was written, in delicate caligraphy:

"G. V. understands the meaning of the advertisement, and will meet L. C. at the entrance of Fern Wood, at eleven o'clock to-morrow morning."

There was a dead silence as we read it; then a tremendous buzz. Cheaply as we held women, I don't think there was one of us who wasn't surprised at Geraldine's doing any clandestine thing like this. He sat with a look of indolent triumph, curling his perfumed moustaches, and looking at the little autograph, which gave us evidence of what he often boasted — Geraldine Vane's regard.

"Let me look at your note," said Fairlie, stretching out his hand.

He soon returned it, with a brief, "Very complimentary indeed!"

When the men left, I chanced to be last, having mislaid my cigar-case. As I looked about for it, Fairlie addressed me in the same brief, stern tone between his teeth with which he spoke to Belle.

"Hardinge, you made this absurd bet with Courtenay, did you not? Is this note a hoax upon him?"

"Not that I know of—it doesn't look like it. You see there is the Vane crest, and the girl's own initials."

"Very true." He turned round to the window again, and leaned against it, looking out into the dawn, with a look upon his face that I was very sorry to see.

"But it is not like Geraldine," I began. "It may be a trick. Somebody may have stolen their paper and crest—it's possible. I tell you what I'll do to find out; I'll follow Belle to-morrow, and see who does meet him in Fern Wood."

"Do," said Fairlie, eagerly. Then he checked himself, and went on tapping an impatient tattoo on the shutter. "You see, I have known the family for years—known her when she was a little child. I should be sorry to think that one of them could be capable of such — — "

Despite his self-command he could not finish his sentence. Geraldine was a great deal too dear to him to be treated in seeming carelessness, or spoken lightly of, however unwisely she might act. I found my cigar-case. His laconic "Good night!" told me he would rather be alone, so I closed the door and left him.

The morning was as sultry and as clear as a July day could be when Belle lounged down the street, looking the perfection of a gentleman, a trifle less bored and *blasé* than ordinary, *en route* to his appointment at Fern Wood (a sequestered part of the Vane estate), where trees and lilies of the valley grew wild, and where the girls were accustomed to go for picnics or sketching. As soon as he had turned a corner, Gower and I turned it too, and with perseverance worthy a better cause, Tom and I followed Belle in and out and down the road which led to Fern Wood—a flat, dusty, stony two miles—on which, in the blazing noon of a hot midsummer day, nothing short of Satanic coercion, or love of Geraldine Vane, would have induced our beauty to immolate himself, and expose his delicate complexion.

"I bet you anything, Tom," said I, confidently, "that this is a hoax, like yesterday's. Geraldine will no more meet Belle there than all the Ordnance Office."

"Well, we shall see," responded Gower. "Somebody might get the note-paper from the bookseller, and the crest seal through the servants, but they'll hardly get Geraldine there bodily against her will."

We waited at the entrance of the wood, shrouded ourselves in the wild hawthorn hedges, while we could still see Belle—of course we did not mean to be near enough to overhear him—who paced up and down the green alleys under the firs and larches, rendered doubly dark by the evergreens, brambles, and honeysuckles,

> which, ripened by the sun,
> Forbade the sun to enter.

He paced up and down there a good ten minutes, prying about with his eye-glass, but unable to see very far in the tangled boughs, and heavy dusky light of the untrimmed wood. Then there was the flutter of something azure among the branches, and Gower gave vent to a low whistle of surprise.

"By George, Hardinge! there's Geraldine! Well! I didn't think she'd have done it. You see they're all alike if they get the opportunity."

It *was* Geraldine herself—it was her fluttering muslin, her abundant folds, her waving ribbons, her tiny sailor hat, and her little veil, and under the veil her face, with its delicate tinting, its pencilled eyebrows, and its undulating bright-colored hair. There was no doubt about it: it was Geraldine. I vow I was as sorry to have to tell it to Fairlie as if I'd had to tell him she was dead, for I knew how it would cut him to the heart to know not only that she had given herself to his rival, but that his little playmate, whom he had thought truth, and honesty, and daylight itself, should have stooped to a clandestine interview arranged through an advertisement! Their retreating figures were soon lost in the dim woodland, and Tom and I turned to retrace our steps.

"No doubt about it now, old fellow?" quoth Gower.

"No, confound her!" swore I.

"Confound her? *Et pourquoi!* Hasn't she a right to do what she likes?"

"Of course she has, the cursed little flirt; but she'd no earthly business to go making such love to Fairlie. It's a rascally shame, and I don't care if I tell her so myself."

"She'll only say you're in love with her too," was Gower's sensible response. "I'm not surprised myself. I always said she was an out-and-out coquette."

I met Fairlie coming out of his room as I went up to mine. He looked as men will look when they have not been in bed all night, and have watched the sun up with painful thoughts for their companions.

"You have been— —" he began; then stopped short, unwilling or unable to put the question into words.

"After Belle? Yes. It is no hoax, Geraldine met him herself."

I did not relish telling him, and therefore told it, in all probability, bluntly and blunderingly—tact, like talk, having, they say, been given to women. A spasm passed over his face. *"Herself!"* he echoed. Until then I do not think he had realized it as even possible.

"Yes, there was no doubt about it. What a wretched little coquette she must have been; she always seemed to make such game of Belle— —"

But Fairlie, saying something about his gloves that he had left behind, had gone back into his room again before I had half done my sentence. When Belle came back, about half an hour afterwards, with an affected air of triumph, and for once in his life of languid sensations really well contented, Gower and I poured questions upon him, as, done up with the toil of his dusty walk, and horrified to find himself so low-bred as to be hot, he kicked off his varnished boots, imbibed Seltzer, and fanned himself with a periodical before he could find breath to answer us.

"Was it Geraldine?"

"Of course it was Geraldine," he said, yawning.

"And will she marry you, Belle?"

"To be sure she will. I should like to see the woman that wouldn't," responded Belle, shutting his eyes and nestling down among the cushions. "And what's more, I've been fool enough to let her make me ask her. Give me some more sherry, Phil; a man wants support under such circumstances. The deuce if I'm not as hot as a ploughboy! It was very cruel of her to call a fellow out with the sun at the meridian; she might as well have chosen twilight. But, I say, you fellows, keep the secret, will you? she don't want her family to get wind of it, because they're bothering her to marry that old cove, Mount Trefoil, with his sixty years and his broad acres, and wouldn't let her take anybody else if they knew it; she's under age, you see."

"But how did she know you were L. C.?"

"Fairlie told her, and the dear little vain thing immediately thought it was an indirect proposal to herself, and answered it; of course I didn't undeceive her. She *raffoles* of me—it'll be almost too much of a good thing, I'm afraid. She's deuced prudish, too, much more than I should have thought *she'd* have been; but I vow she'd only let me kiss her hand, and that was gloved."

"I hate prudes," said Gower; "they've always much more devilry than the open-hearted ones. Videlicet—here's your young lady stiff enough only to give you her hand to kiss, and yet she'll lower herself to a clandestine correspondence and stolen interviews—a condescension I don't think I should admire in *my* wife."

"Love, my dear fellow, oversteps all—what d'ye call 'em?—boundaries," said Belle, languidly. "What a bore! I shall never be able to wear this coat again, it's so ingrained with dust; little puss, why didn't she wait till it was cooler?"

"Did you fix your marriage-day?" asked Tom, rather contemptuously.

"Yes, I was very weak!" sighed Belle; "but you see she's uncommonly pretty, and there's Mount Trefoil and lots of men, and, I fancy, that dangerous fellow Fairlie, after her; so we hurried matters. We've been making love to one another all these three months, you know, and fixed it so soon as Thursday week. Of course she blushed, and sighed, and put her handkerchief to her eyes, and all the rest of it, *en règle*; but she consented, and I'm to be sacrificed. But not a word about it, my dear fellows! The Vanes are to be kept in profoundest darkness, and, to lull suspicion, I'm not to go there scarcely at all until then, and when I do, she'll let me know when she will be out, and I'm to call on her mother then. She'll write to me, and put the letters in a hollow tree in the wood, where I'm to leave my answers, or, rather, send 'em; catch me going over that road again! Don't give me joy, old boys. I know I'm making a holocaust of myself, but deuce take me if I can help it—she is so deuced pretty!"

Fairlie was not at mess that night. Nobody knew where he was. I learnt, long months afterwards, that as soon as I had told him of Geraldine's identity, he, still thirsting to disbelieve, reluctant to condemn, catching at straws to save his idol from being shattered as men in love will do, had thrown himself across his horse and torn off to Fern Dell to see whether or no Geraldine was at home.

His heart beat faster and thicker as he entered the drawing-room than it had done before the lines at Ferozeshah, or in the giant semicircle at Sobraon; it stood still as in the far end of the room, lying back on a low chair, sat Geraldine, her gloves and sailor hat lying on her lap. She sprang up to welcome him with her old gay smile.

"Good God! that a child like that can be such an accomplished actress!" thought Fairlie, as he just touched her hand.

"Have you been out to-day?" he asked suddenly.

"You see I have."

"Prevarication is conviction," thought Fairlie, with a deadly chill over him.

"Where did you go, love?" asked mamma.

"To see Adela Ferrers; she is not well, you know, and I came home through part of the wood to gather some of the anemones; I don't mean anemones, they are over—lilies of the valley."

She spoke hurriedly, glancing at Fairlie all the time, who never took his iron gaze off her, though all the beauty and glory was draining away from his life with every succeeding proof that stared him in the face with its cruel evidence.

At that minute Lady Vane was called from the room to give some directions to her head gardener about some flowers, over which she was particularly choice, and Fairlie and Geraldine were left in dead silence, with only the ticking of the timepiece and the chirrup of the birds outside the open windows to break its heavy monotony.

Fairlie bent over a spaniel, rolling the dog backwards and forwards on the rug.

Geraldine stood on the rug, her head on one side in her old pretty attitude of plaintiveness and defiance, the bright sunshine falling round her and playing on her gay dress and fair hair—a tableau lost upon the Colonel, who though he had risen too, was playing sedulously with the dog.

"Colonel Fairlie, what is the matter with you? How unkind you are to-day!"

Fairlie was roused at last, disgusted that so young a girl could be so accomplished a liar and actress, sick at heart that he had been so deceived, mad with jealousy, and that devil in him sent courtesy flying to the winds.

"Pardon me, Miss Vane, you waste your coquetteries on me. Unhappily, I know their value, and am not likely to be duped by them."

Geraldine's face flushed as deep a rose hue as the geraniums nodding their heads in at the windows.

"Coquetteries?—duped? What do you mean?"

"You know well enough what. All I warn you is, never try them again on me—never come near me any more with your innocent smiles and your lying lips, or, by Heaven, Geraldine Vane, I may say what I think of you in plainer words than suit the delicacy of a lady's ears!"

Geraldine's eyes flashed fire; from rose-hued as the geraniums she changed to the dead white of the Guelder roses beside them.

"Colonel Fairlie, you are mad, I think! If you only came here to insult me——"

"I had better leave? I agree with you. Good morning."

Wherewith Fairlie took his hat and whip, bowed himself out, and, throwing himself across his horse, tore away many miles beyond Norwich, I should say, and rode into the stable-yard at twelve o'clock that night, his horse with every hair wringing and limb trembling at the headlong pace he had been ridden; such a midnight gallop as only Mazeppa, or a Border rider, or Turpin racing for his life, or a man vainly seeking to leave behind him some pursuing ghost of memory or passion, ever took before.

We saw little of him for the next few days. Luckily for him, he was employed to purchase several strings of Suffolk horses for the corps, and he rode about the country a good deal, and went over to Newmarket, and to the Bury horse fair, inspecting the cattle, glad, I dare say, of an excuse to get away.

"I feel nervous, terribly nervous; do give me the Seltzer and hock, Tom. They wonder at the fellows asking for beer before their execution. I don't; and if a fellow wants it to keep his spirits up before he's hanged, he may surely want it before he's married, for one's a swing and a crash, and it's all over and done most likely before you've time to know anything about it; but the other you walk into so deliberately, superintend the sacrifice of yourself, as it were, like that old cove Seneca; feel yourself rolling down-hill like Regulus, with all the horrid nails of the 'domesticities' pricking you in every corner; see life ebbing away from you; all the sunshine of life, as poets have it, fading, sweetly but surely, from your grasp, and Death, *alias* the Matrimonial Black Cap, coming down ruthlessly on your devoted heads. I feel low—shockingly low. Pass me the Seltzer, Tom, do!"

So spake Geraldine's *sposo* that was to be, on the evening before his marriage-day, lying on his sofa in his Cashmere dressing-gown, his gold embroidered slippers, and his velvet smoking-cap, puffing largely at his meerschaum, and unbosoming his private sentiments and emotions to the (on this score) sufficiently sympathetic listeners, Gower and I.

"I don't pity you!" said Tom, contemptuously, who had as much disdain for a man who married as for one who bought gooseberry for champagne, or Cape for comet hock, and did not know the difference—"I don't pity you one bit. You've put the curb on yourself; you can't complain if you get driven where you don't like."

"But, my dear fellow, *can* one help it?" expostulated Belle, pathetically. "When a little winning, bewitching, attractive little animal like that takes you in hand, and traps you as you catch a pony, holding out a sieve of oats, and coaxing you, and so-ho-ing you till she's fairly got the bridle over your head, and the bit between your teeth, what is a man to do?"

"Remember that as soon as the bit is in your mouth, she'll never trouble herself to give you any oats, or so-ho you softly any more, but will take the whip hand of you, and not let you have the faintest phantom of a will of your own ever again," growled the misogamistic Tom.

"Catch a man's remembering while it's any use," was Belle's very true rejoinder. "After he's put his hand to a little bill, he'll remember it's a very green thing to do, but he don't often remember it before, I fancy. No, in things like this, one can't help one's self; one's time is come, and one goes down before fate. If anybody had told me that I should go as spooney about any woman as I have about that little girl Geraldine, I'd have given 'em the lie direct; I would, indeed! But then she made such desperate love to me, took such a deuced fancy to me, you see: else, after all, the women *I* might have chosen——By George! I wonder what Lady Con, and the little Bosanquet, and poor Honoria, and all the rest of 'em will say?"

"What?" said Gower; "say 'Poor dear fellow!' to you, and 'Poor girl, I pity her!' to your wife. So you're going to elope with Miss Geraldine? A man's generally too ready to marry his daughters, to force a fellow to carry them off by stealth. Besides, as Bulwer says somewhere, '*Gentlemen* don't run away with the daughters of gentlemen.'"

"Pooh, nonsense! all's fair in love or war," returned Belle, going into the hock and Seltzer to keep up his spirits. "You see, she's afraid, her governor's mind being so set on old Mount Trefoil and his baron's coronet; they might offer some opposition, put it off till she was one-and-twenty, you know— and she's so distractedly fond of me, poor little thing, that she'd die under the probation, probably—and I'm sure I couldn't keep faithful to her for two mortal years. Besides, there's something amusing in eloping; the excitement of it keeps up one's spirits; whereas, if I were marched to church with so many mourners—I mean groomsmen—I should feel I was rehearsing my own obsequies like Charles V., and should funk it, ten to one I should. No!

I like eloping: it gives the certain flavor of forbidden fruit, which many things, besides pure water, want to 'give them a relish.'"

"Let's see how's the thing to be managed?" asked Gower. "Beyond telling me I was to go with you, consigned ignominiously to the rumble, to witness the ceremony, I'm not very clear as to the programme."

"Why, as soon as it's dawn," responded Belle, with leisurely whiffs of his meerschaum, "I'm to take the carriage up to the gate at Fern Wood—this is what she tells me in her last note; she was coming to meet me, but just as she was dressed her mother took her to call on some people, and she had to resort to the old hollow tree. The deuce is in it, I think, to prevent our meeting; if it weren't for the letters and her maid, we should have been horribly put to it for communication;—I'm to take the carriage, as I say, and drive up there, where she and her maid will be waiting. We drive away, of course, catch the 8.15 train, and cut off to town, and get married at the Regeneration, Piccadilly, where a fellow I know very well will act the priestly Calcraft. The thing that bothers me most of all is getting up so early. I used to hate it so awfully when I was a young one at the college. I like to have my bath, and my coffee, and my paper leisurely, and saunter through my dressing, and get up when the day's *warmed* for me. Early parade's one of the crying cruelties of the service; I always turn in again after it, and regard it as a hideous nightmare. I vow I couldn't give a greater test of my devotion than by getting up at six o'clock to go after her—deuced horrible exertion! I'm quite certain that my linen won't be aired, nor my coffee fit to drink, nor Perkins with his eyes half open, nor a quarter of his wits about him. Six o'clock! By George! nothing should get me up at that unearthly hour except my dear, divine, delicious little demon Geraldine! But she's so deuced fond of me, one must make sacrifices for such a little darling."

With which sublimely unselfish and heroic sentiment the bridegroom-elect drank the last of his hock and Seltzer, took his pipe out of his lips, flung his smoking-cap lazily on to his Skye's head, who did not relish the attention, and rose languidly to get into his undress in time for mess.

As Belle had to get up so frightfully early in the morning, he did not think it worth while to go to bed at all, but asked us all to vingt-et-un in his room, where, with the rattle of half-sovereigns and the flow of rum-punch, kept up his courage before the impending doom of matrimony. Belle was really in love with Geraldine, but in love in his own particular way, and consoled himself for his destiny and her absence by what I dare say seems to mademoiselle, fresh from her perusal of "Aurora Leigh" or "Lucille," very material comforters indeed. But, if truth were told, I am afraid mademoiselle would find, save that from one or two fellows here and there, who go in for love as they go in for pig-sticking or tiger-hunting, with all their might and main, wagering even their lives in the sport, the Auroras and Lucilles are very apt to have their charms supplanted by the points of a favorite, their absence made endurable by the aroma of Turkish tobacco, and their last fond admonishing words, spoken with such persuasive caresses under the moonlight and the limes, against those "horrid cards, love," forgotten that very night under the glare of gas, while the hands that lately held their own so tenderly, clasp wellnigh with as much affection the unprecedented luck "two honors and five trumps!"

Man's love is of man's life a thing apart.

Byron was right; and if we go no deeper, how can it well be otherwise, when we have our stud, our pipe, our Pytchley, our Newmarket, our club, our coulisses, our Mabille, and our Epsom, and they—oh, Heaven help them!—have no distraction but a needle or a novel! The Fates forbid that our *agrémens* should be *less*, but I dare say, if they had a vote in it, they'd try to get a trifle *more*. So Belle put his "love apart," to keep (or to rust, whichever you please) till six A. M. that morning, when, having by dint of extreme physical exertion got himself dressed, saw his valet pack his things with the keenest anxiety relative to the immaculate folding of his coats and the safe repose of his shirts, and at last was ready to go and fetch the bride his line in the *Daily* had procured him.

As Belle went down the stairs with Gower, who should come too, with his gun in his hand, his cap over his eyes, and a pointer following close at his heels, but Fairlie, going out to shoot over a friend's manor.

Of course he knew that Belle had asked for and obtained leave for a couple of months, but he had never heard for what purpose; and possibly, as he saw him at such an unusual hour, going out, not in his usual travelling guise of a wide-awake and a Maude, but with a delicate lavender tie and a toilet of the most unexceptional art, the purport of his journey flashed fully on his mind, for his face grew as fixed and unreadable as if he had had on the iron mask. Belle, guessing as he did that Fairlie would not have disliked to have been in his place that morning, was too kind-hearted and infinitely too much of a gentleman to hint at his own triumph. He laughed, and nodded a good morning.

"Off early, you see, Fairlie; going to make the most of my leave. 'Tisn't very often we can get one; our corps is deuced stiff and strict compared to the Guards and the Cavalry."

"At least our strictness keeps us from such disgraceful scenes as some of the other regiments have shown up of late," answered Fairlie between his teeth.

"Ah! well, perhaps so; still, strictness ain't pleasant, you know, when one's the victim."

"Certainly not."

"And, therefore, we should never be hard upon others."

"I perfectly agree with you."

"There's a good fellow. Well, I must be off; I've no time for philosophizing. Good-bye, Colonel."

"Good-bye—a safe journey."

But I noticed that he held the dog's collar in one hand and the gun in the other, so as to have an excuse for not offering that *poignée de main* which ought to be as sure a type of friendship, and as safe a guarantee for good faith, as the Bedouin Arab's salt.

Belle nodded him a farewell, and lounged down the steps and into the carriage, just as Fairlie's man brought his mare round.

Fairlie turned on to me with unusual fierceness, for generally he was very calm, and gentle, and impassive in manner.

"Where is he gone?"

I could not help but tell him, reluctant though I was, for I guessed pretty well what it would cost him to hear it. He did not say one word while I told him, but bent over Marquis, drawing the dog's leash tighter, so that I might not see his face, and without a sign or a reply he was out of the barracks, across his mare's back, and rushing away at a mad gallop, as if he would leave thought, and memory, and the curse of love for a worthless woman behind him for ever.

His man stood looking at the gun Fairlie had thrown to him with a puzzled expression.

"Is the Colonel gone mad?" I heard him say to himself. "The devil's in it, I think. He used to treat his things a little carefuller than this. As I live, he's been and gone and broke the trigger?"

The devil wasn't in it, but a woman *was*, an individual that causes as much mischief as any Asmodeus, Belphégor, or Mephistopheles. Some fair unknown correspondents assured me the other day, in a letter, that my satire on women was "a monstrous libel." All I can say is, that if it *be* a libel, it is like many a one for which one pays the highest, and which sounds the blackest—a libel that is *true*!

While his rival rode away as recklessly as though he was riding for his life, the gallant bridegroom—as the *Court Circular* would have it—rolled on his way to Fern Wood, while Gower, very amiably occupying the rumble, smoked, and bore his position philosophically, comforted by the recollection that Geraldine's French maid was an uncommonly good-looking, coquettish little person.

They rolled on, and speedily the postilion pulled up, according to order, before the white five-bar gate, its paint blistering in the hot summer dawn, and the great fern-leaves and long grass clinging up round its posts, still damp with the six o'clock dew. Five minutes passed—ten minutes—a quarter of an hour. Poor Belle got impatient. Twenty minutes—five-and-twenty—thirty. Belle couldn't stand it. He began to pace up and down the turf, soiling his boots frightfully with the long wet grass, and rejecting all Tom's offers of consolation and a cigar-case.

"Confound it!" cried poor Belle, piteously, "I thought women were always ready to marry. I know, when I went to turn off Lacquers of the Rifles at St. George's, his bride had been waiting for him half an hour, and was in an awful state of mind, and all the other brides as well, for you know they always marry first the girl that gets there first, and all the other poor wretches were kept on tenter-hooks too. Lacquers had lost the ring, and found it in his waistcoat after all! I say, Tom, devil take it, where can she be? It's forty minutes, as I live. We shall lose the train, you know. She's never prevented coming, surely. I think she'd let me hear, don't you? She could send Justine to me if she couldn't come by any wretched chance. Good Heavens, Tom, what shall I do?"

"Wait, and don't worry," was Tom's laconic and common-sense advice; about the most irritating probably to a lover's feelings that could pretty well be imagined. Belle swore at him in stronger terms than he generally exerted himself to use, but was pulled up in the middle of them by the sight of Geraldine and Justine, followed by a boy bearing his bride's dainty trunks.

On came Geraldine in a travelling-dress; Justine following after her, with a brilliant smile, that showed all her white teeth, at "Monsieur Torm," for whom she had a very tender friendship, consolidated by certain half-sovereigns and French phrases whispered by Gower after his dinners at Fern Chase.

Belle met Geraldine with all that tender *empressement* which he knew well how to put into his slightest actions; but the young lady seemed already almost to have begun repenting her hasty step. She hung her head down, she held a handkerchief to her bright eyes, and to Belle's tenderest and most ecstatic whispers she only answered by a convulsive pressure of the arm, into which he had drawn her left hand, and a half-smothered sob from her heart's depths.

Belle thought it all natural enough under the circumstances. He knew women always made a point of impressing upon you that they are making a frightful sacrifice for your good when they condescend to accept you, and he whispered what tender consolation occurred to him as best fitted for the occasion, thanked her, of course, for all the rapture, &c. &c., assured her of his life-long devotion—you know the style—and lifted her into the carriage, Geraldine only responding with broken sighs and stifled sobs.

The boxes were soon beside Belle's valises, Justine soon beside Gower, the postilion cracked his whip over his outsider, Perkins refolded his arms, and the carriage rolled down the lane.

Gower was very well contented with his seat in the rumble. Justine was a very dainty little Frenchwoman, with the smoothest hair and the whitest teeth in the world, and she and "Monsieur Torm" were eminently good friends, as I have told you, though to-day she was very coquettish and wilful, and laughed *à propos de bottes* at Gower, say what Chaumière compliments he might.

"Ma chère et charmante petite," expostulated Tom, "tes moues mutines sont ravissantes, mais je t'avoue que je préfère tes——"

"Tais-toi, bécasse!" cried Justine, giving him a blow with her parasol, and going off into what she would have called *éclats de rire*.

"Mais écoute-moi, Justine," whispered Tom, piqued by her perversity; "je raffole de toi! je t'adore, sur ma parole! je——Hallo! what the devil's the matter? Good gracious! Deuce take it!"

Well might Tom call on his Satanic Majesty to explain what met his eyes as he gave vent to all three ejaculations and maledictions. No less a sight than the carriage-door flying violently open, Belle descending with a violent impetus, his face crimson, and his hat in his hand, clearing the hedge at a bound, plunging up to his ankles in mud on the other side of it, and starting across country at the top of his speed, rushing frantically straight over the heavy grass-land as if he had just escaped from Hanwell, and the whole hue and cry of keepers and policemen was let loose at his heels.

"Good Heavens! By Jove! Belle, Belle, I say, stop! Are you mad? What's happened? What's the row? I say—the devil!"

But to his coherent but very natural exclamations poor Tom received no answer. Justine was screaming with laughter, the postilion was staring, Perkins swearing, Belle, flying across the country at express speed, rapidly diminishing into a small black dot in the green landscape, while from inside the carriage, from Geraldine, from the deserted bride, peals of laughter, loud, long, and uproarious, rang out in the summer stillness of the early morning.

"By Jupiter! but this is most extraordinary. The deuce is in it. Are they both gone stark staring mad?" asked Tom of his Cuba, or the blackbirds, or the hedge-cutter afar off, or anything or anybody that might turn out so amiable as to solve his problem for him.

No reply being given him, however, Tom could stand it no longer. Down he sprang, jerked the door open again, and put his head into the carriage.

"Hallo, old boy, done green, eh? Pity 'tisn't the 1st of April!" cried Geraldine, with renewed screams of mirth from the interior.

"Eh? What? What did you say, Miss Vane?" ejaculated Gower, fairly staggered by this extraordinary answer of a young girl, a lady, and a forsaken bride.

"What did I say, my dear fellow? Why, that you're done most preciously, and that I fancy it'll be a deuced long time before your delectable friend tries his hand at matrimony again, that's all. Done! oh, by George, he is done, and no mistake. Look at me, sir, ain't I a charming bride?"

With which elegant language Geraldine took off her hat, pulled down some false braids, pushed her hair off her forehead, shook her head like a water-dog after a bath, and grinned in Gower's astonished eyes—*not* Geraldine, but her twin-brother, Pretty Face!

"Do you know me now, old boy?" asked the Etonian, with demoniacal delight,—"do you know me now? Haven't I chiselled him—haven't I tricked him—haven't I done him as green as young gooseberries, and as brown as that bag? Do you fancy he'll boast of his conquests again, or advertise for another wife? So you didn't know how I got Gary Clements, of the Ten Bells, to write the letters for me? and Justine to dress me in Geraldine's things? You know they always did say they couldn't tell her from me; I've proved it now, eh?—rather! Oh, by George, I never had a better luck! and not a creature guesses it, not a soul, save Justine, Nell, and I! By Jupiter, Gower, if you'd heard that unlucky Belle go on swearing devotion interminable, and enough love to stock all Mudie's novels! But I never dare let him kiss me, though my beard is down, confound it! Oh! what jolly fun it's been, Gower, no words can tell. I always said he shouldn't marry her; he'll hardly try to do it now, I fancy! What a lark it's been! I couldn't have done it, you know, without that spicy little French girl;—she did my hair, and got up my crinoline, and stole Geraldine's dress, and tricked me up altogether, and carried my notes to the hollow oak, and took all my messages to Belle. Oh,

Jupiter! what fun it's been! If Belle isn't gone clean out of his senses, it's very odd to me. When he was going to kiss me, and whispered, 'My dearest, my darling, my wife!' I just took off my hat and grinned in his face, and said, 'Ain't this a glorious go? Oh! by George, Gower, I think the fun will kill me!'"

And the wicked little dog of an Etonian sank back among the carriage cushions stifled with his laughter. Gower staggered backwards against a roadside tree, and stood there with his lips parted and his eyes wide open, bewildered, more than that cool hand had ever been in all his days, by the extraordinary finish of poor Belle's luckless wooing; the postilion rolled off his saddle in cachinnatory fits at the little monkey's narrative! Perkins, like a soldier as he was, utterly impassive to all surrounding circumstances, shouldered a valise and dashed at quick march after his luckless master; Justine clapped her plump French-gloved fingers with a million ma Fois! and mon Dieus! and O Ciels! and far away in the gray distance sped the retreating figure of poor Belle, with the license in one pocket and the wedding-ring in the other, flying, as if his life depended on it, from the shame, and the misery, and the horror of that awful sell, drawn on his luckless head by that ill-fated line in the *Daily*.

While Belle drove to his hapless wooing, Fairlie galloped on and on. Where he went he neither knew nor cared. He had ridden heedlessly along, and the Grey, left to her own devices, had taken the road to which her head for the last four months had been so often turned—the road leading to Fern Chase,—and about a mile from the Vane estate lost her left hind-shoe, and came to a dead stop of her own accord, after having been ridden for a couple of hours as hard as if she had been at the Grand Military. Fairlie threw himself off the saddle, and, leaving the bridle loose on the mare's neck, who he knew would not stray a foot away from him, he flung himself on the grass, under the cool morning shadows of the roadside trees, no sound in the quiet country round him breaking in on his weary thoughts, till the musical ring of a pony's hoofs came pattering down the lane. He never heard it, however, nor looked up, till the quick trot slackened and then stopped beside him.

"Colonel Fairlie!"

"Good Heavens! Geraldine!"

"Well," she said, with tears in her eyes and petulant anger in her voice, "so you have never had the grace to come and apologize for insulting me as you did last week?"

"For mercy's sake do not trifle with me."

"Trifle! No, indeed!" interrupted the young lady. "Your behavior was no trifle, and it will be a very long time before I forgive it, if ever I do."

"Stay—wait a moment."

"How can you ask me, when, five days ago, you bid me never come near you with my cursed coquetries again?" asked Geraldine, trying, and vainly, to get the bridle out of his grasp.

"God forgive me! I did not know what I said. What I had heard was enough to madden a colder man than I. Is it untrue?"

"Is what untrue?"

"You know well enough. Answer me, is it true or not?"

"How can I tell what you mean? You talk in enigmas. Let me go."

"I will never let you go till you have answered me."

"How can I answer you if I don't know what you mean?" retorted Geraldine, half laughing.

"Do not jest. Tell me, yes or no, are you going to marry that cursed fool?"

"What 'cursed fool'? Your language is not elegant, Colonel Fairlie!" said Geraldine, with demure mischief.

"Belle! Would you have met him? Did you intend to elope with him?"

Geraldine's eyes, always large enough, grew larger and a darker blue still, in extremest astonishment.

"Belle!—elope with him? What are you dreaming? Are you mad?"

"Almost," said Fairlie, recklessly. "Have you misled him, then—tricked him? Do you care nothing for him? Answer me, for Heaven's sake, Geraldine!"

"I know nothing of what you are talking!" said Geraldine, with her surprised eyes wide open still. "Oblige me by leaving my pony's head. I shall be too late home."

"You never answered his advertisement, then?"

"The very question insults me! Let my pony go."

"You never met him in Fern Wood—never engaged yourself to him—never corresponded with him?"

"Colonel Fairlie, you have no earthly right to put such questions to me," interrupted Geraldine, with her hot geranium color in her cheeks and her eyes flashing fire. "I honor the report, whoever circulated it, far more than it deserves, by condescending to contradict it. Have the kindness to unhand my pony, and allow me to continue my ride."

"You shall *not* go," said Fairlie, as passionately as she, "till you have answered me one more question: Can you, will you ever forgive me?"

"No," said Geraldine, with an impatient shake of her head, but a smile nevertheless under the shadow of her hat.

"Not if you know it was jealousy of him which maddened me, love for you which made me speak such unpardonable words to you?—not if I tell you how perfect was the tale I was told, so that there was no link wanting, no room for doubt or hope?—not if I tell you what tortures I had endured in losing you—what bitter punishment I have already borne in crediting the report that you were secretly engaged to my rival—would you not forgive me then?"

"No," whispered the young lady perversely, but smiling still, the geraniums brighter in her cheeks, and her eyes fixed on the bridle.

Fairlie dropped the reins, let go her hand, and left her free to ride, if she would, away from him.

"Will you leave me, Geraldine? Not for this morning only, remember, nor for to-day, nor for this year, but—for ever?"

"No!" It was a very different "No" this time.

"Will you forgive me, then, my darling?"

Her fingers clasped his hand closely, and Geraldine looked at him from under her hat; her eyes, so like an April day, with their tears, and their tender and mischievous smile, were so irresistibly provocative that Fairlie took his pardon for granted, and thanked her in the way that seemed to him at once most eloquent and most satisfactory.

If you wish to know what became of Belle, he fled across the country to the railway station, and spent his leave Heaven knows where—in sackcloth and ashes, I suppose—meditating on his frightful sell. *We* saw nothing more of him; he could hardly show in Norwich again with all his laurels tumbled in the dust, and his trophies of conquest laughing-stocks for all the troop. He exchanged into the Z Battery going out to India, and I never saw or heard of him till a year or two ago, when he landed at Portsmouth, a much wiser and pleasanter man. The lesson, joined to the late campaign under Sir Colin, had done him a vast amount of good; he had lost his conceit, his vanity, his affectation, and was what Nature meant him to be—a sensible, good-hearted fellow. As luck would have it, Pretty Face, who had joined the Eleventh, was there too, and Fairlie and his wife as well, and Belle had the good sense to laugh it over with them, assuring Geraldine, however, that no one had eclipsed the G. V. whom he had once hoped had answered his memorable advertisement. He has grown wiser, and makes a jest of it now; it may be a sore point still, I cannot say—nobody sees it; but, whether or no, in the old city of Norwich, and in our corps, from Cadets to Colonels, nobody forgets The Line in the "Daily:" who did it, and who was done by it.

HOLLY WREATHS AND ROSE CHAINS

I

THE COLONEL OF THE "WHITE FAVORS" AND CECIL ST. AUBYN

"What are you going to do with yourself this Christmas, old fellow?" said Vivian, of the 60th Hussars: the White Favors we call them, because, after Edgehill, Henriette Maria gave their Colonel a white rosette off her own dress to hang to his sword-knot, and all the 60th have like ribbons to this day. "If you've nothing better to do," continued their present Lieutenant-Colonel, "Come down with me to Deerhurst. The governor'll be charmed to see you; my mother has always some nice-looking girls there; and, as we keep the hounds, I can promise you some good hunting with the Harkaway."

"I shall be delighted," said I, who, being in the — — Lancers, had been chained by the leg at Kensington the whole year, and, of all the woes the most pitiable, had not been able to get leave for either the 12th or the 1st; but while my chums were shooting among the turnips, or stalking royals in Blackmount Forest, I had been tied to town, a solitary unit in Pall-Mall, standing on the forsaken steps of the U. S., or pacing my hack through the dreary desert of Hyde Park—like Macaulay's New Zealander gazing on the ruins of London Bridge.

"Very well," continued Vivian, "come down with me next week, and you can send your horses with Steevens and my stud. The governor could mount you well enough, but I never hunt with so much pleasure as when I'm on Qui Vive; so I dare say you, like me, prefer your own horses. I only hope we shan't have a confounded 'black frost;' but we must take our chance of the weather. I think you'll like my sisters; they're just about half my age. Lots of children came in between, but were providentially nipped in the bud."

"Are they pretty?"

"Can't say, really; I'm too used to them to judge. I can't make love to them, so I never took the trouble to criticise them; but we've always been a good-looking race, I believe. I tell you who's staying there—that girl we met in Toronto. Do you remember her—Cecil St. Aubyn?"

"I should say I did. How did she get here?"

"She's come to live with her aunt, Mrs. Coverdale. You know that over-dressed widow who lives in Hyde Park gardens, and, when she can't afford Brighton, shuts the front shutters, lives in the back drawing-room, and says, 'Not at home to callers?' St. Aubyn is as poor as a rat, so I suppose he was glad to send Cecil here; and the Coverdale likes to have somebody who'll draw men to her parties, which I'm sure her champagne will never do. It's the most unblushing gooseberry ever ticketed 'Veuve Clicquot.'"

"'Pon my life, I'm delighted to hear it," said I. "The St. Aubyn's superb eyes will make the gooseberry go down. Men in Canada would have swallowed cask-washings to get a single waltz with her. All Toronto went mad on that score. You admired her, too, old fellow, only you weren't with her long enough for such a stoic as you are to boil up into anything warmer."

"Oh yes, I thought her extremely pretty, but I thought her a little flirt, nevertheless."

"Stuff! An attractive girl can't make herself ugly or disagreeable, or erect a brick wall round herself, with iron spikes on the top, for fear, through looking at her, any fellow might come to grief. The men followed her, and she couldn't help that."

"And she encouraged them, and she *could* help that. However, I don't wish to speak against her; it's nothing to me how she kills and slays, provided I'm not among the bag. Take care you don't get shot yourself, Ned."

"Keep your counsel for your own use, Syd. You put me in mind of the philanthropist, who ran to warn his neighbor of the dangers of soot while his own chimney was on fire."

"As how? I don't quite see the point of your parable," said Vivian, with an expression of such innocent impassiveness that one would have thought he had never seen her fair face out of her furs in her sledge, or admired her small ankles when she was skating on the Ontario.

The winter before, a brother of mine, who was out there in the Rifles, wrote and asked me to go and have some buffalo-hunting, and Vivian went out with me for a couple of months. We had some very good sport in the western woods and plains, and his elk and bison horns are still stuck up in Vivian's rooms at Uxbridge, with many another trophy of both hemispheres. We had sport of another kind, too, to the merry music of the silvery sledge-bells, over the crisp snow and the gleaming ice, while bright eyes shone on us under delicate lace veils, and little feet peeped from under heaps of sable and bearskin, and gay voices rang out in would-be fear when the horses shied at the shadow of themselves, or at the moon shining on the ice. Who thinks of Canada without in fancy hearing the ringing chimes of the gay sledge bells swinging joyous measure into the clear sunshine or the white moonlight, in tune with light laughter, and soft whispers, and careless hearts?

There we saw Cecil St. Aubyn, one of the prettiest girls in Toronto, then about nineteen. My brother Harry was mad about her, so were almost all the men in the Canada Rifles, and Engineers, and, 61st that were quartered there; and Vivian admired her too, though in a calmer sort of way. Perhaps if he had been with her more than a fortnight he might have gone further. As it was, he left Toronto liking her long Canadian eyes no more than was pleasant. It was as well so, perhaps, for it would not have been a good match for him, St. Aubyn being a broken-down gambler, who, having lost a princely fortune at Crocky's, and the Bads, married at fifty a widow with a little money, and migrated to Toronto, where he was a torment to himself and to everybody else. Vivian, meanwhile, was a great matrimonial *coup*. Coming of a high county family, and being the only son, of course there was priceless value set on his life, which, equally, of course, he imperilled, after the manner of us all, in every way he could—in charges and skirmishes, yachting, hunting, and steeple-chasing—ever since some two-and-twenty years ago he joined as a cornet of fifteen—a man already in muscle and ideas, pleasures and pursuits.

At the present time he had been tranquilly engaged in the House, as he represented the borough of Cacklebury.

He spoke seldom, but always well, and was thought a very promising member, his speeches being in Bernal Osborne's style; but he himself cared little about his senatorial laurels, and was fervently hoping that there would be a row with Russia, and that we should be allowed to go and stick Croats and make love to Bayadères, to freshen us up and make us boys again.

Next week, the first in December, he and I drove to Paddington, put ourselves in the express, and whisked through the snow-covered embankments, whitened fields, and holly hedges on the line down to Deerhurst. If the frost broke up we should have magnificent runs, and we looked at the country with a longing eye. Ever since he was six years old, he told me, he had gone out with the Harkaway Hack on Christmas-eve. When the drag met us, with the four bays steaming in the night air, and the groom warming into a smile at the sight of the Colonel, the sleet was coming down heavily, and the wind blew as keen as a sabre's edge. The bays dashed along at a furious gallop under Vivian's hand, the frosty road cracked under the wheel, the leaders' breath was white in the misty night; we soon flew through the park gate—though he didn't forget to throw down a sovereign on the snow for the old porteress—and up the leafless avenue, and bright and cheery the old manor-house, with its score of windows, like so many bright eyes, looked out upon the winter's night.

"By George! we did that four miles quick enough," said Vivian, jumping down, and shaking the snow off his hair and mustaches. "The old place looks cheery, doesn't it? Ah! there are the girls; they're sure to pounce on me."

The two girls in question having warm hearts, not spoilt by the fashionable world they live in, darted across the hall, and, regardless of the snow, welcomed him ardently. They were proud of him, for he is a handsome dog, with haughty, aristocratic features, and a grand air as stately as a noble about Versailles in the polished "Age doré."

He shook himself free, and went forward to meet his mother, whom he is very fond of; while the governor, a fine-looking, genial old fellow, bade me welcome to Deerhurst. In the library door I caught sight of a figure in white that I recognised as our belle of the sledge drives; she was looking at Vivian as he bent down to his mother. As soon as she saw me though, she disappeared, and he and I went up to our rooms to thaw, and dress for dinner.

By the fire, talking to Blanche Vivian, stood Cecil, when we went down to the drawing-room. She always makes me think of a Sèvres or Dresden figure, her coloring is so delicate, and yet brilliant; and if you were to see her Canadian eyes, her waving chestnut hair, and her instantaneous, radiant, coquettish smiles, you would not wonder at the Toronto men losing their heads about her.

"Why, Cecil, you never told me you knew Sydney!" cried Blanche, as Vivian shook hands with the St. Aubyn. "Where did you meet him? how long have you been acquainted? why did you never tell me?"

"How could I tell Colonel Vivian was your brother?" said Cecil, playing with a little silver Cupid driving a barrowful of matches on the mantelpiece till she tumbled all his matches into the fender.

"You might have asked. Never mind the wax-lights," said Blanche, who, not having been long out, had a habit of saying anything that came into her head. "When did you see him? Tell me, Sydney, if she won't."

"Oh, in Canada, dear!" interrupted Cecil, quickly. "But it was for so short a time I should have thought Colonel Vivian would have forgotten my face, and name, and existence."

"Nay, Miss St. Aubyn," said Vivian, smiling. "Pardon me, but I think you must know your own power too well to think that any man who has seen you once could hope for his own peace to forget you."

The words of course were flattering, but his quizzical smile made them doubtful. Cecil evidently took them as satire. "At least, you've forgotten anything we talked about at Toronto," she said, rather impatiently, "for I remember telling you I detested compliments."

"I shouldn't have guessed it," murmured Vivian, stroking his mustaches.

"And you," Cecil went on, regardless of the interruption, "told me you never complimented any woman you respected; so that speech just now doesn't say much for your opinion of me."

"How dare I begin to like you?" laughed Vivian.

"Don't you know Levinge and Castlereagh were great friends of mine? Poor fellows! the sole object of their desires now is six feet of Crimean sod, if we're lucky enough to get out there." Cecil colored. Levinge's and Castlereagh's hard drinking and gloomy aspect at mess were popularly attributed to the witchery of the St. Aubyn. Canada, while she was in it, was as fatal to the Service as the Cape or the cholera.

"If I talked so romantically, Colonel Vivian, with what superb mockery you would curl your mustaches. Surely the Iron Hand (wasn't that your sobriquet in Caffreland?) does not believe in broken hearts?"

"Perhaps not; but I *do* believe in some people's liking to try and break them."

"So do I. It is a favorite pastime with your sex," said Cecil, beating the hearth-rug impatiently with her little satin shoe.

"I don't think we often attack," laughed Vivian. "We sometimes yield out of amiability, and we sometimes take out the foils in self-defence, though we are no match for those delicate hands that use their Damascus blades so skilfully. We soon learn to cry quarter!"

"To a dozen different conquerors in as many months, then!" cried Cecil, with a defiant toss of her head.

Vivian looked down on her as a Newfoundland might look down on a small and impetuous-minded King Charles, who is hoping to irritate him. Just then three other people staying there came in. A fat old dowager and a thin daughter, who had turquoise eyes, and from whom, being a great pianist, we all fled in mortal terror of a hailstorm of Thalberg and Hertz, and a cousin of Syd's, Cossetting, a young chap, a blondin, with fair curls parted down the centre, whose brains were small, hands like a girl's, and thoughts centred on dew *bouquets* and his own beauty, but who, having a baronetcy, with much tin, was strongly set upon by the turquoise eyes, but appeared himself to lean more towards the Canadian, as a greater contrast to himself, I suppose.

"How do you do, Cos?" said Vivian, carelessly. The Iron Hand very naturally scorned this effeminate *patte de velours*.

"You here!" lisped the baronet. "Delighted to see you! thought you'd killed yourself over a fence, or something, before this— —"

"Why, Horace," burst in energetic little Blanche, "I have told you for the last month that he was coming down for Christmas."

"Did you, my dear child?" said Cos. "'Pon my life I forgot it. Miss St. Aubyn, my man Cléante (he's the handiest dog—he once belonged to the Duc d'Aumale) has just discovered something quite new—there's no perfume like it; he calls it 'Fleurs des Tilleuls,' and the best of it is, nobody can have it. If you'll allow me— —"

"Everybody seems to make it their duty to forget Sydney," muttered Blanche, as the Baronet murmured the rest of his speech inaudibly.

"Never mind, petite; I can bear it," laughed Vivian, leaning against the mantelpiece with that look of quiet strength characteristic of both his mind and body.

Cecil overheard the whisper, and flushed a quick look at him; then turning to Cossetting, talked over the "Fleurs des Tilleuls" as if her whole mind was absorbed in *bouquet*.

When dinner was announced, Vivian troubled himself, however, to give his arm to Cecil, and, tossing his head back in the direction of the turquoise eyes, said to the discomfited Horace, "You sing, don't you, Cosset? Miss Screechington will bore you less than she would me."

"Is it, then, because I 'bore you less' that you do me the honor?" asked Cecil, quickly.

"Yes," said Syd, calmly; "or, rather, to put it more courteously, you amuse me more."

"Monseigneur! je vous remercie," said Cecil, her long almond eyes sparkling dangerously. "You promote me to the same rank with an opera, a hookah, a rat-hunt, and a French novel?"

"And," Vivian went on tranquilly, "I dare say I shall amuse *you* better than that poor little fool with his lisp and his talk of the toilet, and his hands that never pulled in a thorough-bred or aided a rowing match."

"Oh, we're not in the Iliad and Odyssey days to deify physical strength," said Cecil, who secretly adored it, as all women do; "nor yet among the Pawnees to reverence a man according to his scalps. Though Sir Horace may not have followed your example and jeopardised his life on every possible occasion, he is very handsome, and can be very agreeable."

"Is it possible you can endure that fop?" said Vivian, quickly.

"Certainly. Why not?"

The Colonel stroked his moustache contemptuously. "I should have fancied you more difficile, that is all; but Cos is, as you say, good-looking, and very well off. I wish — —"

"What? That you were 'less bored?'"

"That I always wish; but I was thinking of Cos, there—milk-posset, as little Eardley in the troop says they called him at Eton—I was wishing he could see Levinge and Castlereagh, just as *épouvantails*, to make him turn and flee as the French noblesse did when they saw their cousins and brothers strung up à la lanterne."

"Wasn't it very strange," Blanche was saying to me at the same time, "that Cecil never mentioned Sydney? I've so often spoken of him, told her his troop, and all about him. (He has always been so kind to me, though he is eighteen years older—just twice my age.) Besides, I found her one day looking at his picture in the gallery, so she must have known it was the same Colonel Vivian, mustn't she Captain Thornton?"

"I should say so. Have you known her long?"

"No. We met her at Brighton this August with that silly woman, Mrs. Coverdale. All her artifices and falsehoods annoy Cecil so; Cecil doesn't mind saying she's not rich, she knows it's no crime."

"C'est pire qu'un crime, c'est une faute," said I.

"Don't talk in that way," laughed Blanche. "That's bitter and sarcastic, like Sydney in his grand moods, when I'm half afraid of him. I am sure Cecil couldn't be nicer, if she were ever such an heiress. Mamma asked her for Christmas because she once knew Mr. St. Aubyn well, and Cecil is not happy with Mrs. Coverdale. False and true don't suit each other. I hope Sydney will like her—do you think he does?"

That was a question I could not answer. He admired her, of course, because he could not well have helped it, and had done so in Canada; and he was talking to her now, I dare say, to force her to acknowledge that he *was* more amusing than Horace Cos. But he seemed to me to weigh her in a criticising balance, as if he expected to find her wanting—as if it pleased him to provoke and correct her, as one pricks and curbs a beautiful two-year old, just to see its graceful impatience at the check and the glance of its wild eye.

II

THE CANADIAN'S COLD BATH
WARMS UP THE COLONEL

Deerhurst was a capital house to spend a Christmas in. It was the house of an English gentleman, with even the dens called bachelors' rooms comfortable and luxurious to the last extent: a first-rate stud, a capital billiard table, a good sporting country, pretty girls to amuse one with when tired of the pink, the best Chablis and Château Margaux to be had anywhere, and a host who would have liked a hundred people at his dinner-table the whole year round. The snow, confound it! prevented our taking the hounds out for the first few days; but we were not bored as one might have expected, and our misery was the girls' delight, who were fervently hoping that the ice might come thick enough for them to skate. Cecil was invaluable in a country-house; her resources were as unlimited as Houdin's inexhaustible bottle. She played in French vaudevilles and Sheridan Knowles's comedies, acted charades, planned tableaux vivants, sang gay wild chansons peculiar to herself, that made the Screechington bravuras and themes more insupportable than ever; and, what was more, managed to infuse into everybody else some of her own energy and spirit. She made every one do as she liked; but she tyrannised over us so charmingly that we never chafed at the bit; and to the other girls she was so good-natured in giving them the rôles they liked, in praising, and in aiding them, that it was difficult for feminine malice, though its limits are boundless, to find fault with her. Vivian, though he did not relax his criticism of her, was agreeable to her, as he had been in Canada, and as he is always to women when he is not too lazy. He consented to stand for Rienzi in a tableau, though he hates doing all those things, and played in the Proverbs with such a flashing fire of wit in answer to Cecil that we told him he beat Mathews.

"I'm inspired," he said, with a laughing bend of his head to Cecil, when somebody complimented him.

She gave an impatient movement—she was accustomed to have such things whispered in earnest, not in jest. She laughed, however. "Are you inspired, then, to take *Huon's* part? All the characters are cast but that."

"I'm afraid I can't play well enough."

"Nonsense. You cannot think that. Say you would rather not at once."

Vivian stroked his mustaches thoughtfully. "Well, you see, it bores me rather; and I'm not Christian enough to suffer ennui cheerfully to please other people."

"Very well, then, I will give the part to Sir Horace," said Cecil, looking through the window at the church spire, covered with the confounded snow.

Vivian stroked away at his mustaches rather fiercely this time. "Cos! he'll ruin the play. Dress him up as a lord in waiting, he'll be a dainty lay figure, but for anything more he's not as fit as this setter! Fancy that essenced, fair-haired young idiot taking *Huon*—his lisp would be so effective!"

She looked up in his face with one of her mischievous, dangerous smiles, and put up her hands in an attitude of petition. "He must have the part if you won't. Be good, and don't spoil the play. I have set my mind on its being perfect, and—I will have *such* a dress as the *Countess* if you will only do as I tell you."

Cecil, in her soft, childlike moods, could finish any man. Of course Vivian rehearsed "Love" with her that afternoon, a play that was to come off on the 23rd. Cos sulked slightly at being commanded by her to dress himself beautifully and play the *Prince of Milan*.

"To be refused by you," lisped Horace. "Oh, I dare say! No! 'pon my life——"

"My dear Cos, you'll have plenty of fellow-sufferers," whispered Syd, mischievously.

"Do you dare to disobey me, Sir Horace?" cried Cecil. "For shame! I should have thought you more of a preux chevalier. If you don't order over from Boxwood that suit of Milan armor you say one of your ancestors wore at Flodden, and wear it on Tuesday, you shall never waltz with me again. Now what do you say?"

"Nobody can rethitht you," murmured Cos. "You do anything with a fellow that you chooth."

Vivian glanced down at him with superb scorn, and turned to me. "What a confounded frost this is. The weathercock sticks at the north, and old Ben says there's not a chance of a change till the new moon. Qui Vive might as well have kept at Hounslow. To waste all the season like this would make a parson swear! If I'd foreseen it I would have gone to Paris with Lovell, as he wanted me to do."

I suppose the Colonel was piqued to find he was not the only one persuaded into his rôle. He bent over Laura Caldecott's chair, a pretty girl, but with nothing to say for herself, admired her embroidery, and talked with great empressement about it, till Laura, much flattered at such unusual attention, after lisping a good deal of nonsense, finally promised to embroider a note-case for him, "if you'll be good and use it, and not throw it away, as you naughty men always do the pretty things we give you," simpered Miss Laura.

"Hearts included," said Syd, smiling. "I assure you if you give me yours, I will prize it with Turkish jealousy."

The fair brodeuse gave a silly laugh; and Vivian, whose especial detestation is this sort of love-making nonsense, went on flirting with her, talking the persiflage that one whispers leaning over the back of a phaeton after a dinner at the Castle or a day at Ascot, but never expects to be called to remember the next morning, when one bows to the object thereof in the Ring, and the flavor of the claret-cup and the scent of the cigar are both fled with the moonbeams and forgotten.

Cecil gave the Colonel and his flirtation a glance, and let Cossetting lean over the back of her chair and deliver himself of some lackadaisical sentiment (taken second-hand out of "Isidora" or the "Amant de la Lune," and diluted to be suitable for presentation to her), looking up at him with her large velvet eyes, or flashing on him her radiant smile, till Horace pulled up his little stiff collar, coaxed his flaxen whiskers, looked at her with his half-closed light eyes—and thought himself irresistible—and Miss Screechington broke the string of the purse she was making, and scattered all the steel beads about the floor in the futile hope of gaining his attention. Blanche went down on her knees and spent twenty minutes hunting them all up; but as I helped her I saw the turquoise eyes looked anything but grateful for our efforts, though if Blanche had done anything for me with that ready kindness and those soft little white hands, I should have repaid her very warmly. But oh, these women! these women! Do they ever love one another in their hearts? Does not Chloris always swear that Lelia's gazelle eyes have a squint in them and Delia hint that Daphne, who is innocent as a dove, is bad style, and horridly bold?

At last Cecil got tired of Cos's drawling platitudes, and walked up to one of the windows. "How is the ice, will anybody tell me? I am wild to try it, ain't you, Blanche? If we are kept waiting much longer, we will have the carpets up and skate on the oak floors."

I told her I thought they might try it safely. "Then let us go after luncheon, shall we?" said Cecil. "It is quite sunny now. You skate, of course, Sir Horace?"

"Oh! to be sure—certainly," murmured Cos. "We'd a quadrille on the Serpentine last February, Talbot, and I, and some other men—lots of people said they never saw it better done. But it's rather cold—don't you think so?"

"Do you expect to find ice in warm weather?" said Vivian, curtly, from the fire, where he was standing watching the commencement of the note-case.

"No. But I hate cold," said Horace, looking at his snowy fingers. "One looks such a figure—blue, and wet, and shivering; the house is much the best place in a frost."

"Poor fellow!" said Vivian, with a contemptuous twist of his mustaches. "I fear, however fêté you may be in every other quarter, the seasons won't change to accommodate you."

"Oh! you are a dreadful man," drawled Cos. "You don't a bit mind tanning yourself, nor getting drenched through, nor soiling your hands——"

"Thank Heaven, no!" responded Syd. "I'm neither a school-girl, nor—a fop."

"Would you believe it, Miss St. Aubyn?" said the baronet, appealingly. "That man'll get up before daylight and let himself be drenched to the skin for the chance of playing a pike; and will turn out of a comfortable arm-chair on a winter's night just to go after poachers and knock a couple of men over, and think it the primest fun in life. I don't understand it myself, do you?"

"Yes," said Cecil, fervently. "I delight in a man's love for sport, for I idolise horses, and there is nothing that can beat a canter on a fine fresh morning over a grass country; and I believe that a man who has the strength, and nerve, and energy to go thoroughly into fishing, or shooting, or whatever it be, will carry the same will and warmth into the rest of his life; and the hand that is strong in the field and firm in righteous wrath, will be the truer in friendship and the gentler in pity."

Cecil spoke with energetic enthusiasm. Horace stared, the Screechington sneered, Laura gave an affected little laugh. The Colonel swung round from his study of the fire, his face lighting up. I've seen Syd on occasion look as soft as a woman. However, he said nothing; he only took her in to luncheon, and was exceedingly kind to her and oblivious of Laura Caldecott's existence throughout that meal, which, at Deerhurst, was of unusual splendor and duration. And afterwards, when she had arrayed herself in a hat with soft curling feathers, and looped up her dress in some inexplicable manner that showed her dainty high heels artistically, he took her little skates in his hand and walked down by her side to the pond. It was some way to the pond—a good sized piece of water, that snobs would have called the Lake, by way of dignifying their possessions, with willows on its banks (where in summer the sentimental Screechington would have reclined, Tennyson *à la main*), and boats and punts beside it, among which was a tub, in which Blanche confessed to me she had paddled herself across to the saturation of a darling blue muslin, and the agonised feelings of her governess, only twelve months before.

"A dreadful stiff old thing that governess was," said Blanche, looking affectionately at the tub. "Do you know, Captain Thornton, when she went away, and I saw her boxes actually on the carriage-top, I waltzed round the schoolroom seven times, and burnt 'Noel et Chapsal' in the fire—I did, indeed!"

The way, as I say, was long to the pond; and as Cecil's dainty high heels and Syd's swinging cavalry strides kept pace over the snow together, they had plenty of time for conversation.

"Miss Caldecott is looking for you," said Cecil, with a contemptuous glance at the fair Laura, who, between two young dandies, was picking her route over the snow holding her things very high indeed, and casting back looks at the Colonel.

"Is she? It is very kind of her."

"If you feel the kindness so deeply, you had better repay it by joining her."

Vivian laughed. "Not just now, thank you. We are close to the kennels—hark at their bay! Would you like to come and see them? By-the-by, how is your wolf-dog—Leatherstockings, didn't you call him?"

"Do you remember him?" said Cecil, her eyes beaming and her lips quivering. "Dear old dog, I loved him so much, and he loved me. He was bitten by an asp just before I left, and papa would have him shot. Good gracious! what is the matter?—she is actually frightened at that setter!"

The "she" of whom Cecil so disdainfully spoke was Miss Caldecott, who, on seeing a large setter leap upon her with muddy paws and much sudden affection, began to scream, and rushed to Vivian with a beseeching cry of "Save me, save me!" Cecil stood and laughed, and called the setter to her.

"Here, Don—Dash—what is your name? Come here, good dog. That poor young lady has nerves, and you must not try them, or you will cause her endless expenses in sal volatile and ether; But I have no such interesting weaknesses, and you may lavish any demonstrations you please on me!"

We all laughed as she thus talked confidentially to the setter, holding his feathered paws against her waist; while Vivian stood by her with admiration in his glance. Poor Laura looked foolish, and began to caress a great bull-dog, who snapped at her. She hadn't Cecil's ways either with dogs or men.

"What a delightful scene," whispered Cecil to the Colonel, as we left the kennels. "You were not half so touched by it as you were expected to be!"

Vivian laughed. "Didn't you effectually destroy all romantic effect? You can be very mischievous to your enemies."

Cecil colored. "She is no enemy of mine; I know nothing of her, but I do detest that mock sentimentality, that would-be fine ladyism that thinks it looks interesting when it pleads guilty to sal volatile, and screams at an honest dog's bark. Did you see how shocked she and Miss Screechington looked because I let the hounds leap about me?"

"Of course; but though you have not lived very long, you must have learned that you are too dangerous to the peace of our sex to expect much mercy from your own."

A flush came into Cecil's cheeks *not* brought by the wind. Her feathers gave a little dance as she shook her head with her customary action of annoyance.

"Ah, never compliment me, I am so tired of it."

"I wish I could believe that," said Syd, in a low tone. "Your feelings are warm, your impulses frank and true; it were a pity to mar them by an undue love for the flattering voices of empty-headed fools."

Tears of pleasure started into her eyes, but she would not let him see it. She had not forgotten the Caldecott flirtation of the morning enough to resist revenging it. She looked up with a merry laugh.

"Je m'amuse—voilà tout. There is no great harm in it."

A shadow of disappointment passed over Syd's haughty face.

"No, if you do not do it once too often. I *have* known men—and women too—who all their lives through have been haunted by the memory of a slight word, a careless look, with which, unwittingly or in obstinacy, they shut the door of their own happiness. Have you ever heard of the Deerhurst ghost?"

"No," said Cecil, softly. "Tell it me."

"It is a short story. Do you know that picture of Muriel Vivian, the girl with the hawk on her wrist and long hair of your color? She lived in Charles's time, and was a great beauty at the court. There were many who would have lived and died for her, but the one who loved her best was her cousin Guy. The story says that she had plighted herself to him in these very woods; at any rate, he followed her when she went to join the court, and she kept him on, luring him with vague promises, and flirting with Goring, and Francis Egerton, and all the other gay gentlemen. One night his endurance broke down: he asked her whether or no she cared for him? He begged, as a sign, for the rosebud she had in her dress. She laughed at him, and—gave the flower to Harry Carrew, a young fellow in Lunsford's 'Babe-eaters.' Guy said no more, and left her. Before dawn he shot Carrew through the heart, took the rosebud from the boy's doublet, put it in his own breast, and fell upon his sword. They say Muriel lost her senses. I don't believe it: no coquette ever had so much feeling; but if you ask the old servants they will tell you, and firmly credit the story too, that hers and Guy Vivian's ghosts still are to be seen every midnight at Christmas-eve, the day that he fought and killed little Harry Carrew."

He laughed, but Cecil shuddered.

"What a horrible story! But do you believe that any woman ever possessed such power over a man?"

"I believe it since I have seen it. One of my best friends is now hopelessly insane because a woman as worthless as this dead branch forsook him. Poor fellow! they set it down to a coup de soleil, but it was the falsehood of Emily Rushbrooke that did it. But, for myself, I never should lose my head for any woman. I did once when I was a boy, but I know better now."

A wild, desperate idea came into Cecil's mind. She contrasted the passionless calm of his face with the tender gentleness of his tone a few moments ago, and she would have given her life to see him "lose his head for her" as he had done for that other. How she hated her, whoever she had been! Cecil had seen too many men not to know that Syd's cool exterior covered a stormy heart, and in the longing to rouse up the storm at her incantation she resolved to play a dangerous game. The ghost story did not warn her. As Mephistopheles to Faust came Horace Cos to aid the impulse, and Cecil turned to him with one of her radiant smiles. She never looked prettier than in her black hat; the wind had only blown a bright flush into her cheeks—though it had turned Laura blue and the Screechington red—

and the Colonel looked up at her as he put her skates on with something of the look Guy might have given Muriel Vivian flirting gaily with the roistering cavaliers.

"Now, Sir Horace, show us some of those wonderful Serpentine figures," cried Cecil, balancing herself with the grace of a curlew, and whirling here, there, and everywhere at her will as easily as if she were on a chalked ball-room floor. She hadn't skated and sledged on the Ontario for nothing. More than one man had lost his own balance looking after her. Cos wasn't started yet; one pair of skates were too large, another pair too small; if he'd thought of it he'd have had his own sent over. He stood on the brink much as Winkle, of Pickwickian memory, trembled in Weller's grasp. Cecil looked at him with laughing eyes, a shrewd suspicion that he had planted her adorer, and that the quadrille on the Serpentine was an offspring of the Cossetting poetic fancy. Thrice did the luckless baronet essay the ice, and thrice did he come to grief with heels in the air, and his dainty apparel disordered. At last, his Canadian sorceress took compassion upon him, and declaring she was tired, asked him to drive her across the pond. Cos, with an air of languid martyrdom and a heavy sigh as he glanced at his Houbigants, torn and soiled, grasped the back of the chair, and actually contrived to start it. Once started, away went the chair and its Phaeton after it, whether he would or no, its occupant looking up and laughing in the dandy's heated, disconcerted, and anxious face. All at once there was a crash, a plunge, and a shout from Vivian, who was on the opposite bank. The chair had broken the ice, flung Cecil out into the water with the shock, while her charioteer, by a lucky jump backwards, had saved himself, and stood on the brink of the chasm unharmed. Cecil's crinoline kept her from sinking; she stretched out her little hand with a cry—it sounded like Vivian's name as it came to my ears on the keen north wind—but before Vivian, who came across the ice like a whirlwind, could get to her, Cos, valorously determining to wet his wristbands, stooped down, and, holding by the chair, which was firmly wedged in, put his arm round her and dragged her out. Vivian came up two seconds too late.

"Are you hurt?" he said, bending towards her.

"No," said Cecil, faintly, as her head drooped unconsciously on Cos's shoulder. She had struck her forehead on the ice, which had stunned her slightly. The Colonel saw the chestnut hair resting against Cos's arm; he dropped the hand he had taken, and turned to the shore.

"Bring her to the bank," he said, briefly. "I will go home and send a carriage. Good Heavens! that that fool should have saved her!" I heard him mutter, as he brushed past me.

He drove the carriage down himself, and under pretext of holding on the horses, did not descend from the box while Horace wrapped rugs and cloaks round Cecil, who, having more pluck than strength, declared she was quite well now, but nearly fainted when Horace lifted her out, and she was consigned by Mrs. Vivian to her bedroom for the rest of the day.

"It is astonishing how we miss Cecil," remarked Blanche, at dinner. "Isn't it dull without her, Sydney?"

"I didn't perceive it," said the Colonel, calmly; "but I am very sorry for the cause of her absence."

"Well, by Jove! it sounds unfeeling; but I can't say I am," murmured Horace. "It's something to have saved such a deuced pretty girl as that."

"Curse that puppy," muttered Syd to his champagne glass. "A fool that isn't fit for her to look at— —"

Syd's and my room, in the bachelors' wing, adjoin each other; and as our windows both possess the convenience of balconies, we generally smoke in them, and hold a little chat before turning in. When I stepped out into my balcony that night, Syd was already puffing away at his pipe. Perhaps his Cavendish was unusually good, for he did not seem greatly inclined to talk, but leant over the balcony, looking out into the clear frosty night, with the winter stars shining on the wide white uplands and the leafless glittering trees.

"What's that?" said he sharply, as the notes of a cornet playing, and playing badly, Halévy's air, "Quand de la Nuit," struck on the night air.

"A serenade, I suppose."

"A serenade in the snow. Who is romantic idiot enough for that?" said Vivian contemptuously, nearly pitching himself over to see where the cornet came from. It came from under Cecil's windows, where a light was still burning. The player looked uncommonly like Cossetting wrapped up in a cloak with a wide-awake on, under which the moonlight showed us some fair hair peeping.

Vivian drew back with an oath he did not mean me to hear. He laughed scornfully. "Milk-posset, of course! There is no other fool in the house. His passion must be miraculously deep to drag him out of his bed into the snow to play some false notes to his lady-love. It's rather windy, don't you think, Ned. Good night, old fellow—and, I say, don't turn little Blanche's head with your pretty speeches. You and I are bound not to flirt, since we're sworn never to marry; and I don't want the child played with, though possibly (being a woman) she'd very soon recover it."

With which sarcasm on his sister and her sex, the Colonel shut down the window with a clang; and I remained, smoking four pipes and a half, meditating on his last words, for I *had* been playing with the child, and felt (inhuman brute! the ladies will say) that I should be sorry if she *did* recover it.

III
SHOWING THAT LOVE-MAKING ON HOLY GROUND DOESN'T PROSPER

Cecil came down the next morning looking very pretty after her ducking. Vivian asked her how she was with his general air of calm courtesy, helped her to some cold pheasant, and applied himself to his breakfast and some talk with a sporting man about the chances of the frost breaking up.

Horace, who looked upon himself as a preux chevalier, had had his left arm put in a sling on the strength of a bruise as big as a fourpenny-piece, and appeared to consider himself entitled to Cecil's eternal gratitude and admiration for having gone the length of wetting his coat sleeves for her.

"Do you like music by starlight?" he whispered, with a self-conscious smile, after a course of delicate attentions throughout breakfast.

Syd fixed his eyes on Cecil's, steadily but impassively. The color rose into her face, and she turned to Cos with a mischievous laugh.

"Very much, if—I am not too sleepy to hear it; and it isn't a cornet out of tune."

"How cruel!" murmured Horace, as he passed her coffee. "You shouldn't criticise so severely when a fellow tries to please you."

"That poor dear girl really thinks I turned out into the snow last night to give her that serenade," observed Cos, with a languid laugh, when we were alone in the billiard-room. "Good, isn't it, the idea of *my* troubling myself?"

"Whose cracked cornet was it, then, that made that confounded row last night?" I asked.

Horace laughed again; it was rarely he was so highly amused at anything: "It was Cléante's, to be sure. He don't play badly when his hands are not numbed, poor devil! Of course he made no end of a row about going out into the snow, but I made him do it. I knew Cecil would think it was I. Women are so vain, poor things!"

It was lucky I alone was the repository of his confidence, for if Vivian had chanced to have been in the billiard-room, it is highly probable he would then and there have brained his cousin with one of the cues.

Happily he was out of the reach of temptation, in the stables, looking after Qui Vive, who had to "bide in stall," as much to that gallant bay's disquiet as to her owner's; for I don't know which of the two best loves a burst over a stiff country, or a fast twenty minutes up wind alone with the hounds when they throw up their heads.

To the stables, by an odd coincidence, Cecil, putting the irresistible black hat on the top of her chestnut braids, prevailed on Blanche to escort her, vowing (which was nearly, but not quite, the truth) that she loved the sweet pets of horses better than anything on earth. Where Cecil went, Laura made a point of going too, to keep her enemy in sight, I suppose; though Cecil, liking a fast walk on the frosty roads, a game of battledore and shuttlecock with Blanche (when we were out of the house), or anything, in short, better than working with her feet on the fender, and the Caldecott inanities or Screechington scandals in her ear, often led Laura many an unwelcome dance, and brought that luckless young lady to try at things which did not sit well upon her as they did upon the St. Aubyn, who had a knack of doing, and doing charmingly, a thousand things no other woman could have attempted. So, as Vivian and I, and some of the other men, stood in the stable-doors, smoking, and talking over the studs accommodated in the spacious stalls, a strong party of four young ladies came across the yard.

"I'm come to look at Qui Vive; will you show him to me?" said Cecil, softly. Her gentle, childlike way was the most telling of all her changing moods, but I must do her the justice to say that it was perfectly natural, she was no actress.

"With great pleasure," said Syd, very courteously, if not over-cordially; and to Qui Vive's stall Cecil went, alone in her glory, for Laura was infinitely too terrified at the sight of the bay's strong black hind legs to risk a kick from them, even to follow Syd. Helena Vivian stayed with her, and Blanche came with me to visit my hunters.

Cecil is a tolerable judge of a horse; she praised Qui Vive's lean head, full eye, and silky coat with discrimination, and Qui Vive, though not the best-tempered of thorough-breds, let her pat his smooth sides and kiss his strong neck without any hostile demonstration.

Vivian watched her as if she were a spoilt child who bewitched him, but whom he knew to be naughty; he could not resist the fascination of her ways, but he never altered his calm, courteous tone to her—the tone Cecil longed to hear change, were it even into invectives against her, to testify some deeper interest.

"Now show me the mount you will give me when the frost breaks up and we take out the hounds," said Cecil, with a farewell caress of Qui Vive.

"You shall have the grey four-year-old; Billiard-ball, and he will suit you exactly, for he is as light as a bird, checks at nothing, and will take you safe over the stiffest bullfinch. I know you may trust him, for he has carried Blanche."

Cecil threw back her head. "Oh, I would ride anything, Qui Vive himself, if he would bear a habit. I am not like Miss Caldecott, who, catching sight of his dear brown legs, vanished as rapidly as if she had seen Muriel's ghost on Christmas-eve."

The Colonel smiled. "You are very unmerciful to poor Miss Caldecott. What has she done to offend you?"

"Offend me! Nothing in the world. Though I heard her lament with Miss Screechington in the music-room, that I was 'so fast,' and 'such slang style;' I consider that rather a compliment, for I never knew any lady pull to pieces my bonnet, or my bouquet, or my hat, unless it was a prettier one than their own. That sounds a vain speech, but I don't mean it so."

The Colonel looked down into her velvet eyes; she was most dangerous to him in this mood. "No," he said, briefly, "no one would accuse you of vanity, though they might, pardon me, of love of admiration."

Cecil laughed merrily. "Yes, perhaps so; it is pleasant, you know. Yet sometimes I am tired of it all, and I want——"

"A more difficult conquest? To find a diamond, merely, like Cleopatra, to show your estimate of its value by throwing it away."

A flush of vexation came into her cheeks. "Do you think me utterly heartless?" she said impetuously. "No. I mean that I often tire of the fulsome compliments, the flattery, the attention, the whirl of society! I do like admiration. I tell you candidly what every other woman acknowledges to herself but denies to the world; but often it is nothing to me—mere Dead Sea fruit. I care nothing for the voices that whisper it; the eyes that express it wake no response in mine, and I would give it all for one word of true interest, one glance of real——"

Vivian looked down on her steadily with his searching eagle eyes, out of which, when he chose, nothing could be read. "If I dare believe you——" he said, half aloud.

Gentle as his tone was, the mere doubt stung Cecil to the quick. Something of the wild, desperate feeling of the day previous rose in her heart. The same feeling that makes men brave heaven and hell to win their desires worked up in her. If she had been one of us, just at that moment, she would have flinched at nothing; being a young lady, her hands were tied. She could only go to Cos's stalls with him (Cos knows as much about horseflesh as I do about the profound female mystery they call "shopping"), and flirt with him to desperation, while Horace got the steam up faster than he, with his very languid motor powers, often did, being accustomed to be spared the trouble and have all the love made to him—an indolence in which the St. Aubyn, who knows how to keep a man well up to hand, never indulged him.

"Do have some pity on me," I heard Cos murmuring, as she stroked a great brute of his, with a head like a fiddle-case, and no action at all. "I assure you, Miss St. Aubyn, you make me wretched. I'd die for you to-morrow if I only saw how, and yet you take no more notice of me sometimes than if I were that colt."

Cecil glanced at him with a smile that would have driven Cos distracted if he'd been in for it as deep as he pretended.

"I don't see that you are much out of condition, Sir Horace, but if you have any particular fancy to suicide, the horse-pond will accommodate you at a moment's notice; only don't do it till after our play, because I have set my heart on that suit of Milan armor. Pray don't look so plaintive. If it will make you any happier, I am going for a walk, and you may come too. Blanche, dear, which way is it to the plantations?"

Now poor Horace hated a walk on a frosty morning as cordially as anything, being altogether averse to any natural exercise: but he was sworn to the St. Aubyn, and Blanche and I, dropping behind them, he had a good hour of her fascinations to himself. I do not know whether he improved the occasion, but Cecil at luncheon looked tired and teased. I should think, after Syd's graphic epigrammatic talk, the baronet's lisped nonsense must have been rather trying, especially as Cecil has a strong leaning to intellect.

Vivian didn't appear at luncheon; he was gone rabbit-shooting with the other fellows, and I should have been with them if I had not thought lounging in the drawing-room, reading "Clytemnestra" to Blanche, with many pauses, the greater fun of the two. I am keen about sport, too; but ever since, at the age of ten, I conceived a romantic passion for my mother's lady's-maid—a tall and stately young lady, who eventually married a retail tea-dealer—I have thought the beaux yeux the best of all games.

"Mrs. Vivian, Blanche and Helena and I want to be very useful, if you will let us," said Cecil, one morning. She was always soft and playful with that gentlest of all women, Syd's mother. "What do you smile in that incredulous way for? We *can* be extraordinarily industrious: the steam sewing-machine is nothing to us when we choose! What do you think we are going to do? We are going to decorate the church for Christmas. To leave it to that poor little old clerk, who would only stick two holly twigs in the pulpit candlesticks, and fancy he had done a work of high art, would be madness. And, besides, it will be such fun."

"If you think it so, pray do it, dear," laughed Mrs. Vivian. "I can't say I should, but your tastes and mine are probably rather different. The servants will do as you direct them."

"Oh no," said Cecil; "we mean to do it all ourselves. The gentlemen may help us if they like — those, at least, who prefer our society to that of smaller animals, with lop-ears and little bushy tails, who have a fascination superior sometimes to any of our attractions." She flashed a glance at the Colonel, who was watching her over the top of *Punch*, as, when I was a boy, I have watched the sun, though it pained my eyes to do it. "You're the grand seigneur of Deerhurst," said Cecil, turning to him; "will you be good, and order cart-loads of holly and evergreens (and plenty of the Portugal laurel, please, because it's so pretty) down to the church; and will you come and do all the hard work for me? The rabbits would *so* enjoy a little peace to-day, poor things!"

He smiled in spite of himself, and did her bidding, with a flush of pleasure on his face. I believe at that moment, to please her, he would have cut down the best timber on the estates — even the old oaks, in whose shadow in the midsummer of centuries before Guy Vivian and Muriel had plighted their troth.

The way to the church was through a winding walk, between high walls of yew, and the sanctuary itself was a find old Norman place, whose *tout ensemble* I admired, though I could not pick it to pieces architecturally.

To the church we all went, of course, with more readiness than we probably ever did in our lives, regardless of the rose chains with which we were very likely to become entangled, while white hands weaved the holly wreaths.

Vivian had ordered evergreens enough to decorate fifty churches, and had sent over to the neighboring town for no end of ribbon emblazonments and illuminated scrolls, on which Cecil looked with delight. She seemed to know by instinct it was done for *her*, and not for his sisters.

"How kind that is of you," she said, softly. "That is like what you were in Toronto. Why are you not always the same?"

For a moment she saw passion enough in his eye to satisfy her, but he soon mastered it, and answered her courteously:

"I am very glad they please you. Shall we go to work at once, for fear it grow dusk before we get through with it?"

"Can I do anything to help you?" murmured Cos in her ear.

She did not want him, and laughed mischievously. "You can cut some holly if you like. Begin on those large boughs."

"Better not, Cos," said the Colonel. "You will certainly soil your hands, and you might chance to scratch them."

"And if you did you would never forgive me, so I will let you off duty. You may go back to the dormeuse and the 'Lys de la Vallée' if you wish," laughed Cecil.

Horace looked sulky, and curled his blond whiskers in dudgeon, while Cecil, with half a dozen satellites about her, proceeded to work with vigorous energy, keeping Syd, however, as her head workman; and the Colonel twisted pillars, nailed up crosses, hung wreaths, and put up illuminated texts, as if he had been a carpenter all his life, and his future subsistence entirely depended on his adorning Deerhurst church in good taste. It was amusing to me to see him, whom the highest London society, the gayest Paris life bored—who pronounced the most dashing opera supper and the most vigorous debates alike slow—taking the deepest interest in decorating a little village church! I question if Eros did not lurk under the shiny leaves and the scarlet berries of those holly boughs quite as dangerously as ever he did under the rose petals consecrated to him.

I had my own affairs to attend to, sitting on the pulpit stairs at Blanche's feet, twisting the refractory evergreens at her direction; but I kept an occasional look-out at the Colonel and his dangerous Canadian for all that. They found time (as we did) for plenty of conversation over the Christmas decorations, and Cecil talked softly and earnestly for once without any "mischief." She talked of her father's embarrassments, her mother's trials, of Mrs. Coverdale, with honest detestation of that widow's arts and artifices, and of her own tastes, and ideas, and feelings, showing the Colonel (what she did not show generally to her numerous worshippers) her heart as well as her mind. As she knelt on the altar steps, twisting green leaves round the communion rails, Syd standing beside her, his pale bronze cheek flushed, and his eyes never left their study of her face as she bent over her work, looking up every minute to ask him for another branch, or another strip of blue ribbon.

When it had grown dusk, and the church was finished, looking certainly very pretty, with the dark leaves against its white pillars, and the scarlet berries kissing the stained windows, Cecil went noiselessly up into the organ-loft, and played the Christmas anthem. Vivian followed her, and, leaning against the organ, watched her, shading his eyes with his hand. She went on playing—first a Miserere, then Mozart's Symphony in E, and then improvisations of her own—the sort of music that, when one stands calmly to listen to it, makes one feel it whether one likes or not. As she played, tears rose to her lashes, and she looked up at Vivian's face, bending over her in the gloaming. Love was in her eyes, and Syd knew it, but feared to trust to it. His pulses beat fast, he leaned towards her, till his mustaches touched her soft perfumy hair. Words hung on his lips. But the door of the organ-loft opened.

"'Pon my life, Miss St. Aubyn, that's divine, delicious!" cried Cos. "We always thought that you were divine, but we never knew till now that you brought the angels' harmony with you to earth. For Heaven's sake, play that last thing again!"

"I never play what I compose twice," said Cecil, hurriedly, stooping down for her hat.

Vivian cursed him inwardly for his untimely interruption, but cooler thought made him doubt if he were not well saved some words, dictates of hasty passion, that he might have lived to repent. For Guy Vivian's fate warned him, and he mistrusted the love of a flirt, if flirt, as he feared— from her sudden caprices to him, her alternate impatience with, and encouragement of, his cousin—Cecil St. Aubyn would prove. He gave her his arm down the yew-tree walk. Neither of them spoke all the way, but he sent a servant on for another shawl, and wrapped it round her very tenderly when it came; and when he stood in the lighted hall, I saw by the stern, worn look of his face—the look I have seen him wear after a hard fight—that the fiery passions in him had been having a fierce battle.

That evening the St. Aubyn was off her fun, said she was tired, and, disregarding the misery she caused to Cos and four other men, who, figuratively speaking, *not* literally, for they went into the "dry" and comestibles fast enough, had lived on her smiles for the last month, excused herself to Mrs. Vivian, and departed to her dormitory. Syd gave her her candle, and held her little hand two seconds in his as he bid her softly good night at the foot of the staircase.

I did not get much out of him in the balcony that night, and long after I had turned in, I scented his Cavendish as he smoked, Heaven knows how many pipes, in the chill December air. The next day, the 23rd, was the night of our theatricals, which went off as dashingly as if Mr. Kean, with his eternal "R-r-r-richard," had been there to superintend them.

All the country came; dowagers and beauties, with the odor of Belgravia still strong about them: people not quite so high, who were not the rose, but living near it, toadied that flower with much amusing and undue worship; a detachment of Dragoons from the next town, whom the girls wanted to draw, and the mammas to warn off—Dragoons being ordinarily better waltzers than speculations; all the magnates, custos rotulorum, sheriff, members, and magistrates—the two latter portions of the constitution being chiefly remarkable for keenness about hunting and turnips, and an unchristian and deadly enmity against all poachers and vagrants; rectors, who tossed down the still Ai with Falstaff's keen relish; other rectors, who came against their principles, but preferred fashion to salvation, having daughters to marry and sons to start; hunting men; girls who could waltz in a nutshell; dandies of St. James's, and veterans of Pall-Mall, down for the Christmas; belles renewing their London acquaintance, and recalling that "pleasant day at Richmond." But, by Jove! if I describe all the different species presented to view in that ball-room, I might use as many words as an old whip giving you the genealogy of a killing pack in a flying county.

Suffice it, there they all were to criticise us, and pretty sharply I dare say they did it, when they were out of our hearing, in their respective clarences, broughams, dog-carts, drags, tilburies, and hansoms. Before our faces, of course, they only clapped their snowy kid gloves, and murmured "Bravissimo!" with an occasional "Go it, Jack!" and "Get up the steam, old fellow!" from the young bloods in the background; and a shower of bouquets at Cecil and Blanche from their especial worshippers.

Blanche made the dearest little *Catherine* that ever dressed herself up in blue and silver, and when she drew her toy-rapier in the green-room, asked me if I could not get her a cornetcy in ours. As for Cecil, she played *à ravir* as Cos, in his Milan armor, whispered with some difficulty, as the steel gorget pressed his throat uncomfortably. Vestris herself never made a more brilliant or impassioned *Countess*. She and Syd really acquitted themselves in a style to qualify them for London boards, and as she threw herself at his feet—

Huon—my husband—lord—canst thou forgive

The scornful maid? for the devoted wife

Had cleaved to thee, though ne'er she owned thee lord,

I thought the St. Aubyn must be as great an actress as Rachel, if some of that fervor was not real.

Cecil played in the afterpiece, "The wonderful Woman;" the Colonel didn't; and Cos being *De Frontignac,* Syd leaned against one of the scenes, and looked on the whole thing with calm indifference externally, but much disquietude and annoyance within him. He was not jealous of the puppy; he would as soon have thought of putting himself on a par with Blanche's little white terrier, but he'd come to set a price on Cecil's winning smiles, and to see them given pretty equally to him, and to a young fool, her inferior in everything save position, whom he knew in her inmost soul she must ridicule and despise, galled his pride, and steeled his heart against her. His experience in women made him know that it was highly probable that Cecil was playing both at once, and that though, as he guessed, she loved him, she would, if Cos offered first, accept the title, and wealth, and position his cousin, equally with himself, could give her; and such love as that was far from the Colonel's ideal.

"By George! Vivian, that Canadian of yours is a perfect angel," said a man in the Dragoons, who had played *Ulric.* "She's such a deuced lot ove pluck, such eyes, such hair, such a voice! 'Pon my life, I quite envy you. I suppose you mean to act out the play in reality, don't you?"

Vivian lying back in an arm-chair in the green-room crushed up one of the satin playbills in his hand, and answered simply, "You do me too much honor, Calvert. Miss St. Aubyn and I have no thought of each other."

If any man had given Vivian the lie, he would have had him out and shot him instanter; nevertheless, he told this one with the most unhesitating defiance of truth. He did not see Cecil, who had just come off the stage, standing behind him. But she heard his words, went as white as Muriel's phantom, and brushed past us into her dressing room, whence she emerged, when her name was called, her cheeks bright with their first rouge, and her eyes unnaturally brilliant. *How* she flirted with Horace that night, when the theatricals were over! Young ladies who wanted to hook the pet baronet, whispered over their bouquets, "How bold!" and dowagers, seeing one of their best matrimonial speculations endangered by the brilliant Canadian, murmured behind their fans to each other their wonder that Mrs. Vivian should allow any one so fast and so unblushing a coquette to associate with her young daughters.

Vivian watched her with intense earnestness. He had given her a bouquet that day, and she had thanked him for it with her soft, fond eyes, and told him she should use it. Now, as she came into the ball-room, he looked at the one in her hand; it was not his, but his cousin's.

He set his teeth hard; and swore a bitter oath to himself. As *Huon*, he was obliged to dance the first dance with the *Countess*, but he spoke little to her, and indeed, Cecil did not give him much opportunity, for she talked fast, and at random, on all sorts of indifferent subjects, with more than even her usual vivacity, and quite unlike the ordinary soft and winning way she had used of late when with him. He danced no more with her, but, daring the waltzes with which he was obliged to favor certain county beauties, and all the time he was doing the honors of Deerhurst, with his calm, stately, Bayard-like courtesy, his eyes would fasten on the St. Aubyn, driving the Dragoons to desperation, waltzing while Horace whispered tender speeches in her ear, or sitting jesting and laughing, half the men in the room gathered round her—with a look of passion and hopelessness, tenderness and determination, strangely combined.

IV
THE COLONEL KILLS HIS FOX, BUT LOSES HIS HEAD AFTER OTHER GAME

The next day was Christmas-eve; and on the 24th of December the hounds, from time immemorial, had been taken out by a Vivian. For the last few days the frost had been gradually breaking up, thank Heaven, and we looked forward to a good day's sport The meet was at Deerhurst, and it proved a strong muster for the Harkaway; though not exactly up to the Northamptonshire Leicestershire mark, are a clever, steady pack. Cecil and Blanche were the only two women with us, for the country is cramped and covered with blind fences, and the fair sex seldom hunt with the Harkaway. But the St. Aubyn is a first-rate seat, and Blanche has, she tells me, ridden anything from the day she first stuck on to her Shetland, when she was three years old. They were both down in time. Indeed, I question if they went to bed at all, or did any more than change their ball dresses for their habits. As I lifted Blanche on to her pet chestnut, I heard Syd telling Cecil that Billiard-ball was saddled.

"Thank you," said the St. Aubyn, hurriedly. "I need not trouble you. Sir Horace has promised to mount me."

Vivian bent his head with a strange smile, and sprang on Qui Vive, while Cecil mounted a showy roan, thorough-bred, the only good horse Cos had in his stud, despite the thousands he had paid into trainers' and breeders' pockets.

"Stole away—forward, forward!" screamed Vivian's fellow-member for Cacklebury; and, holding Qui Vive hard by the head, away went Syd after the couple or two of hounds that were leading the way over some pasture land, with an ox-rail at the bottom of it, all the field after him. Cecil's roan flew over the grass land, and rose at the ox-rail as steadily as Qui Vive. Blanche's chestnut let himself be kicked along at no end of a pace, his mistress sitting down in her stirrups as well as the gallant M. F. H., her father. I never *do* think of anything but the hounds flying along in front of me, but I could not help turning my head over my shoulder to see if she was all right; and I never admired her so much as when she passed me with a merry laugh: "Five to one I beat you, monsieur!" Away we went over the dark ploughed lands, and the naked thorn hedges, the wide straggling briar fences, and the fields covered with stones and belted with black-looking plantations. Down went Cos with his horse wallowing helplessly in a ditch, after considerately throwing him unhurt on the bank. Syd set his teeth as he lifted Qui Vive over the prostrate baronet, to the imminent danger of that dandy field-sportsman's life. "Take hold of his head, Miss St. Aubyn," shouted the M. F. H.; but before the words had passed his lips, Cecil had landed gallantly a little farther down. Another ten minutes with the hounds streaming over the country—a ten minutes of wild delight, worth all the monotonous hours of every-day life—and Qui Vive was alone with the hounds. We could see him speeding along a quarter of a mile ahead of us, and Cecil's roan was but half a field behind him. She was "riding jealous" of one of the best riders in the Queen's; the M. F. H. just in front of her turned his head once, in admiration of her pluck, to see her lift her horse at a staken-bound fence; but the Colonel never looked round. Away they went—they disappeared over the brow of a hill. Blanche shook her reins and struck her chestnut, and I sawed my hunter's mouth mercilessly with the snaffle. No use—we were too late by three minutes. Confound it! they had just killed their fox after twenty minutes' burst over a stiff country, one of the fastest things I ever saw.

Cecil was pale with over-excitement, and upon my word she looked more ready to cry than anything when the M. F. H. complimented her with his genial smile, and his cordial "Well done, my dear. I never saw anybody ride better. I used to think my little Blanche the best seat in the country, but she must give place to you—eh, Syd?"

"Miss St. Aubyn does everything well that she attempts," answered the Colonel, in his calm, courteous tone, looking, nevertheless, as stern as if he had just slain his deadliest enemy, instead of having seen a fox killed.

Cecil flushed scarlet, and Cos coming up at that moment, a sadly bespattered object for such an Adonis to present, his coat possessing more the appearance of a bricklayer's than any one else's, after its bath of white mud, she turned to him, and began to laugh and talk with rather wild gaiety. It so chanced that the fox was killed on Horace's land, and we, being not more than a mile and a half off his house, the gallant Cos immediately seized upon the idea of having the object of his idolatry up there to luncheon; and his uncle, and Cecil, and Blanche acquiescing in the arrangement, to his house we went, with such of the field as had ridden up after the finish. Cos trotted forward with the St. Aubyn to show us the way by a short cut through the park, and the echoes of Cecil's laughter rang to Vivian in the rear discussing the run with his father.

A very slap-up place was Cos's baronial hall, for the Cossettings had combined blood and money far many generations; its style and appointments were calculated to back him powerfully in the matrimonial market, and that Cecil might have it all was fully apparent, as he devoted himself to her at the luncheon, which made its appearance at a minute's notice, as if Aladdin had called it up. Cecil seemed disposed to have it too. A deep flush had come up in her cheeks; she smiled her brightest smiles on Cos; she drank his Moët's, bending her graceful head with a laughing pledge to her host; she talked so fast, so gaily, such repartee, such sarcasms, such jeux de mots, that it was well no women were at table to sit in judgment on her afterwards. A deadly paleness came over Vivian's face as he listened to her—but he sat at the bottom of the board where Cecil could not see him. His father, the gayest and best-tempered of mortals, laughed and applauded her; the other men were charmed with a style and a wit so new to them; and Cos, of course, was in the seventh heaven.

The horses were dead beat, and Cos's drag, with its four bays very fresh, for they were so little worked, was ordered to take us back to Deerhurst.

"Who'll drive," said Horace. "Will you, Syd?"

"No," said his cousin, more laconically than politely.

"Let *me*," cried Cecil. "I can drive four in hand. Nothing I like better."

"Give me the ribbons," interposed the Colonel, changing his mind, "if you can't drive them yourself, Cos, as you ought to do."

"No, no," murmured Cos. "Mith St. Aubyn shall do everything she wishes in *my* house."

"Let her drive them," laughed Vivian, senior. "Blanche has tooled my drag often enough before now."

Before he had finished, Cecil had sprung up on to the box as lightly as a bird; her cheeks were flushed deeper still, and her gazelle eyes flashed darker than ever. Cos mounted beside her. Blanche and I in the back seat. The M. F. H., Syd, and the two other men behind. The bays shook their harness and started off at a rattling pace, Cecil tooling them down the avenue with her little gauntleted hands as well as if she had been Four-in-hand Forester of the Queen's Bays, or any other crack whip. How she flirted, and jested, and laughed, and shook the ribbons till the bays tore along the stony road in the dusky winter's afternoon—even Blanche, though a game little lady herself, looked anxious.

Cecil asked Horace for a cigar, and struck a fusee, and puffed away into the frosty air like the wildest young Cantab at Trinity. It didn't make her sick, for she and Blanche had had two Queens out of Vivian's case, and smoked them to the last ash for fun only the day before; and she drove us at a mad gallop into Deerhurst Park, past the dark trees and the gleaming water and the trooping deer, and pulled up before the hall door just as the moon came out on Christmas-eve.

We were all rather fast at Deerhurst, so Blanche got no scolding from her mamma (who, like a sensible woman, never put into their heads that things done in the glad innocency of the heart were "wrong"); and Cecil, as soon as she had sprung down, snatched her hand from Cos, and went up to her own room.

The Colonel's lips were pressed close together, and his forehead had the dark frown that Guy wears in his portrait.

It had been done with another, so it was all wrong; but oh! Syd, my friend, if the "dry" that was drunk, and the drag that was tooled, and the weed that was smoked, had been *yours*, wouldn't it have been the most charming caprice of the most charming woman!

That night, at dinner, a letter by the afternoon's post came to the Colonel. It was "On her Majesty's Service," and his mother asked him anxiously what it was.

"Only to tell me to join soon," said he, carelessly, giving me a sign to keep the contents of a similar letter I had just received to myself; which I should have done anyhow, as I had reason to hope that the disclosure of them would have quenched the light in some bright eyes beside me.

"Ordered off at last, thank God!" said Syd, handing his father the letter as soon as the ladies were gone. "There's a train starts at 12.40, isn't there, for town? You and I, Ned, had better go to-night. You don't look so charmed, old fellow, as you did when you went out to Scinde. I say, don't tell my sisters; there is no need to make a row in the house. Governor, you'll prepare my mother; I must bid *her* good-by."

I *did not* view the Crimea with the unmingled, devil-me-care delight with which I had gone out under "fighting Napier" nine years before, for Blanche's sunshiny face had made life fairer to me; and to obey Syd, and go without a farewell of her, was really too great a sacrifice to friendship. But he and I went to the drawing-rooms, chatted, and took coffee as if nothing had chanced, till he could no longer stand seeing Cecil, still excited, singing chansons to Cos, who was leaning enraptured over the instrument, and he went off to his own room. The other girls and men were busy playing the Race game; Blanche and I were sitting in the back drawing-room beside the fire, and the words that decided my destiny were so few, that I cite them as a useful lesson to those novelists who are in the habit of making their heroes, while waiting breathless to hear their fate, recite off at a cool canter four pages of the neatest-turned sentences without a single break-down or a single pull-up, to see how the lady takes it.

"Blanche, I must bid you good-by to-night." Blanche turned to me in bewildered anxiety. "I must join my troop: perhaps I may be sent to the Crimea. I could go happily if I thought you would regret me?"

Brutally selfish that was to be sure, but she did not take it so. She looked as if she was going to faint, and for fear she should, trusting to the engrossing nature of the Race game in the further apartment, I drew nearer to her. "Will you promise to give yourself to nobody else while I am away, my darling?" Blanche's eyes did promise me through their tears, and this brief scene, occupying the space of two minutes, twisted our fates into one on that eventful Christmas-eve.

While I was parting with my poor little Blanche in the library, Vivian was bidding his mother farewell in her dressing-room. His mother had the one soft place in his heart, steeled and made skeptical to all others by that fatal first love of which he had spoken to Cecil. Possibly some of her son's bitter grief was shown to her on that sad Christmas-eve; at all events, when he left her dressing-room, he had the tired, haggard look left by any conflict of passion. As he came down the stairs to come to the dog-cart that was to take us to the station, the door of Blanche's boudoir stood open, and in it he saw Cecil. The fierce tide of his love surged up, subduing all his pride, and he paused to take his last sight of the face that would haunt him in the long night watches and the rapid rush of many a charge. She looked up and saw him; that look overpowered all his calmness and resolve. He turned, and bent towards her, every feature quivering with the passion she had once longed to rouse. His hot breath scorched her cheek, and he caught her fiercely against his heart in an iron embrace, pressing his burning lips on hers. "God forgive you! I have loved you too well. Women have ever been fatal to my race!"

He almost threw her from him in the violence of feelings roused after a long sleep. In another moment he was driving the dog-cart at a mad gallop past the old church in which we had spent such pleasant hours. Its clock tolled out twelve strokes as we passed it, and on the quiet village, and the weird-like trees, and the tall turrets of Deerhurst, the Christmas morning dawned.

Vivian continued so utterly enfeebled and prostrate that there was but one chance for him—return homewards. I was going to England with despatches, and Syd, at his mother's entreaty, let himself be carried down to a transport, and shipped for England. He was utterly listless and strengthless, although the voyage did him a little good. He did not care where he went, so he stayed in town with me while I presented myself at the Horse Guards and war Office, and then we travelled down together to Deerhurst.

Oddly enough it was Christmas-eve again when we drove up the old avenue. The snow was falling heavily, and lay deep on the road and thick on the hedges and trees. The meadows and woods were white against the dark, hushed sky, and the old church, and its churchyard cedars, were loaded too with the clouds' Christmas gift. To me, at least, the English scene was very pleasant, after the heat, and dirt, and minor worries of Gallipoli and Constantinople. The wide stretching country, with its pollards, and holly hedges, and homesteads, the cattle safe housed, the yule fire burning cheerily on the hearths, the cottages and farms nestling down among their orchards and pasture-lands, all was so heartily and thoroughly English. They seemed to bring back days when I was a boy skating and sliding on the mere at home, or riding out with the harriers light-hearted and devil-me-care as a boy might be, coming back to hear the poor governor's cheery voice tell me I was one of the old stock, and to toss down a bumper of Rhenish with a time-honored Christmas toast. The crackle of the crisp snow, the snort of the horses as they plunged on into the darkening night, and the red fire-light flickering on the lattice windows of the cottages we passed, were so many welcomes home, and I double-thonged the off-wheeler with a vengeance as I thought of soft lips that would soon touch mine, and a soft voice that would soon whisper my best "Io triumphe!"

The lodge-gates flew open. We passed the old oaks and beeches, the deer trooping away over the snow as we startled them out of their rest. We were not expected that night, and my man rang such a peal at the bell as might have been heard all over the quiet park. Another minute, and Blanche and I were together again, and alone in the library where we had parted just twelve months before. Of course, for the time being, we neither knew nor cared what was going on in the other rooms of the house. The Colonel had gone to rest himself on the sofa in the dining-room. Half an hour had elapsed, perhaps, when a wild cry rang through the house, startling even us, absorbed though we were in our tête-à-tête. Blanche's first thought was of her brother. She ran out through the hall, and up the staircase, and I followed her. At the top of the stairs, leaning against the wall, breathing fast, and his face ashy white, stood Syd, and at his feet, in a dead faint, lay Cecil St. Aubyn. I caught hold of Blanche's arm and held her back as she was about to spring forward. I thought their meeting had much best be uninterrupted; for, if Cecil's had been mere flirtation I fancied the Colonel's return could scarcely have moved her like this.

Vivian stood looking down on her, all the passion in him breaking bounds. He could not stand calmly by the woman he loved. He did not wait to know whether she was his or another's—whether she was worthy or unworthy of him—but he lifted her up and pressed her unconscious form against his heart, covering her lips with wild caresses. Waking from her trance, she opened her eyes with a terrified stare, and gazed up in his face; then tears came to her relief, and she sank down at his feet again with a pitiful cry, "Forgive me—forgive me!" Weak as Syd was, he found strength to raise her in his arms, and whisper, as he bent over her, "If you love me, I have nothing to forgive."

The snow fell softly without over the woods and fields and the winds roared through the old oaks and whistled among the frozen ferns, but Christmas-eve passed brightly enough to us at home within the strong walls of Deerhurst.

I am sure that all Moore's pictures of Paradise seemed to me tame compared to that drawing-room, with its warmth, and coziness, and luxuries; with the waxlights shining on the silver of the English tea equipage (pleasant to eye and taste, let one love campaigning ever so well, after the roast beans of the Commissariat), and the fire-gleams dancing on the soft brow and shining hair of the face beside me. I doubt if Vivian either ever spent a happier Christmas-eve as he lay on the sofa in the back drawing-room, with Cecil sitting on a low seat by him, her hand in his, and the Canadian eyes telling him eloquently of love and reconciliation. They had such volumes to say! As soon as she knew that wild farewell of his preceded his departure to the Crimea, Cecil, always impulsive, had written to him on the instant, telling him how she loved him, detailing what she had heard in the green-room, confessing that, in desperation, she had done everything she could to rouse his jealousy, assuring him that that same evening she had refused Cos's proposals, and beseeching him to forgive her and come back to her. That letter Vivian had never had (six months from that time, by the way, it turned up, after a journey to India and Melbourne, following a cousin of his, colonel of a line regiment, she in her haste having omitted to put his troop on the address), and Cecil, whose feeling was too deep to let her mention the subject to Blanche or Helena, made up her mind that he would never forgive her, and being an impressionable young lady, had, on the anniversary of Christmas-eve, been comparing her fate with that of Muriel in the ghost legend, and, on seeing the Colonel's unexpected apparition, had fainted straight away in the over-excitement and sudden joy of the moment.

Such was Cecil's story, and Vivian was content with it and gladly took occasion to practise the Christmas duties of peace, and love, and pardon. He had the best anodyne for his wounds now, and there was no danger for him, since Cecil had taken the place of the Scutari nurses. No "Crimean heroes," as they call us in the papers, were ever more fêted and petted than were the Colonel and I.

Christmas morning dawned, the sun shining bright on the snow-covered trees, and the Christmas bells chiming merrily; and as we stood on the terrace to see the whole village trooping up through the avenue to receive the gifts left to them by some old Vivian long gone to his rest with his forefathers under the churchyard cedars, Syd looked down with a smile into Cecil's eyes as she hung on his arm, and whispered,

"I will double those alms, love, in memory of the priceless gift this Christmas has given me. Ah! Thornton and I little knew, when we came down for the hunting, how fast you and Blanche would capture us with your—Holly Wreaths and Rose Chains."

SILVER CHIMES AND GOLDEN FETTERS

I

WALDEMAR FALKENSTEIN AND VALÉRIE L'ESTRANGE

"A quarter to twelve! By Heaven if my luck don't change before the year is out, I vow I'll never touch a card in the next!" exclaimed one of several men playing lansquenet in Harry Godolphin's rooms at Knightsbridge.

There were seven or eight of them, some with long rent-rolls, others within an ace of the Queen's Bench; the poor devils losing in the long run much oftener and more recklessly than the rich fellows; all of them playing high, as that *beau joueur* of the Guards, Godolphin, always did.

Luck had been dead against the man who spoke ever since they had deserted the mess-room for the *cartes* in the privacy of Harry's rooms. If Fortune is a woman, he ought to have found favor in her eyes. His age was between thirty and thirty-five, his figure with grace and strength combined, his features nobly and delicately cut, his head, like Canning's, one of great intellectual beauty, and by the flash of his large dark eyes, and the additional paleness of his cheek, it was easy to see he was playing high once too often.

Five minutes passed—he lost still; ten minutes' luck was yet against him. A little French clock began the Silver Chimes that rang out the Old Year; the twelfth stroke sounded, the New Year was come, and Waldemar Falkenstein rose and drank down some cognac—a ruined man.

"A happy New Year to you, and better luck, Falkenstein," cried Godolphin, drinking his toast with a ringing laugh and a foaming bumper of Chambertin. "What shall I wish you? The richest wife in the kingdom, a cabal that will break all the banks, for Mistletoe to win the Oaks, or for your eyes to be opened to your sinful state, as the parson phrases it—which, eh?"

"Thank you, Harry," laughed Falkenstein. (Like the old Spartans, we can laugh while the wolf gnaws our vitals.) "You remind me of what my holy-minded brother wrote to me when I broke my shoulder-bone down at Melton last season: 'My dear Waldemar, I am sorry to hear of your sad accident; but all things are ordered for the best, and I trust that in your present hours of solitude your thoughts may be mercifully turned to higher and better things.' Queer style of sympathy, wasn't it? I preferred yours, when you sent me 'Adélaïde Méran,' and that splendid hock I wasn't allowed to touch."

"I should say so; but catch the Pharisees giving anybody anything warmer than texts and counsels, that cost them nothing," said Tom Bevan of the Blues. "Apropos of Pharisees, have you heard that old Cash is going to build a chapel-of-ease in Belgravia, to endow that young owl Gus with as soon as he can pull himself through his 'greats?' It is thought that the dear Bella will be painted as St. Catherine for the altar-piece."

"She'll strychnine herself if we're all so hard-hearted as to leave her to St. Catharine's nightcap," laughed Falkenstein.

"Why don't *you* take up with her, old fellow?" said a man in Godolphin's troop. "Not the sangue puro, you'd say; rather sallied with XXX. But what does that signify? you've quarterings enough for two."

"Much good the quarterings do me. No, thank you," said Falkenstein bitterly. "I'm not going to sell myself, though my dear friends would insinuate that I was sold already to a gentleman who never quits hold of his bargains. I've fetters enough now too heavy by half to add matrimonial handcuffs to them."

"Right, old boy," said Harry. "The Cashranger hops and vats, even done in the brightest parvenu *or*, would scarcely look well blazoned on the royal *gules*. Come, sit down. Where are you going?"

"He's going to Eulalie Brown's, I bet," said Bevan. "Nonsense, Waldemar; throw her over, and stay and take your revenge—it's so early."

"No, thank you," said Falkenstein briefly. "By the way, I suppose you all go to Cashranger's to-morrow?"

"Make a point of it, answered Godolphin. I feel I'm sinning against my Order to visit him, but really his Lafitte's so good——I'm sorry you *will* leave us, Waldemar, but I know I might as well try to move the Marble Arch as try to turn you."

"Indeed I never set up for a Roman, Harry. The deuce take this pipe, it won't light. Good night to you all." And leaving them drinking hard, laughing loud, and telling *grivois* tales before they sat down to play in all its delirious delight, he sprang into a hanson, and drove, not to Eulalie Brown's *petit souper*, but to his own rooms in Duke Street, St. James's.

Falkenstein's governor, some two-score years before, had got in mauvaise odeur in Vienna for some youthful escapade at court; powerful as his princely family was, had been obliged to fly the country; and, coming over here, entered himself at the Bar, and, setting himself to work with characteristic energy, had, wonderful to relate, made a fortune at it. A fine, gallant, courtly *ancien noble* was the Count, haughty and passionate at times, after the manner of the house; fond of his younger son Waldemar, who at school had tanned boys twice his size; rode his pony in at the finish; smoked, swam, and otherwise conducted himself, till all the rest of the boys worshipped him, though I believe the masters generally attributed to him more *diablerie* than divinity. But of late, unluckily, his father had been much dominated over by Waldemar's three sisters, ladies of a chill and High Church turn of mind, and by his brother, who in early life had been a prize boy and a sap, and received severe buffetings from his junior at football; and now, being much the more conventional and unimpeachable of the two, took his revenge by carrying many tales to the old Count of his wilder son—tales to which Falkenstein gave strong foundation. For he was restless and reckless, strikingly original, and, above the common herd, too impatient to take any meddling with his affairs, and too proud to explain where he was misjudged; and, though he held a crack government place, good pay, and all but a sinecure, he often spent more than he had, for economy was a dead-letter to him, and if any man asked him a loan, he was too generous to say "No." Life in all its phases he had seen from the time he left school, and you know, mon ami, we cannot see life on a groat—at least, through the bouquet of the wines at Véfours, and the brilliance of the gas-light in Casinos and Redoutes. The fascinations of play were over him—the iron hand of debt pressed upon him; altogether, as he sat through the first hours of the New Year, smoking, and gazing on the flickering fire gleams, there was not much light either in his past or future!

Keenly imaginative and susceptible, blasé and skeptical though he was, the weight of the Old Year and of many gone before it, weighed heavily on his thoughts. Scenes and deeds of his life, that he would willingly have blotted out, rose before him; vague regrets, unformed desires, floated to him on the midnight chimes.

The Old Year was drifting away on the dark clouds floating on to the sea, the New Year was dawning on the vast human life swarming in the costly palaces and crowded dens around him. The past was past, ineffaceable, and relentless; the future lay hid in the unborn days, and Falkenstein, his pipe out, his fire cold and black, took a sedative, and threw himself on his bed, to sleep heavily and restlessly through the struggling morning light of the New Year.

James Cashranger, Esq., of 133, Lowndes Square, was a millionnaire, and the million owed its being to the sale of his entire, which was of high celebrity, being patronised by all the messes and clubs, shipped to all the colonies, blessed by all the H. E. I. C.s, shouted by all the potmen as "Beer-r-r-how," and consumed by all England generally. But Cashranger's soul soared above the snobisms of malt and jack, and à la Jourdain, of bourgeois celebrity, he would have let any Dorante of the beau monde fleece him through thick and thin, and, *en effet*, gave dinners and drums unnumbered to men and women, who, like Godolphin, went there for the sake of his Lafitte, and quizzed him mercilessly behind his back. The first day Harry dined there with nine other spirits worse than himself—Cashranger having begged him to bring some of his particular chums—he looked at the eleventh seat, and asked, with consummate impudence, who it was for?

"Why, really, my dear Colonel, it is for—for myself," faltered the luckless brewer.

"Oh?—ah?—I see," drawled Harry; "you mistook me; I said I'd dine *here*—I didn't say I'd dine with *you*."

That, however, was four or five years before; now, Godolphin having proclaimed his cook and cellar worth countenancing, and his wife, the relict of a lieutenant in the navy, being an admirable adept in the snob's art of "pushing," plenty of exclusive dandies and extensive fine ladies crushed up the stairs on New Year's-night to one of Cashranger's numerous "At homes." Among them, late enough, came Falkenstein. These sort of crushes bored him beyond measure, but he wanted to see Godolphin about some intelligence he had had of an intended illegitimate use of the twitch to Mistletoe, that sweet little chestnut who stood favorite for the Oaks. He soon paid his devoir to madame, who wasn't quite accustomed even yet to all this grandeur after her early struggles on half-pay, and to her eldest daughter, the Bella aforesaid, a showy, flaunting girl with a peony color, and went on through the rooms seeking Harry, stopping, however, for a word to every pretty woman he knew; for though he began to find his game grow stale, he and the beau sexe have a mutual attraction. Little those women guessed, as they smiled in his handsome eyes, and laughed at his witty talk, and blushed at his soft voice, how heartily sick he was of their frivolities, and how often disappointment and sarcasm lurked in his mocking words. To be blasé was no affectation with Falkenstein; it was a very earnest reality, as with most of us who have knocked about in the world, not only from the variety of his manifold experiences, but from the trickery, and censure, and cold water with which the world had treated him.

"You here, old fellow?" said Bevan of the Blues, meeting him in the music-room, where some artistes were singing Traviata airs. "You don't care for this row, do you? Come along with me, and I'll show you something that will amuse you better."

"Show me Godolphin, and I'll thank you. I didn't come to stay—did you?"

"No. Horrid bore, ain't it? But since you are here, you may as well take a look at the dearest little actress I ever saw since I was a boy, and bewitched by Léontine Fay. Sit down." Bevan went on, as they entered a room fitted up like a theatre, "There, it's that one with blue eyes, got up like a Watteau's huntress; isn't she a brilliant little thing?"

"Very. She plays as well as Déjazet. Who is she?"

"Don't know. Can you tell us, Forester?"

"She's old Cash's niece," said Forester, not taking his eyes off the stage. "Come as a sort of companion to the beloved Bella; dangerous companion, I should say, for there's no comparing the two."

"What's her name?"

"Viola—Violet—no, Valérie L'Estrange. L'Estrange, of the 10th, ran away with Cash's sister. God knows why. Horrid low connexion, and no money. She went speedily to glory, and he drank himself to death two years ago in Lahore. I remember him, a big fellow, fourteen stone, pounded Bully Batson once at Moseley, and there wasn't such another hard hitter among the fancy as Bully. When he departed this life, of course his daughter was left to her own devices, with scarcely a rap to buy her bonnets. Clever little animal she is, too; she wrote those proverbs they're now playing; full of dash, and spice, ain't they? especially when you think a girl wrote 'em."

"Introduce me as soon as they're over," said Falkenstein, leaning back to study the young actress and author, who was an engaging study enough, being full of grace and vivacity, with animated features, mobile eyebrows, dark-blue eyes, and chestnut hair. "Anything original would be as great a wonder as to buy Cavendish in Regent-Street that wasn't bird's-eye."

"Valérie's original enough for anybody's money. Hark how she's firing away at Egerton. Pretty little soft voice she has. I do like a pretty voice for a woman," said Forester, clapping softly, with many a murmured bravisima.

"You're quite enthusiastic," smiled Falkenstein. "Pity you haven't a bouquet to throw at her."

"Don't you poke fun at me, you cynic," growled Forester. "I've seen you throw bouquets at much plainer women."

"And the bouquets and the women were much alike in morning light— faded and colorless on their artificial stalks as soon as the gas glare was off them."

"Hold your tongue, Juvenal," laughed Forester, "or I vow I won't introduce you. You'll begin satirising poor little Val as soon as you've spoken to her."

"Oh, I can be merciful to the weak; don't I let *you* alone, Forester?" laughed Waldemar, as the curtain fell.

The proverbs were over, and having put herself in ball-room style, the author came among the audience. He amused himself with watching how she took her numerous compliments, and was astonished to detect neither vanity nor shyness, and to hear her turn most of them aside with a laugh. She was quite as attractive off as on the stage, especially with the aroma of her sparkling proverbs hanging about her; and Falkenstein got his introduction, and consigning Godolphin and Mistletoe to futurity, waltzed with her, and found her dancing as full of grace and lightness as an Andalusian's or Arlésienne's. Falkenstein cared little enough for the saltatory art, but this waltz did not bore him, and when it was over, regardless of some dozen names written on her tablets, he gave her his arm, and they strolled out of the ball-room into a cooler atmosphere. He found plenty of fun in her, as he had expected from her proverbs, and sat down beside her in the conservatory to let himself be amused for half an hour.

"Do you know many of the people here?" she asked him. "Is there anybody worth pointing out? There ought to be, in four or five hundred dwellers in the aristocratic west."

"I know most of them personally or by report, but they are all of the same stamp, like the petals of that camellia, some larger and some smaller, but all cut in the same pattern. Most of them apostles of fashion, martyrs to debt, worshippers of the rising sun. All of them created by art, from the young ladies who owe their roses and lilies to Breidenbach, to the ci-devant jeunes hommes, who buy their figures in Bond Street and their faces from Isidore. All of them actors—and pretty good actors, too—from that pretty woman yonder, who knows her milliner may imprison her any day for the lace she is now drawing round her with a laugh, to that sleek old philanthropist playing whist through the doors there, whose guinea points are paid by the swindle of half England."

She laughed.

"Lend me your lorgnon. I should like to see around me as you do."

"Wait twenty years, you will have it; there are two glasses to it—experience and observation."

"But your glasses are smoked, are they not?" said Valérie, with a quick glance at him; "for you seem to me to see everything en noir."

He smiled.

"When I was a boy I had a Claude glass, but they break very soon; or rather, as you say, grow dark and dim with the smoke of society. But you ask me about these people. You know them, do you not, as they are your uncle's guests?"

She shook her head.

"I have been here but a week or two. For the last two years I have been vegetating among the fens, with a maiden aunt of poor papa's."

"And did you like the country?"

"Like it!" cried Valérie, "I was buried alive. Everything was so dreadfully punctual and severe in that house, that I believe the very cat had forgotten how to purr. Breakfast at eight, drive at two, dinner at five, prayers at ten. Can't you fancy the dreary diurnal round, with a pursy old rector or two, and three or four high-dried county princesses as callers once a quarter? Luckily, I can amuse myself, but oh, you cannot think how I sickened of the monotony, how I longed to *live!* At last, I grew so naughty, I was expelled."

"May I inquire your sins?" asked Falkenstein, really amused for once.

She laughed at the remembrance.

"I read 'Notre-Dame' against orders, and I rode the fat old mare round the paddock without a saddle. I saw no harm in it; as a child, I read and rode everything I came near, but the rough-riding was condemned as unfeminine, and any French book, were it even the 'Génie du Christianisme,' or the 'Petit Carême,' would be regarded by Aunt Agatha, who doesn't know a word of the language, as a powder magazine of immorality and infidelity."

"C'est la profonde ignorance qui inspire le ton dogmatique," laughed Falkenstein. "But surely you have been accustomed to society."

"No, never; but I am made for it, I fancy," said Valérie, with an unconscious compliment to herself. "When I was with the dear old Tenth, I used to enjoy myself, but I was a child then. The officers were very kind to me—gentlemen always are much more so than ladies"—("Pour cause," thought Waldemar, as she went on)—"but ever since then I have vegetated as I tell you, in much the same still life as the anemones in my vase."

"Yet you could write those proverbs," said he, involuntarily.

She laughed, and colored.

"Oh, I have written ever since I could make A B C, and I have not forgotten all I saw with the old Tenth. But come, tell me more of these people; I like to hear your satire."

"I am glad you do," said Falkenstein, with a smile; "for only those who have no foibles to hit have a relish for sarcasm. Do you think Messaline and Lélie had much admiration for La Bruyère's periods, however well turned or justly pointed? but those whom the caps did not fit probably enjoyed them as you and I do. All satirists, from Martial downwards, most likely gain an enemy for each truth they utter, for in this bal masqué of life it is not permitted to tear the masks off our companions."

"Do you wear one?" asked Valérie, quickly. "I fancy, like Monte Cristo, your pleasure is to 'usurper les vices que vous n'avez pas, et de cacher les vertus que vous avez.'"

"Virtues? If you knew me better, you would know that I never pretend to any. If you compare me to Monte Cristo, say rather that I 'prêche loyalement l'égoisme,'" laughed Falkenstein. "Upon my word, we are talking very seriously for a ball-room. I ought to be admiring your bouquet, Miss L'Estrange, or petitioning for another waltz."

"Don't trouble yourself. I like this best," said Valérie, playing with the flowers round her. "And I ought to have my own way, for this is my birthday."

"New Year's-day? Indeed! Then I am sure I wish you most sincerely the realisation of all your ideals and desires, which, to the imaginative author of the proverbs, will be as good as wishing her Aladdin's lamp," smiled Falkenstein.

She smiled too, and sighed.

"And about as improbable as Aladdin's lamp. Did you see the Old Year out last night?"

"Yes," he answered, briefly; for the remembrance of what he had lost watching it out was not agreeable to him.

"There was a musical party here," continued Valérie, "but I got away from it, for I like to be alone when the past and the future meet—do not you?"

"No; your past is pure, your future is bright. Mine are not so; I don't want to be stopped to contemplate them."

"Nor are mine, indeed; but the death of an Old Year is sad and solemn to me as the death of a friend, and I like to be alone in its last hour. I wonder," she continued, suddenly, "what this year will bring. I wonder where you and I shall be next New Year's-night?"

Falkenstein laughed, not merrily.

"*I* shall be in Kensal Green or the Queen's Bench, very likely. Why do you look astonished Miss L'Estrange; one is the destination of everybody in these rooms, and the other probably of one-half of them."

"Don't speak so bitterly—don't give me sad thoughts on my birthday. Oh, how tiresome!" cried Valérie, interrupting herself, "there comes Major D'Orwood."

"To claim you?"

"Yes; I'd forgotten him entirely. I promised to waltz with him an hour ago."

"What the devil brought you here to interrupt us?" thought Falkenstein, as the Guardsman lisped a reproof at Valérie's cruelty, and gave her his arm back to the ball-room. Waldemar stopped her, however, engaged her for the next, and sauntered through the room on her other side. He waltzed a good deal with her, paying her that sort of attention which Falkenstein knew how to make the softest and subtlest homage a woman could have. Amused himself, he amused her with his brilliant and pointed wit, so well, that Valérie L'Estrange told him, when he bid her good night, that she had never enjoyed any birthday so much.

"Well," said Bevan, as they drove away from 133, Lowndes Square, "did you find that wonderful little L'Estrange as charming a companion as actress? You ought to know, for you've been after her all night, like a ferret after a rabbit."

"Yes," said Falkenstein, taking out a little pet briarwood pipe, "I was very pleased with her: she's worth no more than the others, probably, au fond, but she's very entertaining and frank: she'll tell you anything. Poor child! she can't be over-comfortable in Cash's house. She's a lady by instinct; that odious ostentation and snobbish toadying must disgust her. Besides, Bella is not very likely to lead a girl a very nice life who is partially dependent on her father, and infinitely better style than herself."

"The devil, no! That flaunting, flirting, over-dressed Cashranger girl is my detestation. She'll soon find means to worry littil Valérie. Women have a great spice of the mosquito in 'em, and enjoy nothing more than stinging each other to death."

"Well, she must get Forester or D'Orwood—some man who can afford it—to take compassion upon her. All of them finish so when they can; the rich ones marry for a title, and the poor ones for a home," said the Count, stirring up his pipe. "Here's my number; thank you for dropping me; and good night, old fellow."

"Good night. Pleasant dreams of your author and actress, *aux longs yeux bleus*."

Waldemar laughed as he took out his latch-key. "I'm afraid I couldn't get up so much romance. You and I have done with all that, Tom. Confound it, I never saw Godolphin, after all. Well, I must go and breakfast with him to-morrow."

II

FALKENSTEIN BREAKS LANCES WITH THE "LONGS YEUX BLEUS"

He did breakfast with Godolphin, not, however, before he had held a small but disagreeable levee to one or two rather impatient callers whom he couldn't satisfy, and a certain Amadeus Levi, who, having helped him to the payment of those debts of honor incurred in Harry's rooms, held him by Golden Fetters as hard to unclasp as the chains that bound Prometheus. He shook himself free of them at last, drove to Knightsbridge, and had a chat with Godolphin, over coffee and chibouques, went to his two or three hours' diplomatic work in the Deeds and Chronicles Office, and when he came out, instead of going to his club as usual, thought he might as well call on the Cashrangers, and turned his steps to Lowndes Square. Valérie L'Estrange was sitting at a Davenport, done out of her Watteau costume into very becoming English morning dress; he had only time to shake hands with her before Bella and her mamma set upon him. Miss Cashranger had a great admiration for him, and, though his want of money was a drawback, the royal gules of his blazonments, joined to his manifold attractions, fairly dazzled her, and she held him tight, talking over the palace concerts, till a dowager and her daughter, and a couple of men from Hounslow, being ushered in, he was at liberty, and sitting down by Valérie, gave her a book she had said the night before she wished to read.

"'Goethe's Autobiography!' Oh, thank you—how kind you are!"

"Not at all," laughed Falkenstein. "To merit such things I ought to have saved your life at least. What are you doing here; writing some more proverbs, I hope, to give me a part in one?"

She shook her head. "Nothing half so agreeable. I am writing dinner invitations, and answering Belle's letters."

"Why, can't she answer them herself?"

"My motto here is 'Ich Dien,'" she answered, with a flush on her cheeks.

Bella turned languidly round, and verified her words: "Val, Puppet's scratching at the door; let him in, will you?"

Waldemar rose and opened the door for a little slate-colored greyhound, and while Bella lisped out her regrets for his trouble, smiled a smile that made Miss Cashranger color, and looked searchingly at Valérie to see how she took it. She turned a grateful, radiant look on him, and whispered, "Je m'affranchirai un jour."

"Et comment?"

She raised her mobile eyebrows: "Dieu sait! Comme actrice, comme feuilletonniste—j'ai mes rêves, monsieur—mais pas comme institutrice: cela me tuerait bientôt."

"Je le crois," said Falkenstein, briefly, as he took up the autobiography, and began to talk on it.

"I don't like Goethe for one thing," said Valérie; "he loved a dozen women one after the other. That I would pardon him; most men do so; but I don't believe he really loved any one of them."

"Oh yes he did; quite enough, at least, to please himself. He wasn't so silly as to go in for a never-ending, heart-burning, heart-breaking, absorbing passion. We don't do those things."

"Go in for it!" repeated Valérie, contemptuously, "I suppose if he had been of the nature to feel such, he couldn't have helped it."

"I can help going near the fire, can't I, if I don't wish to be burnt?"

"Yes; but a coal may fly out of the fire, and set you in flames, when you are sitting far away from it."

"Then I ought to wear asbestos," said Waldemar, with a merry quizzical smile. "You authors, and poets, and artists think 'the world well lost, and all for love!' but we rational people, who know the world, find it quite the contrary. Those are very pretty ideas for your proverbs, but they don't suit real life. We, when we're boys, worship some parterre divinity, till we see her some luckless day inebriate with eau-de-Cologne, or more unpoetic porter, are cured and disenchanted, wait ten years with Christines and Minna Herzliebs in the interim, and wind up with a rich widow, who keeps us straight and heads our table. You, fresh from the school-room, fasten on some lachrymose curate, or flirting dragoon, as the object of your early romances, walk with him under the limes, work him a smoking-cap, and write him tender little notes, till mamma whispers her hope that Mr. A. or B. is serious, and you, balancing, like a sensible girl, A. or B.'s tangible settlements with the others' intangible love-speeches, forsake the limes, forswear the notes, and announce yourself as 'sold.' That's the love of our day, Miss L'Estrange, and very wise and——"

"Love!" cried Valérie, with supreme scorn. "You don't know the common A B C of love. You might as well call gilt leather-work pure gold."

Falkenstein laughed heartily. "Well, there's a good deal more leather-work than gold about in the world, isn't there?"

"A good deal more, granted; but there is some gold to be found, I should hope."

"Not without alloy; it can't be worked, you know."

"It can't be worked for the base purposes of earth; but it may be found still undefiled before men's touch has soiled it. So I believe in some hearts, undefiled by the breath of conventionality and cant, may lie the true love of the poets, 'lasting, and knowing not change.'"

"Ah! you're too ideal for me," cried Waldemar, smiling at her impetuous earnestness. "You are all enthusiasm, imagination, effervescence — —"

"I am not," she answered, impatiently. "I can be very practical when I like; I made myself the loveliest wreath yesterday; quite as pretty as Bella buys at Mitchell's for five times the sum mine cost me. That was very realistic, wasn't it?"

"No. That exercised your fancy. You wouldn't do—what do you call it?—plain work, with half the gusto; now, would you?"

Valérie made a *moue mutine*, expressive of entire repudiation of such employment.

"I thought so," laughed Falkenstein. "You idealists are like the fire in the grate yonder; you flame up very hot and bright for a moment, but 'the sparks fly upward and expire,' and if they're not fed with some fresh fuel they soon die out into lifeless cinders."

"On the contrary," said Valérie, quickly, "we are like wood fires, and burn red down to the last ash."

"Mr. Falkenstein, come and look at this little 'Ghirlandaio,'" said Bella, turning round, with an angry light in her eyes; "it is such a gem. Papa bought it the other day."

Waldemar rose reluctantly enough to inspect the "Ghirlandaio," manufactured in a back slum, and smoked into proper antiquity to pigeon, under the attractive title of an "Old Master," the brewer and his species, and found Miss Cashranger's ignorant dilettantism very tame after Valérie's animated arguments and gesticulation. But he was too old a hand at such game not to know how to take advantage of even an enemy's back-handed stroke, and he turned the discussion on art to an inspection of Valérie's portfolio, over whose croquis and pastels, and water-colors, he lingered as long as he could, till the clock reminded him that it was time to walk on into Eaton Square, where he was going to dine at his father's. The governor excepted, Falkenstein had little rapport with his family. His brother was as chilly disagreeable in private life as he was popularly considered irreproachable in public, and as pragmatical and uncharitable as your immaculate individuals ordinarily are. His sisters were cold, conventional women, as utterly incapable of appreciating him as of allowing the odor of his Latakia in their drawing-room, and so it chanced that Waldemar, a favorite in every other house he entered, received but a chill welcome at home. A prophet has no honor in his own country, and the hearth where a man's own kin are seated is too often the one to nurture the cockatrice's eggs of ill-nature and injustice against him. Thank Heaven there are others where the fire burns brighter, and the smiles are fonder for him. It were hard for some of us if we were dependent on the mercies of our "own family."

The old Count gave him this night but a distant welcome, for Maximilian was there to "damn" his brother with "faint praise," and had been pouring into his father's ear tales of "poor Waldemar's losses at play." All that Falkenstein said, his sisters took up, contradicted, and jarred upon, till he, fairly out of patience, lapsed into silence, only broken by a sarcasm deftly flung at Maximillian to floor him completely in his orthodoxy or ethics. He was glad to bid the governor good night; and leaving them to hold a congress over his skepticism, radicalism, and other dangerous opinions, he walked through the streets, and swore slightly, with his pipe between his teeth, as he opened his own door.

"Since my father prefers Max to me, let him have him," thought Waldemar, smoking, and undressing himself. "If people choose to dictate to me or misjudge me, let them go; and if they have not penetration enough to judge what I am, I shall not take the trouble to show them."

But, nevertheless, as he thus resolved, Falkenstein smoked hard and fast, for he was fond of the old Count, and felt keenly his desertion; for, steel himself as he might, egotist as he might call himself, Waldemar was quick in his susceptibilities and tenacious in his attachments.

Since Falkenstein had got intimate with Valérie L'Estrange in one ball you are pretty sure that week after week did not lessen their friendship. He was amused, and past memories of women he had wooed, and won, and left, certain passages in his life where such had reproached him, not always deservedly, never presented themselves to check him in his new pursuit. It is pleasant to a naturalist to study a butterfly pinned to the wall;

the rememberance that the butterfly may die of the sport does not occur to him, or, at least, never troubles him.

So Falkenstein called to Lowndes Square, and lent her books, and gave her a little Skye of his, and met her occasionally by accident on purpose in Kensington Gardens, where Valérie, according to Mrs. Cashranger's request, sometimes took one of her cousins, a headstrong young demon of six or seven, for an early walk, to which early walks Valérie made no objection, preferring them to the drawing-rooms of No. 133, and liking them, you may guess, none the less after seeing somebody she knew standing by the pond throwing in sticks for his retriever, and Falkenstein had sat down with her under the bushes by the water, and talked of all the things in heaven and earth; while Julius Adolphus ran about and gobbled at the China geese, and wetted his silk stockings unreproved. He made no love to her, not a bit; he talked of it theoretically, but never practically. But he liked to talk to her, to argue with her, to see her demonstrative pleasure in his society, to watch her coming through the trees, and find the *longs yeux bleus* gleam and darken at his approach. All this amused him, pleased him as something original and out of the beaten track. She told him all she thought and felt; she pleased him, and beguiled him from his darker thoughts, and she began to reconcile him to human nature, which, with Faria, he had learnt to class into "les tigres et les crocodiles à deux pieds."

It was well he had this amusement, for it was his only one. He was going to the bad, as we say; debts and entanglements imperceptibly gathered round him, held him tight, and only in Valérie's lively society (lively, for when with him she was as happy as a bird) could exercise his dark spirit.

You remember the vow he made when the Silver Chimes rang in the New Year? So did not he. We cannot be always Medes and Persians, madam, to resist every temptation and keep unbroken every law, though you, sitting in your cushioned chair, in unattacked tranquillity, can tell us easily enough we should be. One night, when he was dining with Bevan, Tom produced those two little ivory fiends, whose rattle is in the ear of watchful deans and proctors as the singing of the rattlesnake, and whose witchery is more wily and irresistible than the witchery of woman. No beaux yeux, whether of the cassette or of one's first love, ever subjugate a man so completely as the fascinations of play. Once yielded to the charm, the Circe that clasps us will not let us go. Falkenstein, though in much he had the strong will of his race, had no power to resist the beguilements of his Omphale; he played again and again, and five times out of seven lost.

"Well, Falkenstein," cried Godolphin, after five games of écarté at a pony a side, three of which Falkenstein had lost, "I heard Max lamenting to old Straitlace in the lobby, the other night, that you were going to the devil, only the irreproachable member phrased it in more delicate periods."

"Quite true," said Falkenstein, with a short laugh, "if for devil you substitute Queen's Bench."

"Well, we're en route together, old fellow," interrupted Tom Bevan; "and, with all your sins, you're a fat lot better than that brother of yours, who, I believe, don't know Latakia from Maryland. Jesse Egerton told me the other day that his wife has an awful life of it; but who'd credit it of a man who patronises Exeter Hall, and gave the shoeblacks only yesterday such unlimited supply of weak tea, buns, and strong texts?"

"Who indeed! Max is such a moral man," sneered Falkenstein; "though he has done one or two things in his life that I wouldn't have stooped to do. But you may sin as much as you like as long as you sin under the rose. John Bull takes his vices as a ten pound voter takes a bribe; he stretches his hand out eagerly enough, but he turns his eyes away and looks innocent, and is the first to point at his neighbor and cry out against moral corruption. Melville's quite right that there is an eleventh commandment—'Thou shalt not be found out'—whose transgression is the only one society visits with impunity."

"True enough," laughed Jimmy Fitzroy. "Thank Heaven, nobody can accuse us of studying the law and the prophets overmuch. By the way, old fellow, who's that stunning little girl you were walking with by the Serpentine yesterday morning, when I was waiting for the Metcalfe, who promised to meet me at twelve, and never came till half-past one—the most unpunctual woman going. Any new game? She's a governess, ain't she? She'd some sort of brat with her; but she's deuced good style, anyhow."

"That's little L'Estrange," laughed Godolphin: "the beloved Bella's cousin. He's met her there every day for the last three months. I don't know how much further the affair may have gone, or if——"

"My dear Harry, your imagination is running away with you," said Falkenstein, impatiently. "I never made an appointment with her in my life; she's not the same style as Mrs. Metcalfe."

Oh the jesuitism of the most candid men on occasion! He never made an appointment with her, because it was utterly unnecessary, he knowing perfectly that he should find her feeding the ducks with Julius Adolphus any morning he chose to look for her.

"All friendship is it, then?" laughed Godolphin. "Stick to it, my boy, if you can. Take care what you do, though, for to carry her off to Duke Street would give Max such a handle as he would not let go in a hurry;

And to marry (though that of course, will never enter your wildest dreams) with anybody of the Cashranger's race, were it the heiress instead of the companion, would be such a come-down to the princely house, as would infallibly strike you out of Count Ferdinand's will."

Waldemar threw back his head like a thorough-bred impatient of the punishing. "The 'princely house,' as you call it, is not so extraordinarily stainless; but leave Valérie alone, she and I have nothing to do with other, and never shall have. I have enough on my hands, in all conscience, without plunging into another love affair."

"I did hear," continued Godolphin, "that Forester proposed to her, but I don't suppose it's true; he'd scarcely be such a fool."

Falkenstein looked up quickly, but did not speak.

"I think it is true," said Bevan; "and, moreover, I fancy she refused him, for he used to cry her up to the skies, and now he's always snapping and sneering at her, which is beastly ungenerous, but after the manner of many fellows."

"One would think you were an old woman, Tom, believing all the tales you hear," said Godolphin. "She'd better know you disclaim her, Falkenstein, that she mayn't waste her chances waiting for you."

Waldemar cast a quick, annoyed, contemptuous glance upon him. "You are wonderfully careful over her interests," he said, sharply, "but I never heard that having her on your lips, Harry, ever did a woman much good. Pass me that whisky, Conrad, will you?"

The next morning, however, though he "disclaimed" her, Waldemar, about ten, took his stick, whistled his dog, and walked down to Kensington Gardens. Under the beeches just budding their first leaves, he saw what he expected to see—Valérie L'Estrange. She turned—even at that distance he thought he saw the *longs yeux bleus* flash and sparkle—dropped the biscuits she was giving the ducks to the tender mercies of Julius Adolphus, and came to meet him. Spit, the little Skye he had given her, welcoming him noisily.

"Spit is as pleased to see you as I am," said Valérie, laughing. "We have both been wondering whether you would come this morning. I am so glad you have, for I have been reading your 'Pollnitz Memoirs,' and want to talk to you about them. You know I can talk to no one as I can to you."

"You do me much honor," said Falkenstein, rather formally. He was wondering in his mind whether she *had* refused Forester or not.

"What a cold, distant speech! It is very unkind of you to answer me so. What is the matter with you, Count Waldemar?"

She always called him by the title he had dropped in English society; she had a fervent reverence for his historic *antécédens*; and besides, as she told him one day, "she liked to call him something no one else did."

"Matter with me? Nothing at all, I assure you," he answered, still distantly.

"You are not like yourself, at all events," persisted Valérie. "You should be kind to me. I have so few who are."

The tone touched him; he smiled, but did not speak, as he sat down by her poking up the turf with his stick.

"Count Waldemar," said Valérie, suddenly, brushing Spit's hair off his bright little eyes, "do tell me; hasn't something vexed you?"

"Nothing new," answered Falkenstein, with a short laugh. "The same entanglements and annoyances that have been netting their toils round me for many years—that is all. I am young enough, as time counts, yet I give you my word I have as little hope in my future, and I know as well what my life will be as if I were fourscore."

"Hush, don't say so," said Valérie, with a gesture of pain. "You are so worthy of happiness; your nature was made to be happy; and if you are not, fate has misused you cruelly."

"Fate? there is no such thing. I have been a fool, and my folly is now working itself out. I have made my own life, and I have nobody but myself to thank for it."

"I don't know that. Circumstances, temptation, education, opportunity, association, often take the place of the Parcæ, and gild or cut the threads of our destiny."

"No. I don't accept that doctrine," said Falkenstein, always much sterner judge to himself than anybody would have been to him. "What I have done has been with my eyes open. I have known the price I should pay for my pleasures, but I never paused to count it. I never stopped for any obstacle, and for what I desired, I would, like the men in the old legends, have sold myself to the devil. Now, of course, I am hampered with ten thousand embarrassments. You are young; you are a woman; you cannot understand the reckless madness which will drink the wine to-day, though one's life paid for it to-morrow. Screened from opportunity, fenced in by education, position, and society, you cannot know how impossible it is to a man, whose very energies and strength become his tempters, to put a check upon himself in the vortex of pleasure round him——"

"Yes," interrupted Valérie, "I can. Feeling for you, I can sympathise in all things with you. Had I been a man, I should have done as you have done, drunk the ambrosia without heeding its cost. Go on—I love to hear you speak of yourself; and I know your real nature, Count Waldemar, into whatever errors or hasty acts repented of in cooler moments the hot spirit of your race may have led you."

Falkenstein was pleased, despite himself, half amused, half saddened. He turned it off with a laugh. "By Heaven, I wish they had made a brewer of me—I might now be as rich and free from care as your uncle."

"You a brewer!" cried Valérie. Her father, a poor gentleman, had left her his aristocratic leanings. "What an absurd idea! All the old Falkensteins would come out of their crypts, and chanceries, and cloisters, to see the coronet surmounting the beer vats!"

He smiled at her vehemence. "The coronet! I had better have full pockets than empty titles."

"For shame!" cried Valérie. "Yes, bark at him, Spit dear; he is telling stories. You do not mean it; you know you are proud of your glorious name. Who would not rather be a Falkenstein on a hundred a year, than a Cashranger on a thousand?"

"I wouldn't," said Waldemar, wilfully. "If I had money, I could find oblivion for my past, and hope for my future. If I had money, what loads of friends would open their purses for me to borrow the money they'd know I did not need. As it is, if I except poor Tom Bevan, who's as hard up as I am, and who's a good-hearted, single-minded fellow, and likes me, I believe I haven't a friend. Godolphin welcomes me as a companion, a bon vivant, a good card player; but if he heard I was in the Queen's Bench, or had shot myself, he'd say, 'Poor devil! I am not surprised,' as he lighted his pipe and forgot me a second after. So they would all. I don't blame them."

"But I do," cried Valérie, her cheeks burning; "they are wicked and heartless, and I hate them all. Oh! Count Waldemar, I would not do so. I would not desert you if all the world did!"

He smiled: he was accustomed to her passionate ebullitions. "Poor child, I believe you would be truer than the rest," he muttered, half aloud, as he rose hastily and took out his watch. "I must be in Downing Street by eleven, and it only wants ten minutes. If you will walk with me to the gates, I have something to tell you about your MS."

III

"SCARLET AND WHITE" MAKES A HIT, AND FALKENSTEIN FEELS THE WEIGHT OF THE GOLDEN FETTERS

"Tom, will you come to the theatre with me to-night?" said Falkenstein as they lounged by the rails one afternoon in May.

"The theatre! What for? Who's that girl with a scarlet tie, on that roan there? I don't know her face. The ballet is the only thing worth stirring a step for in town. Which theatre is it?"

"I am going to see the new piece Pomps and Vanities is bringing out, and I want you as a sort of claqueur."

"Very well. I'll come," said Tom, who regarded Falkenstein, who had been his school and formfellow, still rather as a Highlandman his chief; "but, certainly, the first night of a play is the very last I should select. But if you wish it — — There's that roan coming round again! Good action, hasn't it?"

Obedient to his chiefs orders, Bevan brushed his whiskers, settled his tie, or rather let his valet do it for him, and accompanied Waldemar to one of the crack-up theatres, where Pomps and Vanities, as the manager was irreverently styled by the habitués of his green-room, reigned in a state of scenic magnificence, very different to the days when Garrick played Macbeth in wig and gaiters.

Bevan asked no questions; he was rather a silent man, and probably knew by experience that he would most likely get no answers, unless the information was volunteered. So settling in his own mind that it was the début of some protégée of Falkenstein's, he followed him to the door of a private box. Waldemar opened it, and entered. In it sat two women: one, a middle-aged lady-like-looking person; the other a young one, in whom, as she turned round with a radiant smile, and gave Falkenstein her hand, Bevan recognised Valérie L'Estrange. "Keep up your courage," whispered Waldemar, as he took the seat behind her, and leaned forward with a smile. Tom stared at them both. It was high Dutch to him; but being endowed with very little curiosity, and a lion's share of British immovability, he waited without any impatience for the elucidation of the mystery, and seeing the Count and Valérie absorbed in earnest and low-toned conversation, he first studied the house, and finding not a single decent-looking woman, he dropped his glass and studied the play-bill. The bill announced the new piece as "Scarlet and White." "Queer title," thought Bevan, a little consoled for his self-immolation by seeing that Rosalie Rivers, a very pretty little brunette, was to fill the soubrette rôle. The curtain drew up. Tom, looking at Valérie instead of the stage, fancied she looked very pale, and her eyes were fixed, not on the actors, but on Falkenstein. The first act passed off in ominous silence. An audience is often afraid to compromise itself by applauding a new piece too quickly. Then the story began to develop itself—wit and passion, badinage and pathos, were well intermingled. It turned on the love of a Catholic girl, a fille d'honneur to Catherine de Médicis, for a Huguenot, Vicomte de Valère, a friend of Condé and Coligny. The despairing love of the woman, the fierce struggle of her lover between his passion and his faith, the intrigues of the court, the cruelty and weakness of Charles Neuf, were all strikingly and forcibly written. The actors, being warmly applauded as the plot thickened and the audience became interested, played with energy and spirit; and when the curtain fell the success of "Scarlet and White" was proclaimed through the house.

"Very good play—very good indeed," said Tom, approvingly. "I hope you've been pleased, Miss L'Estrange." Valérie did not hear him; she was trembling and breathless, her blue eyes almost black with excitement, while Falkenstein bent over her, his face more full of animation and pleasure than Bevan had seen it for many a day. "Well," thought Tom, "Forester *did* say little Val was original. I should think that was a polite term for insane. I suppose Falkenstein's keeper."

At that minute the applause redoubled. Pomps and Vanities had announced "Scarlet and White" for repetition, and from the pit to the gods there was a cry for the author. Falkenstein bent his head till his lips touched her hair, and whispered a few words. She looked up in his face. "Do you wish me?"

"Certainly."

His word was law. She rose and went to the front of the box, a burning color in her cheeks, smiles on her lips, and tears lying under her lashes.

"The devil, Waldemar! Do you mean that—that little thing?" began Bevan.

Falkenstein nodded, and Tom, for once in his life astonished, forgot to finish his sentence in staring at the author! Probably the audience also shared his surprise, in seeing her young face and girlish form, in lieu of the anticipated member of the Garrick or new Bourcicault, with inspiration drawn from Cavendish and Cognac; for there was a moment's silence, and then they received her with such a welcome as had not sounded through the house for years.

She bowed two or three times to thank them; then Falkenstein, knowing that though she had no shyness, she was extremely excitable, drew her gently back to her seat behind the curtain. "Your success is too much for you," he said, softly.

"No, no," said Valérie, passionately, utterly forgetful that any one else was near her; "but I am so glad that I owe it all to you. It would be nothing to me, as you know, unless it pleased you; and it came to me through your hands."

Falkenstein gave a short, quick sigh, and moved restlessly.

"You would like to go home now, wouldn't you?" he said after a pause.

She assented, and he led her out of the box, poor victimised Tom following with her duenna, who was the daily governess at No. 133.

As their cab drove away, Valérie leaned out of the window, and watched Falkenstein as long as she could see him. He waved his hand to her, and walked on into Regent Street in silence.

"Hallo, Waldemar!" began Bevan, at length, "so your protégée's turning out a star. Do you mean that she really wrote that play?"

Falkenstein nodded.

"Well, it's more than I could do. But what the deuce have you got to do with it? For a man who says he won't entangle himself with another love affair, you seem pretty tolerably *au mieux* with her. How did it all come about?"

"Simply enough," answered Falkenstein. "Of course I haven't known her all these months without finding out her talents. She has a passion for writing, and writes well, as I saw at once by those New Year's Night's Proverbs. She has no money, as you know; she wants to turn her talents to account, and didn't know how to set about it. She'd several conversations with me on the subject, so I took her play, looked it over, and gave it to Pomps and Vanities. He read it to oblige me, and put it on the stage to oblige himself, as he wanted something new for the season, and was pretty sure it would make a hit."

"Do the Cashrangers know of it?"

"No; that is why she asked the governess to come with her to-night. That stingy old Pomps wouldn't pay her much, but she thinks it an El Dorado, and I shall take care she commands her own price next time. I count on a treat on enlightening Miss Bella."

"Yes, she'll cut up rough. By George! I quite envy you your young genius."

"She isn't *mine*," said Falkenstein, bitterly.

"She might be if you chose."

"Poor little thing!—yes. But love is too expensive a luxury for a ruined man, even if— — The devil take this key, why won't it unlock? You're off to half a dozen parties I suppose, Tom?"

"And where are you going?"

"Nowhere."

"What! going to bed at half-past ten?"

"There is no particular sin in going to bed at half-past ten, is there?" said Waldemar, impatiently. "I haven't the stuff in me for balls and such things. I'm sick of them. Good-night, old fellow."

He went up-stairs to his room, threw himself on his bed, and, lighting his pipe, lay smoking and thinking while the Abbey clock tolled the hours one after another. The *longs yeux bleus* haunted him, for Waldemar had already too many chains upon him not to shrink from adding to them the Golden Fetters of a fresh passion, and marriage, unless a rich one, was certain to bring about him all his entanglements. He resolved to seek her no more, to check the demonstrative affection which, like Esmeralda, "à la fois naïve et passionnée," she had no thought of concealing from him, and which, as Falkenstein's conscience told him, he had done everything to foster. "What is a man worth if he hasn't strength of will?" he muttered, as he tossed on his bed. "And yet, poor little Valérie— — Pshaw! all women learn quickly enough to forget!"

Some ten days after he was calling in Lowndes Square. True as yet to his resolution, he had avoided the tête-à-tête walks in the Gardens; and Valérie keenly felt the change in his manner, though in what he did for her he was as kind as ever. The successful run of "Scarlet and White," the praises of its talents, its promises of future triumphs—all the admiration which, despite Bella's efforts to keep her back, the *yeux bleus* excited—all were valueless, if, as she vaguely feared, she had lost "Count Waldemar." The play had made a great sensation, and the Cashrangers had taken a box the night before, as they made a point of following the lead and seeing everything, though they generally forswore theatres as not quite *ton*. Pah! these people, "qui se couchent roturiers et se lèvent nobles," they paint their lilies with such superabundant coloring, that we see, at a glance, the flowers come not out of a conservatory but out of an atelier.

They were out, as it chanced, and Valérie was alone. She received him joyously, for unhappy as she was in his absence, the mere sight of his face recalled her old spirits, and Falkenstein, in all probability, never guessed a tithe she suffered, because she had always a smile for him.

"Oh! Count Waldemar," she cried, "why have you never been to the Gardens this week? If you only knew how I miss you — —"

"I have had no time," he answered, coldly.

"You could make time if you wished," said Valérie, passionately. "You are so cold, so unkind to me lately. Have I vexed you at all?"

"Vexed me, Miss L'Estrange? Certainly not."

She was silent, chilled, despite herself.

"Why do you call me Miss L'Estrange?" she said, suddenly. "You know I cannot bear it from *you*."

"What should I call you?"

"Valérie," she answered, softly.

He got up and walked to the hearth-rug, playing with Spit and Puppet with his foot, and for once hailed, as a relief, the entrance of Bella, in an extensive morning toilet, fresh from "shopping." She looked rapidly and angrily from him to Valérie, and attacked him at once. Seeing her cousin's vivacity told, she went in for the same stakes, with but slight success, being a young lady of the heavy artillery stamp, with no light action about her.

"Oh! Mr. Falkenstein," she began, "that exquisite play — you've seen it, of course? Captain Boville told me I should be delighted with it, and so I was. Don't you think it enchanting?"

"It is very clever," answered Falkenstein, gravely.

"Val missed a great treat," continued Bella; "nothing would make her go last night; however, she never likes anything I like. I should love to know who wrote it; some people say a woman, but I would never believe it."

"The witty raillery and unselfish devotion of the heroine might be dictated by a woman's head and heart, but the passion, and vigor, and knowledge of human nature indicate a masculine genius," replied Waldemar.

Valérie gave him such a grateful, rapturous glance, that, had Bella been looking, might have disclosed the secret; but she was studying her dainty gloves, and went on:

"Could it be Westland Marston—Sterling Coyne?"

Falkenstein shook his head. "If it were, they would put their name on the play-bills."

"You naughty man! I do believe you could tell me if you chose. *Are* you not, now, in the author's confidence?"

The corner of Falkenstein's mouth went up in an irresistible smile as he telegraphed a glance at "the author." "Well, perhaps I am."

Bella clapped her hands with enchanting gaiety. "Then, tell me this moment; I am in agonies to know!"

"It is no great mystery," smiled Falkenstein. "I fancy you are acquainted with the unknown."

"You don't mean it!" cried Bella, in a state of ecstasy. "Have you written it, then?"

"I'm afraid I can't lay claim to the honor."

"Who can it be? Oh, do tell me! How enchanting!" cried Miss Cashranger; "I am wild to hear. Somebody I know, you say? Is it—is it Captain Tweed?"

"No, it isn't," laughed Falkenstein. Elliot Tweed—Idiot Tweed, as they all call him—who was hanging after Bella, abhorred all caligraphy, and wrote his own name with one *e*.

"Mr. Dashaway, then?"

"Dash never scrawled anything but I. O. U.s."

"Lord Flippertygibbett, perhaps?"

"Wrong again. Flip took up a pen once too often, when he signed his marriage register, to have any leanings to goose quills."

"Charlie Montmorency, then?"

"Reads nothing but his betting-book and *Bell's Life*."

"Dear me! how tiresome. Who can it be? Wait a moment. Let me see. Is it Major Powell?"

"Guess again. He wouldn't write, save in Indian fashion, with his tomahawk on his enemies' scalps."

"How provoking!" cried Bella, exasperated. "Stop: is it Mr. Beauchamp?"

"No; he scribbles for six-and-eightpences too perseveringly to have time for anything, except ruining his clients."

"Dr. Montressor, then?"

"Try once more. His prescriptions bring him too many guineas for him to waste ink on any other purpose."

"How stupid I am! Perhaps—perhaps—— Yet no, it can't be, because he's at the Cape, and most likely killed, poor fellow. Could it be Cecil Green?"

Falkenstein laughed. "You needn't go so far as Kaffirland; try a little nearer home. Think over the *ladies* you know."

"The ladies! Then it *is* a woman!" cried Bella. "Well, I should never have believed it. Who can she be? How I shall admire her, and envy her! A lady! Can it be darling Flora?"

"No. If your pet friend can get through an invitation-note of four lines, the exertion costs her at least a dram of sal volatile."

"How wicked you are," murmured Miss Cashranger, delighted, after the custom of women, to hear her friend pulled to pieces. "Is it Mrs. Lushington, then?"

"Wrong again. The Lushington has so much business on hand, inditing rose-hued notes to twenty men at once, and wording them differently, for fear they may ever be compared, that she's no time for other composition."

"Lady Mechlin, perhaps—she is a charming creature?"

Falkenstein shook his head. "Never could learn the simplest rule of grammar. When she was engaged to Mechlin, she wrote her love-letters out of 'Henrietta Temple,' and flattered him immensely by their pathos."

"Was there ever such a sarcastic creature!" cried Bella, reprovingly; her interest rather flagged, since no man was the incognito author. "Well, let me see: there is Rosa Temple—she is immensely intellectual."

"But immensely orthodox. Every minute of her life is spent in working slippers and Bible markers for interesting curates. It is to be hoped one of them may reward her some day, though, I believe, till they *do* propose, she is in the habit of advocating priestly celibacy, by way of assertion of her disinterestedness. No! Miss Cashranger, the talented writer of 'Scarlet and White,' is not only of your acquaintance, but your family."

"My family!" almost screamed Bella. "Good gracious, Mr. Falkenstein, is it dear papa, or—or Augustus?"

The idea of the brewer, fat, and round, and innocent of literature as one of his own teams, or of his son just plucked for his "smalls" at Cambridge, for spelling Cæsar, Sesar, sitting down to indite the pathos and poetry of "Scarlet and White," was so exquisitely absurd that Waldemar, forgetting courtesy, lay back in his arm-chair and laughed aloud. The contagion of his ringing laugh was irresistible; Valérie followed his example, and their united merriment rang in the astonished ears of Miss Cashranger, who looked from one to the other in wrathful surprise. As soon as he could control himself, Falkenstein turned towards her with his most courteous smile.

"You will forgive our laughter, I am sure, when I tell you what I am certain *must* give you great pleasure, that the play you so warmly and justly admire was written by your cousin."

Bella stared at him, her face scarlet, all the envy and reasonless spite within her flaming up at the idea of her cousin's success.

"Valérie—Valérie," she stammered, "is it true? I had no idea she ever thought of——"

"No," said Falkenstein, roused in his protégée's defence; "I dare say you are astonished, as every one else would be, that any one so young, and, comparatively speaking, so inexperienced as your cousin, should have developed such extraordinary talent and power."

"Oh, of course—to be sure—yes," said Bella, her lips twitching nervously, "mamma will be astonished to hear of these new laurels for the family. I congratulate you, Valérie; I never knew you dreamt of writing, much less of making so public a début."

"Nor should I ever have been able to do so unless my way had been pioneered for me," said Valérie, resting her eyes fondly on Waldemar.

He stayed ten minutes longer, chatting on indifferent subjects, then left, making poor little Val happy with a touch of his hand, and a smile as "kind" as of old.

"You horrid, deceitful little thing!" began Bella, bursting with fury, as the door closed on him, "never to mention what you were doing. I can't bear such sly people I hate——"

"My dear Bella, don't disturb yourself," said Valérie, quietly; "if you had testified any interest in my doings, you might have known them; as it was, I was glad to find warmer and kinder friends."

"In Waldemar Falkenstein, I suppose," sneered Bella, white with rage. "A nice friend you have, certainly; a man whom everybody knows may go to prison for debt any day."

"Leave him alone," said Valérie haughtily; "unless you speak well of him, in my presence, you shall not speak at all."

"Oh, indeed," laughed Bella, nervously; "how very much interested you are in him! more than he is in you, I'm afraid, dear. He's famed for loving and leaving. Pray how long has this romantic affair been on the tapis?"

"He's met her every day in the Gardens," cried Julius Adolphus, just come in with that fatal apropos of "enfans terribles," much oftener the result of méchanceté than of innocence; "he's met her every day, Bella, while I fed the ducks."

Bella rose, inflated with fury, and summoning all her dignity:

"I suppose, Valérie, you know the sort of reputation you will get through these morning assignations."

Valérie bent over Spit with a smile.

"Of course, it is nothing to *me*," continued Bella, spitefully; "but I shall consider it my duty to inform mamma."

Valérie fairly laughed out.

"Do your duty, by all means."

"And," continued Bella, a third time, "I dare say she will find some means to put a stop to this absurd friendship with an unmarried and unprincipled man."

Valérie was roused; she lifted her head like a little Pythoness, and her blue eyes flashed angry scorn.

"Tell your mamma what you please, but—listen to me, Bella—if you venture to harm him in any way with your pitiful venom, I, girl as I am, will never let you go till I have revenged myself and him."

Bella, like most bullies, was a terrible coward. There was an earnestness in Valérie's words, and a dangerous light in her eyes, that frightened her, and she left the room in silence, while Valérie leaned her forehead on Spit's silky back, and cried bitterly, tears that for her life she wouldn't have shed while her cousin was there.

The next time Falkenstein called at Lowndes Square, the footman told him, "Not at home," and Waldemar swore, mentally, as he turned from the door, for though he could keep himself from seeking her, it was something new not to find her when he wished.

"She's like all the rest," he thought bitterly; "She's used me, and now she's gone to newer friends. I was a fool to suppose any woman would do otherwise. They'll tell her I can't marry; of course she'll go over to D'Orwood, or some of those confounded fools that are dangling after her."

So in his skeptical haste judged Falkenstein, on the strength of a single "Not at home," due to Cashranger malice, and the fierce throbs the mere suspicion gave him showed him that he loved Valérie too much to be able to deceive himself any longer with the assurance that his feelings towards his protégée was simple "friendship." He knew it, but he was loth to give way to it. He had long held as a doctrine that a man could forget if he chose. He had been wearied of so many, been disappointed in so much, he had had idols of the hour, in which, their first gloss off, he had found no beauty, he could not tell; it might not be the same with Valérie. Warm and passionate as a Southern, haughty and reserved as a Northern, he held many a bitter conflict in his solitary vigils at night over his pipe, after evenings spent in society which no longer amused him, or excitement with which he vainly sought to drown his cares. When he did meet Valérie out, which was rarely, as he refused most invitations now, his struggle against his ill-timed passion made his manner so cold and capricious, that Valérie, who could not divine the workings of his heart, began, despite her vehement faith in him, and conviction that he was not wholly indifferent to her, to dread that Bella might be right, and that as he had left others so would he leave her. He gave her no opportunity of questioning him as to his sudden change, for when he did call in Lowndes Square, Bella and her aunt always stationed themselves as a sort of detective police, and Falkenstein now never sought a tête-à-tête.

One evening she met him at a dinner-party. With undisguised delight she watched his entrance, and Waldemar, seeing her radiant face, thought in his haste, "She is happy enough, what does she care for me?" If he had looked at her after he had shaken hands carelessly with her, and turned away to talk to another woman, he would have discovered his mistake. But when do we ever discover half our errors before it is too late? She signed to him to come to her under pretext of looking at some croquis, and whispered hurriedly,

"Count Waldemar, what have I done—why do you never come to see me? You are so changed, so altered——"

"I was not aware of it."

"But I never see you in the Gardens now. You never talk to me, you never call on me."

"I have other engagements."

Valérie breathed hard between her set teeth.

"That are more agreeable to you, I suppose. You should not have accustomed me to what you intended to withdraw when it ceased to amuse you. *I* am not so capricious. Your kindness about my play——"

"It was no kindness; I would have done the same for any one."

She looked at him fixedly.

"General kindness is no kindness," said Valérie, passionately. "If you would do for a mere acquaintance what you would do for your friend, what value attaches to your friendship?"

"I attach none to it," said the Count, coldly.

Valérie's little hands clenched hard. She did not speak, lest her self-possession should give way, and just then D'Orwood came to give her his arm in to dinner; and at dinner Valérie, demonstrative and candid as she was, was gay and animated, for she could wear a mask in the bal d'Opéra of life as well as he; and though she could not believe the coldness he testified was really meant, she felt bitterly the neglect of his manner before others, at sight of which Bella's small eyes sparkled with malicious satisfaction.

IV
SOME GOLDEN FETTERS ARE SHAKEN OFF AND OTHERS ARE PUT ON

"Mrs. Boville told me last night that Waldemar Falkenstein is so dreadfully in debt, that she thinks he'll have to go into court—don't they call it?" lisped Bella, the next morning; "be arrested, or bankrupt, or something dreadful. Should you think it is true?"

"I know it's true," said Idiot Tweed, who was there, having a little music before luncheon. "He's confoundedly hard up, poor devil."

"But I thought he was in such a good position—so well off?" said Bella, observing with secret delight that her cousin's head was raised, and that the pen with which she was writing had stopped in its rapid gallop.

"Ah! so one thinks of a good many fellows," answered the Guardsman; "or, at least, you ladies do, who don't look at a man's ins and outs, and the fifty hundred things there are to bother him. Lots of people—householders, and all that sort of thing—that one would fancy worth no end, go smash when nobody's expecting it."

"And Mr. Falkenstein really is embarrassed?"

The Guardsman laughed outright. "That is a mild term, Miss Cashranger. I heard down at Windsor yesterday, from a man that knows his family very well, that if he don't pay his debts this week, Amadeus Levi will arrest him. I dare say he will. Jews do when they can't bleed you any longer, and think your family will come down handsomely. But they say the old Count won't give Falkenstein a rap, so most likely he'll cut the country."

That afternoon, on his return from the Deeds and Chronicles Office, whose slow red-tapeism ill suited his impatient and vigorous intellect, Waldemar sat down deliberately to investigate his affairs. It was true that Amadeus Levi's patience was waning fast; his debts of honor had put him deep in that worthy's books, and Falkenstein, as he sat in his lodgings, with the August sun streaming full on the relentless figures that showed him, with cruel mathematical ruthlessness, that he was fast chained in the Golden

Fetters of debt, leaned his head upon his arms with the bitter despair of a man whose own hand has blotted his past and ruined his future.

The turning of the handle of his door roused him from his reverie. He looked up quickly.

"A lady wants to speak to you, sir," said the servant who waited on him.

"What name?"

"She'd rather not give it, sir."

"Very well," said Falkenstein, consigning all women to the devil; "show her up."

Resigning himself to his fate, he rose, leaning his hand on the arm of the chair. He started involuntarily as the door opened again.

"Valérie!"

She looked up at him half hesitatingly. "Count Waldemar, don't be angry with me— —"

"Angry! no, Heaven knows; but— —"

Her face and her voice were fast thawing his chill reserve, and he stopped abruptly.

"You wonder why I have come here," Valérie went on singularly shyly for her, "but—but I heard that you—you have much to trouble you just now. Is it true?"

"True enough, Heaven knows."

"Then—then," said Valérie, with all her old impetuosity, "let me do something for you—let me help you in some way—you who have done everything for me, who have been the only person kind to me on earth. Do let me—do not refuse me. I would die to serve you."

He breathed fast as he gazed on her expressive eyes. It was a hard struggle to him to preserve his self-control.

"No one can help me," he answered, hurriedly. "I have made my own fate—leave me to it."

"I will not!" cried Valérie, passionately. "Do not send me away—do not refuse me. What happiness would there be for me so great as serving you—you to whom I owe all the pleasure I have known! Take them. Count Waldemar—pray take them; they have often told me they are worth a good deal, and I will thank Heaven every hour for having enabled me to aid you ever so little." She pressed into his hands a jewel-case.

Falkenstein could not answer her. He stood looking down at her, his lips white as death. She mistook his silence for displeasure, and laid her hands on his arm.

"Do not be offended—do not be annoyed with me. They are my own—an old heirloom of the L'Estranges that only came to me the other day. Take them, Count Waldemar. Do, for Heaven's sake. I spoke passionately to you last night; I have been unhappy ever since. If you will not take them, I shall think you have not yet forgiven me?"

He seized her hands and drew her close to him: "Good Heavens! do you love me like this?"

She did not answer, but she looked up at him. That look shivered to atoms Falkenstein's resolves, and cast his pride and prudence to the winds. He pressed her fiercely against his heart, he kissed her again and again, bitter tears rushing to his burning eyes.

"Valérie! Valérie!" he whispered, wildly, "my fate is at its darkest. Will you share it?"

She leaned her brow on his shoulder, trembling with hysterical joy.

"You do care for me, then?" she murmured, at last.

"Oh! thank Heaven."

In the delirium of his happiness, in the vehemence of feelings touched to the core by sight of the intense love he had awakened, Falkenstein poured out on her all the passion of his impetuous and reserved nature, and in the paradise of the moment forgot every cloud that hung on his horizon.

"Valérie!" he whispered, at length, "I have now nothing to offer you. I can give you none of the riches, and power, and position that other men can——"

She stopped him, putting her hands on his lips. "Hush! I shall have everything that life can give me in having your love."

"My darling, Heaven bless you!" cried Falkenstein, passionately; "but think twice, Valérie—pause before you decide. I am a ruined man—embarrassments fetter me on every side. To-morrow, for aught I know, I may be arrested for debt. I would not lead you into what, in older years, you may regret."

"Regret!" cried Valérie, clinging to him. "How can I ever regret that I have won the one heaven I crave. If you love me, life will always be beautiful in my eyes; and, Count Waldemar, I can work for you—I can help you, be it ever so little. I cannot make much money now, but you have said that I shall gain more year after year. Only let me be with you; let me know your sorrows and lighten them if I can, and I could ask no greater happiness——"

Falkenstein bent over her, and covered with caresses the lips that to him seemed so eloquent; he had no words to thank her for a love that, to his warm and solitary heart, came like water in the wilderness. The sound of voices gay and laughing, on the stairs, startled him.

"That is Bevan and Godolphin; I forgot they were coming for me to go down to the Castle. Good Heavens! they mustn't see you here, love, to jest about you over their mess-tables. Stay," said Falkenstein, hastily, as the men entered the front room, "wait here a moment; they cannot see you in this window, and I will come to you again. Hallo! old fellows!" said he, passing through the folding-doors. "You're wonderfully punctual, Tom. I always give you half an hour's grace; but I suppose Harry's such an awful martinet, that he kept you up to time for once."

"All the credit's due to my mare," laughed Godolphin. "She did the distance from Knightsbridge in four minutes, and I don't think Musjid himself could beat that. Are you ready, I say? because we're to be at the Castle by six, and Fitz don't like waiting for his turbot."

"Give me a brace of seconds, and I shall be with you," said Waldemar.

"Make haste, there's a good fellow. By George!" said Harry, catching sight of the jewel-case, "for a fellow who's so deucedly hard up, you've been pretty extravagant in getting those diamonds, Waldemar. Who are they for—Rosalie Rivers, or the Deloraine; or that last love of yours, that wonderful little L'Estrange?"

Falkenstein's brow grew dark; he snatched the case from the table, with a suppressed oath, and went back to the inner room, slamming the folding-doors after him. Godolphin lounged to the window looking on the street, where he stood for five minutes, whistling A te, o cara. "The devil! what's that fellow about?" he said, yawning. "How impatient Bonbon's growing! Why don't that fool Roberts drive her up and down? By Jove! come here, Tom. Who's that girl Falkenstein's now putting into a cab? That's what he wanted his brace of seconds for! Confound that portico! I can't see her face, and women dress so much alike now, there's no telling one from another. What an infernal while he is bidding her good-by. I shall know another time what his two seconds mean. There, the cab's off at last, thank Heaven!— Very pretty, Falkenstein," he began, as the Count entered. "That's your game, is it? I think you might have confided in your bosom friend. Who is the fair one? Come, make a clean breast of it."

Falkenstein shook his head. "My dear Harry, spare your words. Don't you know of old that you never get anything out of me unless I choose?"

"Oh yes, confound you, I know that pretty well. One question, though—was she pretty?"

"Do you suppose I entertain plain women?"

"No; never was such a man for the beaux yeux. It looked uncommonly like little L'Estrange; but I don't suppose she could get out of the durance vile of Lowndes Square, to come and pay you a tête-à-tête call. Well, are you ready now? because Bonbon's tired of waiting, and so are we. A man in love makes an abominable friend."

"A man in love with himself makes a worse one," said Waldemar; which hit Harry in a vulnerable spot, Godolphin being generally chaffed about the affection he bore his own person.

"That *was* the little L'Estrange, wasn't it?" asked Godolphin, as they leaned out of the window after dinner, apart from the others.

"Yes," said Waldemar, curtly; "but I beg you to keep silence on it to every one."

"To be sure; I've kept plenty of your confidences. I had no idea you'd push it so far. Of course you won't be fool enough to marry her?"

Falkenstein's dark eyes flashed fire. "I shall not be fool enough to consult or confide in any man upon my private affairs."

Godolphin shrugged his shoulders with commiseration, and left Waldemar alone in his window.

Falkenstein called in Lowndes Square the morning after and had an interview with old Cash in the library of gaudy books that were never opened, and told him concisely that he loved his niece, and—that ever I should live to record it!—that little snob, with not two ideas in his head, who couldn't, if put to it, tell you who his own grandfather was, and who owed his tolerance in society to his banking account, refused an alliance with the refined intellect and the blue blood of one of the proud, courtly, historic Falkensteins! He'd been tutored by his wife, and said his lesson properly, refusing to sanction "any such connexion;" of course his niece must act for herself.

Waldemar bowed himself out with all his haughtiest high-breeding; he knew Valérie *would* act for herself, but the insult cut him to the quick. He threw himself into the train, and went down to Fairlie, his governor's place in Devonshire, determining to sacrifice his pride, and ask his father to aid him in his effort for freedom. In the drawing-room he found his sister

Virginia, a cold, proud woman of the world. She scarcely let him sit down and inquire for the governor, before she pounced on him.

"Waldemar, I have heard the most absurd report about you."

"Most reports are absurd."

"Yes, of course; but this is too ridiculous. What do you think it is?"

"I am sure I can't say."

"That you are going to marry."

"Well?"

"Well! You take it very quietly. If you were going to make a good match I should be the first to rejoice; but they say that you are engaged to some niece of that odious, vulgar parvenu, Cashranger, the brewer; that little bold thing who wrote that play that made a noise a little while ago. Pray set me at rest at once, and say it is not true."

"I should be very sorry if it were not."

His sister looked at him in haughty horror. "Waldemar! you must be mad. If you were rich, it would be intolerable to stoop to such a connexion; but, laden with debts as you are, to disgrace the family with such——"

"Disgrace?" repeated Falkenstein, scornfully. "She would honor any family she entered."

"You talk like a boy of twenty," said Virginia, impatiently. "To load yourself with a penniless wife when you are on the brink of ruin—to introduce to *us* the niece of a low-bred, pushing plebeian—to give your name to a bold manœuvring girl, who has the impudence to take her stand before a crowded theatre——"

"Hold!" broke out Waldemar, fiercely: "you might thank Heaven, Virginia, if you were as frank-hearted and as free from guile as she is. She thinks no ill, and therefore she is not, like you fine ladies, on the constant qui vive lest it should be attributed to her. I have found at last a woman too generous to be mistrustful, too fond to wait for the world's advantages, and, moreover, untainted by the breath of your conventionalities, and pride, and cant."

Virginia threw back her head with a curl on her lip. "You are mad, as I said before. I suppose you do not expect me to countenance your infatuation?"

He shrugged his shoulder. "Really, whether you do or not is perfectly immaterial to me."

Virginia was silent, pale with anger, for they were all (pardonably enough) proud. She turned with a sneer to Josephine, a younger and less decided woman, just entering. "Josephine, you are come in time to be congratulated on your sister-in-law."

"Is it true?" murmured Josephine, aghast. "Oh! my dear Waldemar, pause; consider how dreadful for us—a person who is so horribly connected; the man's beer wagon is now standing at the door. Oh, do reflect—a girl, whose name is before the public— —"

"By talent that would grace a queen!" interrupted Waldemar, rising impatiently. "You waste your words; you might know that I am not so weak as to give up my sole chance of happiness to please your pitiful prejudices."

"Very well. *I* shall never speak to her," said Virginia, between her teeth.

"That you will do as you please; you will be the loser."

"But, Waldemar, do consider," began Josephine.

"Your women's tongues would drive a man mad," muttered Falkenstein. "Tell me where my father is."

"In his study," answered Virginia briefly. And in his study Falkenstein found him. He saw at once that something was wrong by his reception; but he plunged at once into his affairs, showing him plainly his position, and asking him frankly for help to discharge his debts.

Count Ferdinand heard him in silence. "Waldemar," he answered, after a long pause, "you shall have all you wish. I will sign you a check for the amount this instant if you give me your word to break off this miserable affair."

Falkenstein's cheek flushed with annoyance; he had expected sympathy from his father, or at least toleration. "That is impossible. You ask me to give up the one thing that binds me to life—the one love I have given me—the one chance of redeeming the future, that lies in my grasp. I am not a boy led away by a passing caprice. I have known and tried everything, and I can judge what will make my happiness. What unfortunate prejudice have you all formed against my poor little Valérie— —"

"Enough" said his father, sternly. "I address you as a man of the world, and a man of sense; you answer me with infatuated folly. I give you your choice: my aid and esteem, in everything you can desire, or the madman's gratification of the ill-placed caprice of the hour."

Falkenstein rose as haughtily as the Count.

"Virtually, then, you give me no choice. I am sorry I troubled you with my concerns. I know whose interference I have to thank for it, and am only astonished you are so easily influenced," said Falkenstein, setting his teeth hard as he closed the door; for his father's easy desertion of him hit him hard, and he attributed it, rightly enough, to Maximilian, who, industriously gathering every grain of evil report against his brother, had taken such a character of Valérie—whom, unluckily, he had seen coming out of Duke street—down to Fairlee, that his father vowed to disinherit him, and his sisters never to speak to him. The doors both of his own home and Lowndes Square were closed to him; and in his adversity the only one that clung to him was Valérie.

If he had been willing to ask them, none of his friends could have helped him. Godolphin, with 20,000*l*. a year, spent every shilling on himself; Tom Bevan, but that he stood for a pocket borough of his governor's, would have been in quod long ago; and for the others, men very willing to take your money at écarté are not very willing to lend you theirs when you can play écarté no longer. Amadeus Levi grew more and more importunate; down on him at once, as Falkenstein knew, would come the Jew's *griffes* if he took any such unprofitable step as a marriage for love; and with all the passion in the world, mesdemoiselles, a man thinks twice before he throws himself into the Insolvent Court.

One night, *nolens volens*, decision was forced on him. He had seen Valérie that morning in the Pantheon, and they had parted to meet again at a ball, one of the lingering stragglers of the past season. About twelve he dressed and walked down Duke Street, looking for a cab to take him to Park Lane. Under a lamp at the corner, standing reading, he saw a man whom he knew by sight, and whose errand he guessed without hesitation. He paused unnoticed close beside him; he stood a moment and glanced over his shoulder; he saw a warrant for his own apprehension at Levi's suit. The man looking, to make sure of the dress, never raised his eyes. Falkenstein walked on, hailed a hansom in Regent street, and in a quarter of an hour was chatting with his hostess.

"Where is Miss L'Estrange?" he asked, carelessly.

"She was waltzing with Tom a moment ago," answered Mrs. Eden. "If you run after her so, I shall believe report. But is anything the matter, Falkenstein? How ill you look!"

"Too much champagne," laughed Waldemar. "I've been dining with Gourmet, and all the Falkensteins inherit the desire of obtaining that gentlemanlike curse, the gout."

"It's not the gout, mon ami," smiled Mrs. Eden.

"Break your engagement and waltz with me," he whispered, ten minutes after, to Valérie.

"I have none. I kept them all free for you!"

He put his arm round her and whirled her into the circle.

"Count Waldemar, you are not well. Has anything fresh occurred?" she asked anxiously, as she felt the quick throbs of his heart, and saw the dark circles of his eyes and the deepened lines round his haughty mouth.

"Not much, dearest. I will tell you in a moment."

She was silent, and he led her through the different rooms into Mrs. Eden's boudoir, which he knew was generally deserted; and there, holding her close to him, but not looking into her eyes lest his strength should fail him, he told her that he must leave England, and asked her if he should go alone.

She caught both his hands and kissed them passionately. "No, no; do not leave me—take me with you, wherever it be. Oh, that I were rich for your sake! I, who would die for you, can do nothing to help you—"

He pressed her fiercely to him. "Oh, Valérie! Heaven bless you for your love, that renders the darkest hour of my life the brightest. But weigh well what you do, my darling. I am utterly ruined. I cannot insure you from privation in the future, perhaps not from absolute want; if I make money, much must go in honor year by year to the payment of my debts, by instalments. I shall take you from all the luxuries and the society that you are formed for; do not sacrifice yourself blindly——"

"Sacrifice myself!" interrupted Valérie. "Oh! Waldemar, if it is no sacrifice to *you*, let me be with you wherever it be; and if you have cares, and toil, and sorrow, let me share them. I will write for you, work for you, do anything for you, only let me be with you——"

He pressed his lips to hers, silent with the tumult of passion, happiness, delirious joy, regret, remorse, that arose in him at her words.

"My guardian angel, be it as you will!" he said, at length. "I must be out of England to-morrow, Valérie. Will you come with me as my wife?"

Early on Sunday morning Falkenstein was married, and out of his host of friends, and relatives, and acquaintance, honest Tom Bevan was the only man who turned him off, as Tom phrased it, and bid him good bye, with few words but much regret, concealed, after the manner of Britons, for the loss of his old chum. Tom's congratulations were the only ones that fell on Valérie's ear in the empty church that morning; but I question if Valérie ever noticed the absence of the marriage paraphernalia, so entirely were her heart, and eyes, and mind, fixed on the one whom she followed into exile. They were out of London before their part of it had begun to lounge down to their late breakfasts; and as they crossed the Channel, and the noon sun streamed on the white line of cliffs, Falkenstein, holding her hands in his and looking down into her eyes, forgot the follies of his past, the insecurity of his future, the tale of his ruin and his flight, that would be on the tongues of his friends on the morrow, and only remembered the love that came to him when all others forsook him.

V
THE SILVER CHIMES RING IN A HAPPY NEW YEAR

One December evening Falkenstein sat in his lodgings in Vienna; the wood fire burnt brightly, and if its flames lighted up a room whose *appanages* were rather different to the palace his grandfather had owned in the imperial city, they at least shone on waving hair and violet eyes that were very dear to him, and helped to teach him to forget much that he had forfeited. From England he had come to Vienna, where, as he had projected, his uncle, one of the cabinet, had been able to help him to a diplomatic situation, for which his keen judgment and varied information fitted him; and in Austria his name gave him at once a brevet of the highest nobility. Of course the knowledge that he was virtually outlawed, and that he was deep in the debt of such sharps as Amadeus Levi, often galled his proud and sensitive nature; but Valérie knew how to soften and to soothe him, and, under her caressing affection or her ready vivacity, the dark hours passed away.

He was smoking his favorite briar-wood pipe, with Valérie sitting at his feet, reading him some copy just going to her publishers in England, and little Spit, not forgotten in their flight, lying on the hearth, when a deep English voice startled them, singing out, "Here you are at last! I give you my word, I've been driving over this blessed city two hours to find you!"

"Tom!" cried Falkenstein.

"Captain Bevan!" echoed Valérie, springing to her feet, while Spit began barking furiously.

Bevan shook hands with them; heartily glad to see his friend again, though, of course he grumbled more about the snow and the stupidity of the Viennese than anything else. "Very jolly rooms you've got," said he at last; "and, 'pon my life, you look better than I've seen you do a long time, Waldemar. Madame has done wonders for you."

"Madame" laughed, and glanced up at Falkenstein, who smiled half sadly.

"She has taught me how to find happiness, Tom. I wish you may get such a teacher."

"Thank you, so do I, if my time ever comes; but geniuses *aux longs yeux bleus* are rare in the world. But you're wondering why I'm here, ain't you?"

"I was flattering myself you were here to see us."

"Well, of course and very glad to see you, too; but I'm come in part as your governor's messenger."

Valérie saw him look up quickly, a flush on his face. "My father?"

"Yes, that rascal—(you know I always said he was good for nothing, a fool that couldn't smoke a Queen without being sick)—I mean, your brother Maximillian—was at the bottom of the Count's row with you. Last week I was dining at old Fitz's, and your father and sisters were there, and when the women were gone I asked him when he'd last heard of you; of course he looked tempestuous, and said, 'Never.' Happily, I'm not easily shut up, so I told him it was a pity, then, for if he did he'd hear you were jollier than ever, and I said your wife was—— Well, I won't say what, for fear we spoil this young lady, and make her vain of herself. The old boy turned pale, and said nothing; but two days after I got a line from him, saying he wasn't quite well; would I go down and speak to him. I found him chained with the gout, and he began to talk about you. I like that old man, Waldemar, I do, uncommonly. He said he'd been too hasty, but that it was a family failing, and that Max had brought him such—well, such confounded lies—about Valérie, that he would have shot you rather than see you give her your name; now he wants to have you back. I'd nothing to do, so I said I'd come and ask you to forgive the poor old boy, and come and see him, for he isn't well. I know you will, Falkenstein, because you never *did* bear malice."

"Oh yes, he will," murmured Valérie, tears in her eyes. "I separated you, Waldemar; you will let me see you reconciled?"

"My darling, yes! Poor old governor!" And Falkenstein stopped and smoked vigorously, for kindness always touched him to the heart.

Bevan looked at him and was silent. "I say," he whispered, when he was a moment alone with Valérie. "I didn't tell Waldemar, because I thought you'd break it to him less blunderingly than I should, but the old Count's breaking fast. I doubt if he'll live another week."

Bevan was right. In another week Falkenstein stood by the death-bed of his father. He had a long interview with him alone, in which the old Count detailed to him the fabricated slanders with which his brother had blackened Valérie's name. With all his old passion he disowned the son capable of such baseness, and constituted Waldemar his sole heir, save the legacies left his daughters. He died in Waldemar's arms the night they arrived in England, with his last word to him and Valérie, whom, despite Virginia's opposition, he insisted on seeing. Falkenstein's sorrow for his father was deep and unfeigned, like his character; but his guardian angel, as he used to call her, was there to console him, and, under the light of her smile, sorrow could not long pursue him.

On his brother, always his own enemy, and now the traducer of the woman he loved, Waldemar's wrath fell heavily, and would, to a certainty, have found some means of wreaking itself, but for the last wishes of his father. As it was, he took a nobler, yet a more complete revenge. The day of the funeral, when they were assembled for the reading of the will, Maximilian, unconscious of his doom, came with his gentle face, and tender melancholy air, to inherit, as he believed, Fairlie, and all the personal property.

Stunned as by a spent ball, horror-struck, disbelieving his senses, he heard his younger brother proclaimed the heir. It was a serious thing to him, moreover, for—for a man of large expenses and great ostentation—his own means were small. To secure every shilling he had schemed, and planned, and lied; and now every shilling was taken from him. Like the dog of Æsopian memory, trying to catch two pieces of meat, he had lost his own!

After the last words were read, Waldemar stood a moment irresolute; then he lifted his head, his dark eyes bright and clear, his mouth fixed and firm, a proud calm displacing his old look of passion and of care.

He went up to his brother with a generous impulse, and held out his hand.

"Maximilian, from our boyhood you never liked me, and of late you have done me a great wrong; but I am willing to believe that you did it from a mistaken motive, and by me, at least, it shall never be recalled. My father, in his wish to make amends for the one harsh act of his life to me, has made a will which I know you consider unjust. I cannot dispute his last desire that I should inherit Fairlie, but I can do what I know he would sanction—divide with you the wealth his energy collected. Take the half of the property, as if he had left it to you, and over his grave let us forget the past!"

On the last day of the year, so eventful to them both, Falkenstein and Valérie drove through the park at Fairlie. The rôle of a country gentleman would have been the last into which Waldemar, with his independent opinions and fastidious intellect, would have sunk; but he was fond of the place from early associations, and he came down to take possession. The tenantry and servants welcomed him heartily, for they had often used to wish that the wild high-spirited child, who rode his Shetland over the country at a headlong pace, and if he sometimes teased their lives out, always gave them a kind word and merry laugh, had been the heir instead of the one to whom they applied the old proverb "still and ill."

The tenantry had been dismissed, the dinner finished, even the briarwood pipe smoked out, and in the wide Elizabethan window of the library Falkenstein stood, looking on the clear bright night, and watching the Old Year out.

"You sent the deed of gift to-day to Maximilian?" said Valérie, clasping both her hands on his arm.

"Yes. He does not take it very graciously; but perhaps we can hardly expect that from a man who has been disinherited. I question if I should accept it at all."

"But you could never have wronged another as he wronged you," cried Valérie. "Oh, Waldemar! I think I never realised fully, till the day you took your generous revenge, how noble, how good, how above all others you are."

He smiled, and put his hand on her lips.

"Good, noble, silly child! those words may do for some spotless Gahlahad or Folko, not for me, who, a month ago, was in debt to some of the greatest blackguards in town, who have yielded to every temptation, given way to every weakness; not with the excuse of a boy new to life, but willfully and recklessly, knowing both the pleasures and their price—I, who but for your love and my father's, should now be a solitary exile, paying for my past follies with——"

"Be quiet," interrupted Valérie, with her passionate vivacity. "As different as was 'Mirabeau jugé par sa famille et Mirabeau jugé par le peuple,' are you judged by your enemies, and judged by those who love you. Granted you have had temptations, follies, errors; so has every man of high spirit and generous temper, and I value you far more coming out of a fiery furnace with so much of pure gold that the flames could not destroy, than if you were some ascetic Pharisee, who has never succumbed because he has never been tempted, and, born with no weaknesses, is born with no warmer virtues either!"

Falkenstein laughed, as he looked down at her.

"You little goose! Well, at least you have eloquence, Valérie, if not truth, on your side; and your sophistry is dear to me, as it springs out of your love."

"But it is not sophistry," she cried, with an energetic stamp of her foot. "If you will not listen to philosophy, concede, at least, to fact. Which is most worthy of my epithets—'noble and good'—Waldemar Falkenstein, or Maximillian? And yet Maximillian has been quiet and virtuous from his youth upwards, and always wins white balls from the ballot of society."

"Well, you shall have the privilege of your sex—the last word," smiled Waldemar, "more especially as the last word is on my side."

"Hark!" interrupted Valérie, quiet and subdued in a second, "the clock is striking twelve."

Silently, with her arms round his neck, they listened to the parting knell of the Old Year, stealing quietly away from its place among men. From the church towers through England tolled the twelve strokes, with a melancholy echo, telling a world that its dead past was laid in a sealed grave, and the stone of Never More was rolled to the door of the sepulchre. The Old Year was gone, with all its sins and errors, its golden gleams and midnight storms, its midsummer days of sunshine for some, its winter nights of starless gloom for others. Its last knell echoed; and then, from the old grey belfries in villages and towns, over the stirring cities and the sleeping hamlets, over the quiet meadows and stretching woodlands and grand old forest trees, rang the Silver Chimes of the New Year.

"It shall be a happy New Year to you, my darling, if my love can make it so," whispered Waldemar, as the musical bells clashed out in wild harmony under the winter stars.

She looked up into his eyes. "I *must* be happy, since it will be passed with you. Do you remember, Waldemar, the night I saw you first, my telling you New Year's-day was my birthday, and wondering where you and I should spend the next? I liked you strangely from the first, but how little I foresaw that my whole life was to hang on yours!"

"As little as I foresaw when, after heavy losses at Godolphin's, I watched the Old Year out in my chambers, a tired, ruined, hopeless, aimless man, with not one on whom I could rely for help or sympathy in my need, that I should stand here now, free, clear from debt, with all my old entanglements shaken off, my old scores wiped out, my darker errors forgotten, my worst enemy humbled, and my own future bright. Oh! Valérie! Heaven bless you for the love that followed me into exile!"

He drew her closer to him as he spoke, and as he felt the beating of the heart that was always true to him, and the soft caress of the lips that had always a smile for him, Falkenstein looked out over the wide woodland that called him master, glistening in the clear starlight, and as he listened to the Silver Chimes—joyous herald of the New-born Year—he blessed in his inmost heart the Golden Fetters of Love.

SLANDER AND SILLERY

I

THE LION OF THE CHAUSSÉE D'ANTIN

Ma mère est à Paris,

Mon père est à Versailles.

Et moi je suis ici.

Pour chanter sur la paille,

L'amour! L'amour!

La nuit comme le jour.

Humming this popular if not over-recherché ditty, a man sat sketching in pastels, one morning, in his rooms at Numéro 10, Rue des Mauvais Sujets, Chaussée d' Antin, Paris.

The band of the national guard, the marchands crying "Coco!" the charlatans puffing everything from elixirs to lead-pencils, the Empress and Mme. d'Alve passing in their carriage, the tramp of some Zouaves just returned from Algeria—nothing in the street below disturbed him; he went sketching on as if his life depended on the completion of the picture. He was a man about thirty-three, middle height, and eminently graceful. He was half Bohemian, half English, and the animation of the one nation and the hauteur of the other were by turns expressed on his chiselled features as his thoughts moved with his pencil. The stamp of his good blood was on him; his face would have attracted and interested in ever so large a crowd. He was very pale, and there was a tired look on his wide, powerful forehead and in his long dark eyes, and a weary line or two about his handsome mouth, as if he had exhausted his youth very quickly; and, indeed, to see life as he had seen it *is* somewhat a fatiguing process, and apt to make one blasé before one's time.

The rooms in which he sat were intensely comfortable, and very provocative to a quiet pipe and idleness. To be sure, if one judged his tastes by them, they were not probably, to use the popular jargon, "healthy," for they had nothing very domestic or John Halifaxish about them, and were certainly not calculated to gratify the eyes of maiden aunts and spinster sisters.

There were fencing-foils, pistols, tobacco-boxes of every style and order, from ballet-girls to terriers' heads. There were three or four cockatoos and parrots on stands chattering bits of Quartier Latin songs, or imitating the cries in the street below. There were cards, dice-boxes, albums à rire, meerschaums, lorgnons, pink notes, no end of De Kock's and Lebrun's books, and all the etcæteras of chambres de garçon strewed about: and there were things, too—pictures, statuettes, fauteuils, and a breakfast-service of Sèvres and silver—that Du Barry need not have scrupled to put in her "petite bon-bonnière" at Luciennes.

So busy was he sketching and singing

"Messieurs les étudiens

Montez á la Chaumière!"

that he never heard a knock at his door, and he looked up with an impatient frown on his white, broad forehead as a man entered *sans cérémonie.*

"Mon Dieu! Ernest," cried his friend, "what the devil are you doing here with your pipe and your pastels, when I've been waiting at Tortoni's a good half-hour, and at last, out of patience, drove here to see what on earth had become of you?"

"My dear fellow, I beg you a thousand pardons," said Vaughan, lazily. "I was sketching this, and you and your horses went clean out of my head, I honestly confess."

"And your breakfast too, it seems," said De Concressault, glancing at the table. "Is it Madame de Mélusine or the little Bluette whose portrait absorbs you so much? No, by Jove! it's a prettier woman than either of 'em. If she's like that, take me to see her this instant. What glorious gold hair! I adore your countrywomen when they've hair that color. Where did you get that face? Is she a duchess, or a danseuse, a little actress you're going to patronise, or a millionnaire you're going to marry?"

"I can't tell you," laughed Vaughan. "I've not an idea who she may be. I saw her last evening coming out of the Français, and picked up her bouquet for her as she was getting into her carriage. The face was young, the smile very pretty and bright, and, as they daguerreotyped themselves in my mind, I thought I might as well transfer them to paper before newer beauties chased them out of it."

"Diable! and you don't know who she is? However, we'll soon find out. That gold hair mustn't be lost. But get your breakfast, pray, Ernest, and let us be off to poor Armand's sale."

"That's the way we mourn our dead friends," said Vaughan, with a sneer, pouring out his coffee. "Armand is jesting, laughing, and smoking with us one day, the next he's pitched out of his carriage going down to Asnières, and all we think of is—that his horses are for sale. If I were found in the Morgue to-morrow, your first emotion, Emile, would be, 'Vaughan's De l'Orme will be sold. I must go and bid for it directly."

De Concressault laughed as he looked up at a miniature of Marion de l'Orme, once taken for the Marquis of Gordon. "I fancy, mon garçon, there'll be too many sharks after all your possessions for me to stand any chance."

"True enough," said Vaughan; "and I question if they'll wait till my death before they come down on 'em. But I don't look forward. I take life as it comes. Vogue la galère! At least, I've *lived*, not vegetated." And humming his refrain,

"L'amour! l'amour!

La nuit comme le jour!"

he lounged down the stairs and drove to a sale in the Faubourg St. Germain, where one of his Paris chums, a virtuoso and connoisseur, had left endless *meubles* to be sold by his duns and knocked down to his friends.

Vaughan was quite right; he *had* lived, and at a pretty good pace, too. When he came of age a tolerably good fortune awaited him, but it had not been long in his hands before he contrived to let it slip through them. He'd been brought up at Sainte Barbe, after being expelled from Rugby, knew all the best of the "jeunesse dorée," and could not endure any place after Paris, where his life was as sparkling and brilliant as the foam off a glass of champagne. Wild and careless, high spirited, and lavish in his Opera suppers, his *cabaret* dinners, his Trois Frères banquets, his lansquenet parties, his bouquets for baronnes, and his bracelets for ballerinas, Ernest gained his reputation as a *Lion*, and—ruined himself, too, poor old fellow!

His place down in Surrey had mortgages thick on every inch of its lands, and the money that kept him going was borrowed from those modern Satans, money lenders, at the usually ruinous interest. "But still," Ernest was wont to say, with great philosophy, "I've had ten years' swing of pleasure. Does every man get as much as that? And should I have been any happier if I'd been a good boy, and a country squire, sat on the bench, amused my mind with turnips, and married some bishop's daughter, who'd have marched me to church, forbidden cigars, and buried me in family boots?"

Certainly that would *not* have been his line, and so, in natural horror at it, he dashed into a diametrically opposite one, and after the favor he had shown him from every handsome woman that drove through Longchamp, wore diamonds at the Tuileries, and supped with dominos noirs at bals d'Opéra, and the favor he showed to cards, the *courses*, and the *coulisses*, few bishops would have imperilled their daughters' souls by setting them to hunt down this wicked *Lion*, especially as the poor *Lion* now wasn't worth the trapping. If he had been, there would have been hue and cry enough after him I don't doubt; but the Gordon Cummings of the beau sexe rarely hunt unless it's worth their while, and they can bring home splendid spoils to make their bosom friends mad with envy; and Ernest, despite his handsome face, his fashionable reputation, and the aroma of conquest that hung about him (they used to say he never wooed ever so negligently but he won), was assuredly neither an "eligible speculation" nor a "marrying man," and was an object rather of terror to English mammas steering budding young ladies through the dangerous vortex of French society with a fierce chevaux de frise of British prejudices and a keen British eye to business. If Ernest was of no other use, however, he was invaluable to his uncles, aunts, and male cousins, as a sort of scapegoat and *épouvantail*, to be held up on high to show the unwary what they would come to if they followed his steps. It was so pleasant to them to exult over his backslidings, and, cutting him mercilessly up into little bits, hold condemnatory sermons over every one of the pieces. "Dans l'adversité de nos meilleurs amis, nous trouvons toujours quelque chose qui ne nous déplait pas;" and Vaughan's friends, like the rest of us pharisees, dearly loved to glance at the publican (especially if he was handsomer, cleverer, or any way better than themselves), and thank God loudly that they were not such men as he. Ernest was a hardened sinner, however; he laughed, put the Channel between him and them, and went on his ways without thinking or caring for their animadversions.

"By Jove! Emile," said he as they sat dining together at Leiter's, "I should like to find out my golden-haired sylphide. She was English, by her fair skin, and though I'm not very fond of my compatriotes, especially when they're abroad (I think touring John Bull detestable wrapped up in his treble plaid of reserve), still I should like to find her out just for simple curiosity. I assure you she'd the prettiest foot and ankle I ever saw, not excepting even Bluette's."

"Ma foi! that's a good deal from *you*. She must be found, then. Voyons! shall we advertise in the *Moniteur*, employ the secret police, or call at all the hotels in person to say that you're quite ready to act out Soulié's 'Lion Amoureux,' if you can only discover the petite bourgeoise to play it with you?"

Vaughan laughed as he drank his demi-tasse.

"Lion amoureux! that's an anomaly; we're only in love just enough pour nous amuser; and of us Albin says, very rightly,

> Si vous connaissiez quelques meilleurs,
>
> Vous porteriez bientôt cette âme ailleurs."

"Very well, then: if you don't know of anything better, let's hunt up this incognita. If she went to the Français, she's most likely at the Odéon to-night," said De Concressault. "Shall we try?"

"Allons!" said Vaughan, rising indolently, as he did most things. "But it's rather silly, I think; there are bright smiles and pretty feet enough in Paris without one's setting off on a wild-goose chase after them."

They were playing the last act of "La Calomnie," as Vaughan and De Concressault took their places, put up their lorgnons, and looked round the house. He swore a few mental "Diables!" and "Sacrés!" as his gaze fell on faces old or ugly, or too brunes or too blondes, or anything but what he wanted. At last, without moving his glass, he touched De Concressault's arm.

"There she is, Emile, in the fourth from the centre, in a white opera cloak, with pink flowers in her hair."

"I see her, mon ami," said Emile. "I found her out two seconds ago (see how well you sketch!) but I wouldn't spoil your pleasure in discovering her. Mon Dieu! Ernest, she's looking at you, and smiles as if she recognised you. Was there ever so lucky a Lauzun?"

Vaughan could have laughed outright to see by the brightness of the girl's expression that she knew the saviour of her bouquet again, for though he was accustomed to easy conquests, such naive interest in him at such short notice was something new to him.

He didn't take his lorgnon off her again, and she was certainly worth the honor, with her soft, lustrous gold hair, the eyes that defy definition—black in some lights, violet in others—a wide-arched forehead, promising plenty of brains, and a rayonnante, animated, joyous expression, quite refreshing to anybody as bored and blasé as Vaughan and De Concressault. As soon as the last piece was over Vaughan slipped out of his loge, and took up his station at the entrance.

He didn't wait in vain: the golden hair soon came, on the arm of a gentleman—middle aged, as Vaughan noticed with a sensation of satisfaction. She glanced up at him as she passed: he looked very handsome in the gas glare. Vaughan perhaps was too sensible a fellow to think of his pose, but even *we* have our weaknesses under certain circumstances, as well as the crinolines. Luckily for him, he chanced to have in his pocket a gold serpent bracelet he had bought that morning for some fair dame or demoiselle. He stopped her, and held it out to her.

"I beg your pardon, mademoiselle," he said in French, "but I think you dropped this?"

She looked up at him with the sunniest of smiles as she answered, in a pure accent, "No monsieur, thank you, it does not belong to me."

The middle-aged man glanced sideways at him with true British suspicion—I dare say a pickpocket, a Rouge, and Fieschi, were all mixed up in his mind as embodied in the graceful figure and bold glance of the *Lion*. He drew the girl on, looking much like a heavy cloud with a bright sun ray after it; but she half turned her head over her shoulder to give him a farewell smile, which Ernest returned with ten per cent. interest.

"Anglais," said Emile, concisely.

"Malheureusement," said Ernest as briefly, as he pushed his way into the air, and saw the gold hair vanish into her carriage. He went quickly up to the cocher.

"Où demeurent-ils, mon ami?" he whispered, slipping a five-franc piece into his hand.

The man smiled. "A l'Hôtel de Londres, monsieur; No. 6, au premier."

"The devil! pourquoir ne allez pas?" said an unmistakably English voice from the interior of the voiture. The man set off at a trot; Ernest sprang into his own trap.

"Au Chateau Rouge! May as well go there, eh, Emile? What a deuced pity la chevelure dorée is English!"

"I wish she were a danseuse, an actress, a fleuriste—anything one could make his own introduction to. Confound it there's the 'heavy father,' I'm afraid, in the case, and some rigorous mamma, or vigilant *béguine* of a governess: but, to judge by the young lady's smiles, she'll be easy game unless she's tremendously fenced in."

With which consolatory reflection Vaughan leaned back and lighted a cheroot, *en route* to spend the night as he had spent most of them for the last ten years, till the fan had begun to be more bore than pleasure.

II
NINA GORDON

"Have you been to the Hôtel de Londres, Ernest?" said De Concressault, as Vaughan lounged into Tortoni's next day, where Emile and three or four other men were drinking Seltzer and talking of how Cerisette had beaten Vivandière by a neck at Chantilly, or (the sport to which a Frenchman takes much more naturally) of how well Rivière played in the "Prix d'un Bouquet;" what a *belle taille* la De Servans had; and what a fool Senecterre had made of himself in the duel about Madame Viardot.

"Of course I have," said Vaughan. "The name is Gordon—general name enough in England. They were gone to the Expiatoire, the portière told me. There *is* the heavy father, as I feared, and a quasi-governess acting duenna; they're travelling with another family, whose name I could not hear: the woman said 'C'était beaucoup trop dur pour les lèvres.' I dare say they're some Brummagem people—some Fudge family or other—on their travels. Confound it!"

"Poor Ernest," laughed De Concressault. "Some gold hair has bewitched him, and instead of finding it belongs to a danseuse, or a married woman, or a fleuriste of the Palais Royal, or something attainable, he finds it turn into an unapproachable English girl, with no end of outlying sentries round her, who'll fire at the first familiar approach."

"It is a hard case," said De Kerroualle, a dashing fellow in one of the "Régiments de famille." "Never mind, mon ami; 'contre fortune bon cœur,' you know: it'll be more fun to devastate one of our countrymen's inviolate strongholds than to conquer where the white flag's already held out. Halloa! here's a compatriot of yours, I'd bet; look at his sanctified visage and stiff choker—a Church of England man, eh?"

"The devil!" muttered Vaughan, turning round; "deuce take him, it's my cousin Ruskinstone! What in the world does *he* do in Paris?"

The man he spoke of was the Rev. Eusebius Ruskinstone, the Dean's Warden of the cathedral of Faithandgrace, a tall, thin young clerical of eight or nine-and-twenty, with goodness enough (it was generally supposed) in his little finger to make up for all Ernest's sins, scarlet though they were.

He had just sat down and taken up the carte to blunder through "Potage au Duc de Malakoff," "Fricassée de volaille à la Princesse Mathilde," and all the rest of it, when his eye lit on his graceless cousin, and a vinegar asperity spread over his bland visage. Vaughan rose with a lazy grace, immensely bored within him: "My dear Ruskinstone, what an unanticipated pleasure. I never hoped Vanity Fair would have had power to lure *you* into its naughty peep-shows and roundabouts."

The Rev. Eusebius reddened slightly; he had once stated strongly his opinion that poor Paris was Pandemonium. "How do you do?" he said, giving his cousin two fingers; "it is a long time since we saw you in England."

"England doesn't want me," said Ernest, dryly. "I don't fancy I should be very welcome at Faithandgrace, should I? The dear Chapter would probably consign me to starvation for my skeptical notions, as Calvin did Castellio. But what *has* brought you to Paris? Are you come to fight the Jesuits in a conference, or to abjure the Wardenship and turn over to them?"

Eusebius was shocked at the irreverent tone, but there was a satirical smile on his cousin's lips that he didn't care to provoke. "I am come," he said, stiffly, "partly for health, partly to collect materials for a work on the 'Gurgoyles and Rose Mouldings of Mediæval Architecture,' and partly to oblige some friends of mine. Pardon me, here they come."

Vaughan lifted his eyes, expecting nothing very delectable in Ruskinstone's friends; to his astonishment they fell on his beauty of the Français! with the outlying sentries of father, governess, and two other women, the Warden's maiden sisters, stiff, maniérées, and prudish, like too many Englishwomen. The young lady of the Français was a curious contrast to them: she started a little as she saw Vaughan, and smiled brilliantly. On the spur of that smile Ernest greeted his cousins with a degree of *empressement* that they certainly wouldn't have been honored by without it. They were rather frightened at coming in actual contact with such a monster of iniquity as a Paris *Lion*, who, they'd heard, had out-Juan'd Don Juan, and gave him but a frigid welcome. Mr. Gordon had doubtless heard, too, of Vaughan's misdemeanors, for he looked stoical and acidulated as he bowed. But the young girl's eyes reconciled Ernest to all the rest, as she frankly returned a look with which he was wont to win his way through women's hearts, 'midst the hum of ball rooms, in the soft tête-à-tête in boudoirs, and over the sparkling Sillery of *petits soupers*. So, for the sake of his new quarry, he disregarded the cold looks of the others, and made himself so charming, that nobody could withstand the fascination of his manner till their dinner was served, and then, telling his cousins he would do himself the pleasure of calling on them the next day, he left the café to drive over to Gentilly, to inspect a grey colt of De Kerroualle's.

"La chevelure dorée is quite as pretty by daylight, Ernest," said De Concressault. "Bon dieu! it is such a relief to see eyes that are not tinted, and a skin whose pink and white is not born from the mysterious rites of the toilet."

Vaughan nodded, with his Manilla between his teeth.

"That cousin of yours is queer style, mon garçon," said Kerroualle. "How some of those islanders contrive to iron themselves into the stiffness and flatness they do, is to me the profoundest enigma. But what Church of England meaning lies hid in his coat-tails? They are, for all the world, like our révérends pères! What is it for?"

"High Church. Next door shop to yours, you know. Our ecclesiastics are given to balancing themselves on a tight rope between their 'mother' and their 'sister,' till they tumble over into their sister's open arms—the Catholics say into salvation, the Protestants into damnation; into neither, I myself opine, poor simpletons. Ruskinstone is fearfully architectural. The sole things he'll see here will be façades, gurgoyles, and clerestories, and his soul knows no warmer loves than 'stone dolls,' as Newton calls them. I say, Gaston, what do you think of *my* love of the Français; isn't she *chic*, isn't she mignonne, isn't she spirituelle?"

"Yes," assented De Kerroualle, "prettier than either Bluette or Madame de Mélusine would allow, or—relish."

Ernest frowned. "I've done with Bluette; she's a pretty face, but—ah, bah! one can't amuse oneself always with a little paysanne, for she's nothing better, after all; and I'm half afraid the Mélusine begins to bore me."

"Better not tell her so, mon ami," said De Kerroualle; "she'd be a nasty enemy."

"Pooh! a woman like that loves and forgets."

"Sans doute; but they also sometimes revenge. Poor little Bluette you may safely turn over; but Madame la Baronne won't so easily be jilted."

Vaughan laughed. "Oh, I'm not going to break her heart. Don't you know, Gaston, 'on a bien de la peine à rompre, même quand on ne s'aime plus.'"

"I shouldn't have said you found it so," smiled De Concressault, "for you change your loves as you change your gloves. La chevelure dorée will be the next, eh?"

"Poor little thing!" said Ernest, bitterly. "I wish her a better fate."

He went to call on la chevelure dorée, nevertheless, the morning after, and found her in the salon alone, greatly to his surprise and pleasure. Nina Gordon *was* pretty *even* in the morning—as Byron says—and she was much more, she was fascinating, and as perfectly demonstrative and natural as any peasant girl out of the meadows of Arles, ignorant of the magic words toilette, cosmétique, and crinoline.

She received him with evident pleasure and perfect unreserve, which even this daring and skeptical *Lion* could not twist or contort into boldness, and began to talk fast and gaily.

"Do I like Paris?" she said, in answer to his question. "Oh yes; or at least I should, if I could see it differently. I detest sight-seeing, crowding one's brains with pictures, statues, palaces, Holy Families jostling Polinchinelle, races, mixing up with grand masses, Versailles, clouding St. Cloud—the Trianon rattled through in five minutes—all in inextricable muddle. *I* should like to see Paris at leisure, with some one with whom I had a 'rapport,' my thoughts undisturbed, and my historical associations fresh and fervent."

"I wish I were honored with the office of your guide," said Ernest, smiling. "Do you think you would have a 'rapport' with me?"

She smiled in return. "Yes, I think I should. I cannot tell why. But as it is, my warmest souvenir of Condé is chilled by the offer of an ice, and my tenderest thought of Louise de la Vallière is shivered with the suggestion of dinner."

Vaughan laughed. "Bravo!" thought he. "Thank God this is no tame English icicle. I would give much," he said, "to be able to take my cousin's place, and show you Paris. We would have no such vulgar gastronomical interruptions; we would go through it all perfectly. I would make you hear the very whispers with which La Vallière, under the old oaks of St. Germain, unknowingly, told her love to Louis. In the forest glades of St. Cloud you should see Cinq-Mars and the Royal Hunt riding out in the *chasse de nuit*; in the gloomy walls of the prisons you should hear André Chénier reciting his last verses, and see Egalité completing his last toilet. The glittering 'Cotillons' on the terraces of Versailles, the fierce canaille surging through the salons of the Tuileries, the Templars dying in the green meadows at the back of St. Antoine—they should all rise up for you under my incantations."

Positively Ernest, bored and blasé, accustomed to look at Paris through the gas-lights of his *Lion's* life, warmed into romance to please the eyes that now beamed upon him.

"Ah! that would be delightful," said the girl, her eyes sparkling. "Mr. Ruskinstone, you know, is terrible to me, for he goes about with 'Ruskin' in one hand, 'Murray' in the other, and a Phrase-book or two in his pocket (of course he wants it, as he's a 'classical scholar'), and no matter whatever associations cling around a place, only looks at it in regard to its architectural points. I beg your pardon," she said, interrupting herself with a blush, "I forgot he was your cousin; but really that constant cold stone does tease me so."

At that moment the heavy father, as Ernest irreverently styled the tall, pompous head of one of the first banks in London, who was worth a million if he was worth a sou, entered, and the Rev. Eusebius after him, who had been spending a lively morning taking notes among the catacombs. He was prepared to be as cold as a refrigerator, and the banker to follow his example, at finding this *bête noire* of the Chaussée d'Antin tête-à-tête with Nina. But Ernest had a sort of haughty high breeding and careless dignity which warned people off from any liberties with him; and Gordon remembered that he knew Paris and its *haute volée* so well that he might be a useful acquaintance if kept at arm's length from Nina, and afterwards dropped. Unlucky man! he actually thought his weak muscles were strong enough to cope with a *Lion's*!

Vaughan took his leave, after offering his box at the Opéra-Comique to Mr. Gordon, and drove to the Jockey Club, pondering much on this new species of the *beau sexe*. He was too used to women not to know at a glance that she had nothing bold about her, and yet he was too skeptical to credit that a girl could possibly exist who was neither a coquette nor a prude. As soon as the door closed on him his friends began to open their batteries of scandal.

"How sad it is to see life wasted as my cousin wastes his," said the Warden, balancing a paper-knife thoughtfully, with a depressed air; "frittered away on mere trifles, as valuless and empty as soap-bubbles, but not, alas! so innocent."

"What do you mean?" Nina asked, quickly.

"What do I mean, Miss Gordon?" repeated Eusebius, reproachfully; "what can I mean but the idle whirl of gaiety, the vitiating pleasures, the debts and the vices which are to be laid at poor Ernest's door. Ever since we were boys together, and he was expelled from Rugby for going to Coventry fair and staying there all night, he has been going rapidly down the road to ruin."

"He looks very comfortable in his descent," smiled the young lady. "Pray why, after all, shouldn't horses, operas, and Manillas, be as legitimate objects to set one's affections upon as Norman arches and Gregorian chants? He has his dissipations, you have yours. Chacun à son goût!"

The Warden had his reasons for conciliating the young heiress, so he made a feeble effort to smile. "You know as well as I that you do not think what you say, Miss Gordon. Were it merely Vaughan's tastes that were in fault it would not be of such fearful consequence, but unfortunately it is his principles."

"He is utterly without any," said Miss Selina Ruskinstone, who, ten years before, had been deeply and hopelessly in love with Ernest, and never forgave him for not reciprocating the passion.

"He is a skeptic, a gambler, a spendthrift; and a more heartlessless flirt never lived," averred Miss Augusta, who hated the whole of Ernest's sex— even the Chapter—*pour cause.*

"Gentlemen can't help seeming flirts sometimes, some women pay such attention to them," said Nina, with a mischievous laugh. "Poor Mr. Vaughn! I hope he's not as black as he is painted. His physiognomy tells a different tale; he is just my ideal of 'Ernest Maltravers.' How kind his eyes are; have you ever looked into them, Selina?"

Miss Ruskinstone gave an angry sneer, vouchsafing no other response.

"My dear Nina, how foolishly you talk, about looking into a young man's eyes," frowned her father. "I am surprised to hear you."

Her own eyes opened in astonishment. "Why mayn't I look at them? It is by the eyes that, like a dog, I know whom to like and whom to avoid."

"And pray does your prescience guide you to see a saint in a ruined *Lion* of the Chaussée d'Antin?" sneered Selina, with another contemptuous sniff.

"Not a saint. I'm not good enough to appreciate the race," laughed Nina. "But I do not believe your cousin to be all you paint him; or, at least, if circumstances have led him into extravagance, I have a conviction that he has a warm heart and a noble character au fond."

"We will hope so," said the Warden, meekly, with an expression which plainly said how vain a hope it was.

"I think we have wasted a great deal too much conversation on a thankless subject," said Selina, with asperity. "Don't you think it time, Mr. Gordon, for us to go to the Louvre?"

That day, as they were driving along the Boulevards, they passed Ernest with Bluette in his carriage going to the Pré Catalan: they all knew her, from having seen her play at the Odéon. Selina and Augusta turned down their mouths, and turned up their eyes. Gordon pulled up his collar, and looked a Brutus in spectacles. Nina colored, and looked vexed. Triumph glittered in Eusebius's meek eyes, but he sighed a pastor's sigh over a lost soul.

III

"LE LION AMOUREUX"

The morning after, as they were going into the Exposition des Beaux Arts, they met Vaughan; and no ghost would have been more unwelcome to the Warden than the distingué figure of his fashionable cousin. Nina was the only one who looked pleased to recognise him, and she, as she returned his smile, forgot that the evening before it had been given to Bluette.

"Are you coming in too?" she asked.

"I was not, but I will with pleasure," said Ernest. And into the Exhibition with them he went, to Ruskinstone's wrath and Gordon's annoyance.

Vaughan was a connoisseur in art. The Warden knew no more than what he took verbatim from the god of his idolatry, Mr. John Ruskin. It was very natural that Nina should listen to the friend of Ingres and Vernet instead of to the second-hand worshipper of Turner. Vaughan, by instinct, dropped his customary tone of compliment—compliment he never used to women he delighted to honor—and talked so charmingly, that Nina utterly forgot the luckless Eusebius, and started when a low, sweet voice said, close beside her, "What, Ernest, you here?"

She turned, and saw a woman about eight-and-twenty, dressed in perfection of taste, with an exquisite figure, and a face of brunette beauty; the rouge most undiscoverable, and the eyes artistically tinted to make them look larger, which, Heaven knows, was needless. She darted a quick look at Vaughan's companion, which Nina gave back with a dash of hauteur. A shade came over his face as he answered her greeting.

"Will you not introduce me to your friend?" said the new comer. "She is of your nation, I fancy, and you know I am entêtée of everything English."

Ernest looked rather gloomy at the compliment, but turning to Nina, begged to introduce her to Madame de Mélusine. The gay, handsome baronne, taking in all the English girl's points as rapidly as a groom at Tattersall's does a two-year-old's, was chatting volubly to Nina, when the others came up. Gordon, though wont to boast that he belonged to the aristocracy of money, was always ready to fall in the dust before the noblesse of blood, and was gratified at the introduction, remembering to have read in the *Moniteur* the name of De Mélusine at the ball at the Tuileries. And the widow was very charming even to the professedly stoical eyes of a Brutus of sixty-two. She soon floated off, however, with her party, giving Vaughan a gay "A ce soir!" and requesting to be allowed the honor of calling on the Gordons.

"Is she a great friend of yours?" asked Nina, when she and he were a little in advance of the others.

"I have known her some time."

"And you are very intimate, I suppose, as she called you by your Christian name?"

He smiled a smile that puzzled Nina. "Oh! we soon get familiar here!"

"Where are you going to see her again this evening?" she persevered, playing with her parasol fringe.

"At her own house—a house that will charm you. By the way, it once belonged to Bussy Rabutin, and it has all Louis Quatorze furniture."

"Is it a dinner?—a ball?"

"No, an Opera supper—she is famed for her Sillery and her mots. Ten to one I shall not go; what amuses one once palls with repetition."

"I don't understand that," said Nina, quickly; "what I like, I like pour toujours."

"Pauvre enfant! you little know life," muttered Ernest. "Ah! Miss Gordon, you are at the happy age when one can believe in the feelings and friendships, and all the charming little romances of existence. But I have passed it, and so that I am amused for a moment, so that something takes time off my hands, I look no further, and expect no more. I know well enough the champagne will cease to sparkle, but I drink it while it foams, and don't trouble myself to lament over it. Qu'importe? when one bottle's empty, there is another!"

"Ah! it is such women as Madame de Mélusine who have taught you that doctrine," cried Nina, with an energy that rather startled Ernest, though his nerves were as strong as any man's in Paris. "My romances, as you term them, still I believe sleep in your heart, but the world you live in has stifled them. Do you think amusement will always be enough for you?—do you think you will never want something better than your empty champagne foam?"

"I hope I shall not, mademoiselle," said Vaughan, bitterly, "for I am certain I do not believe in it, and am quite sure I should never get it. Leave me to the roses of my Tritericæ; they are all I shall ever enjoy, and they, at the best, are withered."

"Nina, love," interrupted Selina, coming up with much amiability, "I was *obliged* to come and tell you not to be *quite* so energetic. All the people in the room are looking at you."

"I dare say they are," said Vaughan, calmly. "It is not often the Parisians have the pleasure of seeing beauty unaffected, and fascinations careless of their own charms. Nature, Selina, is unhappily as rare one side the Channel as the other, and we men appreciate it when we do see it."

When Vaughan parted from them soon after, he swore at himself for three things. First, for having driven Bluette, en plein jour, through the Boulevards, though he had driven Bluette, and such as Bluette, a thousand times before; secondly, for having been so weak as to introduce Madame de Mélusine to the Gordons; and, thirdly, for having—he the thorough-paced *Lion*, whose manual was Rochefoucauld, and tutor in love, De Kock— actually talked romance as if he were Werter or Paul Flemming, or some other sentimental simpleton.

Vaughan, to his great disgust, felt a fit of blue devils stealing on him, hurled one or two rose notes waiting for him into the fire with an oath, smoked half a dozen Manillas fiercely, and then, to get excitement, went to a dinner at the Rocher de Cancale, played écarté with a beau joueur, went to an Opera supper—*not* to the De Mélusine's—then to Mabille and came home at seven in the morning after a night such as would have raised every hair off Brutus's head, given a triumphant glitter to the Warden's small blue eyes, and possibly even staggered the hot faith of his young champion. Pauline de Mélusine was as good as her word—she did call on the Gordons—and Brutus, stoic though he was, was well pleased; for the baronne, though her nobility only dated from the Restoration, and was not received by the exclusive Legitimists of the old Faubourg St. Germain, had a very pleasant set of her own, and figured among the nouvelle noblesse and bourgeois décorés who fill the vacant places of the De Rochefoucauld, the De Rohan, and the Montmorency, in the "imperial" salons of the Tuileries, where once the noblest blood in Europe was gathered.

"It is painful to me to frequent Ernest's society," the Warden was wont to say, "for every word he utters impresses me but more sadly with the conviction of his lost state. But we are commanded to be in the world though not of it, and, if I shun him, how can I hope to benefit him?"

"True; and, as your cousin, it would scarcely be charitable to avoid him entirely, terrible as we know his habits to be. But there is no necessity to be too intimate, and I do not wish Nina to be too much with him," the banker was accustomed to answer.

"*Anglice,* Vaughan gets us good introductions, and makes Paris pleasant to us; we'll use him while we want him: when we don't, we will give him his congé."

That's the reading of most of our dear friends' compliments and caresses, isn't it?

Vaughan knew perfectly well that they would like to make a cat's-paw of him, and was the last man likely to play that simple and certainly not agreeable rôle unless it suited him. But he had reasons of his own for forcing Gordon to be civil and obliged to him, despite the prejudices of that English, and therefore, of course, opinionated gentleman. It amused him to mortify Eusebius, whom he saw at a glance was bewitched with the prospect of Nina's *dot,* and it amused him very much to see Nina's joyous laughter as he leaned over her chair at the Opéra Comique, to hear her animated satire on Madame de Mélusine, for whom, knowing nothing of her, the young lady had conceived hot aversion, and to listen to her enthusiasm when she poured out to him her vivid imaginings.

Gradually the cafés, and the Boulevards, and the boudoirs missed Ernest while he accompanied Nina through the glades of St. Cloud, or down the Seine to Asnières, or up the slopes of Père la Chaise, in his new pursuit; and often at night he would leave the coulisses, or a lansquenet, or the gas-lights of the Maison Dorée, and the Closerie des Lilas, to watch her thorough enjoyment of a vaudeville, her fervent feeling in an opera, or to waltz with her at a ball, and note her glad recognition of him.

To this girl, Ernest opened his heart and mind as he—being a reserved, proud, and skeptical man—had never done to any one; there was a sympathy and confidence between them, and she learned much of his inner nature as she talked to him soft and low under the forest trees of Fontainebleau, such talk as could not be heard in Bluette's boudoir, under the wax-lights of the Quartier Bréda, or in the flow of the Sillery at la Mélusine's soupers. All this was new to the tired *Lion,* and amused him immensely. La chevelure dorée was twisting the golden meshes of its net round him, as De Concressault told him one day.

"Nonsense," said Ernest; "have I not two loves already on my hands more than I want?"

"Dethrone them, and promote la petite."

Vaughan turned on his friend with his eyes flashing.

"Bon Dieu! do you take her for a ballet-girl or a grisette?"

"Well, if you don't like that, marry her then, mon cher. You will satisfy your fancy, and get cinquante mille francs de rente—at a sacrifice, of course; but, que veux-tu? There is no medal without its reverse, though a 'lion marié' is certainly an anomaly, an absurdity, and an intense pity."

"Tais-toi," said Ernest, impatiently; "tu es fou! Caught in the toils of a wretched intrigante, in the power of any tailor in the Rue Vivienne, any jeweller in the Palais Royal, my money spent on follies, my life wasted in play, the turf, and worthless women, I have much indeed to offer to a young girl who has wealth, beauty, genius, and heart!"

"All the more reason why you should make a good coup," said Emile, calmly, after listening with pitying surprise to his friend in his new mood. "You have a handsome face, a fashionable reputation, and a good name. Bah! you can do anything. As for your life, all women like a mauvais sujet, and unless the De Mélusine turn out a Brinvilliers, I don't see what you have to fear."

"When I want your counsel, Emile, I will ask it," said Vaughan, shortly; "but, as I have no intention of going in for the prize, there is no need for you to bet on the chance of the throw."

"Comme tu veux!" said the Parisian, shrugging his shoulders. "That homme de paille, your priestly cousin, will take her back to the English fogs, and make her a much better husband than you'd ever be, mon garçon."

Vaughan moved restlessly.

"The idiot! if I thought so—— The devil take you, Emile! why do you talk of such things?"

At that minute Nina was sitting by one of the windows of their hotel, watching for Ernest, with a bouquet he had sent her on a table by her side; and the Rev. Eusebius was talking in a very low tone to her father. She caught a few words. "Last night—Vaughan at the Frères Provençaux—a souper au cabinet—Mademoiselle Céline, première danseuse—quite terrible," &c., &c.

Nina flushed scarlet, and turned round. "If you blame your cousin, Mr. Ruskinstone, why were you there yourself?"

The Warden colored too. With him, as with a good many, foreign air relaxed the severity of the Decalogue, and what was sin at home, where everybody knew it, was none at all abroad—under the rose. Some dear pharisees will not endanger their souls by a carpet-dance in England, but if a little bird followed them in their holiday across the Channel, it might chance to see them disporting under a domino noir.

"I had been," he stammered, "to see, as you know, a beautiful specimen of the arcboutant in a ruined chapel of the Carmélites, some miles down the Seine. It was very late, and I was very tired, so turned into the Frères Provençaux to take some little refreshment, and I there saw my unhappy cousin in society which *ought*, Miss Gordon, to disqualify him for yours. It is very painful to me to mention such things to you. I never thought you overheard— —"

"Then, if it is very painful to you," Nina burst in, impetuously, her *bouche de rose*, as De Kerroualle called it, curving haughtily, "why are you ceaselessly raking up every possible bit of scandal that you can against your cousin? His life does not clash with yours, his acts do not matter to you, his extravagance does not rob you. I used to fancy charity should cover a multitude of sins, but it seems to me that, now-a-days, clergymen, like Dr. Watt's naughty dogs, only delight to bark and bite."

"You are cruelly unjust," answered the Warden, in those smooth tones that irritate one much more than "hard swearing." "I have no other wish than Christian kindness to poor Ernest. If, in my place as pastor, I justly condemn his errors and vices, it is only through a loving desire to wean him from his downward course."

"Your love is singularly vindictive," said his vehement young opponent, her cheeks hot and her eyes bright. "No good was ever yet done to a man by proclaiming his faults right and left. *I* should like you much better, Mr. Ruskinstone, if you said, candidly, I don't like my cousin, and I have never forgiven him for thrashing me at Rugby, and playing football better than I did."

Eusebius winced at this little touch up of his bygone years, but he smiled a benign, superior, pitying smile. "Such petitesses, I thank Heaven, are utterly beneath me, and I should have fancied Miss Gordon was too generous to suppose them. God forbid that I should envy poor Vaughan his dazzling qualities. I sorrow over him as a relative and a precious human soul, but as a minister of our holy Church I neither can, nor will, countenance his gross violations of all her divinest laws." With which peroration the Warden, with a sigh, took up a work on "The Early English Piscini and Aspersoria," and became immersed therein.

"Poor Mr. Vaughan!" cried Nina, impatiently. "Probably he is too wise to concern himself about what people buzz in his absence, or else he need be cased in mail to avoid being stung to death with the musquito bites of scandal."

Gordon came down on her with his heavy artillery. "Silence, Nina! you do not know what you are defending. I fear that no slander can darken Mr. Vaughan's character more than he merits."

"A gambler—a roué—a lover of married woman, of dancing-girls," murmured Eusebius, in an aside, meant, like those on the stage, to tell killingly with the audience.

Nina flushed as scarlet as the camellias in her bouquet, and put up her head with a haughty gesture. "Here comes the subject of your vituperation, Mr. Ruskinstone, so you can repeat your denunciations, and favor him with a sermon in person—unless, indeed, the secular recollections of Rugby intimidate the religious arm."

I fear something as irreverent as "Little devil!" rose to the Warden's pious lips as he flashed a fierce glance at her from his pale-blue eyes, for he loved not her, but the splendid *dot* which the banker was sure to pay down if his son-in-law were to his taste. He caught his cousin's glance as he came into the salons, and in the superb scorn gleaming in Ernest's dark eyes, Eusebius saw that they were not merely enemies, but—rivals: a Warden with Church principles, all the cardinal virtues, strict morality, and money; and a *Lion* with Paris principles (if any), great fascinations, debts, entanglements, and an empty purse. Which will win, with Nina for the cup and Gordon for the umpire?

IV
MISCHIEF

"Qui cherchez-vous, petite?"

The speaker was la Mélusine, and the hearer was Nina who considerably resented the half-patronising, half mocking, yet intensely amiable manner the widow chose to assume towards her. Gordon was stricken with warm admiration of madame, and never inquired into *her* morality, only too pleased when she condescended to talk to or invite him. They had met at a soirée at some intimate friends of Vaughan's in the Champs Elysées. (Ernest was a favorite wherever he went, and the good-natured French people at once took up his relatives to please him.) He was not there himself, but the baronne's quick eyes soon caught and construed her restless glances through the crowded rooms.

"Je ne cherche personne, madame," said Nina, haughtily. Dressed simply in white tulle, with the most exquisite flowers to be had out of the Palais Royal in the famous golden hair, which gleamed in the gaslight like sunshine, she aroused the serpent which lay hid in the roses of madame's smiles.

Pauline laughed softly, and flirted her fan. "Nay, nay, mignonne, those soft eyes are seeking some one. Who is it? Ah! it is that méchant Monsieur Vaughan n'est-ce pas? He is very handsome, certainly, but

On dit an village

Qu'Argire est volage."

"Madame's own thoughts possibly suggest the supposition of mine," said Nina, coldly.

"Comme ces Anglaises sont impolies," thought the baronne. "No, indeed," she said, laughing carelessly, "I know Ernest too well to let my thoughts dwell on him. He is charming to talk to, to waltz with, to flirt with, but from anything further Dieu nous garde! Lauzun himself were not more dangerous or more unstable."

"You speak as bitterly, madame, as if you had suffered from the fickleness," said Nina, with a contemptuous curl of her soft lips. Sweet temper as she was, she could thrust a spear in her enemy's side when she liked.

Madame's eyes glittered like a rattlesnake's. Nina's chance ball shot home. But madame was a woman of the world, and could mask her batteries with a skill of which Nina, with her impetuous *abandon*, was incapable. She smiled very sweetly, as she answered, "No, petite I have unhappily seen too much of the world not to know that we must never put our trust in those charming mauvais sujets. At your age, I dare say I should not have been proof against your countryman's fascinations, but now, I know just how much his fondest vows are worth, and I have been deaf to them all, for I would not let my heart mislead me against my reason and my conscience. Ah, petite! you little guess what the traitor word 'love' means here, in Paris. We women grow accustomed to our fate, but the lesson is hard sometimes."

"You have been reading 'Mes Confidences,' lately?" asked Nina, with a sarcastic flash of her brilliant eyes.

"How cruel! Do you suppose I can have no *émotions* except I learn them second-hand through Lamartine or Delphine Gay? You are very satirical, Miss Gordon——How strange!" said the baronne, interrupting herself; "your bouquet is the fac-simile of mine! Look! De Kerroualle sent you that I fancy? You know he raffoles of you. I was very silly to use mine, but Mr. Vaughan sent me such a pretty note with it, that I had not the resolution to disappoint him. Poor Ernest!" And Madame sighed softly, as if bewailing in her tender heart the woes her obduracy caused. The blood flamed up in Nina's cheeks, and her hand clenched hard on Ernest's flowers: they *were* the fac-similes of the widow's; delicate pink blossoms, mixed with white azalias. "Is he here to-night, do you know?" madame continued. "I dare say not; he is behind the coulisses, most likely. Céline, the new danseuse from the Fenice, makes her début to-night. Here comes poor Gaston to petition for a valse. Be kind to him, pray."

She herself went off to the ball-room, and the effect of her exordium was to make Nina very disagreeable to poor De Kerroualle, whom she really liked, and who was *entêté* about her. Not long afterwards, Nina saw in the distance Vaughan's haughty head and powerful brow, and her silly little heart beat as quick as a pigeon's just caught in the trap: he was talking to the widow.

"Look at our young English friend," Pauline was saying, "how she is flirting with Gaston, and De Lafitolle, and De Concressault. Certainly, when your Englishwomen do coquet, they go further than any of us."

"Est-ce possible?" said Ernest, raising his eyebrows.

"Méchant!" cried madame, with a chastising blow of her fan. "But, do you know, I admire the petite very much. I believe all really beautiful women had that rare golden hair of hers—Lucrezia Borgia (I could never bear Grisi as *Lucrezia*, for that very reason). La Cenci, the Duchess of Portsmouth, Ænone—and Helen, I am sure, netted Paris with those gold threads. Don't you think it is very lovely?"

"I do, indeed," said Vaughan, with unconscious warmth.

Madame laughed gaily, but there was a disagreeable glitter in her eye. "What, fickle already? Ah well, I give you full leave."

"And example, madame," said Ernest, as he bowed and left her side, glad to have struck the first blow of his freedom from this handsome tyrant, who was as capricious and exacting as she was clever and captivating. But fetters made of fairer roses were over Ernest now, and he never bethought himself of the probable vengeance of that bitterest foe, a woman who is piqued.

"Tout beau!" thought Pauline, as she saw him waltzing with Nina. "Mais je vous donnerai encore l'échec et mat, mon brave joueur."

"Did you give Madame de Mélusine the bouquet she carries this evening?" asked Nina, as he whirled her round.

"No," said Ernest, astonished. "Why do you ask?"

"Because she said you did," answered Nina, never accustomed to conceal anything; "and, besides, it is exactly like mine."

"Infernal woman!" muttered Ernest. "How could you for a moment believe that I would have so insulted you?"

"I didn't believe it," said Nina, lifting her frank eyes to his. "But how very late you are; have you been at the ballet?"

His face grew stern. "Did she tell you that?"

"Yes. But why did you go there, instead of coming to dance with me? Do you like those danseuses better than you do me? What was Céline's or anybody's début, to you?"

Ernest smiled at the native indignation of the question. "Never think that I do not wish to be with you; but—I wanted oblivion, and one cannot shake off old habits. Did you miss me among all those other men that you have always round you?"

"How unkind that is!" whispered Nina, indignantly. "You know I always do."

He held her closer to him in the waltz, and she felt his heart beat quicker, but she got no other answer.

That night Nina stood before her toilette-table, putting her flowers in water, and some hot tears fell on the azalias.

"I will have faith in him," she cried, passionately; "though all the world be witness against him, I will believe in him. Whatever his life may have been, his heart is warm and true; they shall never make me doubt it."

Her last thoughts were of him, and when she slept his face was in her dreams, while Ernest, with some of the wildest men of his set, smoked hard and drank deep in his chambers to drive away, if he could, the fiends of Regret and Passion and the memory of a young, radiant, impassioned face, which lured him to an unattainable future.

"Nina dearest," said Selina Ruskinstone, affectionately, the morning after, "I hope you will not think me unkind—you know I have no wish but for your good—but *don't* you think it would be better to be a little more— more reserved, a little less free, with Mr. Vaughan?"

"Explain yourself more clearly," said Nina, tranquilly. "Do you wish me to send to Turkey for a veil and a guard of Bashi-Bazouks, or do you mean that Mr. Vaughan is so attractive that he is better avoided, like a mantrap or a Maëlstrom?"

"Don't be ridiculous," retorted Augusta; "you know well enough what we mean, and certainly you do run after him a great deal too much."

"You are so *very* demonstrative," sighed Selina, "and it is so easily misconstrued. It is not feminine to court any man so unblushingly."

Nina's eyes flashed, and the blood colored her brow. "I am not afraid of being misconstrued by Mr. Vaughan," she said, haughtily; "gentlemen are kinder and wiser judges in those things than our sex."

"I wouldn't advise you to trust to Ernest's tender mercies," sneered Augusta.

"My dear child, remember his principles," sighed Selina; "his life—his reputation——"

"Leave both him and me alone," retorted Nina, passionately. "I will not stand calmly by to hear him slandered with your vague calumnies. You preach religion often enough; practice it now, and show more common kindness to your cousin: I do not say charity, for I am sick of the cant word, and he is above your pity. You think me utterly lost because I dance, and laugh, and enjoy my life, but, bad as *my* principles are, I should be shocked—yes, Selina, and I should think I merited little mercy myself, were

I as harsh and bitter upon any one as you are upon him. How can *you* judge him?—how can you say what nobility, and truth, and affection—that will shame your own cold pharisaism—may lie in his heart unrevealed?—how can you dare to censure *him*?"

In the door of the salon, listening to the lecture his young champion was giving these two blue, opinionated, and strongly pious ladies, stood Ernest, his face even paler than usual, and his eyes with a strange mixture of joy and pain in them. Nina colored scarlet, but went forward to meet him with undisguised pleasure, utterly regardless of the sneering lips and averted eyes of the Miss Ruskinstones. He had come to go with them to St. Germain, and, with a dexterous manœuvre, took the very seat in the carriage opposite Nina that Eusebius had planned for himself. But the Warden was no match for the *Lion* in such affairs, and, being exiled to the barouche with Gordon and Augusta, took from under the seat a folio of the "Stones of Venice," and read sulkily all the way.

"My dear fellow," said Vaughan, when they reached St. Germain, "don't you think you would prefer to sit in the carriage, and finish that delightful work, to coming to see some simple woods and terraces? If you would, pray don't hesitate to say so; I am sure Miss Gordon will excuse your absence."

The solicitous courtesy of Ernest's manner was boiling oil to the fire raging in the Warden's gentle breast, and Eusebius, besides, was not quick at retorts. "I am not guilty of any such bad taste," he said, stiffly, "though I do discover a charm in severe studies, which I believe you never did."

"No, never," said Ernest, laughing; "my genius does not lie that way; and I've no vacant bishopric in my mind's eye to make such studies profitable. Even you, you know, light of the Church as you are, want recreation sometimes. Confess now, the chansons à boire last night sounded pleasant after long months of Faithandgrace services!"

Eusebius looked much as I have seen a sleek tom-cat, who bears a respectable character generally, surprised in surreptitiously licking out of the cream-jug. He had the night before (when he was popularly supposed to be sitting under Adolphe Monod) tasted rather too many petits verres up at the Pré Catalan, utterly unconscious of his cousin's proximity. The pure-minded soul thus cruelly caught looked prayers of piteous entreaty to Vaughan not to damage his milk-white reputation by further revelation of this unlucky detour into the Broad Road; and Ernest, who, always kind-hearted, never hit a man when he was down, contented himself with saying:

"Ah! well, we are none of us pure alabaster, though some of the sepulchres *do* contrive to whiten themselves up astonishingly. My father, poor man, once wished to put me in the Church. Do you think I should have graced it, Selina?"

"I can't say I do," sneered Selina.

"You think I should *disgrace* it? Very probably. I am not good at 'canting.'" And giving Nina his arm, the Warden being much too confused to forestall him, he whispered: "when is that atrocious saint going to take himself over the water? Couldn't we bribe his diocesan to call him before the Arches Court? Surely those long coats, so like the little wooden men in Noah's Ark, and that straightened hair, so mathematically parted down the centre, look 'perverted' enough to warrant it."

Nina shook her head. "Unhappily, he is here for six months for ill health!—the sick-leave of clergymen who wish for a holiday, and are too holy to leave their flock without an excuse to society."

Vaughan laughed, then sighed. "Six months—and you have been here four already! Eusebius hates me cordially—all my English relatives do, I believe; we do not get on together. They are too cold and conventional for me. I have some of the warm Bohemian blood, though God knows I've seen enough to chill it to ice by this time; but it is *not* chilled—so much the worse for me," muttered Ernest "Tell me," he said, abruptly—"tell me why you took the trouble to defend me so generously this morning?"

She looked up at him with her frank, beaming regard. "Because they dare to misjudge you, and they know nothing, and are not worthy to know anything of your real self."

He pressed his lips together as if in bodily pain. "And what do you know?"

"Have you not yourself said that you talk to me as you talk to no one else?" answered Nina, impetuously; "besides—I cannot tell why, but the first day I met you I seemed to find some friend that I had lost before. I was certain that you would never misconstrue anything I said, and I felt that I saw further into your heart and mind than any one else could do. Was it not very strange?" She stopped, and looked up at him. Ernest bent his eyes on the ground, and breathed fast.

"No, no," he said at last; "yours is only an ideal of me. If you knew me as I really am, you would cease to feel the—the interest that you say——"

He stopped abruptly; facile as he was at pretty compliments, and versed in tender scenes as he had been from his school-days, the longing to make this girl love him, and his struggle not to breathe love to her, deprived him of his customary strength and nonchalance.

"I do not fear to know you as you are," said Nina, gently. "I do not think you yourself allow all the better things that there are in you. People have not judged you rightly, and you have been too proud to prove their error to them. You have found pleasure in running counter to the prudish and illiberal bigots who presumed to judge you; and to a world you have found heartless and false you have not cared to lift the domino and mask you wore."

Vaughan sighed from the bottom of his heart, and walked on in silence for a good five minutes. "Promise me, Nina," he said at length with an effort, "that no matter what you hear against me, you will not condemn me unheard."

"I promise," she answered, raising her eyes to his, brighter still for the color in her checks. It was the first time he had called her Nina.

"Miss Gordon," said Eusebius, hurriedly overtaking them, "pray come with me a moment: there is the most exquisite specimen of the Flamboyant style in an archway— —"

"Thank you for your good intentions," said Nina, pettishly, "but really, as you might know by this time, I never can see any attractions in your prosaic and matter-of-fact-fact study."

"It might be more profitable than— —"

"Than thinking of La Vallière and poor Bragelonne, and all the gay glories of the exiled Bourbons?" laughed Nina. "Very likely; but romance is more to my taste than granite. You would never have killed yourself, like Bragelonne, for the beaux yeux of Louise de la Beaume-sur-Blanc, would you?"

"I trust," said Eusebius, stiffly, "that I should have had a deeper sense of the important responsibilities of the gift of life than to throw it away because a silly girl preferred another."

"You are very impolitic," said Ernest, with a satirical smile. "No lady could feel remorse at forsaking you, if you could get over it so easily."

"He *would* get over it easily," laughed Nina. "You would call her Delilah, and all the Scripture bad names, order Mr. Ruskin's new work, turn your desires to a deanship, marry some bishop's daughter with high ecclesiastical interest, and console yourself in the bosom of your Mother Church—eh, Mr. Ruskinstone?"

"You are cruelly unjust," sighed Eusebius. "You little know— —"

"The charms of architecture? No; and I never shall," answered his tormentor, humming the "Queen of the Roses," and waltzing down the forest glade, where they were walking. "How severe you look!" she said as she waltzed back. "Is *that* wrong, too? Miriam danced before the ark and Jephtha's daughter."

The Warden appeared not to hear. Certainly his mode of courtship was singular.

"Ernest," he said, turning to his cousin as the rest of the party came up, "I had no idea your sister was in Paris. I have not seen her since she was fourteen. I should not have known her in the least."

"Margaret is in India with her husband," answered Vaughan. "What are you dreaming of? Where have you seen her?"

"I saw her in your chambers," answered the Warden, slowly. "I passed three times yesterday, and she was sitting in the centre window each time."

"Pshaw! You dreamt it in your sleep last night. Margaret's in Vellore, I assure you."

"I saw her," said the Warden, softly; "or, at least, I saw some lady, whom I naturally presumed to be your sister."

Ernest, who had not colored for fifteen years, and would have defied man or woman to confuse him, flushed to his very temples.

"You are mistaken," he said, decidedly. "There is no woman in my rooms."

Eusebius raised his eyebrows, bent his head, smiled and sighed. More polite disbelief was never expressed. The Miss Ruskinstones would have blushed if they could; as they could not, they drew themselves bolt upright, and put their parasols between them and the reprobate. Nina, whose hand was still in Vaughan's arm, turned white, and flashed a quick, upward look at him; then, with a glance at Eusebius, as fiery as the eternal wrath that that dear divine was accustomed to deal out so largely to other people, she led Ernest up to her father, who being providentially somewhat deaf, had not heard this by-play, and said, to her cousin's horror, "Papa, dear, Mr. Vaughan wants you to dine with him at Tortoni's to-night, to meet M. de Vendanges. You will be very happy, won't you?"

Ernest pressed her little hand against his side, and thanked her with his eyes.

Gordon was propitiated for that day; he was not likely to quarrel with a man who could introduce him to "Son Altesse Monseigneur le Duc de Vendanges."

V
MORE MISCHIEF—AND AN END

In a little cabinet de peinture, in a house in the Place Vendôme, apart from all the other people, who having come to a déjeûner were now dispersed in the music rooms, boudoirs, and conservatories, sat Madame de Mélusine, talking to Gordon, flatteringly, beguilingly, bewitchingly, as that accomplished widow could. The banker found her charming, and really, under her blandishments, began to believe, poor old fellow, that she was in love with him!

"Ah! by-the-by, cher monsieur," began madame, when she had soft-soaped him into a proper frame of mind, "I want to speak to you about that mignonne Nina. You cannot tell, you cannot imagine, what interest I take in her."

"You do her much honor, madame," replied her bourgeois gentilhomme, always stiff, however enraptured he might feel internally.

"The honor is mine," smiled Pauline. "Yes, I do feel much interest in her; there is a sympathy in our natures, I am certain, and—and, Monsieur Gordon, I cannot see that darling girl on the brink of a precipice without stretching out a hand to snatch her from the abyss."

"Precipice—abyss—Nina! Good Heavens! my dear madame, what do you mean?" cried Gordon—a fire, an elopement, and the small-pox, all presenting themselves to his mind.

"No, no," repeated madame, with increasing vehemence, "I will not permit any private feelings, I will not allow my own weakness to prevent me from saving her. It would be a crime, a cruelty, to let your innocent child be deceived, and rendered miserable for all time, because I lack the moral courage to preserve her. Monsieur, I speak to you, as I am sure I may, as one friend to another, and I am perfectly certain that you will not misjudge me. Answer me one thing; no impertinent curiosity dictates the question. Do you wish your daughter married to Mr. Vaughan?"

"Married to Vaughan!" exclaimed the startled banker; "I'd sooner see her married to a crossing sweeper. She never thought of such a thing.

Impossible! absurd! she'll marry my friend Ruskinstone as soon as she comes of age. Marry Vaughan! a fellow without a penny — —"

Pauline laid her soft, jewelled hand on his arm:

"My dear friend, *he* thinks of it if you do not, and I am much mistaken if dear Nina is not already dazzled by his brilliant qualities. Your countryman is a charming companion, no one can gainsay that; but, alas! he is a roué, a gambler, an adventurer, who, while winning her young girl's affections, has only in view the wealth which he hopes he will gain with her. It is painful to me to say this" (and tears stood in madame's long, velvet eyes). "We were good friends before he wanted more than friendship, while poor De Mélusine was still living, and his true character was revealed to me. It would be false delicacy to allow your darling Nina to become his victim for want of a few words from me, though I know, if he were aware of my interference, the inference he would basely insinuate from it. But you," whispered madame, brushing the tears from her eyes, and giving him an angelic smile, "I need not fear that you would ever misjudge me?"

"Never, I swear, most generous of women!" said the banker, kissing the snow-white hand, very clumsily, too. "I'll tell the fellow my mind directly — an unprincipled, gambling — —"

"Non, non, je vous en prie, monsieur!" cried the widow, really frightened, for this would not have suited her plans at all. "You would put me in the power of that unscrupulous man. He would destroy my reputation at once in his revenge."

"But what am I to do?" said the poor gulled banker. "Nina's a will of her own, and if she take a fancy to this confounded — —"

"Leave that to me," said la baronne, softly. "I have proofs which will stagger her most obstinate faith in her lover. Meanwhile give him no suspicion, go to his supper on Tuesday, and — you are asked to Vauvenay, accept the invitation — and conclude the fiançailles with Monsieur le Ministre as soon as you can."

"But — but, madame," stammered this new Jourdain to his enchanting Dorimène, "Vauvenay is an exile. I shall not see you there?"

"Ah, silly man," laughed the widow, "I shall be only two miles off. I am going to stay with the Salvador; they leave Paris in three weeks. Listen — your daughter is singing 'The Swallows.' Her voice is quite as good as Ristori's."

Three hours after, madame held another tête-à-tête in that boudoir. This time the favored mortal was Vaughan. They had had a pathetic interview, of which the pathos hardly moved Ernest as much as the widow desired.

"You love me no longer, Ernest," she murmured, the tears falling down her cheeks—her rouge was the product of high art, and never washed off—"I see it, I feel it; your heart is given to that English girl. I have tried to jest about it; I have tried to affect indifference, but I cannot. The love you once won will be yours to the grave."

Ernest listened, a satirical smile on his lips.

"I should feel more grateful," he said, calmly, "if the gift had not been given to so many; it will be a great deal of trouble to you to love us all to our graves. And your new friend Gordon, do you intend cherishing his grey hairs, too, till the gout puts them under the sod?"

She fell back sobbing with exquisite *abandon*. No deserted Calypso's *pose* was ever more effective.

"Ernest, Ernest! that I should live to be so insulted, and by you!"

"Nay, madame, end this vaudeville," said he bitterly. "I know well enough that you hate me, or why have you troubled yourself to coin the untruths about me that you whispered to Miss Gordon?"

"Ah! have you no pity for the first mad vengeance dictated by jealousy and despair?" murmured Pauline. "Once there was attraction in this face for you, Ernest; have some compassion, some sympathy——"

Well as he knew the worth of madame's tears, Ernest, chivalric and generous at heart, was touched.

"Forgive me," he said, gently, "and let us part. You know now, Pauline, that she has my deepest, my latest love. It were disloyalty to both did we meet again save in society."

"Farewell, then," murmured Pauline. "Think gently of me, Ernest, for I *have* loved you more than you will ever know now."

She rose, and, as he bent towards her, kissed his forehead. Then, floating from the room, passed the Reverend Eusebius, standing in the doorway, looking in on this parting scene. The widow looked at herself in her mirror that night with a smile of satisfaction.

"C'est bien en train," she said, half aloud. "Le fou! de penser qu'il puisse me braver. Je ne l'aime plus, c'est vrai, mais je ne veux pas qu'elle réussisse."

Nina went to bed very happy. Ernest had sat next her at the déjeûner; and afterwards at a ball had waltzed often with her and with nobody else; and his eyes had talked love in the waltzes though his tongue never had.

Ernest went to his chambers, smoked hard, half mad with the battle within him, and took three grains of opium, which gave him forgetfulness and sleep. He woke, tired and depressed, to hear the gay hum of life in the street below, and to remember he had promised Nina to meet them at Versailles.

It was Sunday morning. In England, of course, Gordon would have gone up to the sanctuary, listened to Mr. Bellew, frowned severely on the cheap trains, and, after his claret, read edifying sermons to his household; but in Paris there would be nobody to admire the piety, and the "grandes eaux" only play once a week, you know—on Sundays. So his Sabbath severity was relaxed, and down to Versailles he journied. There must be something peculiar in continental air, for it certainly stretches our countrymen's morality and religion uncommonly: it is only up at Jerusalem that our pharisees worship. Eusebius dare not go—he'd be sure to meet a brother-clerical, who might have reported the dereliction at home—so that Vaughan, despite Gordon's cold looks, kept by Nina's side though he wasn't alone with her, and when they came back in the *wagon* the banker slept and the duenna dozed, and he talked softly and low to her—not quite love, but something very like it—and as they neared Paris he took the little hand with its delicate Jouvin glove in his, and whispered,

"Remember your promise: I can brave, and have braved most things, but I could not bear your scorn. *That* would make me a worse man than I have been, if, as some folks would tell you, such a thing be possible."

It was dark, but I dare say the moonbeams shining on the chevelure dorée showed him a pair of truthful, trusting eyes that promised never to desert him.

The day after he had, by dint of tact and strategy, planned to spend entirely with Nina. He was going with them to the races at Chantilly, then to the Gaité to see the first representation of a vaudeville of a friend of his, and afterwards he had persuaded Gordon to enter the Lion's den, and let Nina grace a petit souper at No. 10, Rue des Mauvais Sujets, Chaussée d'Antin.

The weather was delicious, the race-ground full, if not quite so crowded as the Downs on Derby Day. Ernest cast away his depression, he gave himself up to the joy of being loved, his wit had never rung finer nor his laugh clearer than as he drove back to Paris opposite Nina. He had never felt in higher spirits than, after having given carte blanche to a cordon bleu for the entertainment, he looked round his salons, luxurious as Eugène Sue's, and perfumed with exotics from the Palais Royal, and thought of one rather different in style to the women that had been wont to drink his Sillery and grace his symposia.

He knew well enough she loved him, and his heart beat high as he put a bouquet of white flowers into a gold bouquetière to take to her.

On his lover-like thoughts the voice of one of his parrots—Ernest had almost as many pets as there are in the Jardin des Plantes—broke in, screaming "Bluette! Bluette! Sacre bleu, elle est jolie! Bluette! Bluette!"

The recollection was unwelcome. Vaughan swore a "sacre bleu!" too. "Diable! she mustn't hear that François, put that bird out of the way. He makes a such a confounded row."

The parrot, fond of him, as all things were that knew him, sidled up, arching its neck, and repeating what De Concressault had taught it: "Fi donc, Ernest! Tu es volage! Tu ne m'aimes plus! Tu aimes Pauline!"

"Devil take the bird!" thought its master; "even he'll be witness against me." And as he went down stairs to his cab, a chorus of birds shouting "Tu aimes Pauline!" followed him, and while he laughed, he sighed to think that even these unconscious things could tell her how little his love was worth. He forgot all but his love, however, when he leaned over her chair in the Gaités and saw that, strenuously as De Concressault and De Kerroualle sought to distract her attention, and many as were the lorgnons levelled at the chevelure dorée, all her thoughts and smiles were given to him.

Ernest had never, even in his careless boyhood, felt so happy as he did that night as he handed her into Gordon's carriage, and drove to the Chaussée d'Antin; and though Gordon sat there heavy and solemn, looming like an iceberg on Ernest's golden future, Vaughan forgot him utterly, and only looked at the sunshine beaming on him from radiant eyes that, skeptic in her sex as he was from experience, he felt would always be true to him. The carriage stopped at No. 10, Rue des Mauvais Sujets. He had given her one or two dinners with the Senecterre, the De Salvador, and other fine ladies—grand affairs at the Frères Provençaux that would have satisfied Brillat-Savarin—but she had never been to his rooms before, and she smiled joyously in his face as he lifted her out—the smile that had first charmed him at the Français. He gave her his arm, and led her across the salle, bending his head down to whisper a welcome. Gordon and Selina and several men followed. Selina felt that it was perdition to enter the *Lion's* den, but a fat old vicomte, on whom she'd fixed her eye, was going, and the "femmes de trente ans" that Balzac champions risk their souls rather than risk their chances when the day is far spent, and good offers grow rare.

Ernest's Abyssinian, mute, subordinate to that grand gentleman, M. François, ushered them up the stairs, making furtive signs to his master, which Vaughan was too much absorbed to notice. François, in all his glory, flung open the door of the salon. In the salon a sight met Ernest's eyes which froze his blood more than if all the dead had arisen out of their graves on the slopes of Père la Chaise.

The myriad of wax-lights shone on the rooms, fragrant with the perfume of exotics, gleamed on the supper-table, gorgeous with its gold plate and its flowers, lighted up the aviary with its brilliant hues of plumage, and showed to full perfection the snowy shoulders, raven hair, and rose-hued dress of a woman lying back in a fauteuil, laughing, as De Cheffontaine, a man but slightly known to Ernest, leaned over her, fanning her. On a sofa in an alcove reclined another girl, young, fair, and pretty, the amber mouthpiece of a hookah between her lips, and a couple of young fellows at her feet.

The brunette was Bluette, who played the soubrette rôles at the Odéon; the blonde was Céline Gamelle, the new première danseuse. Bluette rose from the depths of her amber satin fauteuil, with her little *pétillant* eyes laughing, and her small plump hands stretched out in gesticulation. "Méchant! Comme tu es tard, Ernest. Nous avons été ici si longtemps—dix minutes au moins! And dis is you leetler new Ingleesh friend. How do you do, my dear?"

Nina, white as death, shrank from her, clinging with both hands to Ernest's arms. As pale as she, Vaughan stood staring at the actress, his lips pressed convulsively together, the veins standing out on his broad, high forehead. The bold *Lion* hunted into his lair, for once lost all power, all strength.

Gordon looked over Nina's shoulder into the room. He recognized the women at a glance, and, with his heavy brow dark as night, he glared on Ernest in a silence more ominous than words or oaths, and snatching Nina's arm from his, he drew her hand within his own, and dragged her from the room.

Ernest sprang after him. "Good God! you do not suppose me capable of this. Stay one instant. Hear me——"

"Let us pass, sir," thundered Gordon, "or by Heaven this insult shall not go unavenged."

"Nina, Nina!" cried Ernest, passionately, "do you at least listen!—you at least will not condemn——"

Nina wrenched her hands from her father, and turned to him, a passion of tears falling down her face. "No, no! have I not promised you?"

With a violent oath Gordon carried her to her carriage. It drove away, and Ernest, his lips set, his face white, and a fierce glare in his dark eyes that made Bluette and Céline tremble, entered his salons a second time, so bitter an anguish, so deadly a wrath marked in his expressive countenance, that even the Frenchmen hushed their jests, and the women shrunk away, awed at a depth of feeling they could not fathom or brave.

The fierce anathemas of Gordon, the "Christian" lamentations of Eusebius, the sneers of Selina, the triumphs of Augusta, all these vials of wrath were poured forth on Ernest, in poor little Nina's ears, the whole of the next day. She had but one voice among many to raise in his defence, and she had no armor but her faith in him. Gordon vowed with the same breath that she should never see Vaughan again, and that she should engage herself to Ruskinstone forthwith. Eusebius poured in at one ear his mild milk-and-water attachment, and, in the other, details of Ernest's scene in the boudoir with Madame de Mélusine, or, at least, what he had seen of it, *i. e.* her parting caress. Selina rang the changes on her immodesty in loving a man who had never proposed to her; and Augusta drew lively pictures of the eternal fires which were already being kept up below, ready for the *Lion's* reception. Against all these furious batteries Nina stood firm. All their sneers and arguments could not shake her belief, all her father's commands—and, when he was roused, the old banker was very fierce—could not move her to promise not to see Ernest again, or alter her firm repudiation of the warden's proposals. The thunder rolled, the lightning flamed, the winds screamed all to no purpose, the little reed that one might have fancied would break, stood steady.

The day passed, and the next passed, and there were no tidings of Ernest. Nina's little loyal heart, despite its unhesitating faith, began to tremble lest it should have wrecked itself: but then, she thought of his eyes, and she felt that all the world would never make her mistrust him.

On the *surlendemain* the De Mélusine called. Gordon and Eusebius were out, and Nina wished her to be shown up. Ill as the girl felt, she rose haughtily and self-possessed to greet madame, as, announced by her tall chasseur, with his green plume, the widow glided into the room.

Pauline kissed her lightly (there are no end of Judases among the dear sex), and, though something in Nina's eye startled her, she sat down beside her, and began to talk most kindly, most sympathisingly. She was *chagrinée, désolée* that her *chère* Nina should have been so insulted; every one knew M. Vaughan was quite *entêté* with that little, horrid, coarse thing, Bluette; but it was certainly very shocking; men were such *démons*. The affair was already *répandue* in Paris; everybody was talking of it. Ernest was unfortunately so well known; he could not be in his senses; she almost wished he *was* mad, it would be the only excuse for him; wild as he was, she should scarcely have thought, &c., &c., &c. "Ah! chère enfant," madame went on at the finish, "you do not know these men—I do. I fear you have been dazzled by this naughty fellow; he *is* very attractive, certainly: if so, though it will be a sharp pang, it will be better to know his real character at once. Voyez donc! he has been persuading you that you were all the world to him, while at the same time, he has been trying to make me believe the same. See, only two days ago he sent me this."

She held out a miniature. Nina, who hitherto had listened in haughty silence, gave a sharp cry of pain as she saw Vaughan's graceful figure, stately head, and statue-like features. But, before the widow could pursue her advantage, Nina rallied, threw back her head, and said, her soft lips set sternly:

"If you repulsed his love, why was he obliged to repulse yours? Why did you tell him on Saturday night that 'you had loved him more than he would ever know now?'"

The shot Eusebius had unconsciously provided, struck home. Madame was baffled. Her eyes sank under Nina's, and she colored through her rouge.

"You have played two rôles, madame," said Nina, rising, "and not played them with you usual skill. Excuse my English ill-breeding, if I ask you to do me the favor of ending this comedy."

"Certainly, mademoiselle, if it is your wish," answered the widow, now smiling blandly. "If it please you to be blind, I have no desire to remove the bandage from your eyes. Seulement, je vous prie de me pardonner mon indiscrétion, et j'ai l'honneur, mademoiselle, de vous dire adieu!"

With the lowest of *révérences* madame glided from the room, and, as the door closed, Nina bowed her head on the miniature left behind in the *déroute*, and burst into tears.

Scarcely had la Mélusine's barouche rolled away, when another visitor was shown in, and Nina, brushing the tears from her cheeks, looked up hurriedly, and saw a small woman, finely dressed, with a Shetland veil on, through which her small black eyes roved listlessly.

"Mademoiselle," she said, in very quick but very bad English, "I is come to warn you against dat ver wrong man, Mr. Vaughan. I have like him, helas! I have like him too vell, but I do not vish you to suffer too."

Nina knew the voice in a moment, and rose like a little empress, though she was flushed and trembling. "I wish to hear nothing of Mr. Vaughan. If this is the sole purport of your visit, I shall be obliged by your leaving me."

"But mademoiselle— —"

"I have told you I wish to hear nothing," interposed Nina, quietly.

"Ver vell, ma'amselle; den read dat. It is a copy, and I got de original."

She laid a letter on the sofa beside Nina. Two minutes after, Bluette joined her friend Céline Gamelle in a fiacre, and laughed heartily, clapping her little plump hands. "Ah, mon Dieu! Céline, comme elle est fière, la petite! Je ne lui ai pas dit un seul mot—elle m'a arrêtée si vite, si vite! Mais la lettre fera notre affaire n'est pas? Oui, oui!"

The letter unfolded in Nina's hand. It was a promise of marriage from Ernest Vaughan to Bluette Lemaire. Voiceless and tearless, Nina sat gazing on the paper: first she rose, gasping for breath; then she threw herself down, sobbing convulsively, till she heard a step, caught up the miniature and letter, dreading to see her father, and, instead, saw Ernest, pale, worn, deep lines round his mouth and eyes, standing in the doorway. Involuntarily she sprang towards him. Ernest pressed her to heart, and his hot tears fell on the chevelure dorée, as he bent over her, murmuring, "*You* have not deserted me. God bless you for your noble faith." At last he put her gently from him, and, leaning against the mantelpiece, said, with an effort, between his teeth, "Nina, I came to bid you farewell, and to ask your forgiveness for the wrong I have done you."

Nina caught hold of him, much as Malibran seized hold of *Elvino*: "Leave me! leave me! No, no; you cannot mean it!"

"I have no strength for it now I see you," said Ernest, looking down into her eyes; and the bold, reckless *Lion* shivered under the clinging clasp of her little hands. "I need not say I was not the cause of the insult you received the other night. Pauline de Mélusine was the agent, women willing to injure me the actors in it. But there is still much for you to forgive. Tell me, at once, what have you heard of me?"

She silently put the miniature and letter in his hand. The blood rushed to his very temples, and, sinking his head on his arms, his chest rose and fell with uncontrollable sobs. All the pent-up feelings of his vehement and affectionate nature poured out at last.

"And you have not condemned me even on these?" he said at length, in a hoarse whisper.

"Did I not promise?" she murmured.

"But if I told you they were true?"

She looked at him through her tears, and put her hand in his. "Tell me nothing of your past; it can make no difference to my love. Let the world judge you as it may, it cannot alter me."

Ernest strained her to him, kissing her wildly. "God bless you for your trust! would to God I were more worthy of it! I have nothing to give you but a love such as I have never before known; but most would tell you all *my* love is worthless, and my life has been one of reckless dissipation and of darker errors still, until you awoke me to a deeper love—to thoughts and aspirations that I thought had died out for ever. Painful as it is to confess——"

"Hush!" interrupted Nina, gently. "Confess nothing; with your past life I can have nothing to do, and I wish never to hear anything that it gives you pain to tell. You say that you love me now, and will never love another— that is enough for me."

Ernest kissed the flushed cheeks and eloquent lips, and thanked her with all the fiery passion that was in him; and his heart throbbed fiercely as he put her promise to the test.

"No, my darling! Priceless as your love is to me I will not buy it by concealment. I will not sully your ears with the details of my life. God forbid I should! but it is only due to you to know that I did give both these women the love-tokens they brought you. Love! It is desecration of the name, but I knew none better then! Three years ago, Bluette Lemaire first appeared at the Odéon. She is illiterate, coarse, heartless, but she was handsome, and she drew me to the coulisses. I was infatuated with her, though her ignorance and vulgarity constantly grated against all my tastes. One night at her petit souper I drank more Sillery than was wise. I have a stronger head than most men: perhaps there was some other stimulant in it; at any rate, she who was then poor, and is always avaricious, got from me a promise to marry her, or to pay twenty thousand francs. Three months after I gave it I cared no more for her than for my old glove. France is too wise to have Breach of Promise cases, and give money to coarse and vengeful women for their pretended broken hearts; but I had no incentive to create a scene by breaking with her, and so she kept the promise in her hands. What Pauline de Mélusine is, you can judge. Twelve months ago I met her at Vichy; the love she gave me, and the love I vowed her, were of equal value—the love of Paris boudoirs. That I sent her that picture only two days ago, is, of course, false. On my word, as a man of honor, since the moment I felt your influence upon me I have shunned her. Now, my own love, you know the truth. Will you send me from you, or will you still love and still forgive?"

In an agony of suspense he bent his head to listen for her answer. Tears rained down her cheeks as she put her arms round his neck, and whispered:

"Why ask? Are you not all the world to me? I should love you little if I condemned you for any errors of your past. I know your warm and noble heart, and I trust to it without a fear. There is no doubt between us now!"

Oh, my prudent and conventional young ladies, standing ready to accuse my poor little Nina, are you any wiser in your generation? You who have had all nature taken out of you by "finishing," whose heads are crammed with "society's" laws, and whose affections are measured out by rule, who would have been cold, and dignified, and read Ernest a severe lesson, and sent him back hopeless and hardened to go ten times worse than he had gone before—believe me, that impulse points truer than "the world," and that the dictates of the heart are better than the regulations of society. Take my word for it, that love will do more for a man than lectures; and faith in him be more likely to keep him straight than all your moralising; and before you judge him severely for having drunk a little too deep of the Sillery of life, remember that his temptations are not your temptations, nor his ways your ways, and be gentle to dangers which society and custom keep out of your own path. The stern thorn crows you offer to us when we are inclined to ask your absolution, are not the right means to win us from the rose wreaths of our bacchanalia.

Nina, as you see, loved her *Lion* too well to remember dignity, or take her stand on principle; and gallantly did the young lady stand the bombardment from all sides that sought to break her resolutions and crush her "misplaced affections." Gordon chanced to come in that day and light upon Ernest, and the fury into which he worked himself ill beseemed so respectable a pharisee. Vaughan kept tranquilly haughty, and told the banker, calmly, that he "thanked God he had his daughter's love, and his money he would never have stooped to accept." Gordon forbade him the house, and carried Nina back to England; but before she went they had a parting interview, in which Ernest offered to leave her free. But such freedom would have been worse than death to Nina, and, before they separated, she told him that in three months more she should be of age, and then, come what might, she would be his if he would take her without wealth. Take her he would have done from the arms of Satanus himself, but to disentangle himself from all his difficulties was a task that beat the Augean stables hollow. The three months of his probation he worked hard;

he sold off all his pictures, his stud, and his *meubles*; he sold, what cost him a more bitter pang, his encumbered estates in Surrey; he paid off all his debts, Bluette's twenty thousand francs included; and shaking himself free of the accumulated embarrassments of fifteen years, he crossed the water to claim his last love. No poor little Huguenot was ever persecuted for her faith more than poor little Nina for her engagement. Every relative she had thought it his duty to write admonitory letters, plentifully interspersed with texts. Eusebius and his 4000*l*. a year, and his perspective bishopric, were held up before her from morning to night; the banker, whose deception in the Mélusine had turned him into sharper vinegar than before, told her with chill stoicism that she must of course choose her own path in life, but that if that path led her into the Chaussée d'Antin, she need never expect a sou from him, for all his property would be divided between her two brothers. But Nina was neither to be frightened nor bribed. She kept true to her lover, and disinherited herself.

They were married a week or two after Nina's majority; and Gordon knew it, though he could not prevent it. They did not miss the absence of bridesmaids, bishop, déjeûner, and the usual fashionable crowd. It was a marriage of the heart, you see, and did not want the trappings with which they gild that bitter pill so often swallowed now-a-days—a "mariage de convenance." Nina, as she saw further still into the wealth of deep feeling and strong affection which, at her touch, she had awoke in his heart, felt that money, and friends, and the world's smile were well lost since she had won him. And Ernest—Ernest's sacrifice was greater; for it is not a little thing, young ladies, for a man to give up his accustomed freedom, and luxuries, and careless vie de garçon, and to have to think and work for another, even though dearer than himself. But he had long since seen so much of life, had exhausted all its pleasures so rapidly, that they palled upon him, and for some time he had vaguely wanted something of deeper interest, of warmer sympathy. Unknown to himself, he had felt the "besoin d'être aimé"—a want the trash offered him by the women of his acquaintance could never satisfy—and his warm, passionate nature found rest in a love which, though the strongest of his life, was still returned to him fourfold.

After some months of delicious *far niente* in the south of France, they came back to Paris. Though anything but rich, he was not absolutely poor, after he had paid his debts, and the necessity to exertion rousing his dormant talents, the *Lion* turned *littérateur*. He was too popular with men to be dropped because he had sold his stud or given up his petits soupers. The romance of their story charmed the Parisians, and, though (behind his back) they sometimes jested about the "Lion amoureux," there were not a few who envied him his young love, and the sunshine that shone round them in his inexpensive appartement garni.

Ernest *was* singularly happy—and suddenly he became the star of the literary, as he had been of the fashionable world. His mots were repeated, his vaudevilles applauded, his feuilletons adored. The world smiled on Nina and her *Lion*; it made little difference to them—they had been as contented when it frowned.

But it made a good deal of difference across the Channel. Gordon began to repent. Ernest's family was high, his Austrian connexions very aristocratic: there would be something after all in belonging to a man so well known. (Be successful, ami lecteur, and all your relatives will love you.) Besides, he had found out that it is no use to put your faith in princes, or clergymen. Eusebius had treated him very badly when he found he could not get Nina and her money, and spoke against the poor banker everywhere, calling him, with tender pastoral regret, a "worldly Egyptian," a "Dives," a "whitened sepulchre," and all the rest of it.

Probably, too, stoic though he was, he missed the chevelure dorée; at any rate, he wrote to her stiffly, but kindly, and settled two thousand a year upon her. Vaughan was very willing she should be friends with her father, but nothing would make him draw a sou of the money. So Nina—the only sly thing she ever did in her life—after a while contrived to buy back the Surrey estate, and gave it to him, with no end of prayers and caresses, on the Jour de l'An.

"And you do not regret, my darling," smiled Ernest, after wishing her the new year's wishes, "having forgiven me for once drinking too much Sillery, and all the other naughty things of my vie de garçon?"

"Regret!" interrupted Nina, vehemently—"regret that I have won your love, live your life, share your cares and joys, regret that my existence is one long day of sunshine? Oh, why ask! you know I can never repay you for the happiness of my life."

"Rather can I never repay you," said Vaughan, looking down into her eyes, "for the faith that made you brave calumny and opposition, and cling to my side despite all. I was heart-sick of the world, and you called me back to life. I was weary of the fools who misjudged me, and I let them think me what they might."

"Ah, how happy you make me!" cried Nina. "I should have been little worthy of your love if I had suffered slander to warp me against you, or if any revelations you cared enough for me to make of your past life, had parted us:

> Love is not love
>
> That alters where it alteration finds,
>
> Or bends with the remover to remove.

There, monsieur!" she said, throwing her arms round him with a laugh, while happy tears stood in her eyes—"there is a grand quotation for you. Mind and take care, Ernest, that you never realise the Ruskinstone predictions, and make me repent having caught and caged such a terrible thing as a hunted Paris Lion!"

SIR GALAHAD'S RAID

AN ADVENTURE ON THE SWEET WATERS

For the punishment of my sins may the gods never again send me to Pera! That I might have plenty on my shoulders I am frankly willing to concede; all I protest is, that when one submissively acknowledges the justice of ones future terminating in Tophet, it comes a little hard to get purgatory in this world into the bargain. Purgatory lies *perdu* for one all over the earth. I have had fifty times more than my share already, and the gout still remains an untried experience, a Gehenna grimly waiting to avenge every morsel of white truffle and every glass of comet claret with which I innocently solace my frail mortality. Purgatory!—I have been chained in it fifty times; *et vous*?

When you rush to a Chancellérie, with the English Arms gorgeous above its doorway, on the spur of a frightfully mysterious and autocratic telegram, that makes it life or death to catch the train for England in ten minutes, and have time enough to smoke about two dozen very big cheroots, cooling your heels in the bureau, and then hear (when properly tortured into the due amount of frantic agony for the intelligence to be fully appreciated) that his Excellency is gone snipe-shooting to — —, and that the First Secretary is in his bath, and has given orders not to be disturbed; your informant languidly pricking his cigar with his toothpick, and politely intimating, by his eyebrows, that you and your necessities may go to the deuce— what's *that*? When you are doing the sanitary at Weedon, by some hideous conjunction of evil destinies, in the very Ducal week itself, and thinking of the rush with which Tom Alcroft will land the filly, or the close finish with which Fordham will get the cup, while you are not there to see, are sorely tempted to realize the Parisian vision of Anglo suicide, and load the apple-trees with suspended human fruit;—what's *that*? When, having got leave, and established yourself in cosy hunting-quarters, with some cattle not to be beat in stay, blood, and pace, close to a killing pack that never score a blank day, there falls a bitter, black frost, locking the country up in iron bonds, and making every bit of ridge and furrow like a sheet of glass—what's *that*?

Bah! I could go on ad infinitum, and cite "circles of purgatory" in which mortal man is doomed to pass his time, beside which Dante's Caïna, Antenora, and Ptolomea sink into insignificance. But of all Purgatories, chiefest in my memory, is——Pera. Pera in the old Crimean time—Pera the "beautiful suburb" of fond "fiction"—Pera, with the dirt, the fleas, the murders, the mosquitoes, the crooked streets, the lying Greeks, the stench, the hubbub, the dulness, and the everlasting "Bono Johnny."

"Call a dog Hervey, and I shall love him," said Johnson, so dear was his friend to him:—"call a dog Johnny, and I shall kick him," so abominable grew that word in the eternal Turkish jabber! Tell me, O prettiest, softest-voiced, most beguiling, feminine Æothen, in as romantic periods as you will, of bird-like feluccas darting over the Bosphorus, of curled caïques gliding through fragrant water-weeds; of Arabian Nights reproduced, when up through the darkness peals the roll of the drums calling the Faithful to prayers; of the nights of Ramadan, with the starry clusters of light gleaming all down Stamboul, and flashing, firefly-like, through the dark citron groves;—tell me of it as you will, I don't care; you may think me a Goth, *ce m'est bien égal*, and *you* were not in cavalry quarters at Pera. I wasn't exacting; I did not mind having ants in my jam, nor centipedes in my boots, nor a shirt in six months, nor bacon for a luxury that strongly resembled an old file rusted by sea-water, nor any little trifle of that sort up in the front; all that is in the fortune of war: but I confess that Pera put me fairly out of patience, specially when a certain trusty friend of mine, who has no earthly fault, that I wot of, except that of perpetually looking at life through a Claude glass (which is the most aggravating opticism to a dispassionate and unblinded mind that the world holds), *would* poetize upon it, or at least on the East in general, which came pretty much to the same thing.

The sun poured down on me till (conscience, probably) I remembered the scriptural threat to the wicked, "their brains shall boil in their skulls like pots;"—Sir Galahad, as I will call him, would murmur to himself, with his cheroot in his teeth, Manfred's *salut* to the sun, looking as lovingly at it as any eagle. Mosquitoes reduced me to the very borders of madness,—Sir Galahad would placidly remark, how Buckland would revel here in all those gorgeous beetles. A Greek told crackers till I had to double-thong him like a puppy,—Sir Galahad would shout to me to let the fellow alone, he looked so deuced picturesque, he must have him for a study. I made myself wretched in a ticklish caïque, the size of a cockle-shell, where, when one was going full harness to the Great Effendi's, it was a moral impossibility to be doubled without one's sash swinging into the water, one's sword sticking over the side, and the liveliest sensation of cramp pervading one's body,—Sir Galahad, blandly indifferent, would discourse, with superb Ruskin obscurity, of "tone," and "coloring," and "harmonized light," while he looked down the Golden Horn, for he was a little Art-mad, and painted so well that if he had been a professional, the hanging committee would have shut him out to a certainty.

Now he was a good fellow, a *beau sabreur*, who had fetched some superb back strokes in the battery at Balaclava, who could send a line spinning, and land his horse in a gentleman riders' race, and pot the big game, and lead the first flight over Northamptonshire doubles at home, as well as a man wants to do; but I put it to any dispassionate person, whether this persistent poetism of his, flying in the face of facts and of fleas, was not enough to make anybody swear in that mosquito-purgatorio of Pera?

Sir Galahad was a capital fellow, and the men would have gone after him to the death; the fair, frank, handsome face, a little womanish perhaps, was very pleasant to look at, and he got the Victoria not long ago for a deed that would suit Arthur's Table; but in Pera, I avow, he made me swear hard, and if he would just have set his heel on his Claude glass, cursed the Turks, and growled refreshingly, I should have loved him better. He was philosophic and he was poetic; and the combination of temperaments lifted him in a mortifying altitude above ordinary humanity, that was baked, broiled, grumbling, savage, bitten, fleeced, and holding its own against miserable rats, Greeks, and Bono Johnnies, with an Aristides thieving its last shirt, and a Pisistratus getting drunk at its case-bottle! That sublime serenity of his in Pera ended in making me unholy and ungenerous; if he would but have sworn once at the confounded country, I should have borne it, but he never did, and I longed to see him out of temper, I pined and thirsted to get him disenchanted. "*Tout vient a point, à qui sait attendre*," they say; a motto, by the way, that might be written over the Horse Guards for the comfort of gloomy souls, when, in the words of the Psalmist, "Promotion cometh neither from the south, nor from the east, nor from the west"—by which lament one might conclude David of Israel to have been a sufferer by the Purchase-system!

"Delicious!" said Sir Galahad, sending a whiff of Turkish tobacco into the air one morning after exercise, when he and I, having ridden out a good many miles along the Sweet Waters, turned the horses loose, bought some grapes and figs of an old Turk, dispossessed him of his bit of cocoa-matting, and flung ourselves under a plane-tree. And the fellow looked round him through his race-glass at the cypress woods, the mosques and minarets, the almond thickets, the "soft creamy distance," as he called it in his *argot d'atelier*, and the Greek fishermen near, drawing up a net full of silvery prismatic fishes, with a relish absolutely exasperating. Exasperating—when the sun was broiling one's brain through the linen, and there wasn't a drop of Bass or soda and B to be got for love or money, and one thought thirstily of days at home in England, with the birds whirring up from the stubble in the cool morning, and the cold punch uncorked for luncheon, under the home woods fringing the open.

"One wants Hunt to catch that bit of color," murmured Sir Galahad, luxuriously eying a mutilated Janissary's tomb covered with scarlet creepers.

"Hunt be hanged!" said I (meaning no disrespect to that eminent Pre-Raphaelite, whose "Light of the World" I took at first sight to be a policeman going his night rounds, and come out in his shirt by mistake; by the way, it is a droll idea to symbolize the "light of the world" by a watchman with a dark lantern, *lux in tenebras* with a vengeance!). "Give me the sweet shady side of Pall Mall, and the devil may take the Sweet Waters. What's the Feast of Bairam beside the Derby-day, or your confounded coloring beside a well-done cutlet? What's lemonade by Brighton Tipper, and a veiled bundle by a pretty blonde, and an eternity of Stamboul by an hour of Piccadilly?"

Sir Galahad smiled superior, and shied a date at me.

"Goth! can't you be content to feed like the Patriarchs and live an idyl?"

"No! I'd rather feed like a Parisian and live an idler! Eat grapes if you choose; I agree with Brillat-Savarin, and don't like my wine in pills."

"My good fellow, you're all prose."

"And you're all poetry. You're as bad as that pretty little commissariat girl who lisped me to death last night at the Embassy with platitudes of bosh about the 'poetry of marriage.'"

"The deuce!" said Sir Galahad, with a whistle, "that must be like most other poetry nowadays—uncommon dull prose, sliced up in uneven lengths! Didn't you tell her so?"

"Couldn't; I should have pulled the string for a shower-bath of sentiment! When a woman's bolted on romance you only make the pace worse if you gall her with the curb of common sense. When romance is in, reason's out,—excuse the personality!"

He didn't hear me; he was up like a retriever who scents a wild duck or a water-rat among the sedges, for sweeping near us with soft gliding motion, as pretty as a toy and as graceful as a swan, came a caïque, with the wife of a Pacha of at least a hundred tails in it, to judge by the costliness of her exquisite attire. Now, women were not rare, but then they were always veiled, which is like giving a man a nugget he mustn't take out of the quartz, a case of champagne he mustn't undo, a cover-side he is never to beat, a trout stream in which he must never fling a fly; and Sir Galahad, whose loves were not, I admit, quite so saintly as Arthur's code exacted, lost his head in a second as the caïque drifted past us, and, raising herself on her cushions, the Leilah Duda, or Salya within it, glanced toward the myrtle screen that half hid us, with the divinest antelope eyes in the world, and letting the silver gauze folds of her veil float half aside, showed us the beautiful warm bloom, the proud lips, and the chestnut tresses braided with pearls and threaded with gold, of your genuine Circassian beauty. Shade of Don Juan! what a face it was!

A yataghan might have been at his throat, a bowstring at his neck, eunuchs might have slaughtered, and pachas have impaled him, Galahad would have seen more of that loveliness: headlong he plunged down the slope, crushing through the almond thickets and scattering the green tree-frogs right and left; the caïque was just rounding past as he reached the water's edge, and the beauty's veil was drawn in terror of her guard. But as the little cockle-shell, pretty and ticklish as a nautilus, was moored to a broad flight of marble stairs, the Circassian turned her head towards the place where the Unbeliever stood in the sunlight—her eyes were left her, and with them women speak in a universal tongue. Then the green lattice gate shut, the white impenetrable walls hid her from sight, and Sir Galahad stood looking down the Sweet Waters in a sort of beatific vision, in love for the 1360th time in his life. And certainly he had never been in love with better reason; for is there anything on earth so divine as your antelope-eyed and gold-haired Circassian?

"I shall be inside those walls or know the reason why," said he, whom two gazelle eyes had fired and captured, there by the side of the sunny Sweet Waters, where the lazy air was full of syringa and rose odors, and there was no sound but the indolent beating of the tired oars on the ripples.

"Which reason you will rapidly find," I suggested, "in a knock on the head from the Faithful!"

"Well! a very picturesque way of coming to grief; to go off the scene in the sick-wards, from raki and fruit, would be commonplace and humiliating, but to die in a serail, stabbed through and through by green-eyed jealousy, would be piquant and refreshing to the last degree; do you really think there's a chance of it?" said Galahad, rather anxiously—the eager wistful anxiety of a man who, athirst for the forest, hears of the rumored slot of an outlying deer—while he shouted the Greek fishermen to him, and learned after sore travail through a slough of mixed Italian, Turkish, and Albanian, that the white palace, with its green lattice and its hanging gardens, belonged to a rich merchant of Constantinople, and that this veiled angel was the favorite of his harem, Leilah Derran, a recent purchase in Circassia, and the queen of the Anderùn.

"The old rascal!" swore Galahad, in his wrath, which was not, however, I think, caused by any particular Christian disgust at polygamy. "A fat old sinner, I'll be bound, who sits on his divan puffing his chibouque and stuffing his sweetmeats, as yellow as Beppo, and as round as a ball. Bah! what pearls before swine! It's enough to make a saint swear. Those heavenly eyes!..." And Galahad went into a somewhat earthly reverie, colored with a thirsty jealousy of the purchaser and the possessor of this Circassian gazelle, as he rode reluctantly back towards Pera.

The Circassian was in his head, and did not get out again. He let himself be bewitched by that lovely face which had flashed on him for a second, and began to feel himself as aggrieved by that innocent and unoffending Turkish lord of hers, as if the unlucky gentleman had stolen his own property! The antelope eyes had looked softly and hauntingly sad, moreover: I demonstrated to him that it was nothing more than the way that the eyelashes drooped, but nobody in love (very few people out of it) have any taste for logic; he was simply disgusted with my realism, and saw an instant vision for himself of this loveliest of slaves, captive in a bazaar and sold into the splendid bondage of the harem as into an inevitable fate, mournful in her royalty as a nightingale in a cage stifled with roses, and as little able to escape as the bird. A vision which intoxicated and enraptured Sir Galahad, who, in the teeth of every abomination of Pera, had been content to see only what he wished to see, and had maintained that the execrable East, to make it the East of Hafiz and all the poets, only wanted—available Haidees!

"Hang it! I think it's nothing *but* Hades," said an Aide, overhearing that statement one night, as we stumbled out of a half-café, half-gambling-booth pandemonium into the crooked, narrow, pitch-dark street, where dogs were snarling over offal, jackals screaming, Turkish bands shrieking, cannon booming out the hour of prayer, women yelling alarms of fire, a Zouave was spitting a Greek by way of practice, and an Irishman had just potted a Dalmatian, in as brawling, rowing, pestiferous, unodorous an earthly Gehenna as men ever succeeded in making.

Sir Galahad was the least vain of mortals; nevertheless, being as well-beloved by the "maidens and young widows," for his fair handsome face, as Harold the Gold-haired, he would have been more than mortal if he had not been tolerably confident of "killing," and luxuriously practised in that pleasant pastime. That if he could once get the antelope eyes to look at him, they would look lovingly before long, he was in comfortable security; but how to get into a presence, which it was death for an unbeliever and a male creature to approach, was a knottier question, and the difficulty absorbed him. There were several rather telling Englishwomen out there, with whom he had flirted *faute de mieux*, at the cavalry balls we managed to get up in Pera, at the Embassy costume-ball, on board yacht-decks in the harbor, and in picnics to Therapia or the Monastery. But they became as flavorless as twice-told tales, and twice-warmed entremets, beside the new piquance, the delicious loveliness, the divine difficulty of this captive Circassian. That he had no more earthly business to covet her than he had to covet the unlucky Turkish trader's lumps of lapis-lazuli and agate, never occurred to him; the stones didn't tempt him, you see, but the beauty did. That those rich, soft, unrivalled Eastern charms, "merely born to bloom and drop," should be caged from the world and only rejoice the eyes of a fat old opium-soddened Stamboul merchant, seemed a downright reversal of all the laws of nature, a tampering with the balance of just apportionment that clamored for redress; but, like most other crying injustice, the remedy was hard to compass.

Day after day he rode down to the same place on the Sweet Waters on the chance of the caïque's passing; and, sure enough, the caïque did pass nine times out of ten, and, when opportunity served for such a hideous Oriental crime not to be too perilous, the silver gauze floated aside unveiling a face as fair as the morning, or, when that was impossible, the eyes turned on him shyly and sadly in their lustrous appeal, as though mutely bewailing such cruel captivity. Those eyes said as plainly as language could speak that the lovely Favorite plaintively resisted her bondage, and thought the Frank with his long fair beard, and his six feet of height, little short of an angel of light, though he might be an infidel.

Given—hot languid days, nothing to do, sultry air heavy with orange and rose odors, and those "silent passages," repeating themselves every time that Leilah Derran's caïque glided past the myrtle screen, where her Giaour lay *perdu*, the result is conjectural: though they had never spoken a word, they had both fallen in love. Voiceless *amourettes* have their advantages:— when a woman speaks, how often she snaps her spell! For instance, when the lips are divine but the utterance is slangy, when the mouth is adorably rosebud but what it says is most horrible horsy!

A tender pity, too, gave its spur to his passion; he saw that, all Queen of the Serail though she might be, this fettered gazelle was not happy in her rose-chains, and to Galahad, who had a wonderful twist of the knight-errant and lived decidedly some eight centuries too late, no wiliest temptation would have been so fatal as this.

He swore to get inside those white inexorable walls, and he kept his oath: one morning the latticed door stood ajar, with the pomegranates and the citrons nodding through the opening; he flung prudence to the winds and peril to the devil, and entered the forbidden ground where it was death for any man, save the fat Omar himself, to be found. The fountains were falling into marble basins, the sun was tempered by the screen of leaves, the lories and humming-birds were flying among the trumpet-flowers, altogether a most poetic and pleasant place for an erratic adventure; more so still when, as he went farther, he saw reclining alone by the mosaic edge of a fountain his lovely Circassian unveiled. With a cry of terror she sprang to her feet, graceful as a startled antelope, and casting the silver shroud about her head, would have fled; but the scream was not loud enough to give the alarm—perhaps she attuned it so—and flight he prevented. Such Turkish as he had he poured out in passionate eloquence, his love declaration only made the more piquant by the knowledge that in a trice the gardens might swarm with the Mussulman's guards and a scimitar smite his head into the fountain. But the danger he disdained, *la belle* Leilah remembered; rebuke him she did not, nor yet call her eunuchs to rid her of this terrible Giaour, but the antelope eyes filled with piteous tears and she prayed him begone— if he were seen here, in the gardens of the women, it were his death, it were hers! Her terror at the infidel was outweighed by her fear for his peril; how handsome he was with his blue eyes and fair locks, after the bald, black-browed, yellow, obese little Omar!

"Let me see again the face that is the light of my soul and I will obey thee; thou shalt do with thy slave as thou wilt!" whispered Galahad in the most impassioned and poetical Turkish he could muster, thinking the style of Hafiz understood better here than the style of Belgravia, while the almond-eyed Leilah trembled like a netted bird under his look and his touch, conscious, pretty creature, that were it once known that a Giaour had looked on her, poison in her coffee, or a sullen plunge by night into the Bosphorus, would expiate the insult to the honor of Omar, a master whom she piteously hated. She let her veil float aside, nevertheless, blushing like a sea-shell under the shame of an unbeliever's gaze—a genuine blush that is banished from Europe—his eyes rested on the lovely youth of her face, his cheek brushed the

Loose train of her amber dropping hair,

his lips met her own; then, with a startled stifled cry, his coy gazelle sprang away, lost in the aisles of the roses, and Galahad quitted the dangerous precincts, in safety so far, not quite clear whether he had been drinking or dreaming, and of conviction that Pera had changed into Paradise. For he was in love with two things at once, a romance and a woman; and an anchorite would fairly have lost his head after the divine dawn of beauty in Leilah Derran.

The morrow, of course, found him at the same place, at the same hour, hoping for a similar fortune, but the lattice door was shut, and defied all force; he was just about to try scaling the high slippery walls by the fibres of a clinging fig-tree, when a negress, the sole living thing in sight, beckoned him, a hideous Abyssinian enough for a messenger of Eros; a grinning good-natured black, who had been bought in the same bazaar and of the same owner as the lovely Circassian, to whose service she was sworn. She told him by scraps of Turkish, and signs, that Leilah had bidden her watch for and warn him, that it were as much as both their lives were worth for him to be seen again in the women's gardens, or anywhere near her presence; that the merchant Omar was a monster of jealousy, and that the rest of the harem, jealous of her supremacy and of the unusual liberty her ascendancy procured her, would love nothing so well as to compass her destruction. Further meeting with her infidel lover she pronounced impossible, unless he would see her consigned to the Bosphorus; an ice avalanche of intelligence, which, falling on the tropical Eden of his passion, had the effect, as it was probably meant that it should have, of drowning the lingering remnant of prudence and sanity that had remained to him after his lips had once touched the exquisite Eastern's.

Under the circumstances the negress was his sole hope and chance; he pressed her into his service and made her Mercury and mediatrix in one. She took his messages, sent in the only alphabet the pretty gazelle could read, i. e. flowers, plotted against her owner with true Eastern finesse, wrought on the Circassian's tenderness for the Giaour, and her terrified hatred of her grim lord Omar, and threw herself into the intrigue with the avidity of all womanhood, be it black or be it white, for anything on the face of the earth that has the charm of being forbidden. The affair was admirably *en train*, and Galahad was profoundly happy; he was deliciously in love,—a pleasant spice as difficult to find in its full flavor as it is to bag a sand grouse;—and had an adventure to amuse him that might very likely cost him his head, and might fairly claim to rise into the poetic. The only reward he received (or ever got, for that matter) for the Balaclava brush, where he cut down three gunners, and had a ball put in his hip, had been a cavil raised by a critic, not there, of doubt whether he had ever ridden inside the lines at all; but his Circassian would have recompensed him at once for a score of years of Chersonnesus campaigning, and unprofessional chroniclers: he was perfectly happy, and his soft, careless, *couleur de rose* enjoyment of the paradise was aggravating to behold,—when one was in Pera, and the heat broiled alive every mortal thing that wasn't a negro, and Bass was limited, and there were no Dailies, and one thought even lovingly and regretfully of the old "beastly shells," that had at least this merit, that they scattered bores when they burst!

"Old fellow!—want something to do?" he asked me one day. I nodded, being silent and savage from having had to dance attendance on the Sultan at an Embassy reception. Peace to his *manes* now! but I know I wished him heartily in Eblis at that time.

"Come with me to-night then, if you don't mind a probability of being potted by a True Believer," went on Leilah Derran's lover, going into some golden water Soyer had sent me.

"For the big game? Like it of all things; but you know I'm tied by the leg here."

Galahad laughed. "Oh, I only want you an hour or two. I've got six days' leave for the pigs and the deer: but the hills won't see much of me, I'm going to make a raid in the rose-gardens. It may be hot work, so I thought you would like it."

Of course I did, and asked the programme which Sir Galahad, as lucidly as a man utterly in love can tell anything, unfolded to me. Fortune favored him; it was the night of the Feast of Bairam, when all the world of Turkey lights its lamps and turns out; he had got leave under pretext of a shooting trip into Roumelia, but the game he was intent on was the captive Circassian, who in the confusion and *tintamarre* attendant on Bairam, was to escape to him by the rose-gardens, and being carried off as swiftly as Syrian stallions could take them, would be borne away by her infidel lover on board a yacht, belonging to a man whom he knew who was cruising in the Bosphorus, which would steam them away down the Dardanelles before the Turk had a chance of getting in chase. Nothing could be better planned for everybody but the luckless Mussulman who was to be robbed,—and the whole thing had a fine flavor about it of dash and difficulty, of piquance and poetry, of Mediæval errantry and Oriental coloring, that put Leilah's Giaour most deliciously in his element, setting apart the treasure that he would carry off in that rich, soft, antelope-eyed, bright-haired Circassian loveliness which made all the dreams in Lalla Rookh and Don Juan look pale.

So his raid was planned, and I agreed to go with him to cover the rear in case of pursuit, which was likely enough to be hot and sharp, for the Moslems, for all their apathy, lack the philosophic gratitude which your British husband usually exhibits towards his despoiler—but then, to be sure, an Englishman can't make a fresh purchase unless he's first robbed of the old! Night came; and the nights, I am forced to admit, have a witching charm of their own in the East, that the West never knows. The Commander of the Faithful went to prayer, with the roar of cannon and the roll of drums pealing down the Golden Horn, and along the cypress-clad valleys. The mosques and minarets, starred and circled with a myriad of lamps, gleamed through the dark foliage, and were mirrored in the silvery sheet of the waves. The caïques, as they swept along, left tracks of light in the phosphor-lit waves, and while the chant of the Muezzin rang through the air, the children of Allah, from one end of the Bosphorus to the other, held festival on the most holy eve of Bairam. A splendid night for a lyric of Swinburne's!—a superb scene for an amorous adventure! And as we mingled amongst the crowds of the Faithful, swarming with their painted lanterns, their wild music, their gorgeous colors, their booming guns, in street and caïque, on land and sea, Sir Galahad, though an infidel, had certainly entered the Seventh Heaven. He had never been more intensely in love in his life; and, if the fates should decree that the dogs of Islam should slay him at her feet, in the sanctuary of her rose-paradise, he was ready to say in his pet poet's words, with the last breath of his lips,

It was ordained to be so, sweet and best

Comes now beneath thine eyes and on thy breast.

Still kiss me! Care not for the cowards! Care

Only to put aside thy beauteous hair

My blood will hurt!

In the night of the feast all the world was astir, Franks and Moslems, believers and unbelievers, and we made our way through the press unwatched to where Omar's house was illumined, the cressets, and wreaths, and stars of light sparkling through the black foliage. Under the walls, hidden by a group of planes, we fastened the stallions in readiness, and Galahad, at the latticed door, gave the signal word, "Kef," low whispered. The door unclosed, and, true to her tryst, in the silvery Bosphorus moonlight, crouching in terror and shame, was the veiled and trembling Circassian.

But not in peace was her capture decreed to be made; scarce had the door flown open, when the shrill yell of "Allah hu! Allah hu!" rung through the air; and from the dark aisles of the gardens poured Mussulmans, slaves, and eunuchs, the Turk with a shoal at his back, giving the alarm with hideous bellowings, while their drawn scimitars flashed in the white starlight, and their cries filled the air with their din. "Make off, while I hold the gate!" I shouted to Galahad, who, catching Leilah Derran in his arms before the Moslems could be nigh us, held her close with one hand, while with his right he levelled his revolver, as I did, and backed—facing the Turks. At sight of the lean shining barrels, the Moslems paused in their rush for a second—only a second; the next, shouting to Allah till the minarets gave back the echo, they sprang at us, their curled naked yataghans whirling above their heads, their jetty eyeballs flaming like tigers' on the spring. Our days looked numbered;—I gave them the contents of one barrel, and in the moment's check we gained the outside of the gardens; the swarm rushed after us, their shots flying wide, and whistling with a shrill hiss harmlessly past; we reserved further fire, not wishing to kill, if we could manage to cut our way through without bloodshed, and backed to the plane-trees, where the horses were waiting. There was a moment's blind but breathless struggle, swift and indistinct to remembrance, as a flash of lightning; the Turks swarmed around us, while we beat them off, and hurled them asunder somehow. Omar sprang like a rattlesnake on to his spoiler, his yataghan circling viciously in the air, to crash down upon Galahad's skull, who was encumbered by the clinging embrace of his stolen Circassian. I straightened my left arm with a remnant of "science" that savored more of old Cambridge than of Crimean custom; the Moslem went down like an ox, and keeping the yelling pack at bay with the levelled death-dealer, I threw myself into saddle just as Galahad flung himself on his stallion, and the Syrians, fleet as Arab breeding could make them, tore down the beach in the rich Eastern night, while the balls shrieked through the air past our ears, and the shouts of our laughter, with the salute of a ringing English cheer in victorious farewell, answered the howls of our distant and baffled pursuers.

Sir Galahad's Raid was a triumph!

On we went through the hot fragrant air, through the silvery moonlight, through the deep shade of cypress and pine woods; on we went through gorge, and ravine, and defile, through stretches of sweet wild lavender, of shining sands, of trampled rose-fields, with the phosphor-lit sea gleaming beside us, and the Islam Feast of Bairam left far distant behind. On and on—while the glorious night itself was elixir, and one shouted to the starry silence Robert Browning's grand challenge—

How good is man's life, the mere living! how fit to employ

All the heart, and the soul, and the senses, for ever in joy!

That ride was superb!

We never drew rein till some ten miles farther on, where we saw against the clear skies the dark outline of the yacht with a blue light burning at her mast-head, the signal selected; then Galahad checked the good Syrian, who had proved pace as fleet as the "wild pigeon blue" is ever vouched in the desert, and bent over his prize who, through that long ride, had been held close to his breast, with her arms wound about him, and the beautiful veiled face bowed on his heart. The moon was bright as day, and he stooped his head to uplift the envious veil, and see the radiant beauty that never again would be shrouded, and to meet once more the lips which his own had touched before but in one single caress; he bowed his head, and I thought that my disinterested ungrudging friendship made the friendships of antiquity look small; when——an oath that chilled my blood rang through the night and over the seas, startling the echoes from rock and hill; the veiled captive reeled from the saddle with a wailing scream, hurled to earth by the impetus with which his arms loosed her from him; and away into the night, without word or sign, plunging headlong down the dark defile, riding as men may ride from a field that reeks with death, far out of sight into the heart of the black dank woods, his Syrian bore Sir Galahad. And lo! in the white moonlight, against the luminous sea, slowly there rose before me, unveiled and confessed—The Negress!

The history of that night we never learnt. Whether Leilah Derran herself played the cruel trick on her Giaour lover (but this *he* always scouted), whether Omar himself was a man of grim humor, whether the Abyssinian, having betrayed her mistress, was used as a decoy-bird, dressed like the Circassian, to lure the infidels into the rose-gardens where the Faithful intended to dispatch them hastily to Eblis—no one knows. We could never find out. The negress escaped me before my surprise let me stay her, and the fray made the place too hot for close investigation. Nor do I know where Galahad tore in that wild night-ride, whose spur was the first maddened pain and rage of shame that his life had tasted. I never heard where he spent the six days of his absence; but when he joined us again, six weeks in the sick-wards would not have altered him more; all he said to me was one piteous phrase—"For God's sake don't tell the fellows!"—and I never did; I liked him well enough not to make chaff of him. Unholily had I thirsted to see him disenchanted, ungenerously had I pined to see him goaded out of temper: I had my wish, and I don't think I enjoyed it. I saw him at last in passion that I had much to do to tame down from a deadly vengeance that would have rung through the Allied Armies; and I saw him loathe the East, curse romance, burn all the poets with Hafiz at their head, and shun a woman's beauty like the pestilence. To this day I believe that the image of Leilah Derran haunts his memory, and that a certain remorse consumes him for his lost gazelle, whom *he* always thought paid penalty for their love under the silent waves of the Bosphorus, with those lost ones whose souls, according to the faith of Stamboul, flit ceaselessly above its waters, in the guise of its white-winged unrestful sea-gulls. He is far enough away just now—in which of the death-pots where we are simmering and fritting away in little wretched driblets men and money that would have sufficed Cæsar or Scipio to conquer an Empire, matters not to his story. When he reads this, he will remember the bitterest night of his life, and the fiasco that ended Sir Galahad's Raid!

'REDEEMED'

AN EPISODE WITH THE CONFEDERATE HORSE

Bertie Winton had got the Gold Vase.

The Sovereign, one of the best horses that ever had a dash of the Godolphin blood in him, had led the first flight over the ridge-and-furrow, cleared the fences, trying as the shire-thorn could make them, been lifted over the stiffest doubles and croppers, passed the turning-flags, and been landed at the straight run-in with the stay and pace for which his breed was famous, enrapturing the fancy, who had piled capfuls of money on him, and getting the Soldiers' Blue Riband from the Guards, who had stood crackers on little Benyon's mount—Ben, who is as pretty as a girl, with his *petites mains blanches*, riding like any professional.

Now, I take it—and I suppose there are none who will disagree with me—that there are few things pleasanter in this life than to stand, in the crisp winter's morning, winner of the Grand Military, having got the Gold Vase for the old corps against the best mounts in the Service.

Life must look worth having to you, when you have come over those black, barren pastures and rugged ploughed lands, where the field floundered helplessly in grief, with Brixworth brook yawning gaunt and wide beneath you, and the fresh cold north wind blowing full in your teeth, and have ridden in at the distance alone, while the air is rent by the echoing shouts of the surging crowd, and the best riding-men are left "nowhere" behind. Life must look pleasant to you, if it had been black as thunder the night before. Nevertheless, where Bertie Winton sat, having brought the Sovereign in, winner of the G. M., with that superb bay's head a little drooped, and his flanks steaming, but scarce a hair turned, while the men who had won pots of money on him crowded round in hot congratulation, and he drank down some Curaçoa punch out of a pocket-pistol, with his habitual soft, low, languid laugh, he had that in his thoughts which took the flavor out of the Curaçoa, and made the sunny, cheery winter's day look very dull and gray to him. For Bertie, sitting there while the cheers reeled round him like mad, with a singularly handsome, reckless face, long tawny moustaches, tired blue eyes, and a splendid length and strength of limb, knew that this was the last day of the old times for him, and that he had sailed terribly near the wind of—dishonor.

He had been brought to *envisager* his position a little of late, and had seen that it was very bad indeed—as bad as it could be. He had run through all his own fortune from his mother, a good one enough, and owed almost as much again in bills and one way and another. He had lost heavily on the turf, gamed deeply, travelled with the most expensive adventuresses of their day, startled town with all its worst crim. cons.; had every vice under heaven, save that he drank not at all; and now, having shot a Russian prince at Baden the August before, about Lillah Lis, had received on the night just passed, from the Horse Guards, a hint, which was a command, that his absence was requested from her Majesty's Service—a mandate which, politely though inexorably couched, would have taken a more forcible and public form but for the respect in which his father, old Lion Winton, as was called, was held by the Army and the authorities. And Bertie, who for five-and-thirty years had never thought at all, except on things that pleasured him, and such bagatelles as *barrière* duels abroad, delicately-spiced intrigues, bills easily renewed, the *cru* of wines, and the siege of women, found himself pulled up with a rush, and face to face with nothing less than ruin.

"I'm up a tree, Melcombe," he said to a man of his own corps that day as he finished a great cheroot before mounting.

"Badly?"

"Well, yes. It'll be smash this time, I suppose."

"Bother! That's hard lines."

"It's rather a bore," he answered, with a little yawn, as he got into the saddle; and that was all he ever said then or afterwards on the matter; but he rode the Sovereign superbly over the barren wintry grass-land, and landed him winner of the Blue Riband for all that, though Black Care, for the first time in his life, rode behind him and weighted the race.

Poor Bertie! nobody would have believed him if he had said so, but he had been honestly and truly thinking, for some brief time past, whether it would not be possible and worth while for him to shake himself free of this life, of which he was growing heartily tired, and make a name for himself in the world in some other fashion than by winging Russians, importing new dancers, taking French women to the Bads, scandalizing society, and beggaring himself. He had begun to wonder whether it was not yet, after all, too late, and whether if——when down had come the request from the

Horse Guards for him to sell out, and the rush of all his creditors upon him, and away forever went all his stray shapeless fancies of a possible better future. And—consolation or aggravation, whichever it be—he knew that he had no one, save himself, to thank for it; for no man ever had a more brilliant start in the race of life than he, and none need have made better running over the course, had he only kept straight or put on the curb as he went down-hill. Poor Bertie! you must have known many such lives, or I can't tell where your own has been spent; lives which began so brilliantly that none could rival them, and which ended—God help them!—so miserably and so pitifully that you do not think of them without a shudder still?

Poor Bertie!—a man of a sweeter temper, a more generous nature, a more lavish kindliness, never lived. He had the most versatile talents and the gentlest manners in the world; and yet here he was, having fairly come to ruin, and very nearly to disgrace.

It was little wonder that his father, looking at him and thinking of all he might have been, and all he might have done, was lashed into a terrible bitterness of passionate grief, and hurled words at him of a deadly wrath, in the morning that followed on the Grand Military. Fiery as his comrades the Napiers, of a stern code as a soldier, and a lofty honor as a man, haughty in pride and swift to passion, old Sir Lionel was stung to the quick by his son's fall, and would have sooner, by a thousand-fold, have followed him to his grave, than have seen him live to endure that tacit dismissal from the service of the country—the deepest shame, in his sight, that could have touched his race.

"I knew you were lost to morality, but I did not know till now that you were lost to honor!" said the old Lion, with such a storm of passion in him that his words swept out, acrid and unchosen, in a very whirlwind. "I knew you had vices, I knew you had follies, I knew you wasted your substance with debtors and gamblers like yourself, on courtesans and gaming-tables, in Parisian enormities, and vaunted libertinage, but I did not think that you were so utterly a traitor to your blood as to bring disgrace to a name that never was approached by shame until *you* bore it!"

Bertie's face flushed darkly, then he grew very pale. The indolence with which he lay back in an écarte-chair did not alter, however, and he stroked his long moustaches a little with his habitual gentle indifferentism.

"It is all over. Pray do not give it that tremendous earnestness," he said, quietly. "Nothing is ever worth that; and I should prefer it if we kept to the language of gentlemen!"

"The language of gentlemen is *for* gentlemen," retorted the old man, with fiery vehemence. His heart was cut to the core, and all his soul was in revolt against the degradation to his name that came in the train of his heir's ruin. "When a man has forgot that he has been a gentleman, one may be pardoned for forgetting it also! You may have no honor left for your career to shame; *I* have—and, by God, sir, from this hour you are no son of mine. I disown you—I know you no longer! Go and drag out all the rest of a disgraced life in any idleness that you choose. If you were to lie dying at my feet, I would not give you a crust!"

Bertie raised his eyebrows slightly.

"*Soit!* But would it not be possible to intimate this quietly? A scene is such very bad style—always exhausting, too!"

The languid calmness, the soft nonchalance of the tone, were like oil upon flame to the old Lion's heart, lashed to fury and embittered with pain as it was. A heavier oath than print will bear broke from him, with a deadly imprecation, as he paced the library with swift, uneven steps.

"It had been better if your 'style' had been less and your decency and your honor greater! One word more is all you will ever hear from my lips. The title must come to you; that, unhappily, is not in my hands to prevent. It must be yours when I die, if you have not been shot in some gambling brawl or some bagnio abroad before then; but you will remember, not a shilling of money, not a rood of the land are entailed; and, by the heaven above us, every farthing, every acre shall be willed to the young children. *You* are disinherited, sir—disowned for ever—if you died at my feet! Now go, and never let me see your face again."

As he spoke, Bertie rose.

The two men stood opposite to each other—singularly alike in form and feature, in magnificence of stature, and distinction of personal beauty, save that the tawny gold of the old Lion's hair was flaked with white, and that his blue eyes were bright as steel and flashing fire, while the younger man's were very worn. His face, too, was deeply flushed and his lips quivered, while his son's were perfectly serene and impassive as he listened, without a muscle twitching, or even a gleam of anxiety coming into his eyes.

They were of different schools.

Bertie heard to the end; then bowed with a languid grace. "It will be fortunate for Lady Winton's children! Make her my compliments and congratulations. Good-day to you."

Their eyes met steadily once—that was all; then the door of the library closed on him; Bertie knew the worst; he was face to face with beggary. As he crossed the hall, the entrance to the conservatories stood open; he looked through, paused a moment, and then went in. On a low chair, buried among the pyramids of blossom, sat a woman reading, aristocrat to the core, and in the earliest bloom of her youth, for she was scarcely eighteen, beautiful as the morning, with a delicate thorough-bred beauty, dark lustrous eyes, arched pencilled brows, a smile like sunshine, and lips sweet as they were proud. She was Ida Deloraine, a ward of Sir Lionel, and a cousin of his young second wife's.

Bertie went up to her and held out his hand.

"Lady Ida, I am come to wish you good-bye."

She started a little and looked up.

"Good-bye! Are you going to town?"

"Yes—a little farther. Will you give me that camellia by way of *bon voyage*?"

A soft warmth flushed her face for a moment; she hesitated slightly, toying with the snowy blossom; then she gave it him. He had not asked it like a love gage.

He took it, and bowed silently over her hand.

"You will find it very cold," said Lady Ida, with a trifle of embarrassment, nestling herself in her dormeuse in her warm bright nest among the exotics.

He smiled—a very gentle smile.

"Yes, I am frozen out. Adieu!"

He paused a moment, looking at her—that brilliant picture framed in flowers; then, without another word, he bowed again and left her, the woman he had learned too late to love, and had lost by his own folly for ever.

"Frozen out? What could he mean?—there is no frost," thought Lady Ida, left alone in her hot-house warmth among the white and scarlet blossoms, a little startled, a little disappointed, a little excited with some vague apprehension, she could not have told why; while Bertie Winton went on out into the cold gray winter's morning from the old Northamptonshire Hall that would know him no more, with no end so likely for him as that which had just been prophesied—a shot in a gambling hell.

Facilis descensus Averni—and he was at the bottom of the pit. Well, the descent had been very pleasant. Bertie set his teeth tight, and let the waters close over his head and shut him out of sight. He knew that a man who is down has nothing more to do with the world, save to quietly accept—oblivion.

It was a hot summer night in Secessia.

The air was very heavy, no wind stirring the dense woods crowning the sides of the hills or the great fields of trodden maize trampled by the hoofs of cavalry and the tramp of divisions. The yellow corn waved above the earth where the dead had fallen like wheat in harvest-time, and the rice grew but the richer and the faster because it was sown in soil where slaughtered thousands rotted, unsepulchred and unrecorded. The shadows were black from the reared mountain range that rose frowning in the moonlight, and the stars were out in southern brilliancy, shining as calmly and as luminously as though their rays did not fall on graves crammed full with dead, on flaming homesteads, crowded sick-wards, poisonous waters that killed their thousands in deadly rivalry with shot and shell, and vast battalions sleeping on their arms in wheat-fields and by river-swamps, in opposing camps, and before beleaguered cities, where brethren warred with brethren, and Virginia was drenched with blood. There was no sound, save now and then the challenge of some distant picket or the faint note of a trumpet-call, the roar of a torrent among the hills, or the monotonous rise and fall from miles away in the interior, of the negroes' funeral song, "Old Joe,"—more pathetic, somehow, when you catch it at night from the far distance echoing on the silence as you sit over a watch-fire, or ride alone through a ravine, than many a grander requiem.

It was close upon midnight, and all was very still; for they were in the heart of the South, and on the eve of a perilous enterprise, coined by a bold brain and to be carried out by a bold hand.

It was in the narrow neck of a valley, pent up between rocky shelving ridges, anywhere you will between Maryland and Georgia—for he who did this thing would not care to have it too particularly drawn out from the million other deeds of "derring-do" that the mighty story of the Great War has known and buried. Eight hundred Confederate Horse, some of Stuart's Cavalry, had got driven and trapped and caged up in this miserable defile, misled and intercepted; with the dense mass of a Federal army marching on their rear, within them by bare fifteen miles, and the forward route through the crammed defile between the hills, by which alone they could regain Lee's forces, dammed up by a deep, rapid, though not broad river; by a bridge strongly fortified and barricaded; and, on the opposite bank, by some Federal corps a couple of thousand strong, well under cover in rifle-pits and earthworks, thrown up by keen woodsmen and untiring trench-diggers. It was close peril, deadly as any that Secessia had seen, here in the hot still midnight, with the columns of the Federal divisions within them by eight hours' march, stretching out and taking in all the land to the rear in the sweep of their semicircular wings; while in front rose, black and shapeless in the deep gloom of the rocks above, the barricades upon the bridge, behind which two thousand rifles were ready to open fire at the first alarm from the Federal guard. And alone, without the possibility of aid, caged in among the trampled corn and maize that filled the valley, imprisoned between the two Federal forces as in the iron jaws of a trap, the handful of Southern troopers stood, resolute to sell their lives singly one by one, and at a costly price, and perish to a man, rather than fall alive into the hands of their foes.

When the morning broke they would be cut to pieces, as the chaff is cut by the whirl of the steam-wheels. They knew that. Well, they looked at it steadily; it had no terrors for them, the Cavaliers of Old Virginia, so that they died with their face to the front. There was but one chance left for escape; aid there could be none; and that chance was so desperate, that even to them—reckless in daring, living habitually between life and death, and ever careless of the issue—it looked like madness to attempt it. But one among them had urged it on their consideration—urged it with passionate entreaty, pledging his own life for its success; and they had given their adhesion to it, for his name was famous through the Confederacy.

He had won his spurs at Manasses, at Antietam, at Chancellorsville; he had been in every headlong charge with Stuart; he had been renowned for the most dashing Border raids and conspicuous staff service of any soldier in Secessia; he had galloped through a tempest of the enemy's balls, and swept along their lines to reconnoitre, riding back through the storm of shot to Lee, as coolly as though he rode through a summer shower at a review; and his words had weight with men who would have gone after him to the death. He stood now, the only man dismounted, in true Virginia uniform; a rough riding-coat, crossed by an undressed chamois belt, into which his sabre and a brace of revolvers were thrust, a broad Spanish sombrero shading his face, great Hessians reaching above his knee, and a long silken golden-colored beard sweeping to his waist,—a keen reconnoitrer, a daring raider, a superb horseman, and a soldier heart and soul.

When he had laid before them the solitary chance of the perilous enterprise that he had planned, each man of the eight hundred had sought the post of danger for himself; but there he was, inexorable—what he had proposed he alone would execute. The Federals were ignorant of their close vicinity, for their near approach had been unheard, the trodden maize and rice, and the angry foaming of the torrent above, deadening the sound of their horses' hoofs; and the Union-men, satisfied that the "rebels" were entrapped beyond escape, were sleeping securely behind their earth-works, the passage of the river blockaded by their barricade, while the Southerners were drawn up close to the head of the bridge in sections of threes, screened by the intense shadow of the overhanging rocks; shadow darker from the brilliance of the full summer moon that, shining on the enemy's encampment, and on the black boiling waters thundering through the ravine, was shut out from the defile by the leaning pine-covered walls of granite. It was terribly still, that awful silence, only filled with the splashing of the water and the audible beat of the Federal sentinel's measured tramp, as they were drawn up there by the bridge-head; and though they had cast themselves into the desperate effort with the recklessness of men for whom death waited surely on the morrow, it looked a madman's thought, a madman's exploit, to them, as their leader laid aside his sword and pistols, and took up a small barrel of powder, part of some ammunition carried off from some sappers and miners' stores in the raid of the past day, the sight of which had brought to remembrance a stray, half-forgotten story told him in boyhood of one of Soult's Army—the story on which he was about to act now.

"For God's sake, take care!" whispered the man nearest him; and though he was a veteran who had gone through the hottest of the campaign since Bull's Run, his voice shook, and was husky as he spoke.

The other laughed a little—a slight, soft, languid laugh.

"All right, my dear fellow," he whispered back. "There's nothing in it to be alarmed at; a Frenchman did it in the Peninsula, you know. Only if I get shot, or blown up, and the alarm be given, do you take care to bolt over and cut your way through in the first of the rush, that's all."

Then, without more words, he laid himself down at full length with a cord tied round his ankle, that they might know his progress, and the cask of gunpowder, swathed in green cloth, that it should roll without noise along the ground; and, creeping slowly on his way, propelling the barrel with his head, and guiding it by his hands, was lost to their sight in the darkness. By the string, as it uncoiled through their hands, they could tell he was advancing; that was all.

The chances were as a million to one that his life would pay the forfeit for that perilous and daring venture; a single shot and he would be blown into the air a charred and shapeless corpse; one spark on that rolling mass that he pushed before him, and the explosion would hurl him upward in the silent night, mangled, dismembered, blackened, lifeless. But his nerve was not the less cool, nor did his heart beat one throb the quicker, as he crept noiselessly along in the black shade cast by the parapet of the bridge, with the tramp of the guard close above on his ear, and rifles ready to be levelled on him from the covered earthworks if the faintest sound of his approach or the dimmest streak of moonlight on his moving body told the Federals of his presence. He had looked death in the teeth most days through the last five years; it had no power to quicken or slacken a single beat of his pulse as he propelled himself slowly forward along the black, rugged, uneven ground, and on to the passage of the bridge, as coolly, as fearlessly, as he would have crept through the heather and bracken after the slot of a deer on the moor-side at home.

He heard the challenge and the tramp of the sentinel on the opposite bank; he saw the white starlight shine on the barrels of their breech-loaders as they paced to and fro in the stillness, filled with the surge and rush of the rapid waters beneath him. Shrouded in the gloom, he dragged himself onward with slow and painful movement, stretched out on the ground, urging himself forward by the action of his limbs so cautiously that, even had the light been on him, he could scarcely have been seen to move, or been distinguished from the earth on which he lay. Eight hundred lives hung on the coolness of his own; if he were discovered, they were lost. And, without haste, without excitation, he drew himself along under the parapet until he came to the centre of the bridge, placed the barrel close against the barricades, uncovered the head of the cask, and took his way back by the same laborious, tedious way, until he reached the Virginian Troopers gathered together under the shelving rocks.

A deep hoarse murmur rolling down the ranks, the repressed cheer they dared not give aloud, welcomed him and the dauntless daring of his act; man after man pressed forward entreating to take his place, to share his peril; he gave it up to none, and three times more went back again on that deadly journey, until sufficient powder for his purpose was lodged under the Federal fortifications on the bridge. Two hours went by in that slow and terrible passage; then, for the last time, he wound a saucisson round his body serpent-wise, and, with that coil of powder curled around him, took his way once more in the same manner through the hot, dark, heavy night.

And those left behind in the impenetrable gloom, ignorant of his fate, knowing that with every instant the crack of the rifles might roll out on the stillness, and the ball pierce that death-snake twisted round his limbs, and the rocks echo with the roar of the exploding powder, blasting him in the rush of its sheet of fire and stones, sat mute and motionless in their saddles, with a colder chill in their bold blood, and a tighter fear at their proud hearts, than the Cavaliers of the South would have known for their own peril, or than he knew for his.

Another half-hour went by—an eternity in its long drawn-out suspense—then in the darkness under the rocks his form rose up amongst them.

"Ready?"—"Ready."

The low whisper passed all but inaudible from man to man. He took back his sabre and pistols and thrust them into his belt, then stooped, struck a slow match, and laid it to the end of the saucisson, whose mouth he had fastened to the barrels on the bridge, and rapidly as the lightning, flung himself across the horse held for him, and fell into line at the head of the troop.

There was a moment of intense silence while the fire crept up the long stick of the match; then the shrill, hissing, snake-like sound, that none who have once heard ever forget, rushed through the quiet of the night, and with a roar that startled all the sleeping echoes of the hills, the explosion followed; the columns of flame shooting upward to the starlit sky, and casting their crimson lurid light on the black brawling waters, on the rugged towering rocks, on the gnarled trunks of the lofty pines, and on the wild, picturesque forms and the bold, swarthy, Spanish-like faces of the Confederate raiders. With a shock that shook the earth till it rocked and trembled under them, the pillar of smoke and fire towered aloft in the hush of the midnight, blasting and hurling upward, in thunder that pealed back from rock to rock, lifeless bodies, mangled limbs, smouldering timbers, loosened stones, dead men flung heavenward like leaves whirled by the wind, and iron torn up and bent like saplings in a storm, as the mass of the barricades quivered, oscillated, and fell with a mighty crash, while the night was red with the hot glare of the flame, and filled with the deafening din.

The Federals, sleeping under cover of their intrenchments, woke by that concussion as though heaven and earth were meeting, poured out from pit and trench, from salient and parallel, to see their fortifications and their guard blown up, while the skies were lurid with the glow of the burning barricades, and the ravine was filled with the yellow mist of the dense and rolling smoke. Confused, startled, demoralized, they ran together like sheep, vainly rallied by their officers, some few hundred opening an aimless desultory fire from behind their works, the rest rushing hither and thither, in that inextricable intricacy, and nameless panic, which doom the best regiments that were ever under arms, when once they seize them.

"Charge!" shouted the Confederate leader, his voice ringing out clear and sonorous above the infernal tempest of hissing, roaring, shrieking, booming sound.

With that resistless impetus with which they had, over and over again, broken through the granite mass of packed squares and bristling bayonets, the Southerners, raising their wild war-whoop, thundered on to the bridge, which, strongly framed of stone and iron, had withstood the shock, as they had foreseen; and while the fiery glare shone, and the seething flame hissed, on the boiling waters below, swept, full gallop, over the torn limbs, the blackened bodies, the charred wood, the falling timbers, the exploding powder, with which the passage of the bridge was strewn, and charged through the hellish din, the lurid fire, the heavy smoke, at a headlong pace, down into the Federal camp.

A thousand shots fell like hail amongst them, but not a saddle was emptied, not even a trooper was touched; and with their line unbroken, and the challenge of their war-shout pealing out upon the uproar, they rode through the confusion worse confounded, and cutting their way through shot and sabre, through levelled rifles, and through piled earthworks, with their horses breathing fire, and the roar of the opening musketry pealing out upon their rear, dashed on, never drawing rein, down into the darkness of the front defile, and into the freshness of the starry summer night, saved by the leader that they loved, and—FREE!

"Tarnation cheeky thing to do. Guess they ain't wise to rile us that way," said a Federal general from Vermont, as they discussed this exploit of the Eight Hundred at the Federal head-quarters.

"A splendid thing!" said an English visitor to the Northern camp, who had come for a six months' tour to see the war for himself, having been in his own time the friend of Paget and Vivian and Londonderry, the comrade of Picton, of Mackinnon, and of Arthur Wellesley. "A magnificent thing! I remember Bouchard did something the same sort of thing at Amarante, but not half so pluckily, nor against any such odds. Who's the fellow that led the charge? I'd give anything to see him and tell him what I think of it. How Will Napier would have loved him, by George!"

"Who's the d——d rebel, Jed?" said the General, taking his gin-sling.

"Think he's an Englishman. We'd give ten thousand dollars for him, alive or dead: he's fifty devils in one, that I know," responded the Colonel of Artillery, thus appealed to, a gentlemanlike, quiet man, educated at West Point.

"God bless the fellow! I'm glad he's English!" said the English visitor, heartily, forgetting his Federal situation and companions. "Who is he? Perhaps I know the name."

"Should say you would. It's the same as your own—Winton. Bertie Winton, they call him. Maybe he's a relative of yours!"

The blood flushed the Englishman's face hotly for a second; then a stern dark shadow came on it, and his lips set tight.

"I have no knowledge of him," he said, curtly.

"Haven't you now? That's curious. Some said he was a son of yours," pursued the Colonel.

The old Lion flung back his silvery mane with his haughtiest imperiousness.

"No, sir; he's no son of mine."

Lion Winton sat silent, the dark shadow still upon his face. For five years no rumor even had reached him of the man he had disowned and disinherited; he had believed him dead—shot, as he had predicted, after some fray in a gaming-room abroad; and now he heard of him thus in the war-news of the American camp! His denial of him was not less stern, nor his refusal to acknowledge even his name less peremptory, because, with all his wrath, his bitterness, his inexorable passion, and his fierce repudiation of him as his son, a thrill of pleasure stirred in him that the man still lived—a proud triumph swept over him, through all his darker thoughts, at the magnificent dash and daring of a deed wholly akin to him.

Bertie, a listless man about town, a dilettante in pictures, wines, and women, spending every moment that he could in Paris, gentle as any young beauty, always bored, and never roused out of that habitual languid indolent indifferentism which the old man, fiery and impassioned himself as the Napiers, held the most damnable effeminacy with which the present generation emasculates itself, had been incomprehensible, antagonistic, abhorrent to him. Bertie, the Leader of the Eight Hundred, the reckless trooper of the Virginian Horse, the head of a hundred wild night raids, the hero of a score of brilliant charges, the chief in the most daring secret expeditions and the most intrepid cavalry skirmishes of the South, was far nearer to the old Lion, who had in him all the hot fire of Crawford's school, with the severe simplicity of Wellington's stern creeds. "He is true to his blood at last," he muttered, as he tossed back his silky white hair, while his blue flashing eyes ranged over the far distance where the Southern lines lay, with something of eager restlessness; "he is true to his blood at last!"

There was fighting some days later in the Shenandoah Valley.

Longstreet's corps, with two regiments of cavalry, had attacked Sheridan's divisions, and the struggle was hot and fierce. The day was warm, and a brilliant sun poured down into the green cornland and woodland wealth of the valley as the Southern divisions came up to the attack in beautiful precision, and hurled themselves with tremendous *élan* on the right front of the Federals, who, covered by their hastily thrown-up breastworks, opened a deadly fire that raked the whole Confederate line as they advanced. Men fell by the score under the murderous mitraille, but the ranks closed up shoulder to shoulder, without pause or wavering, only maddened by the furious storm of shot, as the engagement became general and the white rolling clouds of smoke poured down the valley, and hid conflict and combatants from sight, the thunder of the musketry pealing from height to height; while in many places men were fighting literally face to face and hand to hand in a death-struggle—rare in these days, when the duello of artillery and the rivalry of breech-loaders begins, decides, and ends most battles.

On Longstreet's left, two squadrons of Virginian Cavalry were drawn up, waiting the order to advance, and passionately impatient of delay as regiment after regiment were sent up to the attack and were lost in the whirling cloud of dust and smoke, and they were kept motionless, in reserve. At their head was Bertie Winton, unconscious that, on a hill to the right, with a group of Federal commanders, his father was looking down on that struggle in the Shenandoah. Bertie was little altered, save that on his face there was a sterner look, and in his eyes a keener and less listless glance; but the old languid grace, the old lazy gentleness, were there still. They were part of his nature, and nothing could kill them in him. In the five years that had gone by, none whom he had known in Europe had ever heard a word of him or from him; he had cut away all the moorings that bound him to his old life, and had sought to build up his ruined fortunes, like the penniless soldier that he was, by his sword alone. So far he had succeeded: he had made his name famous throughout the States as a bold and unerring cavalry leader, and had won the personal friendship and esteem of the Chiefs of the Southern Confederacy. The five years had been filled with incessant adventures, with ever present peril, with the din of falling citadels, with the rush of headlong charges, with daring raids in starless autumn nights, with bivouacs in trackless Western forests, with desert-thirst in parching summer heats, with winters of such frozen roofless misery as he had never even dreamed—five years of ceaseless danger, of frequent suffering, of habitual renunciation; but five years of *life*—real, vivid, unselfish—and Bertie was a better man for them. What he had done at the head of Eight Hundred was but a sample of whatever he did whenever duty called, or opportunity offered, in the service of the South; and no man was better known or better trusted in all Lee's divisions than Bertie Winton, who sat now at the head of his regiment, waiting Longstreet's orders. An aide galloped up before long.

"The General desires you to charge and break the enemy's square to the left, Colonel."

Bertie bowed with the old Pall Mall grace, turned, and gave the word to advance. Like greyhounds loosed from leash, the squadrons thundered down the slope, and swept across the plain in magnificent order, charging full gallop, riding straight down on the bristling steel and levelled rifles of the enemy's kneeling square. They advanced in superb condition, in matchless order, coming on with the force of a whirlwind across the plain; midway they were met by a tremendous volley poured direct upon them; half their saddles were emptied; the riderless chargers tore, snorting, bleeding, terrified, out of the ranks; the line was broken; the Virginians wavered, halted, all but recoiled; it was one of those critical moments when hesitation is destruction. Bertie saw the danger, and, with a shout to the men to come on, he spurred his horse through the raking volley of shot, while a shot struck his sombrero, leaving his head bare, and urging the animal straight at the Federal front, lifted him in the air as he would have done before a fence, and landed him in the midst of the square, down on the points of the levelled bayonets. With their fierce war-cheer ringing out above the sullen uproar of the firing, his troopers followed him to a man, charged the enemy's line, broke through the packed mass opposed to them, cut their way into the centre, and hewed their enemies down as mowers hew the grass. Longstreet's work was done for him; the Federal square was broken, never again to rally.

But the victory was bought with a price; as his horse fell, pierced and transfixed by the crossed steel of the bayonets, a dozen rifles covered the Confederate leader; their shots rang out, and Bertie Winton reeled from his saddle and sank down beneath the press as his own Southerners charged above him in the rush of the onward attack. On an eminence to the right, through his race-glass, his father watched the engagement, his eyes seldom withdrawn from the Virginian cavalry, where, for aught he knew, one of his own blood and name might be—memories of Salamanca and Quatre Bras, of Moodkee and Ferozeshah, stirring in him, while the fire of his dead youth thrilled through his veins with the tramp of the opposing divisions, and he roused like a war-horse at the scent of the battle as the white shroud of the smoke rolled up to his feet, and the thunder of the musketry echoed through the valley. Through his glass, he saw the order given to the troopers held in reserve; he saw the magnificent advance of that charge in the morning light; he saw the volley poured in upon them; and he saw them under that shock reel, stagger, waver, and recoil. The old soldier knew well the critical danger of that ominous moment of panic and of confusion; then, as the Confederate Colonel rode out alone and put his horse at that leap on to the line of steel, into the bristling square, a cry loud as the Virginian battle-shout broke from him. For when the charger rose in the air, and the sun shone full on the uncovered head of the Southern leader, he knew the fair English features that no skies could bronze, and the fair English hair that blew in the hot wind. He looked once more upon the man he had denied and had disowned; and, as Bertie Winton reeled and fell, his father, all unarmed and non-combatant as he was, drove the spurs into his horse's flanks, and dashing down the steep hill-side, rode over the heaps of slain, and through the pools of gore, into the thick of the strife.

With his charger dead under him, beaten down upon one knee, his sword-arm shivered by a bullet, while the blood poured from his side where another shot had lodged, Bertie knew that his last hour had come, as the impetus of the charge broke above him—as a great wave may sweep over the head of a drowning man—and left him in the centre of the foe. Kneeling there, while the air was red before his sight that was fast growing blind from the loss of blood, and the earth seemed to reel and rock under him, he still fought to desperation, his sabre in his left hand; he knew he could not hold out more than a second longer, but while he had strength he kept at bay.

His life was not worth a moment's purchase,—when, with a shout that rang over the field, the old Lion rode down through the carnage to his rescue, his white hair floating in the wind, his azure eyes flashing with war-fire, his holster-pistol levelled; spurred his horse through the struggle, trampled aside all that opposed him, dashed untouched through the cross-fire of the bullets, shot through the brain the man whose rifle covered his son who had reeled down insensible, and stooping, raised the senseless body, lifted him up by sheer manual strength to the level of his saddle-bow, laid him across his holsters, holding him up with his right hand, and, while the Federals fell asunder in sheer amazement at the sudden onslaught, and admiration of the old man's daring, plunged the rowels into his horse, and, breaking through the reeking slaughter of the battle-field, rode back, thus laden with his prisoner, through the incessant fire of the cannonade up the heights to the Federal lines.

"If you were to lie dying at my feet!"—his father remembered those words, that had been spoken five years before in the fury of a deadly passion, as Bertie lay stretched before him in his tent, the blood flowing from the deep shot-wound in his side, his eyes closed, his face livid, and about his lips a faint and ghastly foam.

Had he saved him too late? had he too late repented?

His heart had yearned to him when, in the morning light, he had looked once more upon the face of his son, as the Virginian Horse had swept on to the shock of the charge; and all of wrath, of bitterness, of hatred, of dark, implacable, unforgiving vengeance, were quenched and gone for ever from his soul as he stooped over him where he lay at his feet, stricken and senseless in all the glory of his manhood. He only knew that he loved the man—he only knew that he would have died for him, or died with him.

Bertie stirred faintly, with a heavy sigh, and his left hand moved towards his breast. Old Sir Lion bent over him, while his voice shook terribly, like a woman's.

"Bertie! My God! don't you know *me*?"

He opened his eyes and looked wearily and dreamily around; he did not know what had passed, nor where he was; but a faint light of wonder, of pleasure, of recognition, came into his eyes, and he smiled—a smile that was very gentle and very wistful.

"I am glad of that—before I die! Let us part friends—*now*. They will tell you I have—redeemed—the name."

The words died slowly and with difficulty on his lips, and as his father's hand closed upon his in a strong grasp of tenderness and reconciliation, his lids closed, his head fell back, and a deep-drawn, labored sigh quivered through all his frame; and Lion Winton, bowing down his grand white crest, wept with the passion of a woman. For he knew not whether the son he loved was living or dead—he knew not whether he was not at the last too late.

Three months further on, Lady Ida Deloraine sat in her warm bright nest among the exotics, gazing out upon the sunny lawns and the green woodlands of Northamptonshire. Highest names and proudest titles had been pressed on her through the five years that had gone, but her loveliness had been unwon, and was but something more thoughtful, more brilliant, more exquisite still than of old. The beautiful warmth that had never come there through all these years was in her cheeks now, and the nameless lustre was in her eyes, which all those who had wooed her had never wakened in their antelope brilliancy, as she sat looking outward at the sunlight; for in her hands lay a camellia, withered, colorless, and yellow, and eyes gazed down upon the marvellous beauty of her face which had remembered it in the hush of Virginian forests, in the rush of headlong charges, in the glare of bivouac fires, in the silence of night-pickets, and in the din of falling cities.

And Bertie's voice, as he bent over her, was on her ear.

"That flower has been on my heart night and day; and since we parted I have never done that which would have been insult to your memory. I have tried to lead a better and a purer life; I have striven to redeem my name and my honor; I have done all I could to wash out the vice and the vileness of my past. Through all the years we have been severed I have had no thought, no hope, except to die more worthy of you; but now—oh, my God!—if you knew how I love you, if you knew how my love alone saved me——"

His words broke down in the great passion that had been his redemption; and as she lifted her eyes upward to his own, soft with tears that had gathered but did not fall, and lustrous with the light that had never come there save for him, he bowed his head over her, and, as his lips met hers, he knew that the redeemed life he laid at her feet was dearer to her than lives, more stainless, but less nobly won.

OUR WAGER; OR, HOW THE MAJOR LOST AND WON

I

INTRODUCES MAJOR TELFER OF THE 50TH DASHAWAY HUSSARS

The softest of lounging-chairs, an unexceptionable hubble-bubble bought at Benares, the last *Bell's Life*, the morning papers, chocolate milled to a T, and a breakfast worthy of Francatelli,—what sensible man can ask more to make him comfortable? All these was my chum, Hamilton Telfer, Major (50th Dashaway Hussars), enjoying, and yet he was in a frame of mind anything but mild and genial.

"The deuce take the whole sex!" said he, stroking his moustache savagely. "They're at the bottom of all the mischief going. The idea of my father at seventy-five, with hair as white as that poodle's, making such a fool of himself, when here am I, at six-and-thirty, unmarried; it's abominable, it's disgusting. A girl of twenty, taking in an old man of his age, for the sake of his money——"

"But are you sure, Telfer," said I, "that the affair's really on the tapis?"

"Sure! Yes," said the Major, with immeasurable disgust. "I never saw her till last night, but the governor wrote no end of rhapsodies about her, and as I came upon them he was taking leave of her, holding her hand in his, and saying, 'I may write to you, may I not?' and the young hypocrite lifted her eyes so bewitchingly, 'Oh yes, I shall long so much to hear from you!' She colored when she saw me—well she might! If she thinks she'll make a fool of my father, and reign paramount at Torwood, give me a mother-in-law sixteen years younger than myself, and fill the house and cumber the estates with a lot of wretched little brats, she'll find herself mistaken, for I'll prevent it, if I live."

"Don't be too sure of that," said I. "From what I know of Violet Tressillian, she's not the sort of girl to lure her quarry in vain."

"Of course she'll try hard," answered Telfer. "She comes of a race that always were poor and proud; she's an orphan, and hasn't a sou, and to catch a man like my father worth 15,000*l*. a year, with the surety of a good dower and jointure house whenever he die, is one of the best things that could chance to her; but I'll be shot if she ever shall manage it."

"*Nous verrons.* I bet you my roan filly Calceolaria against your colt Jockeyclub that before Christmas is out Violet Tressillian will be Violet Telfer."

"Done!" cried the Major, stirring his chocolate fiercely. "You'll lose, Vane; Calceolaria will come to my stables as sure as this mouthpiece is made of amber. Whenever this scheming little actress changes her name, it sha'n't be to the same cognomen as mine. I say, it's getting deuced warm — one must begin to go somewhere. What do you say to going abroad till the 12th? I've got three months' leave — that will give me one away, and two on the moor. Will you go?"

"Yes, if you like; town's emptying gradually, and it is confoundedly hot. Where shall it be? — Naples — Paris — —"

"Paris in July! Heaven forbid! Why, it would be worse than London in November. By Jove! I'll tell you where: let's go to Essellau."

"And where may that be? Somewhere in the Arctic regions, I hope, for I've spent half my worldly possessions already in sherry and seltzer and iced punch, and if I go where it's warmer still, I shall be utterly beggared."

"Essellau is in Swabia, as you ought to know by this, you Goth. It's Marc von Edenburgh's place, and a very jolly place, too, I can tell you; the sport's first-rate there, and the pig-sticking really splendid. He's just written to ask me to go, and take any fellows I like, as he's got some English people — some friends of his mother's. (A drawback that — I wonder who they are.) Will you come, Vane? I can promise you some fun, if only at the trente-et-quarante tables in Pipesandbeersbad."

"Oh yes, I'll come," said I. "I hope the English won't be some horrid snobs he's picked up at some of the balls, who'll be scraping acquaintance with us when we come back."

"No fear," said Telfer; "Marc's as English as you or I, and knows the good breed when he sees them. He'd keep as clear of the Smith, Brown, and Robinson style as we should. It's settled, then, you'll come. All right! I wish I could settle that confounded Violet, too, first. I hope nothing will happen while I'm in Essellau. I don't think it can. The Tressillian leaves town to-day with the Carterets, and the governor must stick here till parliament closes, and it's sure to be late this year."

With which consolatory reflection the Major rose, stretched himself, yawned, sighed, stroked his moustache, fitted on his lavender gloves, and rang to order his tilbury round.

Telfer was an only son, and when he heard it reported that his father intended to give him a *belle-mère* in a young lady as attractive as she was poor, who, if she caught him, would probably make a fool of the old gentleman in the widest sense of the word, he naturally swore very heartily, and anything but relished the idea. Hamilton Telfer, senior, had certainly been a good deal with Violet that season, and Violet, a girl poor as a rat and beautiful as Semele, talked to him, and sang to him, and rode with him more than she did with any of us; so people talked and talked, and said the old member would get caught, and the Major, when he heard it, waxed fiercely wroth at the folly his parent had fallen into while he'd been off the scene down at Dover with his troop, but, like a wise man, said nothing, knowing, both by experience and observation, that opposition in such affairs is like a patent Vesta among hayricks. Telfer was a particular chum of mine: we'd lounged about town, and shot on the moors, and campaigned in India together, and I don't believe there was a better soldier, a cooler head, a quicker eye, or a steadier hand in the service than he was. He was six-and-thirty now, and had seen life pretty well, I can tell you, for there was not a get-at-able corner of the globe that he hadn't looked at through his eye-glass. Tall and muscular, with a stern, handsome face, with the prospect of Torwood (where there's some of the best shooting in England, I give you my word), and 15,000*l*. a year, Telfer was a great card in the matrimonial line, but hadn't let himself be played as yet, for the petty trickery the women used in trying to get him dealt to them disgusted him, and small wonder. Men liked him cordially, women thought him cold and sarcastic; and he was much more genial, I admit, at mess, or at lansquenet, or in the smoking-room of the U. S., than he was in boudoirs and ball-rooms, as the mere knowledge that mammas and their darlings were trying to hook him made him get on his stilts at once.

"I don't feel easy in my mind about the governor," said he, as we drove along to the South-Eastern Station a few days after on our way to Essellau. "As I was bidding him good-bye this morning, Soames brought him a letter in a woman's hand. Heaven knows he may have a score of fair correspondents for anything I care, but if I thought it was the Tressillian, devil take her— —"

"And the devil won't have had a prettier prize since Proserpine was stolen," said I.

"No, confound it, I saw she was handsome enough," swore the Major, disgusted; "and a pretty face always did make a fool of my father, according to his own telling. Well, thank God, I don't take that weakness after him. I never went mad about any woman. You've just as much control over love, if you like, as over a quiet shooting pony; and if it don't suit you to gallop, you can rein up and give over the sport. Any man who's anything of a philosopher needn't fall in love unless he likes."

"Were you never in love, then, old boy?" I asked.

"Of course I have been. I've made love to no end of women in my time; but when one love was died out I took another, as I take a cigar, and never wept over the quenched ashes. You need never fall in love unless it's convenient, and as to caring for a girl who don't care for you, that's a contemptible weakness, and one I don't sympathize with at all. Come along, or the train will be off."

He went up to the carriages, opened a door, shut it hastily, and turned away, with the frigid bow with which Telfer, in common with every other Briton, can say, "Go to the devil," as plainly as if he spoke.

"By Jove!" said I, "what's that eccentric move? Did you see the Medusa in that carriage, or a baby?"

"Something quite as bad," said he, curtly. "I saw the Tressillian and her aunt. For Heaven's sake, let's get away from them. I'd rather have a special train, if it cost me a fortune, than travel with that girl, boxed up for four hours in the same compartment with such a little intrigante."

"Calm your mind, old fellow; if she's aiming at your governor she won't hit you. She can't be your wife and your mother-in-law both," laughed Fred Walsham, a good-natured little chap in the Carabiniers, a friend of Von Edenburgh, who was coming with us.

"I'll see her shot before she's either," said Telfer, fiercely stroking his moustache.

"Hush! the deuce! hold your tongue," said Walsham, giving him a push. For past us, so close that the curling plumes in her hat touched the Major's shoulder, floated the "little intrigante" in question, who'd come out of her carriage to see where a pug of hers was put. She'd heard all we said, confound it, for her head was up, her color bright, and she looked at Telfer proudly and disdainfully, with her dark eyes flashing. Telfer returned it to the full as haughtily, for he never shirked the consequences of his own actions ('pon my life, they looked like a great stag and a little greyhound challenging each other), and Violet swept away across the platform.

"You've made an enemy for life, Telfer," said Walsham, as we whisked along.

"So much the better, if I'm a rock ahead to warn her off a marriage with the governor," rejoined the Major, smoking, as he always did, under the officials' very noses. "I hope I sha'n't come across her again. If the Tressillian and I meet, we shall be about as amicable as a rat and a beagle. Take a weed, Fred. I do it on principle to resist unjust regulations. Why shouldn't we take a pipe if we like? A man whose olfactory nerves are so badly organized as to dislike Cavendish is too great a muff to be considered."

As ill luck would have it, when we crossed to Dover, who should cross, too, but the Tressillian and her party—aunt, cousins, maid, courier, and pug. Telfer wouldn't see them, but got on the poop, as far away as ever he could from the spot where Violet sat nursing her dog and reading a novel, provokingly calm and comfortable to the envious eyes of all the *malades* around her.

"Good Heavens!" said he, "was anything ever so provoking? Just because that girl's my particular aversion, she must haunt me like this. If she'd been anybody I wanted to meet, I should never have caught a glimpse of her. For mercy's sake, Vane, if you see a black hat and white feather anywhere again, tell me, and we'll change the route immediately."

Change the route we did, for, going on board the steamer at Düsseldorf, there, on the deck, stood the Tressillian. Telfer turned sharp on his heel, and went back as he came. "I'll be shot if I go down the Rhine with her. Let's cut across into France." Cut across we did, but we stopped at Brussels on our way; and when at last we caught sight of the tops of the fir-trees around Essellau, Telfer took a long whiff at his pipe with an air of contentment. "I should say we're safe now. She'll hardly come pig-sticking into the middle of Swabia."

II
VIOLET TRESSILLIAN

Essellau was a very jolly place, with thick woods round it, and the river Beersbad running in sight; and his pretty sister, the Comtesse Virginie, his good wines, and good sport, made Von Edenburgh's a pleasant house to visit at. Marc himself, who is in the Austrian service (he was winged at Montebello the other day by a rascally Zouave, but he paid him off for it, as I hope his countrymen will eventually pay off all the Bonapartists for their *galimatias*)—Marc himself was a jolly fellow, a good host, a keen shot, and a capital écarté player, and made us enjoy ourselves at Essellau as he had done before, hunting and shooting with Telfer down at Torwood.

"I've some countrywomen of yours here, Telfer," said Marc, after we'd talked over his English loves, given him tiding of duchesses and danseuses, and messages from no end of pretty women that he'd flirted with the Christmas before. "They're some friends of my mother's, and when they were at Baden-Baden last year, Virginie struck up a desperate young lady attachment with one of them——"

"Are they good-looking?—because, if they are, they may be drysalters' daughters, and I shan't care," interrupted Fred.

Telfer stroked his moustache with a contemptuous smile—*he* wouldn't have looked at a drysalter's daughter if she'd had all the beauty of Amphitrite.

"Come and see," said Marc. "Virginie will think you're neglecting her atrociously."

Horribly bored to be going to meet some Englishwomen who might turn out to be Smiths or Joneses, and would, to a dead certainty, spoil all his pleasure in pig-sticking, shooting, and écarté, by flirting with him whether he would or no, the Major strode along corridors and galleries after Von Edenburgh. When at length we reached the salon where Virginie and her mother and friends were, Telfer lifted his eyes from the ground as the door opened, started as if he'd been shot, and stepped back a pace or two, with an audible, "If that isn't the very devil!"

There, in a low chair, sat the Tressillian, graceful as a Sphakiote girl, with a toilet as perfect as her profile, dark hair like waves of silk, and dark eyes full of liquid light, that, when they looked irresistible, could do anything with any man that they liked. Violet certainly looked as unlike that unlucky ogre and scapegoat, the devil, as a young lady ever could. But worse than a score of demons was she in poor Telfer's eyes: to have come out to Essellau only to be shut up in a country-house for a whole month with his pet aversion!—certainly it *was* a hard case, and the fierce lightning glance he flashed on her was pardonable under the circumstances. But nobody's more impassive than the Major: I've seen him charge down into the Sikhs with just the same calm, quiet expression as he'd wear smoking and reading a novel at home; so he soon rallied, bowed to the Tressillian, who gave him an inclination as cold as the North Pole, shook hands with her aunt and cousins (three women I hate: the mamma's the most dexterous of manœuvrers, and the girls the arrantest of flirts), and then sat down to a little quiet chat with Virginie von Edenburgh, who's pretty, intelligent, and unaffected, though she's a belle at the Viennese court. Telfer was pleasant with the little comtesse; he'd known her from childhood, and she was engaged to the colonel of Marc's troop, so that Telfer felt quite sure she'd no designs upon him, and talked to her *sans géne*, though to have wholly abstained from bitterness and satire would have been an impossibility to him, with the obnoxious Tressillian seated within sight. Once he fixed her with his calm gray eyes, she met them with a proud flashing glance; Telfer gave back the defiance, and *guerre à outrance* was declared between them. It was plain to see that they hated one another by instinct, and I began to think Calceolaria wasn't so safe in my stables after all, for if the Major set his face against anything, his father, who pretty well worshipped him, would never venture to do it in opposition; he'd as soon think of leaving Torwood to the country, to be turned into an infirmary or a museum.

That whole day Telfer was agreeable to the Von Edenburgh, distantly courteous to the Carterets, and utterly oblivious of the very existence of the Tressillian. When we were smoking together, after dinner, he began to unburden himself of his mighty wrath.

"Where the deuce did you pick up that girl, Marc?" asked he, as we stood looking at the sun setting over the woods of Essellau, and crimsoning the western clouds.

"What girl?" asked Marc.

"That confounded Tressillian," answered the Major, gloomily.

"I told you the Carterets were friends of my mother's, and last year, when the Tressillian came with them to Baden, Virginie met her, and they were struck with a great and sudden love for one another, after the insane custom of women. But why on earth, Telfer, do you call her such names? I think her divine; her eyes are something— —"

"I wish her eyes had been at the devil before she'd bewitched my poor father with them," said Telfer, pulling a rose to pieces fiercely. "I give you my word, Marc, that if I didn't like you so well, I'd go straight off home to-morrow. Here have I been turning out of my route twenty times, on purpose to avoid her, and then she must turn up at the very place I thought I was sure to be safe from her. It's enough to make a man swear, I should say, and not over-mildly either."

"But what's she done?" cried Von Edenburgh, thinking, I dare say, that Telfer had gone clean mad. "Refused you—jilted you—what is it?"

"Refused me! I should like to see myself giving her the chance," said the Major, with intense scorn. "No but she's done what I'd never forgive— tried to cozen the poor old governor into marrying her. She's no money, you know, and no home of her own; but, for all that, for a girl of twenty to try and hook an old man of seventy-five, to cheat him into the idea that he's made a conquest, and chisel him into the belief that she's in love with him—faugh! the very idea disgusts one. What sort of a wife would a woman make who could act such a lie?"

As he spoke, a form swept past him, and a beautiful face full of scorn and passion gleamed on him through the *demi-lumière*.

"By Jove! you've done it now, Telfer," said Walsham. "She was behind us, I bet you, gathering those roses; her hands are full of them, and she took that means of showing us she was within earshot. You *have* set your foot in it nicely, certainly."

"*Ce m'est bien égal*," said Telfer, haughtily. "If she hear what I say of her, so much the better. It's the truth, that a young girl who'd sell herself for money, as soon as she's got what she wanted will desert the man who's given it to her; and I like my father too well to stand by and see him made a fool of. The Tressillian and I are open foes now—we'll see which wins."

"And a very fair foe you have, too," thought I, as I looked at Violet that night as she stood in the window, a wreath of lilies on her splendid hair, and her impassioned eyes lighting into joyous laughter as she talked nonsense with Von Edenburgh.

"Isn't she first-rate style, in spite of your prejudice?" I said to Telfer, who'd just finished a game at écarté with De Tintiniac, one of the best players in Europe. If the Major has any weakness, écarté is one of them. He just glanced across with a sarcastic smile.

"Well got up, of course; so are all actresses—on the stage."

Then he dropped his glass and went back to his cards, and seemed to notice the splendid Tressillian not one whit more than he did her pup.

Whether his discourteous speeches had piqued Violet into showing off her best paces, or whether it's a natural weakness of her sex to shine in all times and places that they can, certain it was that I never saw the Tressillian more brilliant and bewitching than she was that night. Waltzing with Von Edenburgh, singing with me, talking fun with Fred, or merely lying back in her chair, playing lazily with her bouquet, she was eminently dangerous in whatever she did, and there wasn't a man in the castle who didn't gather round her, except her sworn foe the Major. Even De Tintiniac, that old campaigner at the green tables, who has long ago given over any mistress save hazard, glanced once or twice at the superb eyes beaming with the *droit de conquête*, but Telfer never looked up from his cards.

Telfer and she parted with the chilliest of "good nights," and met again in the morning with the most frigid of "good mornings," and to that simple exchange of words was their colloquy limited for an entire fortnight. Unless I'd been witness of it, I wouldn't have credited that any two people could live for that space of time in the same country-house and keep so distant. Nobody noticed it, for there were no end of guests at Essellau, and the Tressillian had so many liege subjects ready to her slightest bidding, that the Major's *lèse-majesté* wasn't of such consequence. But when day after day came, and he spent them all boar-hunting, shooting, fishing, or playing rouge-et-noir and roulette at the gaming-tables in Pipesandbeersbad, and when he was in the drawing-rooms at Essellau she saw him amusing and agreeable, and unbending to every one but herself, I don't know anything of woman's nature if I didn't see Violet's delicate cheek flush, and her eyes flash, whenever she caught the Major's cool, contemptuous, depreciating glance, much harder to her sex to bear than spoken ridicule or open war. Occasionally he cast a sarcasm, quick, sharp, and relentless as a Minié ball, at her, which she fired back with such rifle-powder as she had in her flask; but the return shot fell as harmlessly as it might have done on Achilles's breast.

"A man is very silly to marry," he was saying one evening to Marc, "since, as Emerson says, from the beginning of the world such as are in the institution want to get out, and such as are out want to get in."

Violet, sitting near at the piano, turned half round. "If all others are of my opinion, Major Telfer, you will never be tempted, for no one will be willing to enter it with you."

The shot fell short. Telfer neither smiled nor looked annoyed, but answered, tranquilly, —

"Possibly; but my time is to come. When I own Torwood, ladies will be as kind to me as they are now to my father; for it is wonderful what a charm to renew youth, reform rakes, buy love, and make the Beast the Beauty, is 'un peu de poudre d'or,' in the eyes of the *beau sexe.*"

The Tressillian flushed scarlet, but soon recovered herself.

"I have heard," she said, pulling her bouquet to pieces with impatience, "that when people look through smoked glass the very sun looks dusky, and so I suppose, through your own moral perceptions, you view those of others. You know what De la Fayette wrote to Madame de Sablé: '*Quelle corruption il faut avoir dans l'esprit pour être capable d'imaginer tout cela!*'"

"It does not follow," answered Telfer, impassively. "De la Fayette was quite wrong. Suard was nearer the truth when he said that Rochefoucauld, '*a peint les hommes comme il les à vus. Il n'appartenait qu'à un homme d'une réputation bien pure et bien distinguée d'oser flétrir ainsi le principe de toutes les actions humaines.*'"

"And Major Telfer is so unassailable himself that he can mount his pedestal and censure all weaker mortals," said Violet, sarcastically. "Your judgments are, perhaps, not always as infallible as the gods'."

"You are gone very wide of the original subject, Miss Tressillian," answered Telfer, coldly. "I was merely speaking of that common social fraud and falsehood, a *mariage de convenance,* which, as I shall never sin in that manner myself, I am at liberty to censure with the scorn I feel for it."

He looked hard at her as he spoke. The Tressillian's eyes answered the stare as haughtily.

"Some may not be all *mariages de convenance* that you choose to call such. It does not necessarily follow, because a girl marries a rich man, that she marries him for his money. There *may* be love in the case, but the world never gives her the grace of the doubt."

"What hardy hypocrisy," thought Telfer. "She'd actually try to persuade me to my face that she was in love with the poor old governor and his gout!"

"Pardon me," he said, with his most cynical smile. "In attributing disinterested affection to ladies, I think '*quelque disposition qu'ait le monde à mal juger, il fait plus souvent grace au faux mérite qu'il ne fait injustice au véritable.*'"

The Tressillian's soft lips curved angrily; she turned away, and began to sing again, at Walsham's entreaty. Telfer got up and lounged over to Virginie, with whom he laughed, talked, waltzed, and played chess for the rest of the evening.

III

FROM WHICH IT WOULD APPEAR, THAT IT IS SOMETIMES WELL TO BEGIN WITH A LITTLE AVERSION

After this split, Telfer and the Tressillian were rather further off each other than before; and whenever riding, and driving, at dinner, or in lionizing, they came by chance together, he avoided her silently as much as ever he could, without making a parade of it. Violet could see very well how cordially he hated her, and, woman-like, I dare say mine, and Edenburgh's, and Walsham's, and all her devoted friends' admiration was valueless, as long as her vowed enemy treated her with such careless contempt.

One morning the two foes met by chance. Telfer and I, after a late night over at Pipesandbeersbad, with lansquenet, cheroots, and cognac, had betaken ourselves out to whip the Beersbad, whose fish, for all their boiling by the hot springs, are first-rate, I can assure you. Telfer tells you he likes fishing, but I never see that he does much more than lie full length under the shadiest tree he can find, with his cap over his eyes and his cigar in his mouth, doing the *dolce* lazily enough. A three-pound trout had no power to rouse him; and he's lost a salmon before now in the Tweed because it bored him to play it! Shade of old Izaak! is *that* liking fishing? But few things ever did excite him, except it was a charge, or a Kaffir scrimmage; and then he looked more like a concentrated tempest than anything else, and woe to the turban that his sabre came down upon.

That part of the stream we'd tried first had been whipped before us, or the fish wouldn't bite; and I, who haven't as much patience as I might have, went up higher to try my luck. Telfer declined to come; he was comfortable, he said, and out of the sun; he preferred "Indiana" and his cheroot to catching all the fish in the Beersbad, so I bid him good-bye, and left him smoking and reading at his leisure under the linden-trees. I went further on than I had meant, up round a bend of the river, and was too absorbed in filling my basket to notice a storm coming up from the west, till I began to find myself getting wet to the skin, and the lightning flying up and down the hills round Essellau. I looked for the Major as I passed the lime-trees, but he wasn't there, and I made the best of my way back to the castle, supposing he'd got there before me; but I was mistaken.

"I've seen nothing of him," said Marc. "He's stalking about the woods, I dare say, admiring the lightning. That's more than the poor Tressillian does, I bet. She went out by herself, I believe, just before the storm, to get a water-lily she wanted to paint, and hasn't appeared since. By Jove! if Telfer should have to play knight-errant to his 'pet aversion,' what fun it would be."

Marc had his fun, for an hour afterwards, when the storm had blown over, up the terrace steps came Violet and the Major. They weren't talking to each other, but they were actually walking together; and the courtesy with which he put a dripping rose-branch out of her path with his stick, was something quite new.

It seems that Telfer, disliking disagreeable sensations, and classing getting wet among such, had arisen when the thunder began to growl, and slowly wended his way homewards. But before he was halfway to Essellau the rain began to drip off his moustache, and seeing a little marble temple (the Parthenon turned into a summer-house!) close by, he thought he might as well go in and have another weed till it grew finer. Go in he did; and he'd just smoked half a cigar, and read the last chapter of "Indiana," when he looked up, and saw the Tressillian's pug, looking a bedraggled and miserable object, at his feet, and the Tressillian herself standing within a few yards of him. If Telfer had abstained from a few fierce mental oaths, he would have been of a much more pacific nature than he ever pretended to be; and I don't doubt that he looked hauteur concentrated as he rose at his enemy's entrance. Violet made a movement of retreat, but then thought better of it. It would have seemed too much like flying from the foe. So with a careless bow she sank on one of the seats, took off her hat, shook the rain-drops off her hair, and busied herself in sedulous attentions to the pug. The Major thought it incumbent on him to speak a few sentences about the thunder that was cracking over their heads; Violet answered him as briefly; and Telfer putting down his cigar with a sigh, sat watching the storm in silence, not troubling himself to talk any more.

As she bent down to pat the pug she caught his eyes on her with a cold, critical glance. He was thinking how pure her profile was and how exquisite her eyes, and—of how cordially he should hate her if his father married her. Her color rose, but she met his look steadily, which is a difficult thing to do if you've anything to conceal, for the Major's eyes are very keen and clear. Her lips curved with a smile half amused, half disdainful. "What a pity, Major Telfer," she said, with a silvery laugh, "that you should be condemned to imprisonment with one who is unfortunately such a *bête noire* to you as I am! I assure you, I feel for you; if I were not coward enough to be a little afraid of that lightning, I would really go away to relieve you from your sufferings. I should feel quite honored by the distinction of your hatred if I didn't know, you, on principle, dislike every woman living. Is your judgment always infallible?"

Beyond a little surprise in his eyes, Telfer's features were as impassive as ever. "Far from it," he answered, quietly "I merely judge people by their actions."

The Tressillian's luminous eyes flashed proudly. "An unsafe guide, Major Telfer; you cannot judge of actions until you know their motives. I know perfectly well why you dislike and avoid me: you listened to a foolish report, and you heard me giving your father permission to write to me. Those are your grounds, are they not?"

Telfer, for once in his life, *was* astonished, but he looked at her fixedly. "And were they not just ones?"

"No," said Violet, vehemently,—"no, they were most rankly unjust; and it is hard, indeed, if a girl, who has no friends or advisers that she can trust, may not accept the kindness and ask the counsels of a man fifty-five years older than herself without his being given to her as a lover, and the world's whispering that she is trying to entrap him. You pique yourself on your clear-sightedness, Major Telfer, but for once your judgment failed you when you attributed such mean and mercenary motives to me, and supposed, because, as you so generously stated, I had 'no money and no home,' I must necessarily have no heart or conscience, but be ready to give myself at any moment to the highest bidder, and take advantage of the kindness of your noble-minded, generous-hearted father to trick him into marriage." She stopped, fairly out of breath with excitement. Telfer was going to speak, but she silenced him with a haughty gesture. "No; now we are started on the subject, hear me to the end. You have done me gross injustice—an offence the Tressillians never forgive—but, for my own sake, I wish to show you how mistaken you were in your hasty condemnation. At the beginning of the season I was introduced to your father. He knew my mother well in her girlhood, and he said I reminded him of her. He was very kind to me, and I, who have no real friend on earth, of course was grateful to him, for I was thankful to have any one on whom I could rely. You know, probably as well as I do, that there is little love lost between the Carterets and myself, though, by my father's will, I must stay with them till I am of age. I have one brother, a boy of eighteen; he is with his regiment serving out in India, and the climate is killing him by inches, though he is too brave to try and get sick leave. Your father has been doing all he can to have him exchanged;

the letters I have had from him have been to tell me of his success, and to say that Arthur is gazetted to the Buffs, and coming home overland. There is the head and front of my offending, Major Telfer; a very simple explanation, is it not? Perhaps another time you will be more cautious in your censure."

A faint flush came over the Major's bronzed cheek; he looked out of the portico, and was silent for a minute. The knowledge that he has wronged another is a keen pang to a proud man of an honor almost fastidious in his punctilio of right. He swung quickly round, and held out his hand to her.

"I beg your pardon; I have misjudged you, and I am thoroughly ashamed of myself for it," he said, in a low voice.

When the Major does come down from his hauteur, and let some of his winning cordial nature come out, no woman living, unless she were some animated Medusa, could find it in her heart to say him nay. His frank self-condemnation touched Violet, despite herself, and, without thinking, she laid her small fingers in his proffered hand. Then the Tressillian pride flashed up again; she drew it hastily away, and walked out into the air.

"Pray do not distress yourself," she said, with an effort (not successful) to seem perfectly calm and nonchalant. "It is not of the slightest consequence; we understand each other's sentiments now, and shall in future be courteous in our hate like two of the French *noblesse*, complimenting one another before they draw their swords to slay or to be slain. It has cleared now, so I will leave you to the solitude I disturbed. Come, Floss." And calling the pug after her, Violet very gracefully swept down the steps, but with a stride the Major was at her side.

"Nay, Miss Tressillian," he said, gently, "it is true I've given you cause to think me as rude as Orson or Caliban, but I am not quite such a bear as to let you walk home through these woods alone."

Violet made an impatient movement. "Pray don't trouble yourself. We are close to the castle, and—pardon me, but truth-telling seems the order for the day—I much prefer you in your open enmity to your simulated courtesy. We have been rude to each other for three weeks; in another one you will be gone, so it is scarcely worth while to begin politeness now."

"As you please," said Telfer, coldly.

He'd made great advances and concessions for him, and was far too English when repulsed to go on making any more. But he was astonished— extremely so—for he'd been courted and sought since he was in jackets, and couldn't make out a young girl like the Tressillian treating him so lightly. He walked along beside her in profound silence, but though neither of them spoke a word, he didn't leave her side till she was safe on the terrace at

Essellau. The Major was very grave that night at dinner, and occasionally he looked at Violet with a strange, inquiring glance, as the young lady, in the most brilliant of spirits, fired away French repartees with Von Edenburgh and De Tintiniac, her face absolutely *rayonnant* in the gleam of the wax lights. I thought the spirits were a little too high to be real. Late at night, as he and I and Marc were smoking on the terrace, before turning in, Telfer constrained himself to tell us of the scene in the summer-house. He'd abused her to us. Common honor, he said, obliged him to tell us the truth about her.

"I am sorry," said he, slowly, between the whiffs of his meerschaum. "If there is one thing I hate, it is injustice. I was never guilty of misjudging anybody before in my life, that I know of; and, I give you my word, I experienced a new sensation—I absolutely felt humbled before that girl's great, flashing, truthful eyes, to think that I'd been listening to report and judging from prejudice like any silly, gossiping woman."

"It seems to have made a great impression on you, Telfer," laughed Marc. "Has your detestation of Violet changed to something as warm, but more gentle? Shall we have to say the love wherewith he loves her is greater than the hate wherewith he hated her?"

"Not exactly," answered the Major, calmly, with a supercilious twist of his moustaches. "But I like pluck wherever I see it, and she's a true Tressillian."

IV

IN WHICH THE MAJOR PROVOKES A QUARREL IN BEHALF OF THE FAIR TRESSILLIAN

"Well, Telfer," said I, two mornings after, "if you want to be at the moor by the 12th, we must start soon; this is the 6th. It will be sharp work to get there as it is."

"What, do you think of not going at all?" said Telfer, laying down the *Revue des deux Mondes* with a yawn. "We are very well here. Marc bothers me tremendously to stay on another month, and the shooting's as good as we shall get at Glenattock. What do you say, Vane?"

"Just as you like," I answered. "The pigs are as good as the grouse, for anything I know. They put me in mind of getting my first spear at Burampootra. I only thought you wanted to be off out of sight of the Tressillian."

He laughed slightly. "Oh! the young lady's no particular eyesore to me now I don't regard her in the light of a *belle-mère*. Well, shall we stop here, then?"

"*Comme vous voulez.* I don't care."

"No philosopher ever moves when he's comfortable," said the Major, laughing. "I'll write and tell Montague he can shoot over Glenattock if he likes. I dare say he can find some men who'll keep him company and fill the box. I say, old fellow, I've won Calceolaria, but I sha'n't have her, because I consider the bet drawn. Our wager was laid on the supposition that the Tressillian wished to marry the governor, but as she never has had the desire, I've neither lost nor won."

"Well, we'll wait and see," said I. "Christmas isn't come yet. Here comes Violet. She looks well, don't she? Confess now, prejudice apart, that you admire her, *nolens volens.*"

Telfer looked at her steadily as she came into the billiard-room in her hat and habit, as she'd been riding with Lucy Carteret, Marc, and De Tintiniac. "Yes," he said, slowly, under his breath, "she is very good style, I admit."

Lucy Carteret challenged Telfer to a game; she has a tall, *svelte* figure, and knows she looks well at billiards. He played lazily, and let her win easily enough, paying as little attention to the *agaceries* and glances she lavished upon him as if he'd been an automaton. When they'd played it out, he went up to the Tressillian, who was talking to Marc in the window, and, to my supreme astonishment, asked her to have a game.

"Thank you, no," answered Violet, coldly; "it is too warm for billiards."

This was certainly the first time the Major had ever been refused in any of his overtures to her sex, and I believe it surprised him exceedingly. He bent his head, and soon after he went for a walk in the rosery with Lucy Carteret, whom he hates. We always hate those manœuvring, *maniéré* girls, who are everlastingly flinging bait after us, whether or no we want to nibble; and just in proportion as they fixatrice, and crinoline, and cosmetique to hook us, will leave us to die in the sun when they've once trapped us into the basket.

That night, when Telfer sat down to écarté, Violet was singing in another room, out of which her voice came distinctly to us. I noticed he didn't play quite as well as usual. I don't suppose he could be listening, though, for he doesn't care for music, and still less for the Tressillian.

"Mademoiselle," said De Tintiniac, going up to her afterwards, "you can boast of greater conquests than Orpheus. He only charmed rocks, but you have distracted the two most inveterate *joueurs* in Europe."

Telfer looked annoyed. Violet laughed. "Pardon me if I doubt your compliment. If you were so kind as to listen to me, I have not enough vanity to think that your opponent would yield to what *he* would think such immeasurable weakness."

"You are not magnanimous, Miss Tressillian," said Telfer, in a low tone, leaning down over the piano. "You are ceaselessly reminding me of a hasty prejudice, unjustly formed, of which I have told you I am heartily ashamed."

"A hasty prejudice!" repeated Violet. "I beg your pardon, Major Telfer; I think ours is a very strong and lasting enmity, as mutual as it is well founded. Don't contradict me; you know you could have shot me with as little remorse as a partridge."

"But can you never forget," continued Telfer, impatiently, "that my enmity, as you please to term it, was grafted on erroneous opinions and false reports, and will you never credit that when I see myself in the wrong, I am too just to others to continue in it?"

The Tressillian laughed—a mischievous, *provoquant* laugh. "No, I believe neither in sudden conversions nor sudden friendships. Pray do not trouble yourself to be 'just' to me; you see I did not droop and die under the shadow of your wrath."

"Oh no," said Telfer, with a sardonic twist of his moustaches, "one would not accuse you of too much softness, Miss Tressillian."

She colored, and the pride of her family flashed out of her eyes. The Tressillians are all deucedly proud, and would die sooner than yield an inch. "If by softness you mean weakness, you are right," she said, haughtily. "As I have told you, we never forgive injustice."

Telfer frowned. If there was one thing he hated more than another, it was a woman who had anything hard about her. He smiled his chilliest smile. "Those are harsh words from a lady's lips—not so becoming to them as something gentler. You remind me, Miss Tressillian, of a young panther I once had, beautiful to look at, but eminently dangerous to approach, much less to caress. Everybody admired my panther, but no one dared to choose it for a pet."

With this uncourteous allegory the Major turned away, leaving Violet to make it out as best she might. It was good fun to watch the Tressillian's face: I only, standing near, had caught what he said, for he had spoken very low. First she looked haughty and annoyed, then a little troubled and perplexed: she sat quiet a minute, playing thoughtfully with her bracelets; then shook her head with a movement of defiance, and began to sing a Venetian barcarole with more *élan* and spirit than ever.

"By Jove! Telfer," said I, as we sat in the smoking-room that night, "your would-have-been mother-in-law has plenty of pluck. She'd have kept you in good training, and made a better boy of you; it's quite a loss to your morals that your father didn't marry her."

Telfer didn't look best pleased. He stretched himself full length on one of the divans, and answered not.

"I shouldn't be surprised if, with all her beauty, she hangs on hand," said Walsham, "for she hasn't a rap, you know; her governor gamed it all away, and she's certainly a bit of a flirt."

"I don't think so," said Telfer, shortly.

"Oh, by George! don't you? but I do," cried Fred. "Why, she takes a turn at us all, from old De Tintiniac, with his padded figure and coulisses compliments, to Marc, young and beautiful, as the novels say,—but we'll spare his blushes—from Vane, there, with his long rent-roll, to poor me, who she knows goes on tick for my weeds and gloves. She flirts with us all, one after the other, except you, whom she don't dare to touch. Tell me where you get your *noli me tangere* armor, Telfer, and I'll adopt it to-morrow, for the girls make such desperate love to me I know some of them will propose before long."

Telfer smoked vigorously during Fred's peroration, and his brow darkened. "I do not consider Miss Tressillian a flirt," he said, slowly. "She's too careless in showing you her weak points to be trying to trap you. What *I* call a coquette is a woman who is all things to all men, whose every languishing glance is a bait, and whose every thought is a conquest."

"And pray how can you tell but what the Tressillian's naturalness and carelessness may be only a superior bit of acting? The highest art, you know, is to imitate nature so close that you can't tell which is which," laughed Walsham.

Telfer didn't seem to relish the suggestion, but went on smoking fiercely.

"Not that I want to speak against the girl," Fred went on; "she's very amusing, and well enough, I dare say, if she weren't so devilish proud."

"You seem rather inconsistent," said Telfer, impatiently. "First, you accuse her of being too free, and then blame her for being too reserved."

Walsham laughed.

"If I'm inconsistent, you're a perfect weathercock. A month ago you were calling Violet every name you could think of, and now you snap us all off short if we say a word against her."

Telfer looked haughty enough to extinguish Fred upon the spot; Fred being a small, lively little chap, with not the slightest dignity about him.

"I know little or nothing of Miss Tressillian, but as I was the first to prejudice you all against her, it is only common honor to take her part when I think her unjustly attacked."

Fred gave me a wink of intense significance, but remonstrated no further, for Telfer had something of the dark look upon him that our men knew so well when he led them down to the slaughter at Alma and Balaklava.

"I tell you," continued the Major, after a little silence, "that I am disgusted with myself for having listened to whispers and reports, and believed in them just because they suited the bias of my prejudice. It didn't matter to me whom my father married, as far as money went, for beyond 10,000*l*. or so, it must all come in the entail; but I couldn't endure the idea of his being chiselled by some Becky Sharp or Blanche Armory, and I made up my mind that the Tressillian was of that genre. I've changed my opinion now. I don't think she either is an actress or an intrigante; and I should be a coward indeed if I hesitated to say so, out of common justice to a young girl who has no one to defend her."

"Bravo, my boy!" said Walsham; "I thought the Tressillian's bright eyes wouldn't let you hate her long. You're quite right, though 'pon my life it is really horrid how women contrive to damage each other. If there's an unlucky girl who has made the best match of the season—she might be an angel from heaven—her bosom-friends would manage gently to spread abroad the interesting facts that she's a 'dreadful flirt,' 'has a snub nose,' is an awful temper, had a ballet-girl for her mamma, or something detrimental. An attractive woman is the target for all her sex to shoot their sneers at, and if the poor thing isn't so riddled with arrows that she's no beauty left, it isn't her sisters' fault."

"I believe you," said Telfer. "My gauge of a woman's fascinations is the amount of hatred all the others bear her. It often amuses me to hear the tone that ladies take in talking of some girl whom we admire. She's a charming creature—a darling—their particular friend but ... there's always a 'but' to neutralize the praise, and with their honeyed hatred they contrive to damn the luckless object irretrievably. If another man's a good shot, or whip, or billiard-player, we're not spiteful to him for it. We think him a good fellow, and like him the better; but the dear *beau sexe* cannot bear a rival, and never rest while one of their acquaintance has diamonds a carat larger, dresses a trifle more costly, has finer horses, or more conquests. The only style of friend I ever heard women speak well of is some plain and timorous individual, good-natured to foolery, and weak as water, who never comes in their orbit, and whom we never look at; and then what a darling she is, and how eloquently they will laud her to the skies, despising her miserably all the while for not having been born pretty!"

"True enough," Marc began. "Why do the Carterets treat the Tressillian so disagreeably?—only because, though without their fortune, she makes ten times their coups; and get themselves up how they may, they know none of us care to waltz with them if she's in the room. Let's drink her health in Marcobrunnen—she's magnificent eyes."

"And first-rate style," said I.

"And a deuced pretty foot," cried Fred.

"*Et une taille superbe,*" added de Tintiniac, just come in. "*En vérité, elle est chouette cette Violette Anglaise.*"

So we chanted the Tressillian's praises. Telfer drank the toast in silence—I thought with a frown on his brow at the freedom with which we discussed his fair foe.

Little Countess Virginie's wedding was to come off in another month, and Marc begged us so hard to stay on till then, that, Telfer seeming very willing, I consented, though it would be the first September I had ever spent out of the English open since I was old enough to know partridges from pheasants. The Tressillian being Virginie's pet friend, after young ladies' custom of contracting eternal alliances (which ordinarily terminate in a quarrel about the shade of a ponceau ribbon, or a mauve flower, or a cornet's eyes, some three months after the signing and sealing thereof), was of course to be one of the *filles d'honneur*. So, as I said to Telfer, he'd have time for a few more battles before the two enemies parted to meet again—nobody could tell when.

I began to think that the Major had really been wounded, and that his opponent's bright eyes wouldn't let him come out of the fight wholly scathless, as I saw him leaning against the wall at a ball in the Redoute at Pipesandbeersbad, watching Violet with great earnestness as she whirled round in a *deux temps*, bewitching as was her wont all the frequenters of the Bad. Rich English dyspeptics, poverty-stricken princes, Austrian diplomats, come to cure their hypochondria; French *décorés*, to try their new cabals and martingales; British snobs, to indulge the luxury of grumbling,—all of them found some strange attraction in the "Violette Anglaise."

Violet sank on a seat after her valse. Telfer quietly displaced a young dragoon from Lucca, and sat down by her.

"I am going to stay on another month, Miss Tressillian; are you not sorry to hear it?" he said, with a smile, but I thought a little anxiety in his eyes.

The color flushed over her face, and she answered, with a laugh, not quite a real one: "Of course I am very sorry. I would go away myself to let you enjoy your last week in peace if I were not engaged to Virginie. Cannot you get me leave of absence from her? I know you would throw your whole heart into the petition."

Telfer curled his moustaches impatiently.

"Truth has come out of her well at last," he said, with a dash of bitterness, "and has disguised herself in Miss Tressillian's tulle illusion."

Violet colored brighter still.

"Well," she said, quickly, "was it not your decision that we should never waste courtesy on one another? Was not your own desire *guerre à outrance*?"

"No," answered Telfer, his brow darkening; "that I certainly must deny. I did you injustice, and I offered you an apology. No man could do more than acknowledge he was in the wrong. I offered you the palm-branch once; you were pleased to refuse it. I am not a man, Miss Tressillian, to run the chance of another repulse. My friendship is not so cheap that I shall intrude it where it is undesired." He spoke with a laugh, but his eyes had a grave anger in them that Violet didn't quite relish.

She looked a little bit frightened up at him. The proud, brilliant Tressillian was as pale and quiet as a little child after a good scolding. But she soon rallied, and flashed up haughtier than ever.

"Major Telfer, you make one great error—one very common to your sex. You drop us one day, and take us up the next, and then think that we must be grateful to you for the supreme honor you do us. You are cold to us, absolutely rude, as long as it pleases your lordly will, and then, at the first word of courtesy and kindness, you expect us to rise and make you a *révérence* in the utmost humiliation and thanksgiving. You men"— and Violet began destroying her bouquet with immense energy—"treat us exactly as a cat will treat a mouse. You yourself, for instance, in a moment's hasty judgment, construed all my actions by the light of your own unjust suspicions, and believing everything, no matter how unfounded, spoke against me to all your acquaintance, and treated me with, as you must admit, but scanty courtesy, for one whom I have heard piques himself on his high breeding. And now, when you discover that your suspicions had no foundation, and your hatred no grounds, you wonder that I find it difficult to be as grateful as you seem to think I should be for your having so kindly misjudged me."

As the young lady gave all this forth with much vehemence and spirit, Telfer's lips set, and the blood forced itself through the bronze of his cheeks. He bent towards her till his moustache touched her hair.

"You have no mercy, Violet Tressillian," he said, between his teeth. "Take care that no one is as pitiless to you in return."

She started, and her bouquet fell to the ground. Telfer gave it her back without looking at her, and turned round to an Austrian with his usual impassive air.

"Do you know where De Tintiniac is, Staumgaurn? In the roulette room? All right. I am going there now."

He did go there, and I've a notion that the croupier of Pipesandbeersbad made something that night out of the Major's preoccupation.

Violet, meanwhile, was waltzing with Staumgaurn and a dozen others, but looked rather white—not using any rouge but what nature had given her—and by the end of the evening her bouquet had utterly come to grief. Days went on till a fortnight of our last month had gone, and Telfer, to my sorrow (not surprise, for I always thought the Tressillian was a dangerous foe, and that, like Ringwood, he'd find himself unhorsed by a woman), grew grave and stern, haunted with ten times more recklessness than usual, and threw away his guineas at the Redoute in a wild way, quite new with him, for though he liked play *pour s'amuser*, he had too much control over his passions ever to let play get ascendancy over him. I used to think he had the strongest passions and the strongest will over them of any man I knew; but now a passion least undesired and most hopeless of any that ever entered his soul, seemed to have mastered him. Not that he showed it; with the Tressillian he was simply distantly courteous; but I, who was on the *qui vive* for his first sign of being conquered, saw his eyebrows contract when somebody was paying her desperate court, and his glance lighten and flash when she passed near him. They had never been alone since the night of the ball, and Violet was too proud to try for a reconciliation, even if she'd cared for one.

One night we were at a ball at the Prince Humbugandschwerinn's. The Tressillian had been waltzing with all her might, and had all the men in the room, Humbugandschwerinn himself included, round her. Telfer leaned against a console ten minutes, watching her, and then abruptly left the ball-room, and did not return again. He came instead into the card-room, and sat down to *écarté* with De Tintiniac, and lost two games at ten Napoleons a side. Generally, he played very steadily, never giving his attention to anything but the game; but now he was listening to what a knot of men were saying, who were laughing, chatting, and sipping coffee, while they talked about—the Tressillian.

"I mark the king and play," said Telfer, his eyes fixed fiercely on a young fellow who was discussing Violet much as he'd have discussed his new Danish dog or English hunter. He was Jack Snobley, Lord Featherweight's son, who was doing the grand, a confounded young parvenu, vulgar as his cotton-spinning ancestry could make him, who could appreciate the Tressillian about as much as he could Dannecker's Ariadne, which work of art he pronounced, in my hearing, "a pretty girl, but the dawg very badly done—too much like a cat." "I take your three to two," continued Telfer, his brow lowering as he heard the young fool praising and criticising Violet with small ceremony. The Major had the haughtiest patrician principles, and to hear a snob like this sandy-haired honorable, speaking of the woman *he* chose to champion as he might have done of some ballerina or Chaumière belle, was rather too much for Telfer's self-control.

When the game was done, he rose, and walked quietly over to where Snobley stood. He looked him down with that cold, haughty glance that has cowed men bolder than Lord Featherweight's hopeful offspring, and said a word or two to him in a low tone, which caused that gentleman to flush up red and look fierce with all his might.

"What's the girl to you, that I mayn't speak as I choose of her?" he retorted; the Sillery, of which he'd taken a good deal too much, working up in his weak brain. "I've heard that she jilted you, and that was why you've been setting them all against her, and saying she wanted to hook your old governor."

The Sillery must have indeed obscured Jack's reason with a vengeance to make him venture this very elegant and refined speech with the Major, most fastidious in his ideas of good breeding, and most direful in his wrath, of any man I ever knew. Telfer's cheek turned as white with passion as the bronze would let it; his gray eyes grew almost black as they stared at the young snob. He was so supremely astonished that this ill-bred boy had actually dared thus to address him!

"Mr. Snobley," he said, with his chilled and most ironical smile, and his quietest, most courteous voice, "you must learn good manners before you venture to parley with gentlemen. Allow me to give you your first lesson." And stooping, as if to a very little boy—young Snobley was a good foot shorter than he—the Major struck him on the lips with his left-hand French kid glove. It was a very gentle blow—it would scarcely have reddened the Tressillian's delicate skin—but on the Hon. Jack it had electric effect. He was beginning to swear, to look big, to talk of satisfaction, insult, and all the rest of it; but Telfer laughed, bent his head, told him he was quite ready to satisfy him to any extent he required; and, turning away, sat down to *écarté* calm and impassive as ever, and pleased greatly with himself for having silenced this silly youth. The affair was much less exciting to him than it was to any other man in the room. "It's too great an honor for him, the young brute, for me to be called out by him, as if he were one of us. I hate snobs; Lord Featherweight's grandfather was butler to mine, and he himself was a cotton-spinner in Lancashire, and then this little contemptible puppy dares to——"

Telfer finished his sentence with a puff of smoke from his meerschaum, as he sat in his bedroom after the ball, into which sanctuary I had followed him to talk a little before turning in.

"To discuss the Tressillian," said I. "But that surprises me less, old fellow, than that you should champion her. What's it for? Has hate turned to the other thing? Have you come to think that, though she'd make a very bad mother-in-law, she'd make a charming wife? 'Pon my life, if you have— —"

"Hush! Don't jest!"

I knew by the tone of those three little monosyllables that the Major was done for—caught, conquered, and fettered by his dangerous foe.

Telfer sat silent for some minutes, looking out of the window where the dawn was rising over the hills, with a settled gloom upon his face. Then he rose, and began swinging about the room with his firm cavalry tread, his arms crossed on his chest, and his head bent down.

"By Heaven! Vane," he said at length, in a tone low, but passionate and bitter, "I have gone on like a baby or a fool, playing with tools till they have cut me. Against my will, against my judgment, against reason, hope, everything, I have lingered in that girl's fascinations till I am bound by them hand and foot. I cannot deceive myself, I cannot shut the truth out; it was not honor, nor chivalry, nor friendship that made me to-night insult the man who spoke jestingly of her; it was love—love as mad, as reckless, as misplaced, as ever cursed a man and drove him to his ruin." He paused, breathing hard, with his teeth set, then broke out again: "I, who held love in such disdain, who have so long kept my passions in such strong control, who thought no woman had the power to move me against my will—I love at last, despite myself, though I know that she is pitiless, that nothing I have said has been able to touch her into softer feeling, and that, mad as my passion is for her, if her nature be as hard and haughty as I fear, I dare not, if I could, make her my wife. No, Vane, no," he went on, hastily, as I interrupted. "She does not love me, she has no gentler feeling in her; I thought she had, but I was mistaken. I tried her several times, but she will never forgive my first injustice to her; and to one with so little softness in her nature I dare not trust my peace. It were a worse hell even than that I now endure, to have her with me, loving her as I do, and feel that her cold heart gave no response to mine; to possess her glorious beauty, and yet know that her love and her soul were dead in their chill pride to me— —"

He paused again, and leaned against the window, his chest heaving, and hot tears standing in his haughty eyes, wrung from the very anguish of his soul. The pride that had never before bent to any human thing, was now cast in the dust before a woman who never did, and probably never would, love him in return.

V
THE DUEL, AND ITS CONSEQUENCES

The contemptible young puppy, for whom Telfer considered the honor of a ball from his pistol a great deal too good in the morning, sent Heavysides, of the 40th, a chum of his found up at the Bad, to claim "satisfaction," the valor produced in him by Sillery over night having been kept up since by copious draughts of cognac and Seltzer. Having signified to Heavysides that the Major would do Mr. Snobley the favor of shooting him in the retired valley of Königshöhle at sunrise the next day, I went to tell Telfer, who had a hearty laugh at the young fellow's challenge.

"I'd give him something to shoot me through the heart," said he, bitterly, "but I don't suppose he will. He's practised at pigeons, not at men, probably. I won't hurt him much, but a little lesson will do him good. Mind nobody in the house gets wind of the affair. Though I make a fool of myself in her defence, there is no need that she or others should know it. But if the boy should do for me, tell her, Vane—tell her," said the Major, shading his eyes with his hand, "that I have learnt to love her as I never dreamt I should love any woman, and that I do not blame her for the just lesson she has read me for the rudeness and the unjust prejudice I indulged in so long towards her. She retaliated fairly upon me, and God forbid that she should have one hour of her life embittered through remorse for me."

His voice sank into a whisper as he spoke; then, with an effort, he forced himself into calmness, and went to play billiards with Marc. This was the man who, three months before, had told me with such contemptuous decision that "we need never fall in love unless it's convenient; and as to caring for a girl who doesn't care for us, that was a weakness with which he couldn't sympathize at all!"

Late that night, Telfer and I, coming down the stairs, met the Tressillian going up them to her room. The Major stopped her, and held out his hand, with a softened light in his eyes. "Will you not bid me good-bye? I may not see you again."

There was a sadness in his smile bitterly significant to me, but very likely she didn't see it, not having any key to it, as I had.

Violet turned pale, and I fancied her lips twitched, but it might be the flickering of the light of the staircase lamps on her face. At any rate, being a young lady born and bred in good society, she put her hand in his, with a simple "What! are you going away?"

"Perhaps. At any rate, let us part in peace."

The proud man laughed as he said it, though he was enduring tortures. Violet heard the laugh, and didn't see the straining anxiety in his gaze.

She drew her hand rapidly away. "Certainly. *Bon voyage*, Major Telfer, and good night," she answered, carelessly; and, with a graceful bend, the Tressillian floated on up the stairs with the dignity of a young empress.

Telfer looked after the white gossamer dress and the beautiful head, with its wreath of scarlet flowers, and an iron sternness settled on his face. All hope was gone now. She could not have parted with him like this if she had cared for him one straw more than for the flowers in her hair. Yet, in the morning, he was going to risk his life for her. Ah, well! I've always seen that in love there's one of the two who gives all and gets nothing.

In the morning, by five o'clock, in the valley of Königshöhle, a snug bit of pasture land between two rocks, where no gendarme could pounce upon us, young Snobley made his appearance to enjoy the honor of being a target for one of the best shots in Europe. Snobley had a good deal of swagger and would-be dash, and made a great show of pluck, which your man of true pluck never does. Telfer stood talking to me up to the last minute, took his pistol carelessly in his hand, and, without taking any apparent aim, fired.

If Telfer made up his mind to shoot off your fifth waistcoat-button, your fifth waistcoat-button would be irrevocably doomed; and therefore, having determined to himself to lodge a bullet in this young puppy's left wrist, in the left wrist did the ball lodge. Snobley was "satisfied," very amply satisfied, I fancy, by his looks. He'd fired, and sent his shot right into the trunk of a chestnut growing some seven yards off his opponent, to Heavyside's supreme scorn.

"That'll teach him not to talk of young ladies in his Mabille slang," said Telfer, lighting his cigar. "I hope the little snob may be the better for my lesson. Now I am *en route*, I'll go over to Pipesandbeersbad, breakfast at the Hôtel de France, and go and see Humbugandschwerinn: he wants me to look at some English racers Brookes has just sent him over. Make my excuses at Essellau; and I say, Vane, see if you can't get us away in a day or two; have some call home, or something, for I shall never stand this long."

With which not over-clear speech the Major mounted his horse and cantered off towards the Bad.

I rode back; went to my own room, had some chocolate, read Pigault le Brun, and about noon, seeing Virginie, the Tressillian, and several others out on the terrace, went to join them. Marc slipped his arm through mine and drew me aside.

"I say, Vane, what's all this about Telfer striking some fellow for talking about the Tressillian? Staurmgaurn was over here just now, and told me there was a row in the card-room at Humbugandschwerinn's between Telfer and another Englishman. I knew nothing about it. Is it true?"

"So far true," I answered, "that Telfer put a ball in the youth's wrist at seven o'clock this morning; and serve him right too—he's an impudent young snob."

"By Jove!" cried Marc, "what in the world made him take the Tressillian's part? Have the *beaux yeux* really made an impression on the most unimpressionable of men?"

"The devil they have," said I, crossly; "but I wish she'd been at the deuce first, for he's too good a fellow to waste his best years pining after a pair of dark eyes."

Marc shrugged his shoulders. "*C'est vrai*; but we're all fools some time or other. The idea of Telfer's chivalry! I declare it's quite like the old days of Froissart and Commines—fighting for my lady's favor." And away he went, singing those two famous lines from Alcyonée:

Pour mériter son cœur, pour plaire à ses beaux yeux,

J'ai fait la guerre aux rois: je l'aurais faite aux dieux;

and I thought to myself that if the Tressillian proved a De Longueville, I could find it in my soul to shoot her without remorse.

But as I turned away from Marc, I came upon her, looking pale and ill enough to satisfy anybody. The color flushed into her cheeks as she saw me; we spoke of the weather, the chances of storm, Floss's new collar, and other trifles; then she asked me, bending over her little dog,—

"Is Captain Staurmgaurn's news true, that your friend has—has been quarrelling with a young Englishman?"

"Yes," I answered. "I wonder Staurmgaurn told you; it is scarcely a topic to interest ladies. Telfer has given the young gentleman a well-merited lesson."

"Have they fought?" she asked, breathlessly, laying her hand on my arm, and looking as white as a ghost.

"Yes, they have," said I; "and he fought, Miss Tressillian, for one who gave him a very cold adieu last night."

Her head drooped, she trembled perceptibly, and the color rushed back to her cheeks.

"Is he safe?" she asked, in the lowest of whispers.

"Quite," I answered, quickly, as De Tintiniac lounged up to us; and I left my words, like a prudent diplomatist, to bear fruit as best they might.

I wondered if she cared for him, or if it was merely a girl's natural feeling for a man who had let himself be shot at, rather than hear a light word spoken of her. But they were both so deuced proud, Heaven's special intervention alone seemed likely to bring them together.

The Major didn't come home from Pipesandbeersbad till between two and three that night, and he's told me since that being *un peu fou* with his self-willed and vehement passion, never went to bed at all, but sat and walked about his room smoking, unable to sleep, in a frame of mind that, when sane, a few months before, he would have pronounced spoony and contemptible in the lowest degree. At eight he strode forth into the park, brushing off the dew with his impatient steps, glad of the fresh morning air upon his brow, which was as burning as our first headache from "that cursed punch of Jones's," the day after our "first wine," which acute suffering any gentleman who ever tasted that delicious *mélange* of rum and milk and lemons, will keenly recall among other passed-away passages of his green youth.

Telfer strode on and on, over the molehills and through the ferns, down this slope and up that, under the oaks, and lindens, and fir-trees gleaming red beneath the October sun, with very little notion of where he was going or what he was doing, a great stag-hound of Marc's following at his heels. The path he took, without thinking, led him to the top of a rock overhanging the Beersbad, where that historic stream was but a few yards in width; and here Telfer, lying down with his head against a plane-tree, struck a fusee and lighted a cigar—for a weed's a pleasant companion in any stage of existence: if we're happy we smoke in the fulness of our hearts, and build airy castles on each fragrant cloud; and if we're unhappy, we smoke to console ourselves, and draw in with each whiff philosophy and peace. So the Major smoked and thought, till a bark from the staghound made him look up. On the top of the cliffs on the other side of the stream, looking down into the valleys below, with her head turned away from him, stood Violet Tressillian; and at the sight of that graceful figure, with its indescribable high-bred air, I don't doubt the Major's once unimpressive heart beat faster than it had ever done in a charge or a skirmish. She was full twenty feet above him, and the rocks on which she stood sloped precipitately down to a ledge exactly opposite that on which he lay smoking—a ledge in reality but a few inches wide, but to which the treacherous boughs and ferns waving over it gave a semblance of a firm broad footing—a semblance which (like a good many other things one meets with) it utterly failed to carry out when you came to try it.

Violet, not seeing Telfer lying *perdu* among the grass at the foot of his plane-tree, walked along to the edge of the cliff, her eyes on the ground, so deep in thought that she never noticed the river beneath, but began to descend the slope, little Floss coming with exceeding trepidation after her. Telfer sprang up to warn her. "Violet! Violet! go back! go back! Oh! my God, do you not hear?"

His passionate tones startled her. Never dreaming he was there, she looked hurriedly up; her foot slipped; unable to stay her descent, she came down the steep cliff with an impetus which, to a certainty, would send her over the narrow ledge into the river below—a fall of full thirty feet. To see her perish thus before his eyes—die thus while he stood calmly by! A whole age of torture was crowded into the misery of that one brief moment. There was but one way to save her. He sprang across the gulf that parted them, while the river in its straitened bed hissed and foamed beneath him, and, standing on the narrow ledge, where there seemed scarce footing for a dog, he caught her as she fell in his iron grasp, as little swayed by the shock as the rock on which he stood. Holding her tight to him with one arm, he swung himself down by the other to a less dangerous position, on a flat plateau of cliff, and leaning against one of the linden-trees on its summit, he bent over her; his eyes dim, and his pulses beating with the emotions he had controlled while he wanted cool thought and firm nerve to save her, but over which he had no more power now. He pressed her to his heart, forgetting pride, and doubt, and fear; and Violet, by way of answer, only burst into a passion of tears. Who would have recognized the proud, brilliant Tressillian, in the pale, trembling woman who sobbed on his breast with the *abandon* of a child, and who, at his passionate kisses, only blushed like a wild rose?

Telfer evidently thought the transformation complete, for he forgot all his reserve resolutions and hauteur, and poured out the tenderest love for a girl who, three months before, he had wished at the devil! And the Tressillian was conquered at last; she was pitiless no longer, and, having vanquished him, was, woman-like, ready to be a slave to her captive; and her eyes were never more dangerous than now, when, shy and softened, they looked up through their tears into Telfer's.

What old De Tintiniac said of her was true, that all her beauty wanted to make it perfect was for her to be in love!

So at least I thought, when, several hours afterwards, I met them coming across the park, and I knew by the gleam of the Major's eyes that he had lost Calceolaria and won Violet.

"How strange it is," laughed Telfer that evening, when they were alone in the conservatory, "that you and I, who so hated each other, should now be so dear to one another. Oh, Violet! how ashamed I have been since of my unjustifiable prejudices, my abominable discourtesy——"

"You *were* dreadfully rude," said the Tressillian, smiling; "and judged me very cruelly by all the false reports that women chose to gossip of me. But you are wrong. I never hated you. Your father had spoken of you as so generous, so noble, so chivalrous a soldier, so kind a son, that I was prepared to admire you immensely, and when you looked so sternly on me at our first introduction, and I overheard your bitter words about me at the station, I really was never more vexed and disappointed in my life. And then a demon entered into me, and I thought—forgive me, Hamilton—that I would try to make you repent your hasty judgment and recant your prejudices. But I could not always fight you with the coolness I wished; your indifference began to pique me more and more. Wounds from you ranked as they did from no one else, and something besides pride made me feel your neglect so keenly. I had meant—yes, I must tell you all," and the Tressillian, in her soft repentance, looked, Telfer thought, more bewitching than in her most brilliant moments—"I had wished," she went on in a whisper, with her color bright, "to make you regret your injustice, to conquer your stubborn pride, and to revenge myself on you for all the wrong you had done me in thoughts and words. But, you see, I wasn't so strong as I fancied; I thought I could fence with the buttons on, but I was mistaken, and—and—when I heard that you had fought for me, I knew then that——" And Violet stopped with a smile and a sigh; the sigh for the past, I suppose, and the smile for the present.

"Well, *nous sommes quittes*, dearest," smiled Telfer. "Thank Heaven! we no longer need reproach each other. Too many elevate the one they love into an ideal of such superhuman excellence, that at the first shadow of mortality they see their poor idol is shivered from its pedestal. But we have seen the worst side of each other's character, Violet, and henceforth love shall cover all faults, and subdue all pride between us."

Telfer kept his word. They had had their last quarrel, and buried their last suspicion before their marriage, and were not, like the generality, doves first and tigers after. The governor, of course, was charmed that a match on which he had secretly set his heart had brought itself about so neatly without his interference. He had begun to despair of his son's ever giving Torwood a mistress, and the diamonds he gave Violet, in the excess of his pleasure, brought her no end of female enemies, for they were some of the finest water in the kingdom. Seldom, indeed, has slander been productive of such good fruits, for rarely, *very* rarely, does that Upas-tree put forth any but Dead Sea apples.

Violet Tressillian *was* Violet Telfer before the Christmas recess, but I considered the bet drawn. So Telfer and I exchanged the roan filly and the colt, and Calceolaria in the Torwood stables, and Jockey Club in my stalls, stand witnesses to this day of Our Wager, and how the Major Lost and Won.

OUR COUNTRY QUARTERS

I remember well the day that we (that is the 110th Lancers) were ordered down to Layton Rise. Savage enough we all were to quit P—— for that detestable country place. Many and miserable were the tales we raked up of the *ennui* we had experienced at other provincial quarters; sadly we dressed for Lady Dashwood's ball, the last *soirée* before our departure. And then the bills and the *billets-doux* that rained down upon our devoted heads!

However, by some miracle we escaped them all; and on a bright April morning, 184-, we were *en route* for this Layton Rise, this *terra incognita*, as grumpy and as seedy as ever any poor demons were. But there was no help for it; so leaving, we flattered ourselves, a great many hearts the heavier for this order from the Horse Guards, we, as I said, set out for Layton Rise.

The only bit of good news that provoking morning had brought was that my particular chum, Drummond Fane, a captain of ours, who had been cutting about on leave from Constantinople to Kamtchatka for the last six months, would join us at Layton. Fane was really a good fellow, a perfect gentleman (*ça va sans dire*, as he was one of *ours*), intensely plucky, knew, I believe, every language under the sun, and, as he had been tumbling about in the world ever since he went to Eton at eight years old, had done everything, seen everything, and could talk on every possible subject. He was a great favorite with ladies: I always wonder they did not quite spoil him. I have seen a young lady actually neglect a most eligible heir to a dukedom, that her mamma had been at great pains to procure for her, if this "fascinating younger son" were by. For Fane *was* the younger son of the Earl of Avanley, and would, of course, every one said, one day retrieve his fortunes by marriage with some heiress in want of rank.

He has been my great friend ever since I, a small youth, spoiled by having come into my property while in the nursery, became his fag at Eton: and when I bought my commission in the 110th, of which he was a captain, our intimacy increased.

But *revenons à nos moutons.* On the road we naturally talked of Layton, wondering if there was any one fit to visit, anybody that gave good dinners, if there was a pack of hounds, a billiard-room, or any pretty girls. Suddenly the Honorable Ennuyé L'Estrange threw a little light on the matter, by recollecting, "now he thought of it, he believed that was where an uncle of his lived; his name was Aspi—Aspinall—no! Aspeden." "Had he any cousins?" was the inquiry. He "y'ally could not remember!" So we were left to conjure up imaginary Miss Aspedens, more handsome than their honorable cousin, who might relieve for us the monotony of country quarters. The sun was very bright as we entered Layton Rise; the clattering and clashing that we made soon brought out the inhabitants, and, lying in the light of a spring day, it did not seem such a very miserable little town after all. Our mess was established at the one good inn of the one good street of the place, and I and two other young subs fixed our residence at a grocer's, where a card of "Lodgings to let furnished" was embordered in vine-leaves and roses.

As I was leaning out of the window smoking my last cigar before mess, with Sydney and Mounteagle stretched in equally elegant attitudes on equally hard sofas, I heard our grocer, a sleek little Methodist, addressing some party in the street with—"I fear me I have done evil in admitting these young servants of Satan into mine habitation!" "Well, Nathan," replied a Quaker, "thou didst it for the best, and verily these officers seem quiet and gentlemanly youths." "Gentlemanlike," I should say we were, *rather*—but "quiet!"—how we shouted over the innocent "Friend's" mistake. Here the voices again resumed. "Doubtless, when the Aspedens return, there will be dances and devices of the Evil One, and Quelps will make a good time of it; however, the custom of ungodly men I would not take were it offered!" So these Aspedens were out—confound it! But the clock struck six; so, flinging the remains of my cigar on the Quaker's broad-brimmed hat, adorned with which ornament he walked unconsciously away, we strolled down to the mess-room.

A few hours later some of them met in my room, and having sent out for some cards, which the grocer kindly wrapped in a tract against gambling, we had just sat down to loo, when the door was thrown open, and Captain Fane announced. A welcome addition!

"Fane, by all that's glorious!"—"Well, young one, how are you?" were the only salutations that passed between two men who were as true friends as any in England. Fane was soon seated among us, and telling us many a joke and tale. "And so," said he, "we're sent down to ruralize? (Mounteagle, you are 'loo'd.') Any one you know here?"

"Not a creature! I am awfully afraid we shall be found dead of *ennui* one fine morning. I'll thank you for a little more punch, Fitzspur," said Sydney. "I suppose, as usual, Fane," he continued, "you left at the very least twelve dozen German princesses, Italian marchesas, and French countesses dying for you?"

"My dear fellow," replied Fane, "you are considerably under the mark (I'll take 'miss,' Paget!); but really, if women *will* fall in love with you, how *can* you help it? And if you *will* flirt with them, how can they help it?"

"I see, Fane, *your* heart is as strong as ever," I added, laughing.

"Of course," answered the gallant captain; "disinterested love is reserved for men who are too rich or too poor to mind its attendant evils. (The first, I must say, very rarely profit by the privilege!) No! I steel myself against all bright eyes and dancing curls not backed by a good dowry. Heiresses, though, somehow, are always plain; I never could do my duty and propose to one, though, of course, whenever I *do* surrender my liberty, which I have not the smallest intention of at present, it will be to somebody with at least fifty thousand a year. Hearts trumps, Mount?"

"Yes—hurrah! Paget's loo'd at last.—Here, my dear, let us have lots more punch!" said Mounteagle, addressing the female domestic, who was standing open-mouthed at the glittering pool of half-sovereigns.

I will spare the gentle reader—if I *may* flatter myself that I entertain a *few* such—a recital of the conversation which followed, and which was kept up until the very, very "small hours;" also I will leave it to her imagination to picture how we spent the next few days, how we found out a few families worth visiting, how we inspired the Layton youths with a vehement passion for smoking, billiards, and the cavalry branch of the service, and how we and our gay uniforms and our prancing horses were the admiration of all the young damsels in the place.

One morning after parade, Fane and I, having nothing better to do, lighted our cigars and strolled down one of those shady lanes which almost reconcile one to the country—*out* of the London season. Seeing the gate of a park standing invitingly open, we walked in and threw ourselves down under the trees. "Now we are in for it," said Fane, "if we are trespassing, and any adventurous-minded gamekeeper appears. Whose park is this?"

"Mr. Aspeden's, Ennuyé told me. It's rather a nice place," I replied.

"And that castle, of which mine eyes behold the turrets afar off?" he asked.

"Lord Linton's, I believe; the father of Jack Vernon, of the Rifles, you know," I answered.

"Indeed! I never saw the old gentleman, but I remember his daughter Beatrice,—we had rather a desperate flirtation at Baden-Baden. She's a showy-looking girl," said the captain, stretching himself on the grass.

"Why did you not allow her the sublime felicity of becoming Lady Beatrice Fane?" I asked, laughing.

"My dear fellow, she had not a *sou*! That old marquis is as poor as a church-mouse. You forget that I am only a younger son, with not much besides my pay, and cannot afford to marry anywhere I like. I am not in your happy position, able to espouse any pretty face I may chance to take a fancy to. It would be utter madness in me. Do you think *I* was made for a little house, one maid-servant, dinner at noon, and six small children? *Very much obliged to you, but love in a cottage is not* my *style, Fred; besides* j'aime à vivre garçon!" added Fane.

"*Et moi aussi!*" said I. "Really the girls one meets seem all tarlatan and coquetry. I have never seen one worth committing matrimony for."

"Hear him!" cried Fane. "Here is the happy owner of Wilmot Park, at the advanced age of twenty, despairing of ever finding anything more worthy of his affection than his moustaches! Oh, what will the boys come to next? But, eureka! here comes a pretty girl if you like. Who on earth is she?" he exclaimed, raising his eye-glass to a party advancing up the avenue who really seemed worthy the attention.

Pulling at the bridle of a donkey, "what wouldn't go," with all her might, was indeed a pretty girl. Her hat had fallen off and showed a quantity of bright hair and a lovely face, with the largest and darkest of eyes, and a mouth now wreathing with smiles. Unconscious of our vicinity, on she came, laughing, and beseeching a little boy, seated on the aforesaid donkey, and thumping thereupon with, a large stick, "not to be so cruel and hurt poor Dapple." At this juncture the restive steed gave a vigorous stride, and toppling its rider on the grass, trotted off with a self-satisfied air; but Fane, intending to make the rebellious charger a means of introduction, caught his bridle and led him back to his discomfited master. The young lady, who was endeavoring to pacify the child, looked prettier than ever as she smiled and thanked him. But the gallant captain was not going to let the matter drop *here*, so, turning to the youthful rider, he asked him to let him put him on "the naughty donkey again." Master Tommy acquiesced, and, armed with his terrible stick, allowed himself to be mounted. Certainly Fane was a most unnecessary length of time settling that child, but then he was talking to the young lady, whom he begged to allow him to lead the donkey home.

"Oh! no, she was quite used to Dapple; she could manage him very well, and they were going farther." So poor Fane had nothing for it but to raise his hat and gaze at her through his eye-glass until some trees hid her from sight.

"'Pon my word, that's a pretty girl!" said he, at length. "I wonder who she can be! However, I shall soon find out. Have another weed, Fred?"

There was to be a ball that night at the Assembly Rooms, which we were assured only the "*best* families" would attend for Layton was a very exclusive little town in its way. Some of us who were going were standing about the mess-room, recalling the many good balls and pretty girls of our late quarters, when Fane, who had declined to go, as he said he had a horror of "bad dancing, bad perfumes, bad ventilation, and bad champagne, and really could not stand the concentration of all of them, which he foresaw that night," to our surprise declared his intention of accompanying us.

"I suppose, Fane, you hope to see your heroine of the donkey again?" asked Sydney.

"Precisely," was Fane's reply; "or if not, to find out who she is. But here comes Ennuyé, got up no end to fascinate the belles of Layton!"

"The Aspedens are home; I saw 'em to-day," were the words of the honorable cornet, as he lounged into the room. "My uncle seems rather a brick, and hopes to make the acquaintance of all of you. He will mess with us to-morrow."

"Have you any *belles cousines*?"—"Are they going to-night?" we inquired.

"Yaas, I saw one; she's rather pretty," said L'Estrange.

"Dark eyes—golden hair—about eighteen?" demanded Fane, eagerly.

"Not a bit of it," replied the cornet, curling his moustache, and contemplating himself in the glass with very great satisfaction; "hair's as dark as mine, and eyes—y'ally I forget. But, let's have loo or whist, or something; we need not go for ages!" So down we sat, and soon nothing was heard but "Two by honors and the trick!" "Game and game!" &c., until about twelve, when we rose and adjourned to the ball-room.

No sooner had we entered the room than Fane exclaimed, "There's my houri, by all that's glorious! and looking lovelier than ever. By Jove! that girl's too good for a country ball-room!" And there, in truth, waltzing like a sylph, was, as Sydney called her, the "heroine of the donkey." The dance over, we saw her join a party at the top of the room, consisting of a handsome but *passée* woman, a lovely Hebe-like girl with dancing eyes, and a number of gentlemen, with whom they seemed to be keeping up an animated conversation.

"Ennuyé is with them—he will introduce me," said Fane, as he swept up the room.

I watched him bow, and, after talking a few minutes, lead off his "houri" for a *valse*; and disengaging myself from a Cambridge friend whom I had met with, I professed my intention of following his example.

"What? Who did you say? That girl at the top there? Why, man, that's my cousin Mary, and the other lady is my most revered aunt, Mrs. Aspeden. Did you not know I and Ennuyé were related? Y'ally I forget how, exactly," he continued, mimicking the cornet. "But do you want to be introduced to her? Come along then."

So, following my friend, who was a Trinity-man, of the name of Cleaveland, I soon made acquaintance with Mrs. Aspeden and her daughter Mary.

"*Who* is he?" I heard Mrs. Aspeden ask, in a low tone, of Tom Cleaveland, as I led off Mary to the *valse*.

"A very good fellow," was the good-natured Cantab's reply, "with lots of tin and a glorious place. The shooting at Wilmot is really——"

"*Bien!*" said his aunt, as she took Lord Linton's arm to the refreshment-room, satisfied, I suppose, on the strength of my "lots of tin," that I was a safe companion for her child.

I found Mary Aspeden a most agreeable partner for a *dance*; she was lively, agreeable, and a coquette, I felt sure (women with those dancing eyes always are), and I thought I could not do better than amuse myself by getting up a flirtation with her. What an intensely good opinion I had of myself then! So I condescended to dance, though it was not Almack's, and actually permitted myself to be amused. Strolling through the rooms with Mary Aspeden on my arm, we entered one in which was an alcove fitted up with a *vis-à-vis* sofa (whoever planned that Layton ball-room had a sympathy in the bottom of his heart for *tête-à-tête*), and here Fane was seated, talking to his "houri" with the soft voice and winning smiles which had gained the heart, or at least what portion of that member they possessed, of so many London belles, and which would do their work *here* most assuredly.

"There is my cousin Florence—ah! she does not observe us. Who is the gentleman with her?" said Miss Aspeden.

"My friend, Captain Fane," I replied. "You have heard of their rencontre this morning?"

"Indeed! is he Tommy's champion, of whom he has done nothing but talk all day, and of whom I could not make Florence say one word?" asked Mary. "You must know our donkey is the most determined and resolute of animals: if she 'will, she will,' you may depend upon it!" she continued.

"Do you honor those most untrue lines upon ladies by a quotation?" I asked.

"I do not think they *are* so very untrue," laughed Mary, "except in confining obstinacy to us poor women and exempting the 'lords of the creation.' The Scotch adage knows better. 'A wilful *man* — —' You know the rest."

"Quite well," I replied; "but another poet's lines on *you* are far more true. 'Ye are stars of the— —'" I commenced.

"Mary, my love, let me introduce you to Lord Craigarven," said Mrs. Aspeden, coming up with Lord Linton's heir-apparent.

At the same time I was introduced to Mr. Aspeden, a hearty Englishman, loving his horses, his dogs, and his daughter; and as much the inferior of his aristocratic-looking wife in *intellect* as he was her superior in *heart*. When we parted that night he gave Fane and me a most hospitable general invitation, and, what was more, an especial one for the next night. As we walked home "i' the grey o' the morning," I asked Fane who his "houri" was.

"A niece of Mr. Aspeden's, and cousin to your friend Cleaveland," was the reply. "Those Aspedens really seem to be uncle and aunt to every one. She is staying there now."

"So is Tom Cleaveland," said I. "But, pray, are your expectations quite realized? Is she as charming as she looks, this Miss Florence— —"

"Aspeden?" added Fane. "Yes, quite. But here are my quarters; so good night, old fellow."

We had soon established ourselves as *amis de la maison* at Woodlands, the Aspedens' place, and found him, as his nephew had stated, "rather a brick," and her daughter and niece something more. All of us, especially Fane and I, spent the best part of our time there, lounging away the days between the shady lanes, the little lake, and the music or billiard-rooms. Fane seemed entirely to appropriate Florence, and to fascinate her as he had fascinated so many others. I really felt angry with him; for, as Tom Cleaveland had candidly told me that poor Florie had not a rap—her father had run through all his property and left her an orphan, and a very poor one too—of course Fane could not marry her, but would, I feared, "ride away" some day, like the "gay dragoon," heartwhole *himself*—but would *she* come out as scatheless? Poor Mounteagle, too, was getting quite spooney about Florence, and, owing to Fane, she paid him no more heed than if he had been an old dried-up Indianized major. *He*, poor fellow! followed her about everywhere, asked her to dance in quite an insane manner, and made the most horrible revokes in whist and mistakes in pool that can be imagined.

"By George! she is pretty, and no mistake!" said Sydney, as Florence rode past us one day as we were sauntering down Layton, looking charmingly *en amazone.*

"Pretty! I should rather think so. She is more beautiful than any other woman upon earth!" cried Mounteagle.

"Y'ally! well, I can't see *that*," replied Ennuyé. "She has tolerably good eyes, but she is too *petite* to please me."

"Ah! the adjutant's girls have rendered L'Estrange *difficile*. He cannot expect to meet *their* equals in a hurry!" said Fane, in a very audible aside.

Poor Ennuyé was silenced—nay, he even blushed. The adjutant's girls recalled an episode in which the gallant cornet had shone in a rather verdant light. Fane had effectually quieted him.

"I wonder if Florence Aspeden will marry Mount?" I remarked to Fane, when the others had left us. "She does not seem to pay him much heed *yet*; but still——"

"The devil, no!" cried Fane, in an unusually energetic manner. "I would stake my life she would not have such a muff as that, if he owned half the titles in the peerage!"

"You seem rather excited about the matter," I observed. "It would not be such a bad match for her, for you know she has no tin; but I am sure, with your opinion on love-matches, you would not counsel Mount to such a step."

"Of course not!" replied Fane, in his ordinary cool tones. "A man has no right to marry for love, except he is one of those fortunate individuals who own half a county, or some country doctor or parson of whom the world takes no notice. There may be a few exceptions. But yet," he continued, with the air of a person trying to convince himself against his will, "did you ever see a love match turn out happily? It is all very well for the first week, but the roses won't bloom in winter, and then the cottage walls look ugly. Then a fellow cannot live as he did *en garçon*, and all his friends drop him, and altogether it is an act no wise man would perpetrate. But I shall forget to give you a message I was intrusted with. They are going to get up some theatricals at Woodlands. I have promised to take *Sir Thomas Clifford* (the piece is the 'Hunchback'). and they want you to play *Modus* to Mary Aspeden's *Helen*. Do, old fellow. Acting is very good fun with a pretty girl——"

"Like the *Julia* you will have, I suppose," I said. "Very well, I will be amiable and take it. Mary will make a first-rate *Helen*. Come and have a game of billiards, will you?"

"Can't," replied the gallant captain. "I promised to go in half an hour with—with the Aspedens to see some waterfall or ruin, or something, and the time is up. So, *au revoir, monsieur.*"

Many of ours were pressed into the service for the coming theatricals, and right willingly did we rehearse a most unnecessary number of times. Many merry hours did we spend at Woodlands, and I sentimentalized away desperately to Mary Aspeden; but, somehow or other, always had an uncomfortable suspicion that she was laughing at me. She never seemed the least impressed by all my gallantries and pretty speeches, which was peculiarly mortifying to a moustached cornet of twenty, who thought himself irresistible. I began, too, to get terribly jealous of Tom Cleaveland, who, by right of his cousinship, arrived at a degree of intimacy I could not attain.

One morning Fane and I (who were going to dine there that evening), the Miss Aspedens, and, of course, that Tom Cleaveland, were sitting in the drawing-room at Woodlands. Fane and Florence were going it at some opera airs (what passionate emphasis that wicked fellow gave the loving Italian words as his rich voice rolled them out to her accompaniment!), the detestable Trinity-man had been discoursing away to Mary on boat-racing, outriggers, bumping, and Heaven knows what, and I was just taking the shine out of him with the description of a shipwreck I had had in the Mediterranean, when Mary, who sat working at her *broderie,* and provokingly giving just as sweet smiles to the one as to the other, interrupted me with—

"Goodness, Florie, there is Mr. Mills coming up the avenue. He is my cousin's admirer and admiration!" she added, mischievously, as the door opened, and a little man about forty entered.

There was all over him the essence of the country. You saw at once he had never passed a season in London. His very boots proclaimed he had never been presented; and we felt almost convulsed with laughter as he shook hands with us all round, and attempted a most *empressé* manner with Florence.

"Beautiful weather we have now," remarked Mrs. Aspeden.

"She is indeed!" answered the little squire, with a gaze of admiration at Florence.

Fane, who was leaning against the mantelpiece, looking most superbly haughty and unapproachable, shot an annihilating glance at the small man, which would have quite extinguished him had he seen it.

"The country is very pretty in June," said Mrs. Aspeden, hazarding another original remark.

"Lovely—too lovely!" echoed Mr. Mills, with a profound sigh, at which the country must have felt exceedingly flattered.

"Glorious creature your new mare is, Mr. Mills," cried the Cantab; "splendid style she took the fences in yesterday."

"Wilkins may well say she is the *belle* of the county!" continued Mr. Mills, dreamily. "I beg your pardon, what did you say? my mother took the fences well? No, she never hunts."

"Pray tell Mrs. Mills I am very much obliged for the beautiful azalias she sent me," interposed Florence, with her sweet smile.

"I—I am sure anything we have *you* are welcome to. I—I—allow me——" And the poor squire, stooping for Florence's thimble, upset a tiny table, on which stood a vase with the azalias in question, on the back of a little bull of a spaniel, who yelled, and barked, and flew at the squire's legs, who, for his part, became speechless from fright, reddened all over, and at last, stammering out that he wanted to see Mr. Aspeden, and would go to him in the grounds, rushed from the room.

We all burst out laughing at this climax of the poor little man's misery.

"I will not have you laugh at him so," said Florence, at length. "I know him to be truly good and charitable, for all his peculiarities of manner."

"It is but right Miss Aspeden should defend a *soupirant* so charming in every way," said the captain, his moustache curling contemptuously.

"Oh! Florie's made an out-and-out conquest, and no mistake!" cried Tom Cleaveland.

Florence did not heed her cousin, but looked up in Fane's face, utterly astonished at his sarcastic tones. No man could have withstood that look of those large, beautiful eyes, and Fane bent down and asked her to sing "*Roberto, oh tu che adoro!*"

"Yes, that will just do. Robert is his name; pity he is not here to hear it. 'Robert Mills, *oh tu che adoro!*'" sang the inexorable Cantab, as he walked across the room and asked Mary to have a game of billiards. For once I had the pleasure of forestalling him, but he, nevertheless, came and marked for us in a very amiable manner. "How well you play, Mary," said he. "Really, stunningly for a woman. Do you know Beauchamp of Kings won three whole pools the other day without losing a life!"

"Indeed!" said Mary. "What good fun it is to see Mr. Mills play; he holds his queue as if he were afraid of it."

"I say, Mary," said Cleaveland, "you don't think that Florence will marry that contemptible little wretch, do you? Hang it, I should be savage if she had not better taste. There's a cannon."

"She has better taste," replied Mary, in a low tone, as Mrs. Aspeden and Fane entered the room.

I never could like Mrs. Aspeden—peace be with her now, poor woman—but there was such a want of delicacy and tact, and such open manœuvring in all she did, which surprised me, clever woman as she was.

No sooner had she approached the billiard-table that day, than she began:

"Florence was called away from her singing to a conference with her uncle, and—with somebody else, I fancy." (Fane darted a keen look of inquiry at her.) "Poor dear girl! being left so young an orphan, I have always felt such a great interest and affection for her, and I shall rejoice to see her happily settled as—as I trust there is a prospect of now," she continued.

Could she mean Florence Aspeden had engaged herself to Mr. Mills? A roguish smile on Mary's face reassured me, but Fane walked hastily to the window, and stood with folded arms looking out upon the sunny landscape.

Inveterate flirt that he was, his pride was hurt at the idea of a rival, and *such* a rival, winning in a game in which *he* deigned to have *ever* so small a stake, *ever* such a passing interest!

The dinner passed off heavily—*very* heavily—for gay Woodlands, for the gallant captain and Florence were both of them *distraits* and *gênés*, and he hardly spoke to the poor girl. Oh, wicked Fane!

We sat but little time after the ladies had retired, and Tom and Mr. Aspeden going after some horse or other, Fane and I ascended to the drawing-room alone. It was unoccupied, and we sat down to await them, I amusing myself with teaching Master Tommy, the young heir of Woodlands, some comic songs, wherewith to astonish his nurse pretty considerably, and Fane leaning back in an arm-chair, with Florence's dog upon his knee in *that*, for *him*, most extraordinary thing, a "brown study."

Suddenly some voices were heard in the next room.

"Florence, it is your duty, recollect."

"Aunt, I can recollect nothing, save that it would be far, far worse than death to me to marry Mr. Mills. I hold it dread sin to marry a man for whom one can have nothing but contempt. Once for all, I cannot,—I will not."

Here the voice was broken with sobs. Fane had raised his head eagerly at the commencement of the dialogue, but now, recollecting that we were listeners, rose, and closed the door. I did not say a word on the conversation we had just heard, for I felt out of patience with him for his heartless flirtation; so, taking up a book on Italy, I looked over the engravings for a little time, and then, Tommy having been conveyed to the nursery in a state of rebellion, I reminded Fane of a promise he had once made to accompany me to Rome the next winter, and asked him if he intended to fulfil it.

"Really, my dear fellow, I cannot tell what I may possibly do next winter; I hate making plans for the future. We may none of us be alive then," said he, in an unusually dull strain for him: "I half fancy I may exchange into some regiment going on foreign service. But *l'homme propose*, you know. By the by, poor Castleton" (his elder brother) "is very ill at Brussels."

"Yes. I was extremely sorry to hear it, in a letter I had from Vivian this morning," I replied. "He is at Brussels also, and mentions a *belle* there, Lady Adeliza Fitzhowden, with whom, he says, the world is associating *your* name. Is it true, Fane?"

"*Les on dit font la gazette des fous!*" cried the captain, impatiently, stroking Florence's little King Charles. "I saw Lady Adeliza at Paris last January, but I would not marry her—no! not if there were no other woman upon earth! I thought, Fred, really you were too sensible to believe all the scandal raked up by that gossiping Vivian. I do hope you have not been propagating his most unfounded report?" asked my gallant friend, in quite an excited tone.

At this moment the ladies entered. Florence with her dark eyes looking very sad under their long lashes, but they soon brightened when Fane seated himself by her side, and began talking in a lower tone, and with even more *tendresse* than ever.

I had the pleasure of quite eclipsing Tom Cleaveland, I thought, as I turned over the leaves of Mary's music, and looked unutterable things, which, however, I fear were all lost, as Mary *would* look only at the notes of the piano, and I firmly believe never heard a word I said.

How Florence blushed as Fane whispered his soft good night; she looked so happy, poor girl, and he, heartless demon, talked of going into foreign service! By the by, what put that into his head, I wonder?

The night of our grand theatricals at length arrived, and we were all assembled in the library, converted for the time into a green-room. Mounteagle was repeating to himself, for the hundredth time, his part of *Lord Tinsel*; I, in my *Modus* dress, which I had a disagreeable idea was not becoming, was endeavoring to make an impression on the not-to-be impressed Mary, and Florence was looking lovelier than ever in her rich old-fashioned dress, when Fane entered, and bending, offered her a bouquet of rare flowers. She blushed deeply as she took it. Oh! Fane, Fane, what will you have to answer for?

We were waiting the summons for the first scene, when, to Mary's horror, I suddenly exclaimed that I could not play!

"Good Heavens! why not?" was the general inquiry.

"Why!" I said. "I never thought of it until now, but certainly *Modus* ought to appear without moustaches, and, hang it, I cannot cut mine off."

"Take my life, but spare my moustaches!" cried Mary, in tragic tones. "Certainly though, Mr. Wilmot, you are right; *Modus* ought not to be seen with the characteristic 'musk-toshes,' as nurse calls them; of an English officer. What is to be done?"

"Please, sir, will you come? Major Vaughan says the group is agoing to be set for the first scene, and you are wanted, sir," was a flunkey's admonition to Fane, who went off accordingly, after advising me to add a dishevelled beard to my tenderly cared-for moustaches, which would seem as if *Modus* had entirely neglected his toilette.

There was a general rush for part books, a general cry for things that were not forthcoming, and a general despair on the parts of the youngest amateurs at forgetting their cues just when they were most wanted.

Fane, when he came off the stage after the first scene, leant against a pillar to watch the pretty one between *Julia* and *Helen*, so near that he must have been seen by the audience, and presented a most handsome and interesting spectacle, I dare say, for young ladies to gaze at. Fixing his eyes on Florence, whose rendering of the part was really perfect as she uttered these words, "Helen, I'm constancy!" he unconsciously muttered aloud, "I believe it!"

"So do I!" I could not help saying, "and therefore more shame to whoever wins such a heart to throw it away. 'Beneath her feet, a duke—a duke might lay his coronet!'" I quoted.

"Are you in love yourself, Fred?" laughed the captain; then, stroking his moustaches thoughtfully for some minutes, he said at last, as if with an effort, "You are right, young one, and yet——"

If I was right, what need was there for him to throw such passion into his part—what need was there for him to say with such *empressement* those words:

A willing pupil kneels to thee,

And lays his title and his fortune at thy feet?

If he intended to go into foreign service, why did he not go at once? Though I confess it seemed strange to me why Fane—the courted, the flattered, the admired Fane—should wish to leave England.

Reader, mind, the gallant captain is a desperate flirt, and I do not believe he will go into foreign service any more than I shall, but I *am* afraid he will win that poor girl's heart with far less thought than you buy your last "little darling French bonnet," and when he is tired of it will throw it away with quite as little heed. But I was not so much interested in his flirtation as to forget my own, still I was obliged to confess that Mary Aspeden did not pay me as much attention as I should have wished.

I danced the first dance with her, after the play was over—(I forgot to tell you we were very much applauded)—and Tom Cleaveland engaging her for the next, I proposed a walk through the conservatories to a sentimental young lady who was my peculiar aversion, but to whom I became extremely *dévoué*, for I thought I would try and pique Mary if I could.

The light strains of dance music floated in from the distance, and the air was laden with the scent of flowers, and many a *tête-à-tête* and *partie carrée* was arranged in that commodious conservatory.

Half hidden by an orange-tree, Florence Aspeden was leaning back in a garden-chair, close to where we stood looking out upon the beautiful night. Her fair face was flushed, and she was nervously picking some of the blossoms to pieces; before her stood Mounteagle, speaking eagerly. I was moving away to avoid being a hearer of his love-speech, as I doubted not it was, but my companion, with many young-ladyish expressions of adoration of the "sublime moonlight," begged me to stay "one moment, that she might see the dear moon emerge like a swan from that dark, beautiful cloud!" and in the pauses of her ecstatics I heard poor Mount's voice in a tone of intense entreaty.

At that moment Fane passed. He glanced at the group behind the orange-trees, and his face grew stern and cold, and his lips closed with that iron compression they always have when he is irritated. His eyes met Florences, and he bowed haughtily and stiffly as he moved on, and his upright figure, with its stately head, was seen in the room beyond, high above any of those around him. A heavy sigh came through the orange boughs, and her voice whispered, "I—I am very sorry, but——"

"Oh! *do* look at the moonbeams falling on that darling little piece of water, Mr. Wilmot!" exclaimed my decidedly *moonstruck* companion.

"Is there no hope?" cried poor Mount.

"None!" And the low-whispered knell of hope came sighing over the flowers. I thought how little she guessed there was none for her. Poor Florence!

"Oh, this night! I could gaze on it forever, though it is saddening in its sweetness, do not you think?" asked my romantic demoiselle. "Ah! what a pretty *valse* they are playing!"

"May I have the pleasure of dancing it with you?" I felt myself obliged to ask, although intensely victimized thereby, as I hate dancing, and wonder whatever idiot invented it.

Miss Chesney, considering her devotion to the moon, consented very joyfully to leave it for the pleasures (?) of a *valse à deux temps*.

As we moved away, I saw that Florence was alone, and apparently occupied with sad thoughts. She, I dare say, was grieving over Fane's cold bow, and poor Mount had rushed away somewhere with his great sorrow. Fane came into my room next morning while I was at breakfast, having been obliged to get up at the unconscionable hour of ten, to be in time for a review we were to have that day on Layton Common for the glorification of the country around.

The gallant captain flung himself on my sofa, and, after puffing away at his cigar for some minutes, came out with, "Any commands for London? I am going to apply for leave, and I think I shall start by the express to-morrow."

"What's in the wind now?" I asked. "Is Lord Avanley unwell?"

"No; the governor's all right, thank you. I am tired of rural felicity, that is all," replied Fane. "I must stay for this review to-day, or the colonel would make no end of a row. He is a testy old boy. I rather think I shall set out, or exchange into the Heavies."

"What in the world have you got into your head, Fane?" I asked, utterly astonished to see him diligently smoking an extinguished cigar. "I am sorry you are going to leave us. The 110th will miss you, old fellow; and what *will* the Aspedens say to losing their *preux chevalier*? By the way, speaking of them, poor Mount received his *congé* last night, I expect."

"What! are you sure? What did you say?" demanded Fane, stooping to relight his cigar.

I told him what I had overheard in the conservatory.

"Oh! well—ah! indeed—poor fellow!" ejaculated the captain. "But there's the bugle-call! I must go and get into harness."

And I followed his example, turning over in my mind, as I donned my uniform, what might possibly have induced Fane to leave Layton Rise so suddenly. Was it, at last, pity for Florence? And if it were, would not the pity come too late?

Layton Rise looked very pretty and bright under the combined influence of beauty and valor (that is the correct style, is it not?). The Aspedens came early, and drew up their carriages close to the flag-staff. Fane's eye-glass soon spied them from our distant corner of the field, and, as we passed before the flagstaff, he bent low to his saddle with one of those fascinating smiles which have gone deep to so many unfortunate young ladies' hearts. Again I felt angry with him, as I rode along thinking of that girl, her whole future most likely clouded for ever, and he going away to-morrow to enjoy himself about in the world, quite reckless of the heart he had broken, and —
— But in the midst of my sentimentalism I was startled by hearing the sharp voice of old Townsend, our colonel, who was a bit of a martinet, asking poor Ennuyé "what he lifted his hand for?"

"There was a bee upon my nose, colonel."

"Well, sir, and if there were a whole hive of bees upon your nose, what right have you to raise your hand on parade?" stormed the colonel.

There was a universal titter, and poor Ennuyé was glad to hide his confusion in the "charge" which was sounded.

On we dashed our horses at a stretching gallop, our spurs jingling, our plumes waving in the wind, and our lances gleaming in the sunlight. Hurrah! there is no charge in the world like the resistless English dragoons'! On we went, till suddenly there was a piercing cry, and one of the carriages, in which the ponies had been most negligently left, broke from the circle and tore headlong down the common, at the bottom of which was a lake. One young lady alone was in it. It was impossible for her to pull in the excited little grays, and, unless they *were* stopped, down they would all go into it. But as soon as it was perceived, Fane had rushed from the ranks, and, digging his spurs into his horse, galloped after the carriage. Breathless we watched him. We would not follow, for we knew that he would do it, if any man could, and the sound of many in pursuit would only further exasperate the ponies. Ha! he is nearing them now. Another moment and they will be down the sloping bank into the lake. The girl gives a wild cry; Fane is straining every nerve. Bravo! well done—-he has saved her! I rushed up, and arrived to find Fane supporting a half-fainting young lady, in whose soft face, as it rested on his shoulder, I recognized Florence Aspeden. Her eyes unclosed as I drew near, and, blushing, she disengaged herself from his arms. Fane bent his head over her, and murmured, "Thank God, I have saved you!" But perhaps I did not hear distinctly.

By this time all her friends had gathered round them, and Fane had consigned her to her cousin's care, and she was endeavoring to thank him, which her looks, and blushes, and smiles did most eloquently; Mr. Aspeden was shaking Fane by the hand, and what further might have happened I know not, if the colonel (very wrathful at such an unseemly interruption to his cherished manœuvres) had not shouted out, "Fall in, gentlemen—fall in! Captain Fane, fall in with your troop, sir!" We did accordingly fall in, and the review proceeded; but my friend actually made some mistakes in his evolutions, and kept his eye-glass immovably fixed on the point in the circle, and behaved altogether in a *distrait* manner—Fane, whom I used to accuse of having too much *sang froid*—whom nothing could possibly disturb—whom I never saw agitated before in the whole course of my acquaintance!

What an inexplicable fellow he is!

The review over, we joined the Aspedens, and many were the congratulations Florence had heaped upon her; but she looked *distraite*, too, until Fane came up, and leaning his hand on the carriage, bent down and talked to her. Their conversation went on in a low tone, and as I was busy laughing with Mary, I cannot report it, save that from the bright blushes on the one hand, and the soft whispered tones on the other, Fane was clearly at his old and favorite work of winning hearts.

"You seem quite *occupé* this morning, Mr. Wilmot," said Mary, in her winning tones. "I trust you have had no bad news—no order from the Horse Guards for the Lancers to leave off moustaches."

"No, Miss Aspeden," said Sydney; "if such a calamity as that had occurred, you would not see Wilmot here, he would never survive the loss of his moustaches—they are his first and only love."

"And a first affection is never forgotten," added that provoking Mary, in a most melancholy voice.

"It would be a pity if it were, as it seems such a fertile source of amusement to you and Miss Aspeden," I said, angrily, to Sydney, too much of a boy then to take a joke.

"Captain Fane has an invitation for you and Mr. Sydney," said Mary, I suppose by way of *amende*. "We are going on the river, to a picnic at the old castle;—you will come?"

The tones were irresistible, so I smoothed down my indignation and my poor moustache, and replied that I would have that pleasure, as did Sydney.

"*Bien!* good-bye, then, for we must hasten home," said Mary, whipping her ponies. And off bowled the carriage with its fair occupants.

"You won't be here for this picnic, old fellow," I remarked to Fane, as we rode off the ground.

"Well! I don't know. I hardly think I shall go just yet. You see I had six months' leave when I was in Germany, before I came down here, and I hardly like to ask for another so soon, and — —"

"It is so easy to find a reason for what one *wishes*," I added, smiling.

"Come and look at my new chestnut, will you?" said Fane, not deigning to reply to my insinuation. "I am going to run her against Stuckup of the Guards' bay colt!"

That beautiful morning in June! How well I remember it, as we dropped down the sunlit river, under the shade of the branching trees, the gentle plash of the oars mingling with the high tones and ringing laughter of our merry party, on our way to the castle picnic.

"How beautiful this is," I said to Mary Aspeden; "would that life could glide on calmly and peacefully as we do this morning!"

"How romantic you are becoming!" laughed Mary. "What a pity that I feel much more in mood to fish than to sentimentalize!"

"Ah!" I replied, "with the present companionship I could be content to float on forever."

"Hush! I beg your pardon, but *do* listen to that dear thrush," interrupted Mary, not the least disturbed, or even interested, by my pretty speeches.

I was old enough to know I was not the least in love with Mary Aspeden, but I was quite too much of a boy not to feel provoked I did not make more impression. I was a desperate puppy at that time, and she served me perfectly right. However, feeling very injured, I turned my attention to Fane, who sat talking of course to Florence, and left Mary to the attentions of her Cantab cousin.

"Miss Aspeden does not agree with you, Fred," said Fane. "She says life was not intended to glide on like a peaceful river; she likes the waves and storms," he added, looking down at her with very visible admiration.

"No, not for myself," replied Florence, with a sweet, sad smile. "I did not mean *that*. One storm will wreck a *woman's* happiness; but were I a man I should glory in battling with the tempest-tossed waves of life. If there be no combat there can be no fame, and the fiercer, the more terrible it is, the more renown to be the victor in the struggle!"

"You are right," answered Fane, with unusual earnestness. "That used to be *my* dream once, and I think even now I have the stuff in me for it; but then," he continued, sinking his voice, "I must have an end, an aim, and, above all, some one who will sorrow in my sorrow, and glory in my glory; who will be — —"

"Quite ready for luncheon, I should think; hope you've enjoyed your boating!" cried Mr. Aspeden's hearty voice from the shore, where, having come by land, he now stood to welcome us, surrounded by a crowd of anxious mammas, wondering if the boating had achieved the desirable end of a proposal from Captain A——; hoping Mr. B——, who had nothing but his pay, had not been paying too much attention to Adelina; and that Honoria had given sufficient encouragement to Mr. C——, who, on the strength of 1000*l.* a year, and a coronet in prospect, was considered an eligible *parti* (his being a consummate scamp and inveterate gambler is nothing); and that D—— has too much "consideration for his family" to have any "serious intentions" to Miss E——, whom he is assisting to land. However, whatever proposals have been accepted or rejected, here we all were ready for luncheon, which was laid out on the grass, and Fane will be obliged to finish his speech another time, for little now is heard but *bons mots*, laughter, and champagne corks. The captain is more brilliant than ever, and I make Mary laugh if I cannot make her sigh. Luncheon over, what was to be done? See the castle, of course, as we were in duty bound, since it was what we came to do; and the *tête-à-tête* of the boats are resumed, as ladies and gentlemen ascended the grassy slopes on which the fine old ruins stood. I looked for Mary Aspeden, feeling sure that I should conquer her in time (though I did not *want* to in the least!), but she had gone off somewhere, I dare say with Tom Cleaveland; so I offered my arm to that same sentimental Miss Chesney who had bored me into a *valse à deux temps* the night of the theatricals, and I have no doubt her mamma contemplated her as Mrs. Wilmot, of Wilmot Park, with very great gratification and security. Becoming rather tired of the young lady's hackneyed style of conversation, which consisted, as usual, of large notes of exclamation about "the *sweet* nightingales!" "the *dear* ruins!" "the *darling* flowers!" &c. &c., I managed to exchange with another sub, and strolled off by myself.

As I was leaning against an old wall in no very amiable frame of mind, consigning all young ladies to no very delightful place, and returning to my old conclusion that they were all tarlatan and coquetry, soft musical voices on the other side of the wall fell almost unconsciously on my ear.

"Oh! Florence, I am so unhappy!"

"Are you, darling? I wish I could help you. Is it about Cyril Graham?"

"Yes!" with a tremendous sigh. "I am afraid papa, and I am sure mamma, will never consent. I know poor dear Cyril is not rich, but then he is so clever, he will soon make himself known. But if that tiresome Fred Wilmot should propose, I know they will want me to accept him." (There is one thing, I never, *never will!*) "I do snub him as much as ever I can, but he is such a puppy, I believe he thinks I am in love with him—as if Cyril, were not worth twenty such as he, for all he is the owner of Wilmot Park!"

Very pleasant this was! What a fool I must have made of myself to Mary Aspeden, and how nice it was to hear one's self called "a puppy!"

"Of course, dear," resumed Florence, "as you love Cyril, it is impossible for you to love any one ever again; but I do not think Mr. Wilmot a puppy. He is conceited, to be sure, but I do not believe he would be so much liked by—by those who are his friends, if he were not rather nice. Come, dear, cheer up. I am sure uncle Aspeden is too kind not to let you marry Cyril when he knows how much you love one another. *I* will talk to him, Mary dear, and bring him round, see if I do not! But—but—will you think me *very* selfish if I tell you"—(a long pause)—"he has asked me—I mean—he wishes—he told me—he says he does love me!"

"Who, darling? Let me think—Lord Athum?—Mr. Grant?"

"No, Mary—Drummond—that is, Captain Fane—he said——Oh, Mary, I am so happy!"

At this juncture it occurred suddenly to me that I was playing the part of a listener. (But may not much be forgiven a man who has heard himself called "a puppy"?) So I moved away, leaving the fair Florence to her blushes and her happiness, unshared by any but her friend. Between my astonishment at Fane and my indignation at Mary, I was fairly bewildered. Fane actually had proposed! *He*, the Honorable Drummond Fane, who had always declaimed against matrimony—who had been proof-hardened against half the best matches in the country—that desperate flirt who we thought would never fall in love, to have tumbled in headlong like this!

Well, there was some satisfaction, I would chaff him delightfully about it; and I was really glad, for if Florence had given her heart to Fane, she was not the sort of girl to forget, nor he the sort of man to be forgotten, in a hurry. But in what an awfully foolish light I must have appeared to Mary Aspeden! There was one thing, she would never know I had overheard her. I would get leave, and go off somewhere—I would marry the first pretty girl I met with—she should *not* think I cared for *her*. No, I would go on flirting as if nothing had happened, and then announce, in a natural manner, that I was going into the Highlands, and then *she* would be the one to feel small, as she had made so *very* sure of my proposal. And yet, if I went away, that was the thing to please her. *Hang* it! I did not know *what* to do! My vanity was most considerably touched, though my heart was not; but after cooling down a little, I saw how foolishly I should look if I behaved otherwise than quietly and naturally, and that after all *that* would be the best way to make Mary reverse her judgment.

So, when I met her again, which was not until we were going to return, I offered her my arm to the boat where Fane and his *belle fiancée* were sitting, looking most absurdly happy; and the idea of my adamantine friend being actually caught seemed so ridiculous, that it almost restored me to my good humor, which, sooth to say, the appellation of "puppy" had somewhat disturbed.

And so the moon rose and shed her silver light over the young lady who had sentimentalized upon her, and a romantic cornet produced a concertina, and sent forth dulcet strains into the evening air, and Florence and her captain talked away in whispers, and Mary Aspeden sat with tears in her eyes, thinking, I suppose, of "Cyril" and I mused on my "puppyism;" and thus, wrapped each in our own little sphere, we floated down the river to Woodlands, and, it being late, with many a soft good night, and many a gentle "*Au revoir,*" we parted, and Mr. Aspeden's castle picnic was over!

I did not see Fane the next day, except at parade, until I was dressing for mess, when he stalked into my room, and stretching himself on a sofa, said, after a pause,

"Well, old boy, I've been and gone and done it."

"Been and gone and done what?" I asked, for, by the laws of retaliation, I was bound to tease him a little.

"Confound you, what an idiot you are!" was the complimentary rejoinder. "Why, my dear fellow, the truth is, that, like most of my unfortunate sex, I have at last turned into that most tortuous path called love, and surrendered myself to the machinations of beautiful woman. The long and the short of it is—I am engaged to be married!"

"Good Heavens! Fane!" I exclaimed, "what next? *You* married! Who on earth is she? I know of no heiress down here!"

"She is no heiress," said the captain; "but she is what is much better— the sweetest, dearest, most lovable— —"

"Of *course!*" I said, "but no heiress! My dear Fane, you cannot mean what you say?"

"I should be sorry if I did not," was the cool reply; "and you must be more of a fool, Fred, than I took you for, if you cannot see that Florence Aspeden is worth all the heiresses upon earth, and is the embodiment of all that is lovely and winning in woman——"

"No doubt of it, *tout cela saute aux yeux*," I answered. "But reflect, Fane; it would be utter madness in *you* to marry anything but an heiress. Love in a cottage is not *your* style. *You* were not made for a small house, one maid-servant, and dinner——"

"Ah!" laughed Fane, "you are bringing my former nonsense against me. Some would say I was committing worse folly now, but believe me, Fred, the folly even of the heart is better than the calculating wisdom of the world. I do not hesitate to say that if Florence had fortune I should prefer it, for such a *vaurien* as I was made to spend money; but as she has not, I love her too dearly to think about it, and my father, I have no doubt, will soon get me my majority, and we shall get on stunningly. So marry for *love*, Fred, if you take my advice."

"A *rather* different opinion to that which you inculcated so strenuously a month ago," I observed, smiling; "but let me congratulate you, old fellow, with all my heart. 'Pon my word, I am very glad, for I always felt afraid you would, like Morvillier's *garçon*, resist all the attractions of a woman until the '*cent mille écus*,' and then, without hesitation, declare, '*J'épouse*.' But you were too good to be spoiled."

"As for my goodness, there's not much of *that*," replied Fane; "I am afraid I am much better off than I deserve. I wrote to the governor last night: dear old boy! he will do anything *I* ask him. By the by, Mary will be married soon too. I hope you are not *épris* in that quarter, Fred?—pray do not faint if you are. *My* Florence, who can do anything she likes with anybody (do you think any one *could* be angry with *her*?) coaxed old Aspeden into consenting to Mary's marriage with a fellow she really is in love with—Graham, a barrister. I think she would have had more difficulty with the lady-mother, if a letter had not most opportunely come from Graham this morning, announcing the agreeable fact that he had lots of tin left him unexpectedly. I wish somebody would do the same by me. And so this Graham will fly down on the wings of love—represented in these days by the express train— to-morrow evening."

"And how about the foreign service, Fane?" I could not help asking. "And do you intend going to London to-morrow?"

"I made those two resolutions under very different circumstances to the *present*, my dear fellow," laughed Fane: "the first, when I determined to cut away from Florence altogether, as the only chance of forgetting her; sad the second, when I thought poor Mount was an accepted lover, and I confess that I did not feel to have stoicism enough to witness his happiness. But how absurd it seems that *I* should have fallen in love," continued he; "*I*, that defied the charms of all the Venuses upon earth—the last person any one would have taken for a marrying man. I am considerably astonished myself! But I suppose love is like the whooping-cough, one must have it some time or other." And with these words the gallant captain raised himself from the sofa, lighted a cigar, and, strolling out of the room, mounted his horse for Woodlands, where he was engaged of course to dinner that evening.

And now, gentle reader, what more is there to tell? I fear as it is I have written too "much about nothing," and as thou hast, I doubt not, a fine imagination, what need to tell how Lord Avanley and Mr. Aspeden arranged matters, not like the cross papas in books and dramas, but amicably, as gentlemen should; how merrily the bells pealed for the double wedding; how I, as *garçon d'honneur*, flirted with the bridesmaids to my heart's content; how Fane is my friend, *par excellence*, still, and how his love is all the stronger for having "come late," he says. How all the young ladies hated Florence, and all the mammas and chaperones blessed her for having carried off the "fascinating younger son," until his brother Lord Castleton dying at the baths, Fane succeeded of course to the title; how she is, if possible, even more charming as Lady Castleton than as Florence Aspeden, and how they were *really* heart-happy until the Crimean campaign separated them; and how she turns her beautiful eyes ever to the East and heeds not, save to repulse, the crowd of admirers who seek to render her forgetful of her soldier-husband.

True wife as she is, may he live to come back with laurels hardly won, still to hold her his dearest treasure.

May 1, 1856.—Fane *has* come back all safe. I hope, dear reader, you are as glad as I am. He has distinguished himself stunningly, and is now lieutenant-colonel of the dear old 110th. You have gloried in the charge of ours at Balaklava, but as I have not whispered to you my name, you cannot possibly divine that a rascally Russian gave me a cut on the sword-arm that very day in question, which laid me *hors de combat*, but got me my majority.

Well may I, as well as Fane, bless the remembrance of Layton Rise, for if I had never made the acquaintance of Mary Aspeden—I mean Graham—I might never have known her *belle-sœur* (who is now shaking her head at me for writing about her), and whom, either through my interesting appearance when I returned home on the sick-list, and my manifold Crimean adventures, or through the usual perversity of women, who will fall always in love with scamps who do not deserve half their goodness—(Edith, you shall *not* look over my shoulder)—I prevailed on to accept my noble self and Lancer uniform, with the *"puppyism"* shaken pretty well out of it! And so here we are *very happy of course.*—"As yet," suggests Edith.

Ah! Fane and I little knew—poor unhappy wretches that we were—what our fate was preparing for us when it led us discontented *blasés* and *ennuyés* down to our Country Quarters!